MW01384406

3 TEEN BOOKS BOXED
Phoebe Matthews
LostLoves Books
Book Club Edition

Boxed Set includes:

Boxed Set Book Club Edition 2013
Copyright © Phoebe Matthews
Cover Design Copyright © LostLoves Books

This is a work of fiction that includes three novels by Phoebe Matthews. With the exception of well-known historical personages, any resemblance to persons living or dead is purely coincidental. All Rights Are Reserved. No part of this book may be used or reproduced in any manner whatsoever without written permission from the author.

that BOY on the COVER
First published as an Avon Flare novel
by Phoebe Matthews

CHAPTER 1

The first time I saw Tommy Dalton was on a book cover.

He was gazing out toward the photographer, his head tilted slightly down, so that he was looking up, and the first time I picked up the book, I felt as though he were looking straight at me.

His dark, gray-brown eyes reflected a glow so mysterious it could have been moonlight. His upper lashes were short, stiff, black, matching the long, straight line of his brows, but his lower lashes were soft little curves of shadow. He had thick, neatly styled dark hair with a touch of a wave to it, brushed across his forehead and halfway down in front of his ears. His nose had this firm arch that contradicted the hint of insecurity in his questioning look. His mouth was slightly open, as though he were about to ask a question. His face was thin, but he had a beautifully squared chin.

"Isn't he gorgeous?" I said, handing the paperback book to Belinda Gray, my lifelong best friend.

Belinda wasn't anything like me. Maybe that's why we got along so well, because we balanced each other. She wore her straight hair in a neat, shoulder-length cut and was big on discreet (her word for invisible) makeup.

"Look at that guy's face!" I said. "Tell me you've ever seen anyone that wonderful in your whole life!"

After carefully studying the book cover, front and back and even the spine, Belinda said, "Is it any good?"

"What? The book? I dunno, I haven't read it yet. Belinda, I bought it because of him, the boy on the cover. As soon as I saw him, I knew he was for me. It's right there, in his look. I know, I am absolutely certain, that if I could meet him, we would discover that we are perfect for each other."

"That's crazy, Cyndi."

Snatching the book back from her, I cradled it in my hands and looked into his eyes. "Why is it crazy?"

"Because," she said, in her careful, point-by-point way that drove me wild, "first, he's a model. Second, he probably lives in New York. Third, you don't know his name."

"Maybe I could write to him."

"How?"

The bell rang for the end of lunch hour.

Just as well. I didn't have an answer. Crumpling my lunch bag into a ball, I tossed it into the trash can by the door of the cafeteria as we hurried out.

"Just because he's had his photo put on a book cover doesn't mean you can write to him," Belinda pointed out. We shouldered our way through the crowd in the corridor.

"Why not?"

"Cyndi, honestly! You have left this planet! Have you any idea how many girls must write to those models? And anyway, where would you mail your letter to?"

"I'll figure it out," I said.

"Just because you spell your name like Cyndi Superstar doesn't mean a male model will answer your letter," she warned.

I glared at her. She shrugged, waved good-bye, and headed away from me toward her next class in the gym.

My next class was math. Fortunately, math was my easy subject, partly because the rest of the sophomore class was unbelievably stupid at it, which meant the teacher explained everything multiple times. Aside from that, I grew up knowing that fingers were for putting nail decorations on, not for counting on. So right here, before I sound like I'm bragging, I'll admit that I can't spell, can't punctuate, and as for history, it's strictly in the forgotten past, especially on my quiz papers. But I am fairly good at art and, when it comes to math, I'm a whiz.

Predictably, the math teacher, Ms. Childer, explained the same problem five times. This gave me most of the period to prop up my paperback inside my math book and concentrate on the boy on the cover. In my mind he became The Boy. He had a name in the story, but of course that wasn't his real name. He was a model. Maybe he was an actor who modeled between parts. I closed my eyes and tried to remember if I had ever seen him in a movie or on TV.

Impossible. If I'd seen that face before, I'd remember. He was to other boys what diamonds are to pebbles.

On a sheet of notebook paper I jotted down my attack plan. First, I had to contact him, but how? I lived nowhere near New York City. Everybody else in the world lived in New York or Hollywood, but I had the fate to be born in a small town that probably isn't even on any maps sold outside our state, that's how boring it is. It is so boring, even boring sitcoms never used us as a locale. And as for rock concerts, to attend one I'd have to travel three hundred miles, which my parents wouldn't let me do, so they certainly wouldn't let me go to New York, which was much further away than that. I wasn't exactly sure how far as I've never been any good at geography, either.

My only alternative was to hope he'd come to me. Hope might take too long. I needed a speedier plan.

I headed the sheet of paper, Write a Letter.

At that moment Ms. Childer got tired of stupid answers and called on me. "Cyndi, can you give us the answer?"

From her tone, I knew that she'd already received at least three wrong answers. I glanced up at the chalkboard, did a quick take of the problem, and said, "C equals thirty-seven."

"All right! Now does everyone know how we got that answer? Can we go on to the next problem?" she shouted happily.

From the groans and protests I knew she'd have to go back over that one four or five more times, which gave me plenty of time to work on my problem.

Under the heading, I began with a 1, followed by the question Where? Was there any sort of address? Turning the book over in my hands, I checked the back cover. It had this dumb paragraph all about the fictional characters in the story. But who cared? I wanted to know about him, the real guy whose photograph was on the cover.

Turning the book back over, I began at the front, after a brief pause to look him in the eyes and reassure myself that he was worth the trouble.

Inside the book I found the publisher's name and address. I copied it down.

After school I met Belinda at our usual place, on the front steps of our high school. We always stood there and let the bus-catchers race by. It was the one sure lookout for anyone we wanted to see, plus a no-fail way to spot anyone new. The whole school, except those who stayed after for activities, came down those stairs to head for the curb where the buses wait.

Even the football players caught the bus in the spring, or at least enough did to keep the crowd interesting. Some had cars. But the bus route went right by the shopping mall, so the rest rode that far.

Just when I spotted a guy I'd seen around but not met and wanted to, and his eyes met mine through the crowd, and I started to smile, Ralph Lowe stepped between us.

"Hi," Ralph grinned. Ralph always grinned. He didn't know anything to do with his mouth except open it full width. I'd known Ralph since kindergarten and there'd been a time when I held out hope that he'd turn into an adult, but I was ready to accept defeat. True, he'd grown taller than me, and his unruly hair was a warm brown that matched his eyes. But his face was still as round and childish as it had been in kindergarten.

"Hi, Ralph," I said peering over his shoulder. The guy I hoped to meet had disappeared.

"Whatcha doing?" Ralph asked. He always asked that.

"Nothing," I said, as I always said.

"You guys want to go to the mall?" he asked.

"We have to go straight home," I said.

"Oh. Well, see you around," Ralph said, which sounded like a closing line, but Belinda and I knew better. Ralph stood next to us, waving and grinning to everyone who went by, which made it impossible for us to make any important eye contacts ourselves. What guy would join us while we were grouped with old Ralph?

Belinda sighed, I shrugged, and we headed home, leaving Ralph on the steps, still grinning.

Belinda and I live in the same neighborhood, half a mile from school, which is about as exciting as living half a mile from the police station, though it does have one advantage. Because we walked home, we could take our time. If the guys were out on the athletic field, we could stand around watching them do warm-ups.

It was spring, track time, and the field was covered with guys. Also, half the track team was girls, but if I wanted to watch girls warm up, I could do that in gym class. I am not the boring kind of girl who only likes boys and thinks they are all that matters. Honestly, my close friends are almost all girls. But when it came to plain old standing and watching, I chose boys.

While the coach shouted, "Backs straight, from the gut, arms out!" and the field stretched in unison, I said to Belinda, "There's an address in the book."

"Yeah?" she said, thinking about Louis. I knew she was thinking about Louis because he was in the second row of the exercisers, and whenever Belinda saw him, she thought about him.

"You think if I write to the publishers they'll tell me his name?"

"Whose name?"

"The boy on the cover."

"What for?" She was still watching Louis.

"So I can write to him!" I shouted.

She reluctantly turned away from Louis to give me the attention a best friend is supposed to deserve. "What are you talking about?"

"Belinda, there is an address in this book, and if I write to the publisher, do you think they'll give me the address of the boy on the cover?"

"You're still ballistic about a book cover?"

"It's important."

"Well," she said slowly, "I don't think they will. I mean, probably models want their addresses kept secret."

"But I've got to find him."

"I wonder if he has any idea who I am," she muttered.

I caught her elbow and dragged her away. As long as Louis was in view, I was talking to myself. We shouldered our bookbags and headed home.

"What'll I say in my letter?" I asked.

"To the publisher? I dunno, ask for the model's name, I guess."

"But that won't give me his address."

"You're not going to get his address. Face it. But maybe he's got an agent, like actors do. Maybe you can buy his autographed photo, or something like that."

"How would I find that out?"

"If he does that kind of thing, wouldn't the publisher send your name to the guy's agent?"

It was worth a try. Her suggestion also proved what sensible friends are good for. Anyone who wore a shoulder-length bob, no eye makeup, only a touch of lipstick, and a navy wool cardigan sweater with a white blouse and and ironed jeans had a well-organized mind. Given a question, she'd eventually produce a useful answer.

"Now tell me how to make Louis know I'm alive," Belinda said.

"Paint your name on a balloon and tie it to his locker door."

"You probably would," she sighed. "Me, I'd die first."

Belinda wanted a sensible suggestion. Sensible wasn't my style. Besides, when I wanted to attract a guy, I wanted to attract him, not just get his attention. Belinda didn't want Louis for a boyfriend. In fact, weird as it was, Belinda didn't want anyone for a boyfriend. What she wanted was a new debate partner for next season. Louis was a junior and next year he probably would be president of the debating team.

Debate season overlapped track by a few weeks. Louis was on both teams. Some people make school involvement their whole lives.

"Okay," I said. "Let's think. If you're both on the same team, how come he doesn't know you're a terrific debater?"

"I am in junior debate," she sighed, so I knew she'd explained that before. "He is in senior. Probably he does know my name, but that's all. He doesn't know my scores because I hardly ever win."

The way I got it from Belinda, she debated as half of a team with a guy who anybody could see was a washout, though Belinda never said that. The deal was, they both got some sort of ratings from the judges, but they were scored as a team, so although Belinda earned great points, her partner's zeros kept them from win, place, or show, or whatever debaters got.

Belinda did not want to be stuck with the same partner again next year.

I said, "Maybe you could get Louis's attention by doing something with the track team."

Belinda shot me a horrified glare.

"I didn't mean you should pole-vault. But what about scorekeepers? Don't they need scorekeepers? Or trainers? Inger Wells works with the coach. I've seen her at basketball games. She runs around with bandages."

"The one who tapes up ankles? Are you putting me on? You ever watch a track meet? People fall down and get huge scrapes on their hands and knees, full of dirt and blood, and Inger cleans them up, and you want me to do that?"

Belinda could faint at the sight of spilled catsup.

"Maybe Louis already has a debate partner," I said.

"The teams for next year haven't been announced."

"What about his partner from this year?"

"She's moving. I know that for a fact. She won't be here next year."

"But you'll still be a junior and he'll be a senior next year."

"Cyndi," she said, carefully enunciating her words, which probably she learned to do in debate because although she'd never been one to slur, she was becoming more emphatic daily, "let me say this once more. Beginning debaters are on junior level. Experienced debaters are in senior division. It has nothing to do with class level. It's how long you've been debating. Next year both Louis and I will be senior debaters."

We parted at the corner after promising to think about each other's problems. She shouted Seeya and I shouted Arrivederci, which was what my favorite musician, Cyndi Superstar, always said at the end of her shows. At home I picked up the mail and put fresh water in the cats' outside dish before going indoors.

Instead of doing my Language Arts homework, I spent the afternoon at the kitchen table writing a letter to the publisher of the paperback book. I explained that what I really wanted was to contact the boy on the cover.

"If you'll send my name to his agent, I'd like to get a photo of him," I said in my first draft.

It wasn't another picture I wanted. But if I had the name of an agency, maybe I could google its phone number. How much would a call to New York cost? Did I have the nerve to phone his agent and ask for his address, once I'd learned his name from the photo? I suspected they would ignore an e-mail query.

First I had to get the picture. Or his name. Or something. Anything. A face on a book cover wasn't much of a starting place. I gazed at him again, then wrote a second draft.

When I finished my letter, I phoned Belinda.

"Let me read this aloud to you," I said.

"What about Louis?" she said.

"As soon as this is in the envelope and stamped, I will concentrate all my powers on solving your problem."

"Promise?"

"Belinda, my mother will be walking through the door any minute, and I can't read this aloud once she's home."

"Okay, go ahead," she said.

I pushed aside the kitchen curtain to see the garage. No sign of my mother's car yet, and she came home a half hour before my father.

"Dear Sir," I read aloud. "I enjoyed reading this terrific book you-"

"You've already read it?" Belinda interrupted.

"No, but I will, and I think I ought to say that, so they won't think all I care about is the cover."

"I guess so."

"Shut up and let me read," I said and continued, "I am interested in the boy in the cover photo. Does he have an agent who sends out his picture? Would you please send my name to his agent? Thank you. Cyndi Carlisle."

"Sounds okay," Belinda said.

"If you think of something else I should say, call me back. My mom just drove in."

"You think about Louis," Belinda said.

I hung up and returned to the kitchen table and opened my Lit book by the time Mom pushed open the back door and shouted. Jumping up, I ran to help her with the groceries.

She did her automatic glance at my homework spread out on the table and smiled. Her glance continued up to my hair and she gave a small shudder. She'd stopped actually mentioning it.

"Have a good day at school?" she asked as we unloaded the groceries into the refrigerator.

"Fine."

"Been home long?"

"Belinda and I stopped for a few minutes to watch the track team work out."

Mom smiled again at the mention of Belinda. If I didn't look quite the way Mom wanted her daughter to look, at least I had a best friend who did. Mom's hair was cut close to her head and shaped in neat waves. She wore a dark gray suit and a white blouse. On weekends she wore cardigan sweaters with tailored slacks. She was beyond salvation. Other than that, she is a nice mom.

A couple of hours later, after my favorite TV show and a shower, I returned to my letter writing. Wrapped in my terry robe, a towel around my head, I curled up on my bed and checked back over what I'd written.

Maybe the publisher received thousands of letters. Probably they threw them away. Who'd want to answer all those letters? If I wanted them to do what I requested, I had to give them a good reason.

I chewed on my pencil while I thought.

It hit me like an inspiration. Why not give them the truth? Oh, not the bit about knowing that The Boy was meant for me, but the other truth-why not tell them that?

Taking out a clean sheet of paper, I started over, using the same explanation about wanting to contact The Boy's agent. What I added was my attention-getter, the line to keep me out of the wastebasket.

"I think his agent would like to know about me because the truth is, I look exactly like Cyndi Superstar. I am enclosing a snapshot of myself so you can see what I mean."

We had exactly the same oval face and blue eyes and full mouth. Our noses were a little different, but how much does a nose count? I plucked my eyebrows to match hers, and I made up my lids in crescents of lavender and green shading, exactly the way she did, and although her hair was bleached to an almost white, which my parents absolutely forbid, at least my cut was like hers, and on weekends, which was when I'd had the snapshot taken, my parents let me add a temporary orange tint on the tips of my brown hair, exactly the way she tipped her blond hair.

Everyone said I looked like her, which was no surprise to me. I'd known that the first time I saw her on TV. And when I saw her name, the same as mine, though mine was spelled C-I-N-D-Y, I knew fate meant her to be my role model. On that day a year ago, I changed the spelling of my name, had my hair cut, and spent a couple of hours in the drugstore finding all the makeup I needed.

I'd also spray-painted my T-shirts and jeans with stars, which were Cyndi's symbol, and copied everything else I could. I watched her TV specials and Belinda said I walked exactly like her. I couldn't sing, but I could play the guitar a little.

There was no reason to explain all that. All I wanted the publisher to do was see the photo, think that the agent might be interested, and send my name there.

I stamped the letter, kissed it for luck, and the next day, on the way to school, dropped it in a mailbox.

Step one toward finding the boy on the cover was accomplished.

CHAPTER 2

Two and a half weeks later I'd gone through steps one, two, and three, and I'd started on four.

Step one was a bummer. All I received from the publisher was a catalog of available books, no letter or anything personal. Right away I knew they'd stuck my name and address in their computer mailing list and thrown away my letter.

I took the catalog to school to show Belinda what became of thoughtful letters to publishers. She was a little late meeting me on the front steps after school. There I stood thinking that the buds on the trees could forget about leafing because who cared in such a miserable world, when Ralph grinned his way up to me and said his usual, "Hi, whatcha doing?"

"Hi, Ralph," I said and tried to peer past his shoulder in the hope of discovering a reason to go on existing.

"Whatcha got?" he said, lifting the catalog off the top of the notebook I was holding in my arm.

I didn't bother to answer. Ralph's one virtue was that he could carry on a conversation alone, leaving me free to think of other things.

"Hey, that's neat!" Ralph leafed through the catalog. "Hey, it's addressed to you? I never get catalogs addressed to me. I never get any mail at all."

"There's an e-mail address. You can get their catalog online if you want," I said. The star of the girls' gymnastics team wandered past, her arm linked through the arm of a guy I didn't know by name. "Who's that guy with Barbara?"

Ralph looked where I was pointing. "Hal Nuen, junior, honor student, why?"

Correction: Ralph had two virtues. His second virtue was that he knew who everyone was.

I shrugged. Ralph carried on his one-person conversation, leafing through my catalog and reading aloud book titles until Belinda showed up and we headed home.

"What am I going to do?" I wailed when we were out of Ralph's or anyone else's hearing.

"Let me see the book," Belinda said.

Reluctantly I handed it to her. I'd reached a point where I almost hated to let that cover out of my possession. We sat on a curb, our feet in the gutter, which was still slightly damp from the midday downpour, our knees bent up almost to our chins. Belinda flipped through the pages. She could go right past that cover without being mesmerized.

"What are you looking for?"

"I was reading a paperback the other day and- yes! There's one in this book, too! Look, they have an address where you can order new books."

"I don't want to order books. Now, if they sold the covers in poster size, I'd be interested."

"Sure, but it's a different department, don't you see? Why not write to it?"

"Why would a book order department send me The Boy's address?"

Belinda sighed. "I don't know, Cyndi, but figure it this way. It's a different person opening the mail. Maybe it will be some very kind person. Whoever it is has to work for the publisher and must know the address of that model's agent."

"What about an e-mail address?"

"They give their webpage. That's all. You can order books online, not models' names."

That was step two. I put it into action that night with another letter. But the next day I had doubts. What if the order department was also run by a computer?

Was there anyone in the world who wasn't run by a computer? That question became the major concern of my life. It filled my mind through history and Language Arts, though in both classes I at least kept my book opened to the right page. When it didn't rain and we had to go outside for gym, I chugged slowly around the track and held a mental picture of The Boy as inspiration.

Beside me a girl gasped out a question. "Didn't I see you with an orange tint on your hair?"

"On weekends," I puffed back. Neither of us was a natural athlete.

"It comes off that easy?"

"With shampoo."

"Honest? Where do you get it?"

I slowed to walking speed but kept up a jogging bounce to avoid confrontations with the gym teacher while I gave her the name of the hair coloring and the drugstore where I bought it.

"That's terrific," she said. "Anyone ever tell you that you look exactly like Cyndi Superstar?"

"Do you think so?" I said, trying to sound surprised and offhand, neither of which was easy to do out of breath.

In math class I set my paperback in front of me in my propped-up math book and gave it full thought. Ms. Childer only interrupted me twice and I could answer without fully losing touch with my thoughts about The Boy. Maybe it was the natural connection between math and computers that gave me my next inspiration. What I needed was the name of a real live person, someone who didn't just copy names off envelopes onto mailing lists.

The only name in the book was that of the author. True, there was no address for the author, but surely there had to be some way to write to authors. Inspired, I thought of a use for my Language Arts teacher, who until then had only made my life difficult by red-penciling all over my papers.

Mr. Kessle was as amazed to see me drop by his room voluntarily after school as I was amazed to be there, but we both hid our surprise with good manners. I started right out with a please.

"Mr. Kessle, could I please ask you a question? It's not about Language Arts, exactly, but it is about a book."

Mr. Kessle's forehead wrinkled, but he said in a normal tone, "Of course, Cyndi, what book is it?"

I had this impression that he didn't believe I read books. I did, even the books he assigned, but I didn't understand his books. When he asked, I almost blurted out the title. Mr. Kessle was my grandfather's age, honestly. He probably thought romance books were a waste of time.

Thinking fast, I said, "Umm, gosh, I've forgotten, something about a-um-boy. Anyway, I wanted to write to the author. Can people write to authors?"

"If the author is still alive."

For the first time I had a glimmer of why I didn't understand the books he assigned. They must all have been written by dead authors. I said, "It's a new book."

"In that case, write to the author in care of the publisher."

Despite his opinion of my punctuation, the man had some smarts. I thanked him and made a fast getaway before he could ask any questions.

That night I shot off a letter to the author.

That was step three, a letter to the author telling him I'd read his book, because I didn't think he'd be very impressed if I said I'd only looked at the cover, and asking if he knew The Boy's name.

In two weeks I had written three letters, more than I usually wrote in a year. Had Mr. Kessle known, he'd have been stunned.

Impressed with myself, I challenged my father again on our usual combat zone. It was an argument we went through about once a week, although he said we weren't arguing. He said I was the one arguing and he wasn't, as he was simply stating policy and wasn't attempting to change anything.

"Can I use one of those spray-on lighteners that work with a blow-dryer?" I asked casually, sitting down beside him on the couch.

He was reading the paper. He didn't look away from the page. He said a flat no.

"They aren't dyes," I said. "You don't wash them in like bleaches. They just bring out highlights."

"No."

"Why not?"

"For the same reason that I've said you can't use a bleach or dye or rinse or anything by any other name that will change the color of your hair," he said, lowering the paper to make firm parental eye contact.

"It doesn't change it. It just lightens," I wailed.

"Cyndi, my darling," he said, "the rule still holds. When you are eighteen you may do anything you like to your hair, shave it off even, but until then, I expect your haircuts to be limited to weird shapes, no shaving, and the color to remain what God gave you, and any deviation from that rule will ground you."

"That's so old-fashioned!" I cried.

In his calm tone, he added, "And when your grandparents visit, would you please wear matching earrings? Also, be sure to wash off those fake tattoos. You are causing your grandmother emotional stress."

I went to my room, closed the door, sat on my bed, and stared at the boy on the cover. From the sincerity of his gaze I just knew that he would love the way I looked. My father didn't seem to believe that Cyndi Superstar was adored by millions all around the world, partly for her voice, but also partly for the way she looked. Lots of girls at school tried to look like her. I was the only one who really did.

Was there anyone else I could write to, now that I had letter writing practically perfected? Maybe I needed to snow New York City with my letters, the way the media did blitzes. I sat in the kitchen with my books spread out, in case a parent wandered through, and phoned Belinda to ask. She had no more suggestions.

"It's too bad I don't know the address of the photographer who took the picture." While I talked, my cat Sunny climbed onto my knees.

"Do you know who the photographer is?"

"Yeah, well, his name is inside the book. No address. I don't have an address."

"What if you did?"

"You think he's in New York City?" My other cat, Shadow, joined Sunny.

"Maybe. Why?"

I had this idea in my mind that I didn't think Belinda would approve of, at least not at first, and I didn't want her shrieking with shock. Her mother might hear and ask for an explanation.

I changed subjects. "If Louis hadn't gone out for track, we could have watched for him on the front steps and maybe thought of something to say to him."

Sunny nipped at Shadow's tail.

"Yeah, I thought of that," Belinda said.

Shadow hissed at Sunny.

Pushing both cats off my legs, I said, "How come you don't know Louis better? Even if you are in different debate classes, you go to the same tournaments."

The cats chased each other around the kitchen and under the table. I opened the back door. They streaked out.

"Junior debaters go with Mr. Bowman, the junior debate coach, and senior debaters go with Ms. Frazier, because she's their coach, and there are enough of us for two vans, so they split us up that way," Belinda explained.

"All right," I conceded. "Let's try this. Let's go to the mall tomorrow after school for a couple hours and then take the bus back to school and by then the track team should be done practicing and be heading home and we can watch for Louis and you can say hi to him."

"Wouldn't it be easier to stay at school?"

"And do what?"

"We could study in the library."

Nobody but a debater would think of spending a perfectly good afternoon studying in the school library. Still, it had one point in its favor. My parents didn't like me going to the mall after school. They might not give permission. But they'd probably cheer when I told them I'd be home late because I was studying at the school library.

Belinda added, "The library windows face the field. We'd know exactly when they finish."

Having committed myself to the plan, there was nothing for it but to spend an hour and a half after school the next day sitting quietly at a library table reading the history assignment. Every five minutes Belinda and I took turns faking a trip to a bookshelf by way of the windows.

When she returned after her tenth trip to whisper, "They're going in now!" I slammed my book closed, clapped my hands in relief, and jumped from my chair. An hour and a half glued to a chair to study was not Cyndi Carlisle style.

We waited on the front steps, very nonchalantly, keeping up conversation so that anyone spotting us would think we just happened to have stopped there to visit and not that we were waiting for anyone.

Belinda said, "When he appears, you wave at him and say hello."

"Me? I don't know him."

"Right, so he'll wonder who you are, and you can explain that you recognized him from somewhere."

"From where?"

"Cyndi! You'll think of something!"

"Let's get this right. I'm not the one who wants Louis for a debate partner. And if you say hello, you can call to him by name, and that'll lead right in to explaining that you're on the debate team."

"And make him admit he doesn't know all the debate team?"

"Belinda, can we discuss this calmly?" I was probably the only person who would say that to Belinda. She always looked much more calm than I did, and only a best friend would know that beneath the sleek, straight bob was a frantic brain.

"Help!" she whispered.

"Okay, now this is what you say. You say, 'Hi, aren't you on the debate team?' and when he says yes you say, 'Oh sure, you're on senior debate. I'll be in senior debate next year.' Now isn't that simple?"

"And then what do I say?"

"Am I right in believing that debaters stand up in front of judges and speak their thoughts and present all sorts of brilliant arguments?"

"Uh, yes, sort of."

"Then why am I, who have never received more than a C in a speech class in my life, telling a debater what to say?"

Belinda laughed, and that was good because for some reason this whole business of saying a simple hello was upsetting her.

I asked, "Is there more to this than a debate partner? Do you want to date Louis?"

"No!" she exclaimed. "He's not my type at all!"

"So why are you so worried?"

She started to answer, let out a screech, and pointed past my shoulder. I swung around in time to see Louis climbing into a car with some other guys.

In the late afternoon sun, his blond hair was unmistakable.

"They came out the side door!"

"And we wasted a whole afternoon in the library!"

Shouldering our bookbags, we headed home. The whole subject of Louis was too depressing to consider. The spring sky was striped with clouds and bright blue clearings. The grass and budded trees rustled in a breeze that smelled lemon-clean, like shampoo. And we'd wasted the afternoon in the library. And I couldn't complain about it because Belinda was far more upset than I was, and not about a wasted afternoon.

To give her something else to think about, I said, "You know the name of that photographer in New York that's in the book?"

She made an uh-huh noise, eyes downcast.

"Isn't there some way I can get his address?"

She shook her head. "Only if he has a webpage and then all you'll get is a way to order something."

"Oh. Aren't there some sites where you can get phone numbers? I could phone him."

"You're going to phone long-distance to New York?" She quit worrying about Louis and stared at me. "Don't you have a limited cell phone plan?"

I'd been right not to mention my idea to her over the phone the previous night. She would have screeched. I'd also been right to mention it now. Count on Belinda to see the flaw.

"There must be some way to phone without having it show up on the bill," I said.

"Use a pay phone," she said.

"How much would that cost?"

Belinda, who like all debaters always knew where to find information, said, "Look in the front of the phone book. It has a chart of long-distance charges. And it also tells what number to call for directory assistance."

That evening after supper I closed myself in my room with my nail stuff and the phone book. I did three coats of glitter polish on my fingernails. While the last coat was drying, I found the directory assistance number and wrote it down.

If I could get his number, I could use a pay phone at the mall.

I phoned directory assistance and gave them the photographer's name. Just my luck, they had a bunch of listings with similar names, but none exactly right.

"All right," I said, thinking fast and saying the first thing that came to mind. "What I need is his place of business. I forget the name, but it's a modeling agency."

Information regretted that he could not supply a number without a name.

And then I had an inspiration.

I said, "It's either his name or something like Talent or Teenage, or maybe just Models, Incorporated."

I mean, I was desperate. And desperate minds are creative minds. The way I figured it, with no real lead, at least if I could talk to a modeling agency, any agency, I might reach someone who could tell me how to locate a specific model.

I made up those agency names out of thin air.

To my amazed joy, directory assistance had a number listed for a place called Teen Models.

All I needed was a pay phone.

Step four had to wait until Saturday, our usual day for going to the mall. Belinda knew of several pay phones, most of them in open locations, hanging right out on walls where any passerby could overhear.

But one was in a small booth in an alcove behind a coffee shop whose customers all looked like grandparents.

I spread out several dollars' worth of change on the ledge.

While I punched in the number, Belinda propped her notepad against the inside of the door. We were kind of twisted around each other in the small space.

"Is this going to work?" I asked.

"Do you think you can sort change, ask questions, and write down answers at the same time?" Belinda said. "I'd be delighted to wait outside."

"No, please don't leave me," I said quickly.

We were both afraid that someone we knew would see us and think we were weird, jammed into that little booth together. I kept glancing toward the coffee shop. Actually, I didn't know anyone who would stop in that shop, but wasn't life like that, with that very moment being the one picked by the school's biggest blabbermouth to walk into that very alcove?

"Just speed it up so we can get out," Belinda suggested.

The phone went through a series of tones and ringings until a voice told me how much to deposit. I listened to the clink as the coins echoed down the slot.

A dead silence.

Then a voice. "Good morning, Teen Model, may I help you?"

"Is this Teen Model?" She'd just said it was. I made a face at Belinda, who was making faces at me, and hurried on. "Could you give me your address?"

The voice on the other end gave me an address, which I repeated aloud, and then she gave me a cross street. What I was meant to do with that, I didn't know, but I told Belinda anyway.

Next I asked, "Does your place do book cover photos?"

Long pause. "I'm sorry, could you repeat your question?"

I repeated it.

Another pause. "We supply models for a variety of assignments."

I gave Belinda a pleading look. She'd heard the answer. She mouthed, "Ask her. Maybe she knows?"

"Please," I said, "could I ask you a question then? On the cover of a particular book there's a-"

Belinda shook her head frantically. Right. I didn't want to sound as though I were some nutty fan trying to track down a guy.

I said, "There is a-a photo. Of a boy. Uh, would he be a professional model?"

"I don't know what photo you're referring to."

"Well, it's on this book and it's a very good photo, I think, and I wondered, is there some way to find out what studio took a particular photo, and uh, who the model's agent is?" I said it quickly, praying she wouldn't hang up on me.

"Oh," she said slowly, sounding friendlier. "Are you interested in becoming a model?"

Belinda nodded.

I said yes.

The voice said, "You want to talk to Ms. Jeffrey. She interviews prospective models. However, her office is closed today. If you'll call back on Monday and ask for Ms. Jeffrey's office, she can set up an appointment for you."

I was looking out of the phone booth, wondering what to ask next, because so far she hadn't told me anything useful, and at the same time watching the coffee shop so that we could turn our heads if anyone we knew walked by, when I saw him.

I honestly saw him.

It was him. It was the boy on the book cover.

CHAPTER 3

The voice from the receiver thanked me. There was a dial tone. Belinda told me to hang up. I did.

Belinda said, "I don't think it's going to do any good, even if you could call back on Monday."

He walked by again, looking around, as though he wasn't sure where he was. He paused, straight in my line of vision, and turned slowly, that questioning look on his face.

Belinda said, "Even if you get the name of his agent-"

I whispered, "He's there."

"-they won't tell you his name," she said, and then she added, "Who's where?"

We bumped against each other trying to untangle. I peered over her elbow. He was gone. "What is it?" Belinda demanded.

I was afraid to breathe.

"Are you sick? Don't get sick in here, there's not enough room. Come on, get out. Take a deep breath."

Outside the booth, I grabbed Belinda's hands. I had to hang onto something. "Belinda! I saw him! It was him, he was right there, and he looked right at me!"

"Hey, that hurts!" Belinda said, twisting her hands free from my clutches.

"Oh, sorry! Oh, gosh, I think I'll faint!"

"Stop it! What's wrong?"

I caught her arm, just above the elbow, and tried not to squeeze too hard, because I knew I did that when I was excited though I didn't mean to. But if I didn't grab her, she wouldn't follow. I rushed toward the front of the coffee shop while I explained.

"It was him, honestly, I saw him, so he can't have gone very far, come on!"

We ducked between shoppers. The mall was so crowded on Saturday we had to stay on the right-hand side, like cars on a street, to avoid bumping into oncoming walkers. Several times I thought I spotted him in front of me, but I wasn't sure. Backs of heads kind of look alike and he didn't turn.

"Who are we following?"

"That boy! The one on the cover!"

Belinda did a lot of gasping about impossible and ridiculous, but she kept up with me, probably because I was still clinging to her arm. We dashed half the length of the mall before I realized I'd lost him. I stopped, swung around and stared at all the open archways into shops.

The mall is like a big covered street with a glass ceiling high above it instead of sky, open shops on both sides, and rows of benches and potted palms running the full length of the center of the walkway to divide the traffic. A person could spend months in that mall and not see every corner of every store.

A person could also very quickly lose sight of another person.

"He's gone," I said. "But it was him, I know it was."

"It was somebody who looked like him," Belinda said.

"Belinda, stop that! I am not blind! I know what I saw and I tell you, I saw the boy on the cover! He looked right toward the phone booth. And I am sure I saw him out here, in front of us."

"What was he doing?" she asked.

"Walking. That way."

"By himself?"

I chewed my lip to help me think. "Maybe he was with some people, some old people, well, not real old, like maybe parents."

"Not with anyone we know?"

"No," I said, and then as if mentioning knowing someone could put a hex on us, up popped Ralph with his grin and his, "Hi, whatcha doing?"

Rather than explain, I decided to go to the juice bar. It was completely open, with tables and benches on the walkway. We bought three orange juices and sat facing the traffic to spot friends.

"Buy something?" Belinda asked Ralph, pointing to a sack he set down on the table.

"Yeah," he grinned. Ralph has round eyes like a puppy, the same sort of warm brown, and his hair is more like shaggy fur than hair.

From a distance he looked like an average guy, a little taller than Belinda or me, but up close all I could see was that little kid face. Sometimes I thought of him as a pet, like a mascot. Other times he was a pest.

He pulled out a couple of CDs. Belinda and I leaned toward him to read the labels.

"Oh, I like that group," Belinda said.

"Yeah, me, too," Ralph said.

Although I discussed bands with them, my mind was really on watching the mall. Somewhere out in that crowd was the boy who was maybe meant to be the most important person in my life. What if I never saw him again?

Coming out of a far archway I saw Louis Turner. He had an unmistakable walk that almost looked like a swagger, shoulders held back, blond head high, and there was a girl on each side of him. Louis was talking, like a typical debater, and the girls were both listening and peering up at him.

"Who are those girls with Louis?" I asked Ralph.

"Jen Something and Maureen Bush, sophomores, relay team," Ralph said.

"I told you you should go out for track," I said to Belinda, and then to Ralph, "How well do you know them?"

"Want to meet them?" he grinned and started to lift his hand to wave.

Belinda ducked backward on the bench, hiding her head behind Ralph's back and grabbing at his arm. "Don't!" she hissed.

Ralph gave me a puzzled look.

"Come out," I said to Belinda. "They're not looking this way."

She sat up straight and checked.

"Ralph could call to the girls and they'd come over and we could talk to everyone," I said sensibly, at least that seemed like a sensible suggestion to me. I very carefully did not mention Louis, although he would surely walk over with the girls.

Belinda enunciated through stiff, unmoving lips. "Don't you dare. This is not the place."

If the mall wasn't the place to talk to people, where was? I shrugged and said, "Okay, what do you want to do?"

"Go someplace else."

And right then I had a wonderful new inspiration. If Belinda wasn't ready to face-to-face it with Louis, I might as well charge on with my project. Wasn't it possible that The Boy, being a professional model and maybe a famous actor, was also on some other book cover, or even in a magazine?

"Let's go to the bookstore," I said.

At the front of the mall bookstore, near the cash-register desk, was a wall covered with rows of magazines. We stood there thumbing through them while I kept an eye on the people out in the mall. I glanced through all the teen magazines, the movie and rock magazines, and even a couple of sports magazines on a wild hope, although I didn't think he looked like a jock.

"Let's check the teen books," I said. They were way in the back, past rows of shelves and tables filled with all kinds of other junk, on a wall marked Young Adult. The books were racked on metal wire holders that turned around.

I spun one slowly, checking top to bottom on each of its four sides, looking for that face.

Then it hit me. He could be out there now, in plain sight, but how could I see him from the back of the shop? I said, "Be back," to Belinda and raced to the front of the store.

The Language Arts teacher once said something about not seeing the tree because of the forest, and I knew what he meant. There was such a forest of people, ail moving, that it was hard to spot any one person.

When I returned to the back of the store, Belinda held out a book.

"That him?" she asked.

"That who?" Ralph asked, sticking his head in between our shoulders.

"Oh, no, nothing like!"

"I guess not," she agreed.

"These books are all dumb love stories," Ralph said.

"You could go look at something else."

"That's okay, I don't have any more money, anyway," he said.

I turned another rack and checked each cover. Then I did another fast dash to the front to check the mall. If I kept it up, zigzagging between display tables and customers, I'd be the one ready to go out for track, probably for something like hurdles.

When I returned, Ralph and Belinda had moved farther back in the store to look at the science fiction books. They had covers that were paintings, of no use to me at all. I stayed with the romances, with their photo covers, checking a row and then checking the front walk.

On my fifth dash, I almost floored him. I'd picked up speed with each trip. I must have shot out of the archway at a dead run. We nearly collided. I skidded to a stop.

He wasn't ten inches away, so close I could even see those soft, curving lower lashes and the color of his eyes, grayer than in the photo, and across the bridge of that fabulous nose, a pale scattering of freckles. I hadn't known about the freckles at all, but then models and actors always cover freckles with makeup.

His eyes widened in that questioning way.

I couldn't breathe. My own mouth was hanging open but I couldn't make a single sound come out. I wanted to say "Hello," or "Excuse me," or anything.

He looked as though he expected me to say something. He waited.

I even thought of Ralph's "Hi, whatcha doing?" but I couldn't make a sound.

He was exactly like the picture, the thin, tanned face, the firm chin, plus a softness to his lower lip that the photographer had missed completely, and the eyebrows were a little thicker, the hair darker, all tricks of makeup and lighting, and if anything, he was much handsomer in person than in a tiny photo. He was Ralph's height, maybe taller, with squarer shoulders.

While I gaped, frozen, a voice behind me said, "Come on, Tommy, we're late."

He moved his head slightly, not exactly a nod to me, but not exactly not, either, and walked on by. I turned, following him with my gaze. Yes, his shoulders were square, his build both solid and graceful, with narrow hips and long legs, and where his arms showed beneath the short sleeves of his T-shirt, the muscles were firm.

I'd never been so aware of anyone before in my life.

Belinda said, "What are you doing?"

I was standing in the middle of the mall staring at the backs of the crowd that had closed in between me and him.

"His name is Tommy," I said slowly.

"Whose name?"

"I almost touched him. He was here. With his father. And his name is Tommy."

"Start at the top," she said, but Ralph popped up between us.

"Later," I said.

Although we wandered the length of the mall a dozen times, with Ralph asking repeatedly where we were going, I didn't see The Boy again.

At supper I asked if I could go back to the mall on Sunday and received a firm no.

"One day is plenty," Dad said.

After supper I phoned Belinda. If I couldn't look for The Boy, I could at least talk about him. Sitting on my bed clutching my cell phone, I said, "Did I tell you he has freckles?"

"You did," she said. "I've never been that crazy about freckles."

"They're real light, just a thin band beneath his eyes and across his nose."

"I guess that'd be okay."

"And his eyes are grayer and his hair darker than in the picture, and he's really better-looking."

"I do remember you saying that," she said.

"Oh, I've said that before?"

"All the way home. Listen, Cyndi, honestly, I don't think it could have been him. I mean, what would he be doing in our mall?"

"I see your point," I said. "How would anyone from New York City even find this town? Or if they did, why would they stay long enough to spend a Saturday at the mall?"

"That's not what I meant."

"I'm sure it was him," I said, before she could say she was sure it couldn't have been.

All the way home on the bus Belinda had given me her theories about why I imagined him. But would I have imagined a boy named Tommy? Derrick or Banning or Jason, maybe, but Tommy was the sort of name my parents liked.

On Sunday afternoon my mother shocked me by poking her head into my room, where I had stretched out on the floor to play with my cats, and saying, "Cyndi, I have to go out to the mall today after all, so if you want to come with me-"

I jumped straight up, shouting, "Yes, yes, yes!"

I switched into my best jeans and my most terrific shirt, touched up my makeup, did a quickie spray job on my hair, and was out in the car before she was.

It was for nothing.

Mom had a list of shopping errands for an office party-somebody was getting married-and she rushed from store to store. The trouble with Mom was that she knew what she wanted. No browsing around. No telling clerks she was just looking. Instead she'd head straight for a clerk, ask for an item, and charge down the aisles without hesitating.

I ran after her, swiveling my head in hopes of seeing Tommy. At the speed I swiveled, my hair would have been windblown if it hadn't been so well sprayed.

"Mom," I gasped, "wouldn't you like a nice healthy glass of orange juice?"

She laughed. "Would you?"

Although there were all sorts of snack shops, the juice bar had the best view of the mall. I bypassed a milkshake just so that I could watch for Tommy.

My mother could also drink an orange juice with quick efficiency. Ten minutes later we raced through her last errand and headed out to the car. As I had seen no one I knew, except Louis Turner who, as usual, was flanked by girls and not the same ones I'd seen Saturday, that extra trip to the mall was a bummer.

Was it possible that Belinda was right? Had I imagined seeing The Boy? Had my fevered brain done one of those hallucination things, like fevered brains are always doing in Saturday-night late movies?

Could I really have dreamed up a fine line of freckles and the name Tommy?

If I wasn't crazy, suppose he'd been in town for one day? Maybe his parents had friends in my town, hard as that was to believe. If so, would he be back?

I wrote a letter that very night, telling him where I lived and how very much I'd like to meet him, and reminding him that I'd almost knocked him down in the mall.

It was my last chance. It had to be lucky.

I addressed the envelope to "Tommy, the model on the cover," listed the title and author, and addressed it to the publisher. I wrote in large letters, PLEASE FORWARD.

CHAPTER 4

On Monday morning while I stood on the steps in front of the high school watching the buses unload, Belinda and Ralph argued about the ending of a Sunday-night TV cop show.

"The guy in the helicopter wasn't working for the mobster," Ralph said.

"Oh, Ralph," Belinda sighed, "you weren't listening. Right at the point when they lined them up, the policeman explained that."

"Did you get that, Cyndi?" Ralph asked.

I shrugged. We'd watched the same show at our house, but I'd been thinking about Tommy and hadn't really been paying attention.

Across from the high school was a small park. It cut through the center of the block, with houses on both sides, so that what it was was a square of grass about as large as four vacant lots. In the middle of the grass stood a statue of George Washington with paths leading up to and around it.

For a crazy minute that tall bronze statue of George Washington on a pedestal, gleaming away in the morning sun, shimmered out of focus and turned into Tommy.

I could see him standing tall, facing the high school, immortalized in bronze. He wasn't just a model anymore, he was a world-famous rock star and the only one who'd ever made a personal appearance in our town.

"What do you think?" Ralph asked, nudging me with his elbow.

"No good asking her. She's off in Cloud Land," Belinda said.

And I was. Which is why, when what happened next did actually happen, I didn't believe it. I thought I was dreaming again.

If I took my experiences as a math problem, they'd come out something like this: First, I saw a picture on a book cover of a guy who lived probably hundreds, maybe thousands, of miles away from me, and I knew he was meant for me. Second, I thought I saw the guy in the local mall, but no one else saw him. Third, the statue of George Washington turned into that guy. Fourth, my best friend said I was hallucinating.

If I had to put that into an equation, one, two, and three would equal four, which was mathematically impossible, proving that Belinda was right.

I shrugged, the statue became George Washington again, and the bell rang. The buses had all unloaded. Everyone of interest had gone by us up the stairs and into the building.

Ralph and Belinda followed after them.

I paused, not more than a second after they turned, to take a last glance back at George Washington. As the last bus pulled away, a car pulled in behind it.

The door opened on the curb side. As I told Belinda later, it must have been fate that kept me frozen in place. I was meant to be standing there, the first person he saw when he climbed out of the car, said good-bye to whoever was driving, and looked up the steps toward our school.

It was the boy I'd seen at the mall. Tommy. The boy on the cover.

He was still in town.

I knew that my mouth was hanging open but I couldn't do anything about it. He was not only at my school, looking up the walkway and straight at me, he looked as though he intended to stay. He wore jeans and a sweater, and he was carrying a notebook. He looked like he was a student. But he couldn't be. If he'd been at our school all along, I'd have seen him. Our school isn't that large.

He had that puzzled look on his face again.

And if he was puzzled, I was in a state of shock. I figured my mind was going for sure. A couple of other students rushed up the steps and one of them brushed against me as she went by. I came out of my trance, closed my mouth, swung around, and fled into the building.

I didn't hear a word anyone said for the rest of the morning. If there were any quizzes, I must have flunked them. Over and over in my mind, I pictured Saturday at the mall and then that fifteen minutes on the steps before school. Was I crazy?

By noontime I'd come up with a possible explanation. Suppose Tommy Whoever was a student at my school and had been all year. Maybe he was a senior, in which case I might have only seen him once or twice in a crowd. Less believable to me was that I wouldn't have remembered him, but I tried to believe it because otherwise I'd have to believe that I was losing my mind.

And even less believable than that was the idea that he had just moved to our town. Why would anyone move from exciting New York to our dull town? So, accepting that he'd just recently caught my eye, suppose I'd then seen the book cover. No wonder I'd been so attracted to it! It reminded me of someone I'd already seen.

So I wasn't crazy and there was a perfectly logical explanation and I went to lunch feeling much better.

When I told Belinda my theory, she said, "That figures."

Belinda likes neat, reasonable explanations. She was reality-centered, my Dad once said, which meant that if I told her about what had happened to the statue, she'd think I'd flipped, so I kept my mouth shut.

"Now all I've got to do is find out who he is," I said.

We had to lean so close to each other to talk our heads were almost touching, but it was the only way to keep a conversation private. The cafeteria was crowded. A couple of girls sitting near us didn't have anyone to talk to. They stared at their lunches while listening in on everyone else.

"Ask Ralph," Belinda suggested.

"I will if I ever see this guy when Ralph is around."

Belinda didn't answer. She was frowning.

"You have another idea?" I asked.

"No, it's not that. It's this morning. Honestly, it was so awful. Sometimes I think I ought to drop out."

"Drop out of what?"

"We did another practice match in debate class and the other team tromped us. I was so embarrassed."

"Your partner blew it?"

"I know he tries," she sighed. "And if I were better, I could cover for him. But when he gets the evidence backward and then gives the wrong references, well, I get all churned up inside, you know? And then I get my evidence wrong, and it gets worse and worse."

"Sounds like me in Language Arts."

"Yes," she said slowly, picking her words with typical Belinda-like care. "But the thing is, this isn't just a class. I wouldn't mind if it were just a class. But I have to do this at meets, in front of judges, and here it is almost the end of the season and I thought by now we'd at least do okay if not great. And instead, we're getting worse."

"It just seems that way," I said. "Probably you're better."

"We're not. And we still have another tournament. And I think I'd be happy if I got the flu, because then I wouldn't have to go."

A statement like that, from Belinda, who felt about debating the way I felt about Cyndi Superstar's videos, was a shocker. Whatever else I did, before the end of this year I just had to help my best friend get a better partner.

"We're having extra practice after school, so I won't be walking home with you," Belinda said.

"I'll call you tonight."

She gave me this pathetic smile. She'd held up well until now. All I could figure was that she'd kept herself above her team's poor record by pinning her hopes on a terrific show at the last tournament. This morning had undone her.

Out of habit I waited on the steps after school while the buses loaded. It wasn't much fun without Belinda. I would even have welcomed Ralph. He didn't show up, either.

My mom wouldn't be home for another hour. There was nothing on afternoon TV worth watching. With nothing else to do, I wandered past the athletic field and watched the track team do their stretches. I wasn't sure how long Belinda's debate practice would last. Maybe if I hung around, they'd finish.

Or it could be hours before they went home. Not much point waiting. Bored, I turned away from the field to head home.

And there he was again, his back to me, walking under the sun and moving shadows cast by the curb trees. He was across the street and half a block away, swinging along, not hurrying, but not pausing either, turning his head occasionally to look at the houses he passed.

Why hadn't I ever seen him walking home from school before? Belinda and I went that way every day. I swung my bookbag onto my shoulder and hurried after him.

I didn't have the nerve to shout, "Hey, Tommy, wait up!"

I wanted to, but I couldn't. He headed right down my old route, even paused to pat the retriever who bounded down from the porch of an old house to greet every passerby. I always patted that retriever. And he paused to sniff a new yellow bud from the forsythia that hung over the walk. I always did that, too.

When he reached a corner, instead of going straight on toward my house, he turned right. I was still half a block behind him. Whenever he paused, I paused. He never once looked back over his shoulder.

If he had, I might have waved.

But what if I waved and he pretended he didn't see me? I wished fervently that Belinda was with me. Together we could have casually speeded up, caught up with him, and said, "Hi."

He kept on going, three blocks past my corner, turned another corner, and disappeared. I rushed forward to peer around a hedge that lined the sidewalk, terrified that I'd lose him. But no, there he was, still walking, his back to me. Could it be the wrong boy? It was the right build, the right height, the right long legs, oh, and of course, the right sweater. That couldn't all be coincidence.

As I followed, I took a quick look at my surroundings. At fifteen, I'd feel stupid if I had to knock on some stranger's door to admit that I was lost and ask my way home. I'd never had a friend on this particular street. It was unfamiliar, with different houses and hedges, yet it didn't look too different from my own street.

There were grass lawns and dusty old hedges overhung by gnarled trees. There were daffodils at doorsteps. Friendly dogs and suspicious cats slept in the shafts of sunlight on front porches. Occasionally an old house had been torn down and replaced by a newer one with a deck instead of a porch and a front yard of gravel, tanbark, and small shrubs.

He turned up a walk. I heard the front door slam. By the time I reached the walk, there was no sign of him. The house wasn't new but it looked newly painted. Its lawn and hedges were carefully trimmed. It didn't tell me a thing.

And if I stood staring at it, he'd see me and think I was following him. I could imagine him inside, looking through a window, wondering who was that weird girl who'd trailed after him from school.

"So what did you do then?" Belinda asked when I told her about it over the phone after supper.

"You're not going to believe this," I whispered. I was sitting in the kitchen, books spread out on the table, watching the door. I suspected that my father, who was in the front room with my mother, would not approve of me tailing guys. My parents were reading. Without the TV going, I was afraid they might hear me.

"I already don't believe it," Belinda said.

"I think I know his last name."

"You finally remembered where you saw him before? So you were right, he's been at school all year?"

"No, not that. Listen, I took this quick last look at the house and there it was, really bright on the mailbox, as though somebody just newly painted it. It said Dalton."

"His name is Tommy Dalton?"

"Unless it wasn't his house. I can't be sure."

"Ask Ralph," she said. "If there's a Tommy Dalton in school, Ralph will know."

"Okay. How was debate practice?""Don't ask," she said. "Let me just say I won't be walking home with you tomorrow, either."

If debate practice had been that bad, I had two requests to make of Ralph. To his amazement, I went looking for him before school, spotted him getting off his bus, and I popped up next to him.

"Hiya," I said. "Whatcha doing?"

Ralph gave me a startled grin. "Hiya, Cyndi! Where's Belinda?"

"Don't know. I haven't seen her yet. Listen, Ralph, I've got a favor to ask."

The grin widened, which wasn't what usually happened when I asked favors of people. In his way, Ralph was a sweetie.

"Actually, I've got two favors."

That didn't worry him, either.

I continued, "Both are very confidential, so don't tell anyone why you're doing them."

He shifted his books to his far hand and leaned closer to me as we walked up the stairs so that I could talk more softly. He even did a quick glance over his shoulder to check for eavesdroppers.

"Ralph, have you ever heard of a boy named Tommy Dalton?"

"Don't think so. Why do you want to know?"

"I just do," I said, and he nodded, accepting that as a good explanation. "And the other thing I want to know is this. Does Louis Turner have anybody picked out to be his debate partner next year?"

"Right," Ralph said. "First I identify one Tommy Dalton, and second I check out the future debate plans of one Louis Turner. Any other orders?".

"That's it for now."

Ralph saluted and gave another one of his ear-to-ear grins before we headed for our classrooms.

Throughout the morning I did a lot of peering around people in the corridors and at lunch in the cafeteria, hoping to glimpse Tommy

Dalton. Belinda warned me I was going to get a stiff neck.

When that didn't stop me, she pointed out, "You are also spilling chocolate milk down your shirt, which does not add to your glamour rating."

"Oh, Belinda, I wish you'd been with me yesterday! I wish you could see him!"

"Me, too," she said. "Seeing would be believing."

"You still think I've made him up."

Although she denied that, I knew she wouldn't really believe in Tommy Dalton until she met him up close with the book cover in her hand for comparison. After dumping our lunch trays on the cleanup counter, we headed for our afternoon classes. I continued my peer-around-people maneuvers over Belinda's protests.

It paid off. I saw him.

"There," I hissed, "look there toward the windows."

It gave me fantastic satisfaction to hear Belinda gasp with astonishment. She whispered, "You're right, that's him! That's the same guy who's on the book cover!" But being a debater, she then refused to accept the evidence of her own eyes without proof. Backing down, she added, "Or his double."

I elbowed her in the ribs, lightly, though she deserved worse.

After she turned away to head for the gym I almost went to math. But what was I thinking of? There he was, in the same corridor. This was my chance. Shrugging off my conscience, I tailed him.

Naturally his next class was at the far end of the building, nowhere near the math room. I'd never been in that room. There was a label in the small metal frame mounted beneath the door window, but it wasn't readable from any distance.

What else could I do but hang around across the corridor, ducked halfway behind the edge of a row of lockers so that hie wouldn't spot me, and wait till the bell rang? The last person went into the room and closed the door. I looked up and down the hallway to check for anyone who might see me and doubt my sanity before approaching the door in a crouch that kept my head below the window.

The label read LANGUAGE ARTS 6, which was junior level. So Tommy Dalton was a junior and had probably been walking through that door every day all year and I hadn't known. Maybe he'd even touched that door. I put my palms flat against it, half-expecting to feel his vibrations.

My mind popped back into focus. I remembered where I was supposed to be and hurried away.

If Ms. Childer sent me for a tardy slip, I wouldn't blame her. What sort of excuse would I give the office? "Sorry, I didn't get to class in time because I was feeling a door for vibrations."

I tried to slip quietly into the math room. Ms. Childer was at the board, pointing to a problem. She stopped, looked straight at me, and said, "Oh, Cyndi, there you are." My heart sank. She went on, "Good, get your book open and tell the class what you did with this problem."

With my breathing resumed, I took my seat and gave her the right answer.

Ralph met me on the steps after school. While we watched the buses load, he told me what he'd found out. "There's a Tom Dalton in school. He's a junior."

"I know," I said.

"If you know, why did you ask me?"

"That's all I know. Anything else you tell me will be news."

"Okay, here goes. He transferred in today from New York, he lives over on Park Street, and I've got his class schedule if you want it. About Turner, his partner won't be here next year and he hasn't made any decision about next year because team assignments have to go through the coaches after the season's over and not before."

I jumped up and down, clapping my hands.

"Ralph, you're a miracle!"

I didn't ask him where he got his information because then he could ask me why I wanted it. Having known each other since kindergarten, we had a few unspoken understandings.

Ralph ducked his head and did a phony aw shucks act followed by his normal grin.

"Can I really have his class schedule?"

He handed it to me. "Whatcha going to do now?"

Although I practically drowned Ralph in thanks, I didn't answer his question.

What else would I do? I did what any normal girl would do who had been handed the class schedule of the most terrific guy in town and probably in the whole world. I figured out exactly what his route would be from class to class and at what points my route could cross his without making me conspicuously late to my classes.

CHAPTER 5

When I explained to Belinda what I was doing, she said, "You need new batteries! Your brain's quit!"

"Why?" I asked her over the phone.

"Guys don't like girls who stalk them."

"How do you know?" I asked.

"Everybody knows that," she said and sighed. "I'll think about that," I said and hung up.

What I thought, after I'd danced my way through Cyndi Superstar's newest album, was that Belinda might be partly right. It was a wonder how much better I could think when I spent an hour or two after school dancing around our empty house wearing my iPod. Maybe it let my brain cool down from the day's strain.

If Tom Dalton realized I was following him, I decided, he might think I was the sort of geek no guy would want to know. The alternative to that was to be always in his line of vision, busily chatting up some other guy.

The trouble with that idea was that I'd once known a girl who did that. The guy she wanted to attract saw her all right. And he figured she had so many boyfriends he'd prefer a girl with more free time.

What I needed was a way to be in his line of vision but not looking at him. I'd have to do it as though our paths crossed by accident. That meant I better skip walking home behind him and stick to crossing his path at the same time twice a day on my way to class. And I couldn't do too much hanging around with friends while watching him out of the corner of my eye. I had to be really subtle.

But if I was too subtle, would he ever notice me? I phoned Belinda again.

"Cyndi," Belinda said in her patient tone, "you are visible at the minimum of a mile."

That was not true. Although I did my best to be an individual, so did lots of girls. Worse yet, maybe he liked the cheerleader types, with their parent-approved clothes and haircuts.

"If only I could wear something really different," I moaned.

Belinda said, "How about a pierced eyebrow?"

"Elinor Stokes has one."

"I was joking! I didn't mean it!"

"It wouldn't be a bad idea if it weren't for Elinor Stokes."

"It would, too! Cyndi, if this guy comes from New York, like Ralph said, he's probably very sophisticated. He's seen every kind of piercing. And before you say it, the same goes for tattoos."

She was right. That's what it came down to. What would interest a guy who'd lived in New York City? He'd probably been to lots of rock concerts. He'd seen everything live, not just on TV. Maybe he'd even attended that famous high school for talented teenagers.

And there I was, with a wardrobe of small-town clothes that I'd had to paint and bleach and tear and adapt myself to make them look like anything special, and a headful of dumb brown hair.

If I was allowed to bleach my hair, I could have be twice as visible. There was one girl at school who had almost black hair. She'd streaked the top pink. There was no missing her.

Why didn't I have parents who'd let me do that?

I passed Tom in the hall twice the next day. If he saw me, he kept a good secret.

By the time I walked home alone after school, I was desperate. And evening consultations on the phone with Belinda weren't enough. Her mind was on her debate practice. She couldn't concentrate on me. I'd have to solve my own problems.

Stopping by the corner drugstore, I wandered through and checked out all the lipsticks. Really boring colors. I had a better range at home. Then I went on to the eyeshadow. Nothing there. To get new shades, I had to shop the mall, which I couldn't do again until Saturday. By then Tom would probably have fallen in love with Elinor Stokes or the girl with the pink streaks, or the captain of the cheerleading squad.

The lower I felt the more desperate I got. And when I get desperate enough, I don't always make the best decisions. So what I did next was maybe not too smart. And if Belinda had been with me, instead of at debate practice, I wouldn't have done it because she would have pointed out the risks.

But there I was, thinking about how I'd walked right past him twice and how he hadn't even looked at me. In fact, it was worse than that. I suspected he did see me. Because as I approached him the second time, he turned away, almost as though he was intentionally avoiding me. And if he was, then he thought I was stalking, and he wanted me to quit.

With all this misery in my mind, I found myself in front of the hair-dye shelf. I looked past bleaches and dyes, which even in that state I remembered were forbidden. But on a lower shelf was the stuff I'd mentioned to my father. It wasn't a dye. It wasn't on the shelf marked "Permanent Color."

It was in a different kind of package and it was called Sunbright Girl. The girl on the front had hair that was pure gold. On the back the instructions said the stuff worked with a hair dryer.

'To bring out your highlights," it said. Not a word about dye. "Apply after shampooing," it said. "Blow dry. No messy bleach. No waiting. Brightens and lightens. Puts sunshine in your hair."

Now who could object to a little sunshine in my hair?

My father could. I knew that. But first he'd have to see it. And I would be very discreet.

I went straight home, shampooed, sprayed the top of my hair very lightly, and blow-dried it. Only by leaning very close to the mirror and peering analytically could I see that my hair was any lighter. In fact, the change was so small, I wasn't sure that there was a change.

I decided that if the difference was invisible, I'd better give it another try. I did a second shampoo and spray.

My mother did a lot of sideways glancing at me during supper. Not wanting to encourage her to blurt out any suspicions, I pretended not to notice. But I was nervous. Because the truth was, the second time I could see the difference.

It wasn't a Wow! I'm a blonde! change. It was more of a Gee, I've got highlights! change. Would Dad notice highlights? Were highlights the same as a dye job in his elderly opinion?

When he didn't say anything, I figured I was home free.

And when I met Belinda on the steps before school, she didn't notice.

However, Tom Dalton did stop in his tracks on an approach down the hall in my direction. I saw him at corridor length do a U-turn. And I also was sure he'd stared right at me for a split second. But my hair couldn't have been the reason, or someone else would have mentioned it.

At noon, Belinda and I took our lunches outside to sit on the grass by the front walk with the rest of the school. Although the trees were barely in leaf, the sun was midsummer hot, filling the air with the scent of lawn. We rolled up our sleeves and jeans to give our tans a start.

"Tomorrow it will probably snow," Belinda said.

"They should close school for the rest of the day," I said.

"What did you do to your hair?" she asked.

"Huh?"

"There hasn't been that much sun."

I clapped my hands on the top of my head. "Is it that obvious? Dad didn't notice."

"He didn't? Did he see you outside?"

"No."

"It sure shows up out here. Did you bleach it?"

"Of course I didn't! That's not allowed! I simply used some spray stuff that is supposed to bring out highlights."

In her dead calm voice, Belinda said, "I think it contains something that's not allowed. Did you read the ingredients?"

"The ingredients?"

"Look for the word peroxide."

"Belinda, you are ruining my whole day."

"Sorry," she said, then smiled. "I've just seen something to brighten your day. Turn your head very slowly to the left, don't jerk, just let your eyes slide that way, over by the maples, uh-huh, a little more to the left. See him?"

And there he was, sitting at the edge of a group of guys, not listening to what they were saying, but instead staring at me.

"He's watching you," she said.

"I see that," I said. "It must be my hair."

"It's not that obvious, Cyndi. No, he's watching you, plain old watching you, no look of shocked amazement on his face."

My eyeballs were beginning to ache, I had them swiveled so far to the side. "So what's it mean?"

"I don't know," she said slowly. 'Tell you what. When I say look you swing around and look him right in the eyes."

"I can't!" I hissed.

"Turn!"

I did. My eyes met Tom Dalton's gaze for as long as it took him to blink and look in another direction.

"I was right!" Belinda said. "He really was watching you, not just glancing over this way, and he doesn't want you to know he's watching."

"But why?"

"You haven't been writing him anonymous letters or something?"

I frowned, remembering the letter I'd written to the publisher with Tommy's name on it. I'd dropped that in the mail on Monday morning on the way to school.

When I told Belinda about it, she said, "This is only Thursday, and to have seen it, he'd have to have got it yesterday. A letter can't get to New York and be forwarded back here that fast."

"Oh my gosh," I moaned.

"Now what's wrong?"

"Belinda, when I wrote that letter, I thought he was in town for the weekend. I didn't know he was moving here!"

"So?"

"How can you be so cool! Think! If he lived in New York and got my letter and thought it was dumb and that I was a nerd to write to models, he'd wad it up and throw it away, right? But here he is living in the same town! If he thinks terrible things about me, he is going to be thinking them right here in the same school that I have to attend every day!"

"Maybe he'll like your letter."

"But I can't take that chance! Belinda, you know everything, tell me this. Is there some way I can get the post office to watch for that letter and return it to me?"

"No," she said.

"What do you mean, no?"

"I mean no, the post office delivers letters to the names on them and not to anyone else and those are federal laws passed by the Congress of the United States and they won't break them for you."

"You don't want to help me?"

"I do," she said, "but the post office won't."

"Let me think about this," I said.

The bell was ringing. We collected our notebooks and lunch sacks from the grass and headed back toward the building. For all I cared, it could blizzard tomorrow. And if it did, I hoped a sack of mail got lost in the blizzard.

"If you're thinking about cutting school for the next week to watch his mailbox, don't do it," she said.

"I hadn't thought of it, but it's a good idea."

"It's a federal offense to take mail out of someone else's box."

"Sometimes I wish you didn't know so much."

The school corridors were gloomy after the outdoor brightness, or maybe that was just my change of mood. Before we headed to our separate classes, Belinda reminded me that she wouldn't be walking home with me after school.

"You haven't all week."

"I know," she sighed. 'Two more horrible days to go before my execution."

"Huh?"

"Saturday is it." With a sad wave, she left.

I'd been too wrapped up in my own thoughts. Now I remembered. Saturday was the last debate tournament of the season, and it would take place right there in our school. Ralph had suggested that he and I go to watch Belinda, but she'd told me not to.

"I'd rather not make a complete idiot of myself in front of my friends," she'd said, which was why I'd let the tournament slip from my mind.

At least at that moment Belinda and I felt exactly the same way. We were both alternating between depression and terror.

With the rest of the afternoon to think about it, I decided that my best choice was to quit following Tom Dalton. Although I knew we were made for each other, I also knew that once he received that letter, he wasn't going to think so. To avoid humiliation, my only course was to avoid him. He might still tell other people about my letter, making my stupidity public, but at least they wouldn't all whisper, "Yeah, I've seen her tailing after him ever since he moved here."

So it was all for nothing, the letters, the long distance phone call, the weeks of daydreams.

And wasn't that exactly what Cyndi Superstar said in her songs? One of them went, "Love makes you crazy," and another warned, "Never trust your heart! It lies!" Now why hadn't I taken her advice?

I didn't bother standing on the steps after school to watch the buses load, that's how depressed I was. I headed straight home after school, "all by my lonesome," which was another Cyndi Superstar song line. When I'd first picked her as my model I hadn't meant to live by her saddest song lines. All I needed to complete my gloom was rain.

Instead the sun shone down on me, warming me and casting clear shadows.

I wandered slowly, my thoughts muddled. If only Belinda were with me, I thought, to listen to my problems and figure a way out.

As I bent over my favorite retriever to scratch his ears, I noticed someone on the walk behind me, about a block away. But when I straightened up and looked, no one was there.

"See you tomorrow," I told the dog and continued on my way.

An early flowering tree hung over the sidewalk. I stopped to reach up and pick a blossom. This time I glanced back without turning my head. Yes, there was someone, and I was almost sure it was Tom Dalton. But when I swung around, he was gone. What was he doing? Why should he duck away every time I looked in his direction? Was he avoiding me or was he playing some sort of game? If all he wanted to do was avoid me, he could walk home by another route.

Was it possible that Belinda was wrong about how long it took a letter to do a round trip to New York? Suppose he'd already received that letter. Then probably he thought I was some ditzy airhead, or even a dangerous crazy. No wonder he wanted to decide which I was.

A car drove by and honked. Startled, I discovered I was standing in the street, a step past the curb, daydreaming my way through my worries. I hurried on again. What I might have to do was figure out a way to avoid going to school for the next few days. Or maybe I needed a new route to my classes to insure that my path did not cross his. What a switch, after all my planning.

I walked faster and even tried to watch where I was walking, but my thoughts kept charging off to new problems.

And then there he was, standing at the side of the walk, right in front of me. I was so startled I almost screamed.

He said, "Hi, is that your dog?" And he looked right at me. And I'd been right, his eyes were dark gray, outlined with black lashes.

"What dog?" I stammered, turning.

The retriever had followed me. He gazed up at me hopeful-eyed, his tail wagging.

"That one," Tom Dalton laughed. "I just moved here last week and I wondered whose dog that was."

"Not mine," I said, "though I wouldn't mind if he was. I see him every day."

Inside I was shaking with nerves but outside I must have looked calm. Was that all he wanted, to ask about the dog? If so, he hadn't received the letter and he didn't think I was odd. But then why had he been shadowing me? All at once I knew that's what he'd been doing. There had been that quick U-turn at school. And a few minutes earlier he'd been behind me. To get ahead of me and be waiting on the walk, he must have cut through lawns behind shrubs. Would he do all that to ask about a dog?

"Do you live around here?" he asked.

"Yes, that way." I pointed.

"I live on Park Street. I guess we go to the same high school."

"There's only one high school," I said.

"Oh yeah, that's right! I moved here from New York, and it has a lot of high schools. I've never lived in a town before, with a backyard and everything. We never had a place for a dog in the city- at least not a big one like that."

So maybe he had stopped me to ask about the dog. I didn't know whether to be relieved or disappointed.

"Do you know what kind of dog that is?" he asked.

"It's a Labrador retriever."

"It's very friendly."

"Uh-huh, retrievers are. Very gentle, too."

"That's important. My little brother is only five."

"Oh, you have a little brother?"

"And two sisters in between. I'm the oldest," he said.

"Retrievers are very good with children, I think. Are you planning to get a dog?"

"Probably. And how about you? Do you have a dog? Any brothers? Sisters? A name?" He ran his questions rapid-fire past me. He had this slight accent, very cute, and like something I'd heard on TV, but not anything I'd heard in my town before. When I hesitated, he charged right on. "Smart, Tom, real smart! I did that backward, didn't I? I should introduce myself first. I'm Tom Dalton."

I laughed. "I'm Cyndi Carlisle, I don't have a dog, and I don't have any brothers or sisters."

"What a quiet home you must have," he said. "This whole town is so quiet. I can't believe it. I leave my windows open at night and I can hear the trees rustling."

"Don't they have trees in New York?"

"Yeah, but our apartment was right above an intersection and all we could hear from the windows was the traffic."

"That sounds so exciting," I said.

"Exciting? Really? I think this place is exciting. I can jog for miles without bumping into anyone. Or I can lie on the grass right in our backyard and be all by myself. And there's that neat lake right outside town. We drove there Sunday. We had a picnic in that park where there's tables and we were the only people there."

I'd spent my whole life going to picnics in that park. Of course there was no one there. All the park had was a small sandy beach and a bunch of tables under the trees and nothing at all to do. It was about as boring as a place could get.

"You going home now?" he asked.

I nodded.

"Mind if I walk along? I've been going a different way every day, trying to see more of this town. It's fantastic. I can't believe all these trees and bushes. They hang right out over the sidewalks! And grass everywhere! It's like living in Central Park, like everyone in the whole town lives in a park! Now if I turned down that way, I'd end up at the grade school, wouldn't I?"

The most exciting thing about Tom Dalton was watching him be excited. His eyes sparkled and he had a wonderful smile and this quick little laugh, almost like an indrawn breath of surprise, and I'd never met anyone who talked so fast. After that Sunday picnic his family had gone for a drive in the country. His description of the farms was really funny. I mean, I'd never before known anyone over six years old who flipped over seeing a herd of cows.

When we reached my house he said, "You live here! Wow, what a gorgeous garden! All those tulips! We don't have any at our house. We'll have to get some. I really like tulips. And I'll bet you even have your own room, your house is so big. Hey, I have my own room now, too, I always had to share with my little brother in the apartment, well, for the past five years, anyway, and it's great to have privacy, you don't know what little brothers are like. You didn't tell me you had a cat!"

"We have two cats," I said, leading him up to the front porch where our yellow cat slept on the porch rail. "This is Sunny and the other one's a gray tiger, we call her Shadow, but she hides when anyone else but family is around."

"Maybe we should get a cat, too. You must love living here. Imagine growing up in a place like this!"

"The nearest rock concert is three hundred miles away," I said.

"You like rock? Me, too."

"I bet you went to lots of concerts in New York," I said.

"Not really," he said. "You have to stand in line for days and then pay a fortune for tickets, and then when you get inside, the stage is a mile away. It's a lot better watching them on TV where you can really see. Is it okay if I pet your cat?"

"Scratch his ears and you'll never get rid of him," I said and laughed.

"Honest? Oh yeah, I can see he likes that, hey, he's purring! What a nice cat!"

I could have purred myself. What a nice boy! He was as gorgeous as his picture but a lot friendlier.

"Maybe you'd like a drink. I can't ask anybody in when my folks aren't home, but I could bring it out here."

"Who'd want to go in? It's so great outside. But you don't have to get me anything."

"I want one myself," I said. Leaving him on the porch petting Sunny, I took my books and jacket into the house, made a quick stop in front of the mirror in the hallway to finger-comb my hair, grabbed two cans of cola from the refrigerator, and headed back out.

He'd sat down on the porch stairs with Sunny cradled in his arms and they were both making purring noises. When I handed him the cola, he tilted his head back and smiled up at me.

"I've got to confess," he said. "Didn't we almost run into each other last Saturday at the shopping mall?"

"Did we?" I said. It wouldn't do to have him think I'd been remembering that encounter all week.

"You've forgotten but I remember," he said.

"I was at the mall Saturday," I admitted.

"So it was you. I've seen so many new faces this week, I wasn't positive. Anyway, then I saw you at school and I thought I recognized you, but you didn't say anything, and I'm new here and I wasn't sure how people here acted, so I thought that if I came charging up to you at school and reminded you, you might not like that, or maybe it wasn't even you, do you know what I'm saying?"

He'd talked so fast he'd talked himself right out of breath.

"You've been following me?"

He did his short, nervous laugh. I felt wonderful. With his looks and coming from a city and having had a career in modeling, he could have been conceited. But he wasn't. He was just a normal guy, not quite sure what to say.

"A couple times, but then I thought you'd noticed and I didn't want to annoy you, only then when I saw that you walked home in the same direction I did, hey, I had to talk to you," he said.

"I'm glad you did. I've never known anyone who lived in New York. Tell me about it. Was your school huge?"

We spent the rest of the afternoon sitting in the sun on the porch. He told me about his school and how he had to walk his sisters to their school first every day because no one let children walk alone, and how they had lived in a building with a doorman to keep strangers out and how on Halloween they could only trick-or-treat at the apartments in their own building.

It was like hearing about another world. I loved it. I tried to imagine all those people and feeling crowded, the way he described it, but instead I kept thinking, what a lot to do! How exciting!

It seemed to me like we'd only been talking for a few minutes when my mother's car turned into the drive. She saw me, waved, got out, and went around to open the trunk.

"I have to help her with the groceries," I said.

Tom put Sunny down and followed me.

"This is Tom Dalton," I said to Mom.

The way she smiled at him, I knew she liked the neat haircut. I'd been so busy checking out the color of his eyes and that line of pale freckles, I hadn't noticed that he wore a plain dark blue shirt with jeans and loafers. No mottos, no cutout sleeves, nothing my mother wouldn't have picked for him.

"Hi, Mrs. Carlisle, nice to meet you, can I help?" he said, reaching into the trunk to pick up a grocery sack. As the three of us walked along the side of the house to the kitchen door, he continued, "I live over on Park Street. We just moved here last week."

"It must be hard, moving so late in the school year," Mom said, "switching classes and leaving all your friends."

I hadn't even thought of that and Tom hadn't mentioned it.

"I don't mind the classes," he said. "This school is a lot smaller and I'm going to like it better, I think, but I do miss my friends."

"I'm sure you do," Mom said.

Was there a girlfriend in New York City that he missed?

"I'll get back there to visit in the summer," he said. "Right now, I figure it's a tradeoff. Like I've been telling Cyndi, the great thing about living here is that we can get pets, and another is that I'll get to learn to drive."

"You don't know how to drive?" I exclaimed. Everyone at our school took Driver's Ed as soon as they were sixteen. I'd be taking it the next year.

And as Tom was a junior, I figured he already had his license.

"Where would I drive? In New York we didn't have a car. It costs almost as much to rent a garage as an apartment."

"How did you get places?"

"Cabs, buses, subway. A few times when we went on summer trips my dad rented a car. But now we own one."

"He's even excited because they've got a backyard full of grass and trees," I told Mom.

Mom smiled at Tom. "Don't mind Cyndi. For the last year or two she's preferred parking lots to parks."

"If you're talking about the mall parking lot, it's a lot more exciting than the lake," I said. "It has things moving around in it."

Of course I didn't mean that exactly the way I said it. I knew a tree was prettier than a car. But a tree stays in the same place and does the same thing every year, while the parking lot of the mall offered a stream of different people walking through and there were always new things to see.

Probably Tom and my mother knew what I meant, but they

laughed at me, anyway.

Mom walked back out to the car with us to close the trunk and pick up her purse and some books from the backseat. She asked Tom, "Are you and Cyndi in a class together?"

She was probably hoping that he was in my composition class, was as straight A as he looked, and would help me.

He said, "No, I'm just another stray who followed her home."

She looked startled.

Tom pointed toward the front hedge. We all looked. And there was my friend, the Labrador retriever, peeking around the hedge, his tail tucked between his legs as though he expected us to shoo him away.

Laughing, Mom said, "Where did that come from?"

"He lives between here and school," I said. "I didn't know he followed us."

"Me, either," Tom said. "I just now saw him. I'll take him home on my way."

We walked to the hedge together and patted the retriever. Tom started out with a whistle to the dog. It trotted after him, its tail wagging. Tom had walked a few places past our house when he turned back. The dog did an identical turn, following him until they were facing me.

He said, "I forgot to ask, do you like fantasy films?"

"Fantasy?"

"Yeah, there's a new one out about a barbarian. It opens this week."

"Oh, that!" I said. I'd seen the ad, too, for the theater at the mall. "Sure, I like that kind."

"Is there any way to get there without a car?" he asked.

"Sure, there's a bus."

"Hey, I don't suppose, uh, you would like to go with me? Saturday? Or sometime?" Bent forward to pet the retriever, his head was at the same level as mine, his face tilted slightly down. He looked up. There was this expression on his face that was such a total switch from his confident smile. He looked unsure. Insecure. Questioning. Exactly

like the cover photo on my book.
   My heart skidded to a full stop.

CHAPTER 6

Belinda said, "Tell me again exactly what he said."

I was home, sitting in the kitchen, staring at my laptop propped open on the table. Because Dad was at a dinner meeting, Mom had decided to shower before she and I heated up a couple of frozen dinners. "He said, and I give you this word for word, 'Would you like to go to the movie with me Saturday?' How about that?"

"And you said?"

"Oh, come on, Belinda! What do you think I said? After I regained my voice, I said I would. You think I'd say no?"

"No, but what do you mean, regained your voice?"

That was more than I could explain. "I solemnly hope you someday fall in love so that you will know what I'm talking about."

"I haven't got time for love," she said sharply. "I don't really even have time to talk to you, but I'm so depressed, I've got to or I'll go to pieces. What I should be doing is practicing my rebuttals."

"You're probably better than you think."

"I'm not. This afternoon was a catastrophe. I was poor and my partner was awful. And I couldn't help him. He's driving me crazy."

"Isn't there some saying in the theater about a poor rehearsal being a sign of a good performance?"

"We have been rehearsing and performing all year and there has never been a good anything," she sighed. "Let's not talk about it anymore. Tell me something different. Tell me about Tom and what you talked about."

"Tell me what to wear. Everything I have is a thousand years out of date."

"In the future." She giggled, which I might have resented at another time, but considering how depressed she was, I let it go.

"You think I should wear something different? You want me to borrow a white blouse with a round collar and a plain gray cardigan from my mother?"

"I don't think so," she said. "He must like you the way you are or he wouldn't have followed you home and asked you for a date."

Asked me for a date! Yes! That's what he had done. I hadn't put it in words in my mind until then, but it was true. Tom Dalton had asked me for a date. The boy on the cover, my dream boy, had asked me, Cyndi Carlisle, for a date. We were meant for each other.

"You're right, Belinda. I think I'll wear my black miniskirt and my long black shirt, the one with the white stars." I'd done the stars with white fabric paint. It was one of my best jobs. I'd turned it in as an art project before wearing it, and my art teacher loved it. "But what about my hair? Maybe I could mousse it flat on one side, up on the other. Yeah, and then do my mouth and nails in midnight blue."

After what seemed to me a lengthy pause, Belinda said, "Maybe you don't have to be quite that much yourself."

"Have you seen Cyndi Superstar's new video? She's wearing a shirt a lot like mine. And she's got a big white star painted on one side of her face."

"I know," Belinda said. "Listen, I could be wrong, but maybe you should wear the same kind of makeup you wear to school, not too wild, at least until you know Tom better. That's the way he's seen you, so maybe that's what he likes."

Belinda's logic was hard to ignore. How she could ever lose a debate was beyond me to figure.

After supper I spent about an hour pulling all my clothes out of my closet and spreading them around on my bed, trying to put together a new combination that would be sensational but not too much. I didn't want to make a mistake. My problem was that I'd never been on an actual date before and it was making me very nervous and I knew that when I was nervous, I didn't do my best thinking.

Probably what I didn't want to do was look as though this were my first date. If I went way out with all new makeup and a different hairstyle, it would look as though I were auditioning for something and everybody who saw me would know it was my first date.

While I thought about it, I showered and washed my hair. Belinda was right, I decided. I'd stick with my usual hairstyle.

With all that settled in my mind, and my preference veering toward a lighter lip liner, I put on my robe and dried my hair. Staring at myself in the mirror, I considered a slightly different combination of eyeshadow stripes, nothing so drastic he wouldn't recognize me, but something just a bit brighter.

And while I was leaning forward, wondering if I could use a blue mascara and then tip the ends of my lashes with green, I noticed my hair.

It fluffed up and out in the hot air blast of the dryer, catching light.

I flipped off the dryer.

It wasn't possible. I hadn't put anything on it.

But there it was. Blond. Not white-blond like Cyndi Superstar's hair, but a kind of brownish golden, three or four shades lighter on the top, where I'd sprayed it yesterday, than on the sides. But why had it suddenly changed so much?

I ran into my room and hunted up the container from the back of my dresser drawer and carefully read the label. It said the spray would bring out highlights when dried, which it had, sort of, nothing so drastic as to alarm a father, though. And then I read the next line.

"Sun exposure not required but greatly increases effectiveness."

Effectiveness? That wasn't the word. What had Belinda said? She'd asked if the color contained peroxide. I spun the box around until I found the list of ingredients, which was several lines of very small print, but there it was, that word, in among the others, peroxide.

And I'd spent the noon hour and several hours after school out in very bright sun.

What was I going to do? My father would go straight through the ceiling.

Maybe I could wear a scarf until it grew out. Definitely I could go to bed early and avoid seeing him that evening. Possibly by the next day I'd have thought of some brilliant way to handle him.

But when I woke in the morning, I hadn't. I dressed quickly, thinking that maybe I could make a fast dash through breakfast and be out the door before he came down. That would put me at school about an hour before they unlocked the doors, which would mean sitting outside on the steps alone, but that was better than an hour's lecture from my father.

Or I could stop by the drugstore and find a darker dye and put it on in the girls' room at school.

I made it in and out of the bathroom and down to the kitchen and even to the front door, and I had my hand out reaching for the handle. That's how close I was.

He said, "Cyndi!"

He didn't have to say more. It was all right there in his voice. I spun around. He was standing on the stairs, this tight look on his face that he gets sometimes.

I tried to say "Good-morning," but nothing came out.

And then I had this funny feeling that he was having the same problem. I felt like we stood there forever.

When he spoke, his voice was very low and controlled. He didn't yell. I'd been prepared for yelling.

Instead he said, "All right, Cyndi, we won't discuss this because I don't want to hear excuses. We'll just get the ground rules straight now. Until that is grown out, you will not leave this house after supper any evening and you will not go to the mall."

I might as well be dead, I thought, but I didn't say it, because when my father made a rule, intervention from the United Nations couldn't change it. And I was too stunned to think of any arguments, anyway. How could this be happening?

My father turned calmly away, as though we'd had nothing more than a discussion about the weather, and went into the kitchen while I stood by the front door and saw my whole life disintegrating.

The most wonderful boy in the world had miraculously moved to my impossibly boring town and amazingly noticed me and fantastically asked me for a date and now none of that counted because I wasn't allowed out.

My desperation shocked me into action. I raced to the kitchen. "Dad, could I go into quarantine on Sunday?"

My mother didn't look up from her plate. I thought she was smiling. But it didn't matter. She wouldn't have told him about my hair, if she'd noticed, but she also wouldn't side with me against his rules.

He looked me straight in the eye and said, "No."

"But, Dad! This guy asked me to go to the movies on Saturday!"

"You'll have to tell him you can't go."

"I've already told him I can!"

"Then you'll have to apologize and tell him you were wrong."

"I can't do that!" I shouted.

By the time I rushed out into the street, I was sobbing. The man was unreasonable! He was a dictator! Who did he think he was, supreme commander of the universe?

I ran all the way to school and I think I was crying all the way, because I didn't even think about where I was until I sank down on the steps and cried myself dry. When the tears ran out, my throat ached.

The buses would be arriving soon. I looked around at the empty walks and lawns. There I'd be like a statue on the steps with a bright red nose and flaming eyes and streaked makeup for everyone to stare at. Digging into my bookbag, I pulled out my plastic makeup kit. In my hand mirror I saw exactly what I expected, a real mess. Lucky for me that I'd left home so early. I needed all that time to get my face cleaned up and redone. There wasn't anything I could do about the red in my eyes, but at least I hid the tear streaks.

My morning was a nightmare. I bumbled through, not hearing anyone, going over and over in my mind what I could say to my father to change his mind. And nothing was good enough.

When I told Belinda at noon, she was as dismayed as I was. She said, "I don't know what you can do."

Ralph popped up between us with his ear-to-ear grin and said, "Hiya, whatcha doing?"

I said, "Go away, Ralph," because I wanted Belinda's mind free to consider my problem.

He said, "Changed your mind about Saturday? Want to come to the meet to watch Belinda?"

Belinda said, "Go away, Ralph," this time, though she was usually more patient with him than I was.

After he gave up on us and wandered away, Belinda said, "That's all I need at the back of the room when I'm trying to make a point, good old Ralph and his gleaming teeth."

"Wish we could trade places. I'd debate for you if you break my date with Tom for me. What can I say to him?"

"The truth, Cyndi. Anything else and he'll think you are making up excuses."

"It doesn't matter what he thinks. Do you know how long it takes hair to grow out? He's not going to wait around. He'll find another girl."

"Not if you're really meant for each other," Belinda said.

"Do you believe that?"

"No, but I thought maybe it would make you feel better."

Nothing could make me feel better. My life had bottomed out. I dragged through the rest of the day somehow. When the last bell rang, I headed home alone, carefully avoiding Ralph, who was standing at our usual watch-the-buses spot in front of school.

I decided that I would phone Tom. It would be awful enough breaking our date that way. If I had to look him in the face, I'd go to pieces. What would he think of me, grounded by some parental rule? He'd think I was too young to date, that's what he'd think. He'd decide I was a baby and he'd find a girl whose parents allowed her to be an adult.

"Hey, Cyndi!" Tom shouted.

I went stiff. I stopped walking and stood still but I couldn't turn around to face him. His footsteps pounded behind me, running to catch up.

"Where you going in such a rush?" he gasped.

Still not looking at him, I said, "Home."

"You must have taken off sprinting as soon as the bell rang."

I nodded.

"Hey, another wonderful day!" he said.

Until then I hadn't noticed the blue skies. I was mad at the sun.

"And it's Friday and there's a whole great weekend coming up!" he continued, then rattled off a list of plans his family had for the weekend, ending with, "What time shall I come over Saturday? You better decide because you know the bus schedules."

Tears choked me. I kept my face turned away from him, staring at blurred front gardens.

He stopped walking. I continued on.

He hurried to catch up, went past me, and stopped in front of me. I kept my head down. Standing still facing him, I stared at his long, jeans-covered legs.

"Did I say something wrong?" he asked.

I shook my head.

"Then why won't you talk to me?"

I blurted, "I can't go Saturday."

He didn't say anything. I wanted to run past him, away, up to my room to hide, anywhere but there. And then I realized what he must think. It wasn't fair to make him miserable just because I was.

Forcing myself to look up at him, I said, "My father's grounded me. I want to go, but I can't."

"Grounded you? When did that happen?"

"This morning," I said.

"Is it something to do with me?"

"No, of course not."

"Something must have happened between yesterday afternoon and this morning," he said.

"It's that dumb sun!" I sobbed.

"Hey, you're crying! Please don't cry! It's okay about Saturday, it doesn't matter, we'll go some other time. The sun?"

"Yes, if it hadn't been-so-bright-"

"You're grounded because the sun was bright?"

When he put it that way, I giggled. It is not easy to giggle and cry at the same time, which is why I hiccuped, and then he laughed, which made me hiccup more.

It's also hard to laugh and sound sympathetic, which is what he was trying to do.

He even tried to brush away my tears with his fingertips. I was so surprised when he touched me, I took a big gulp of air and the hiccups stopped. And the tears.

He waited while I dried my face on my sleeve.

"How long are you grounded?" he asked.

"Until my hair grows out."

"Until what!"

"I can't go out at night or to the mall at all until my hair grows out," I said. "And there is no changing his mind because once my father makes a decision it becomes a federal law."

"How long does your hair have to get?" Tom asked.

"Long enough for me to get all the bleached part cut off, and as he will also ground me if I shave my head, don't bother suggesting that."

"I wasn't going to! What's wrong with your hair? It's pretty-oh! Bleached? Sun? They go together?"

I explained about the spray and my father's rules.

Tom hooked his thumbs in his pockets and settled into a thinking stance, elbows out, one knee bent. I kept remembering the way his fingertips had felt, brushing away my tears. After today he'd probably never look at me again, much less touch me.

"So you knew you weren't supposed to use that bleach before you used it?" he said slowly.

"So I blew it!" I exclaimed. I was getting tired of thoughtful friends pointing out my errors.

He raised his eyebrows and gave me his puzzled look. "Okay, don't be mad at me."

"I'm not. I'm mad at myself. Anyhow, it's you who should be mad, because I'm wrecking your plans."

He did that funny, quick laugh. "Don't worry about that. I can have a magical Saturday night taking my kid sisters to the movies instead."

"I have wrecked your weekend!"

"No, stop worrying. Listen, it doesn't matter and maybe by next week your father will have cooled down."

"Cooled down, yes. Changed his mind, no."

Tom walked home with me, probably because he couldn't think of a polite way to desert me, but he didn't stay around or accept my offer of a soda. He said he'd promised to get home early from school to babysit his little brother. It was a reasonable excuse.

"Why waste time on a girl who's been as good as sent to prison?" I asked Belinda when I phoned her after supper.

"I wish somebody'd ground me through tomorrow afternoon," she said sadly. "Anything would be better than that meet."

"At least you won't have to imagine me at the mall having fun without you," I said.

During supper my father and I eyed each other without conversing past the "Please pass the butter" stage. He didn't want to argue. I didn't want to cry. Neither of us was good at pretense. Mom often said we were alike, equally stubborn, but I couldn't believe that.

Throughout the meal she carried on a one-person conversation, rushing from topic to topic. As we were clearing up, she said, "How's Belinda doing in debate?"

"Terrible," I said. I'd been giving one-word answers right along.

"What do you mean, terrible? I thought she was a good debater."

"She is."

"So then what's terrible? I don't understand." She was trying so hard to make conversation, I felt guilty.

"Belinda is good but her partner isn't," I explained. "And Saturday is the last tournament."

"Oh, where will she be going?"

"It's here this time. At our school."

"I hope she does well," Mom said. "Belinda is so nice. It'll be a shame if she doesn't get a fair chance."

"She'll feel rotten," I agreed.

"Would it cheer her up if you were there?" Mom asked.

I looked at Dad, who was loading the dishwasher. I said in my flattest tone, as though I didn't care, "I'm not sure that's allowed."

He said, equally calmly, "You may not go to the mall anytime or out at night anywhere. You may go to school during the day any day, including Saturday."

"I can?" I exclaimed.

He gave me a very calm but searching look. "Don't stretch things by using the tournament as an excuse to go on a date."

"What if I go with a couple of other people?" I asked.

"It would be nice for Belinda," Mom said.

Dad liked Belinda. "But you're to come home right afterward, in time for supper," he said.

After we finished clearing, I waited until my parents had settled in the front room with the TV on before phoning Tom. The occasional Saturday afternoon at educational events would not be his idea of dating, I thought. But even so, if one day was all I got in my whole life with the perfect boy, then I'd have to hope he'd accept. Later he'd find someone else, and I couldn't stop that, but I'd have had one day with him.

A girl answered.

"Is Tom there?" I asked.

She said he was. I heard her shout his name. She added, "It's a girl for you!"

My heart raced. Would he think I was terrible, phoning him?

His voice said, "Hello?"

"It's me. Cyndi." I remembered that he'd refused to stop for a soda. Maybe he didn't want to talk to me anymore.

"Hi! How are you? Everything okay?" He sounded pleased to hear from me.

"Not perfect, but better," I said and explained about the debate tournament. "I have to go with a crowd, so that means going with Ralph, if you want to go, too."

"Is Ralph the retriever?" he asked.

"The retriever? Oh no! Ralph is, uh, a friend. A friend of Belinda's." Although I hadn't phoned him, I knew Ralph would go.

"Sounds fun," he said.

"I don't know how much fun a debate tournament is, and I have to be home before supper."

He didn't seem to mind. We arranged to meet at school. Next I phoned Ralph.

He said what I expected him to say. "Hiya, Cyndi. Whatcha doing? The debate meet? You want to go? Terrific!"

My third call was to Belinda. She wouldn't be as thrilled. I broke it to her with careful explanations. "Belinda, if you don't want us to watch you, I'll take the guys into other rooms. How will I know what to avoid?"

"There's a list posted at the sign-up table in the front hall. It tells you who's debating in which room. And you be sure to check it."

"I will. I promise."

"I wouldn't so much mind you there, Cyndi, but if I have to debate with Ralph there watching me, I'll die."

Ralph's grin could be unnerving. In Belinda's present state, I could see how she'd not want any distractions.

CHAPTER 7

Tom, Ralph, and I agreed to meet at one. Saturday I wore my black outfit with the white stars. For Belinda's sake I refrained from tipping my hair orange. When I reached school I was glad I hadn't gone wild with my hair. Unbelievable as it was, the school was filled with people in Belinda-type outfits and three-piece suits. And though I wouldn't have minded brightening up their lives, Belinda might have been uneasy.

Ralph was already at the sign-up tables, checking the postings.

"Belinda's in Room 126."

"Then we can go to any other room," I said, looking through the crowd for Tom.

"But I came to watch Belinda."

"Ralph, Belinda especially asked that we not watch her. It would make her nervous."

"Gotcha," Ralph said. "So who will we watch?"

Tom appeared near the doorway. I waved him over and introduced him to Ralph. When they stood side by side, I saw I'd been right, they were about the same height and coloring, and they were even both wearing jeans and sweatshirts. But right after that, the similarity stopped. Where Ralph's face was round and childish, Tom's was adult. Ralph grinned. Tom smiled. Ralph bounced nervously, unable to stand still, and didn't know where to put his hands. He crossed and uncrossed his arms repeatedly. Tom leaned back on his heels, shoulders squared, and looked slowly around, his thumbs hooked in his pockets.

Tom said, "So this is a debate tournament. I've never been to one. Hey, I'm glad you asked me."

Ralph blurted, "Whatcha gonna do now?"

I bent over the postings and ran my finger down the list. "Louis Turner. Good enough. Let's go watch Louis."

"Yeah, all the girls watch Louis," Ralph said.

"Ralph, Louis Turner is a king-size bore and I am only interested in observing his debate ability."

Ralph backed off. "Sure, Cyndi, gotcha."

To Tom I explained, "My friend Belinda needs a new debate partner for next year and she's thinking about Louis, because his partner's leaving. We might as well check him out."

"That's fine," Tom said. "I've never seen anyone debate. I don't know how this is done, but it looks complicated, with all those lists and people checking in."

"Each team does six rounds in this tournament. Each round is against a different team and they get points and then at the end the points are totaled to see who goes into finals. This will be the fifth round."

"The fifth round already?"

"They start meets on Fridays after school, so they did two rounds yesterday and two this morning."

We found the room with Louis Turner and his partner. Louis posed casually in front of the far windows where the light made a pale halo of his hair. I was beginning to think that Louis was very conceited and also girl-crazy, which was an odd choice for Belinda to have made.

The judge sat at a front desk, facing a table where the four debaters spread out their gear. They had real briefcases, like my parents carry to work, and also metal file boxes. The judge spoke to them. They all dug through their papers, rearranging things.

Taking chairs at the back of the room, we tried to be quietly inconspicuous. Debate wasn't like other sports. Debaters wanted silence and no distractions. Applause was not allowed.

The other team spoke first, arguing about some legislation affecting water table levels.

Next was Louis's turn. He looked very dignified, stood very straight and still in his gray suit, and made hand gestures like a politician.

I glanced at Tom. He leaned forward, elbows on his desk, chin on his fists, eyes narrowed with concentration. It seemed to me that Louis was talking faster than anyone could follow, but then I remembered that Tom spoke rapidly, too.

When the round was over, Tom whispered, "Who won?"

"Beats me," Ralph said.

Tom said, "They sounded very closely matched, didn't they?"

"Yes, but the scoring is very complicated." I knew that from Belinda.

"Let's find Belinda," Ralph said and headed for the door. Tom and I followed. There would be a wait between rounds while the judges turned in scores and teams were matched for the final round. The hall was jammed with debaters arguing with their teammates about results.

"Can you believe that rebuttal?"

"Where did they pull that evidence?"

"What kind of case was that? Talk about squirrelly!"

We found Belinda huddled against the wall across from the sign-up tables, staring at a handful of three-by-five cards.

"How'd it go?" Ralph asked her.

"So far past gruesome there's no word for it," she moaned.

"Tom, this is my friend Belinda," I said.

"It probably wasn't that bad," he said.

"I don't want to discuss it," she said. "Did you watch any debates?"

"Louis Turner."

"I'm glad you watched a good debate. I wish I had," she said.

"It was interesting," Tom said. "I'm sorry I don't know more about the topic. Maybe if I could watch a different topic, I'd understand better what they were doing."

"Everybody debates the same topic," Belinda said. "Except my team. We're never talking about what anyone else is discussing. You wouldn't believe! He pulled out an argument we tried way last autumn and decided to drop. I don't know why he still had it in his evidence box. And then he went round and round and couldn't think to go on to different evidence, and I should have pulled him out but my mind went blank with shock and if I live through this next round, which I don't think I will, I am going to burn my briefcase and take up football."

"Next round's gotta be better," Ralph said.

"I don't see why. We've become progressively worse throughout the season, hit new lows today, and in a few minutes will set an historic record for lowest possible point total."

"We'll see you after," Ralph said.

Belinda gave him a look of pure pain before hurrying off to check the postings.

"She's better than she says," I told Tom. "Really very good. Just nervous."

When the debaters had moved away from the tables to rush to their next room assignments, we read the list until we found a junior team other than Belinda's to watch. The difference between junior and senior teams was interesting, though we didn't know the scores of the teams or how they compared. The junior teams spoke more slowly and paused more often.

Afterward, in the corridor, we discussed what we'd seen and agreed that what we needed was a demonstration round with someone explaining what was going on.

Louis Turner brushed past us, talking loudly to his partner. "That was a power match! I know it was!"

"Could be," Ralph grinned and shrugged. He had no more idea what a power match was than I did. "Let's find Belinda."

"Let's do something to cheer her up," Tom said.

"Like what?"

"Like all go out for pizza?"

"Oh, I'd like to! Only I'm not sure."

Ralph nodded agreement so enthusiastically I thought his head might fall off. I didn't want to explain to Ralph that I was grounded. While we hunted for Belinda, I tried to think up quick excuses. What I didn't want to say was that I had to be home by six, which sounded like rules for infants. It was already almost five o'clock.

When we found Belinda, standing near the judges' table, I knew from one look at her that if I'd been her, I'd have been sobbing.

Belinda held things in. Her face was rigid with her effort to hide her feelings.

Rushing toward her, Ralph said, "We're going out for pizza. You wanna come?"

"Maybe you're supposed to go with the team," I said.

"I don't think I could bear to," she whispered. "He knocked over the evidence box. All our cards! All over the floor!"

"Can you leave now?" Tom asked.

She nodded yes.

"Let's go," he said.

I almost followed. Why not go out for pizza? I'd head right home afterward and be an hour late at most. I could say the debates ran late, couldn't I? Who'd know?

Instead I said, "I've got to phone home first. Can you wait a sec?"

"We'll be outside," Tom said.

I leaned against the wall in the corridor and pulled out my cell phone.

My father answered, which struck me as unlucky.

"How'd Belinda do?" he asked.

"Terrible. Her partner knocked over her box of three-by-fives right in the middle of their last debate."

"She must be very upset."

"Yeah. Tom and Ralph are going to take her to the pizza place."

"What about you?"

"I guess I'll wait at the bus stop with them until their bus arrives and then I'll walk home."

"Does Belinda want to go for pizza with two boys?" Dad asked.

"She wants to do anything except go out with the debate team."

"She'll feel better if you're there, too. You'd better go along, Cyndi, but I'll expect you home by eight."

"Honest?" I shouted. "Oh yeah! Okay! Thank you. I will!" and slammed down the phone and dashed outside to find my friends. At rare moments my father could stun me with disbelief at his reasonableness.

The pizza place was tacky medieval, with beamed ceilings, black-iron lighting fixtures, and formica-topped tables. On a Saturday night the noise level almost shook the beams. We picked up pizza and root beers at the counter before finding a

place. Belinda and I sat on one side of the table facing Tom and Ralph.

It was practically like a double date, so I pretended it was, because with my restricted social life, that's as close to a date as I'd get. I couldn't imagine Belinda dating Ralph, but why stick to reality in a daydream?

"Do they subtract points for knocking evidence on the floor?" Ralph asked.

"No, but they don't allow time to refile, either," Belinda moaned. "I couldn't find any of the cards I needed and my partner was too upset to try."

My mother always says that if you can't fix something, forget it. I switched subjects.

"Tell us about New York City," I said to Tom.

He gave a shrug. "It's tall, crowded, noisy, and smells like exhaust fumes, your typical small-town America."

"It sounds so exciting," I said.

"Exhaust fumes are exciting?" Ralph asked.

"No, the tall, crowded, noisy is exciting, dummy."

"Hey, sometimes," Tom admitted, and told us about all the magical places he'd been, places I'd heard about or seen on TV, but until then they had been movie sets, not places real people got to go to. He'd even been to Bloomingdale's!

"You want to hear about Bloomingdale's?" He did his puzzled look and I nudged Belinda.

She gave a weak smile.

Tom saw it and did his best to cheer her. "Listen, if they don't have it in Bloomingdale's, they don't have it anywhere, and the same goes for losing little sisters. I've tried to misplace them at Central Park and the zoo and dozens of other

places, but the only time I actually managed to lose those two was at Bloomie's. Most rewarding day of my life."

"Did you ever work for Bloomingdale's?" I asked, thinking perhaps he'd done modeling for catalogs.

"Work there? No, but I've ridden the Staten Island ferry and been inside the Statue of Liberty and bought streusel from Mrs. Petowski, and of the three, the only one worth doing more than once is Mrs. Petowski's streusel."

"I've never heard of Mrs. Petowski or her streusel. Is that something world famous?"

"It was, in my neighborhood."

"Don't you love it?" I said to Belinda, who was finally relaxing.

"I'd have to taste it to tell you," she said. As Belinda rarely made jokes, that was a sure sign that she felt better.

"Want another pizza?" Ralph asked.

We chipped in a couple of dollars each and sent him to get a pepperoni.

"Is it hard to find a job?" I asked Tom. "In New York?"

"I guess so. Why, is it here?"

"I mean, there must be special opportunities in a city."

"Think so?" He looked puzzled, a look that practically knocked me out every time he did it. "Hey, that reminds me, I knew this guy at school who figured he'd make money walking dogs, see, so he printed up this notice to put near mailboxes, only when he went to do that, the doormen wouldn't let him leave his flyers, and in places where there aren't doormen, there are foyers but you can't get to the foyer without a key, so here he had these three hundred notices..."

Tom talked faster and faster, spinning out this long story, smiling at Belinda and me. I knew he was doing it to cheer Belinda, which was fabulous of him. Only why did he switch subjects every time I mentioned jobs? Or was that my imagination?

After Ralph returned with the pizza, Tom told us a couple more stories. Ralph and I remembered some stories of our own, dumb things we'd done in grade school. And finally, by the time we'd made it through another pizza, Belinda was laughing.

Time to try again to uncover Tom's glamorous past, I decided. "You said your friend walked dogs. Did you have a job?"

"I have never been a dog walker, I swear," Tom said. "I'd rather take care of a dog here, where it wouldn't have to be on a leash all the time."

"You've never had any kind of job? Ever?"

"What, you're afraid to have an unemployed bum as a friend? Actually, I have been employed. I had a summer job once."

"You've never had a job," Ralph said to me. "Why should Tom?"

"I didn't mean it that way. I just meant, I wondered."

"Okay, to satisfy your curiosity, yes, I have been gainfully employed."

"Doing what?" I blurted.

"Hey, you are curious! I spent two months last summer sweeping floors and washing counters for the neighborhood deli, nothing glamorous, but I hope it meets your requirements, whatever they are."

What else could I say? To ask further would be to sound like a snob, as though I judged friends by their summer jobs. And I couldn't demand to know if he'd worked as a model. Obviously there was some reason he didn't want to talk about that.

I said, "All I wanted to know was what kind of jobs teenagers could get in New York. Working in a deli sounds fun. What's a deli?"

"What's a deli! You don't know what a deli is?"

"Not exactly," I said. "They sell food, right? I've heard the word, but how is it different from a restaurant?"

"Are you telling me this town has no deli?"

"This town has no deli," I said, using a very solemn, Belinda-type tone of voice.

Tom couldn't believe it.

"I told you this was a boring town," I said.

"A deli isn't exactly exciting," he laughed. "But I thought everyplace had one. A deli has long glass counters filled with stuff that's all ready to eat, salads, cold cuts, like that, so you pick what you want and they put it in little cartons to take home and you've got your supper all made."

To Belinda I said, "Do you realize there's a huge world out there filled with things we don't know about?"

"Actually, I did know what a deli is," Belinda said.

"But that's only a start!"

"Cyndi expects life to be like those romance books she reads," Ralph said.

I almost went into shock, unable to figure what he was talking about. "What romance books?"

"I saw you carrying one around the other day," he said.

What if the next thing he said was the title of the book? Then Tom would know I'd seen his picture on it. And he obviously didn't want to tell us about his modeling career. If Ralph remembered the title of the book with Tom's photo, it could end my relationship with Tom before it started.

"I read a lot of books," I said quickly and rushed on to ask Tom the name of his favorite book.

It was a fantasy, which I should have guessed because he'd wanted to go to a fantasy film.

Which reminded me that I was grounded. "What time is it?"

"Seven-thirty."

"I've got to be home by eight. I've got to leave now!"

"But there's still two slices of pizza!" Ralph said.

"I can't be late!"

I didn't mean to sound desperate, but I guess I did, because Tom said, "Bring them along, Ralph. You can eat them on the bus."

Tom didn't ask why I had to be home. He knew. And he was very nice about it. We dashed out of the pizza place. There wasn't any bus in sight. I hopped up and down because I was too upset to stand still. Ralph calmly munched away at two huge slices of pizza balanced on his palms. Tom kept saying that there ought to be a bus soon, though we all knew that he knew nothing about our bus schedules. And Belinda looked from Ralph to Tom to me and started laughing again.

The bus arrived in time to get me to the corner four blocks from my house with all of eight minutes left before eight o'clock.

"I'll never make it!" I wailed as we headed down the walk.

"Hang on, I'll get you there!" Tom said, catching my hand in his. He started to run, pulling me along.

Behind us Ralph said, "What's the rush?"

"Wait there, I'll be back," Tom called over his shoulder.

Belinda shouted, "See you tomorrow, Cyndi!"

Their footsteps stopped. Ours pounded together, matching my racing heart, until my breath burned in my throat. We ran past gardens and walks and shadowed drives, faster and faster, until it was all I could do to keep from stumbling. I concentrated on staring ahead into the darkness. Every inch of me ached except my hand, and it had its own life, warm in Tom's grip.

When we reached my porch I was too winded to speak.

"Two minutes to spare." Tom dropped my hand so that he could press the light button on his watch.

'That's okay, then," I managed to gasp. I'd been leaning forward to catch my breath. When I straightened and looked up, the sky startled me with its dazzle of star patterns.

"Beautiful, huh?" Tom said.

"I can't ever remember any of the constellations except the dippers."

"I never could see them because of the city lights."

"Really?"

"So that's something else you've got here. Stars. And you've got so many extras, they've even stuck to your shirt."

I'd forgotten that I was wearing my shirt with the white stars.

"Loose glue. They fall," I said.

"From the sky?" Tom did a cowboy drawl, complete with his New York accent. "Sure is a lot out here in the open spaces for a city boy to learn, ma'am."

I giggled. "That's your next assignment. Memorize three constellations by Friday quiz time."

"I'll do that. And I'll check them nightly to be sure they haven't lost any of their stars." He touched a painted star on my shoulder with his fingertip. "Though I don't know but that they look prettier on you than in the sky."

I didn't know what to say to that. And I don't think Tom did either. It was one of those comments that slipped out, more personal than he'd meant it to be, and having said it, he couldn't take it back.

Finding my voice, I said, "Guess I'd better get in."

"Uh-huh."

I ran up the stairs.

From the walk, Tom said, "Hey, Cyndi?"

"Yes?"

"Thanks for asking me today. It was fun."

"I'm sorry about the movie," I said.

"That doesn't matter. See you Monday."

Inside, I closed the door but watched through the window as he walked away into the night.

From the living room my mother called, "Is that you, Cyndi?"

"Yes, I'm back," I said.

I pressed my face against the glass to look outside. All I could see was the front garden between the house and the long black shadow of the hedge. But I could imagine Tom striding easily, shoulders squared, beneath the star-filled sky. And I could still feel the warmth of his hand holding tightly to mine.

CHAPTER 8

"You think there's some secret reason why Tom won't talk about being a model?" I asked Belinda Monday during lunch hour.

"Like what?"

"I don't know. Maybe something terrible happened. Maybe he had a nervous breakdown. People in show business are always having nervous breakdowns."

"He doesn't look to me like anyone who's been sick," she said.

"No, I guess not."

"You could come right out and ask him why he quit modeling," she suggested.

"But he obviously wants it kept a secret! I couldn't possibly do that!"

"In that case, you'll have to go on wondering," she said with boring Belinda-logic. I thought up several other possibilities during my afternoon classes. Not that it mattered. I didn't expect to see much of Tom, as fantastic as Saturday had been. No boy would remain interested in a girl who had to keep the same hours as his younger sisters.

If I wanted someone to cheer me up, I'd picked the wrong person to walk home with. We stopped near the athletic field to watch the track team go through their stretches. To the casual observer, Belinda was the model of organization, her shoulder- length bob smooth, her cardigan, white blouse, and even her jeans neatly ironed, her loafers polished. But up close she was a picture of confusion, her face twisted into a worried frown as she chewed the last of her coral lipstick off her lower lip.

She was, of course, staring at Louis. His blond head bobbed up and down in unison with his teammates. They were sitting on the grass, scissor-legged, reaching first for one foot, then the other.

"Now is the time to tell him you're looking for a new debate partner for next year," I said.

"Now? Out on the field?"

"Only if you want to impress the whole team. Otherwise, phone him at home tonight."

"Now is the time to give up debate entirely," she said sadly, turning away and heading down the walk.

Hurrying to catch up with her, I said, "Why? What's such a big deal about a phone call?"

"Nothing except that I can't do it."

I started to ask if she'd like me to phone him for her but before I had the chance, we heard Tom calling, "Hey, wait up!"

Belinda said under her breath, "Maybe he doesn't know anyone else who lives in this direction. If you're lucky, your hair could grow out before he gets to know the neighbors."

"Thanks, best friend," I hissed back at her.

What was it about Tom that made my heart do backflips? One close look at that face and I went numb all over.

He fell into step beside us, shortening his long stride. "You two should be on the track team, as fast as you are getting away from school."

"Exactly what I've been telling Belinda. She should definitely go out for track."

"Really?" He leaned forward to look past me to Belinda. "What event are you interested in?"

Belinda actually blushed.

I said, "It's not events that matter, it's participating with other team members."

"Ignore her, she's talking crazy," Belinda said.

When we reached the corner where Belinda and I parted directions, Tom said, "See you tomorrow," to Belinda and continued along with me. Pulling a leaf off a hedge as we passed it, Tom concentrated on ripping it along its veins until he had a confetti-like pile of bits in his hand.

"Were you back on time Saturday?" he asked.

"Sure, fine," I said.

He kept his gaze on the leaf bits, not looking at me. "Any problem with me walking home with you after school?"

I tried to sound equally casual. "No, it's just my evenings and weekends that are dead."

"Uh-huh," he said and tossed the leaf confetti away.

I wished I knew the definition of uh-huh. Were all these questions plain old curiosity, or nothing more than talk to fill in silences, or was there something more? I wanted to ask why he wanted to know. But what would he think of that? Instead I asked him about how his new classes were and what he thought of school and then later, sitting on the porch steps holding the sodas I'd brought out from the kitchen, we discussed the best sort of dog to get.

Sunny leaned against Tom, purring noisily, anticipating a good ear scratch. Tom picked up my silly cat and cradled it in his arms.

"I don't know if I like dogs or cats better," he said.

"Maybe you'll have to get both."

We talked until Mom came home without running out of things to say. I'd never known I could feel so comfortable with a boy.

Tom said hello to my mother. She asked him how his family was settling into their new home. And then I walked with him to the street.

I said, "Arrivederci."

He said, "See you."

I said, "Sure."

He said, "Weekdays from three to five."

He was halfway down the block, his back to me, striding away, before I realized what he meant.

"He said it like we had a daily appointment," I told Belinda over the phone that evening.

"Maybe that's the way he meant it."

"He can't know how long it takes hair to grow out!"

"Maybe he thinks your father will change his mind."

"If that's so, he doesn't know anything about fathers, either. Or mine, anyway," I added glumly.

"So enjoy him until he finds out," Belinda said.

It was so easy for Belinda to come up with such a calm suggestion.

She wasn't the one who was in danger of dying of a broken heart. Add to that my relationship with my father, and my life was misery. Because although things were going better with Tom than I'd thought they could, I simply could not bring myself to speak more than four-word sentences to a father who was willing to destroy his only daughter's chance for happiness.

Mealtimes were the worst, with Mom and Dad talking to each other, and me limited to saying, "Please pass the butter."

And as my evening phone calls had always been restricted to fifteen minutes apiece, I spent most nights alternating between studying and gazing at my book with Tom's picture.

Why would anyone give up such an exciting career, I wondered. Belinda was right, Tom didn't look like a person who had suffered a nervous breakdown. Still, there could have been some tragedy. Had he been photographed in one of those gossip papers that sold in the grocery store, innocently involved in some scandalous love triangle? Those papers made up that sort of stuff all the time. And had his parents wanted to protect his reputation, maybe even keep him out of a lawsuit?

No, that didn't make sense. Why move the whole family? They could have sent Tom off to a boarding school.

But what if he'd been promised a lead in some big sitcom? Maybe they'd all counted on a fantastic income. Maybe they'd run up debts, or simply run up their hopes. And then some dishonest producer had given the part to a nephew. And the whole family had been so crushed, they decided to get Tom out of show business.

Or maybe he had a weak heart! How about that? Maybe he had some tragic secret illness, and the doctors forbid him to continue with his career.

When I told Belinda all my ideas, she said I was crazy. "Did it ever occur to you that his family may have moved here because they wanted a small town in which to raise four children?"

"But in that case, they tore Tom away from his career! He must be devastated!"

"He doesn't look devastated to me," she pointed out.

"So why is he keeping it a secret?"

My best friend said patiently, "Cyndi, it is possible that Tom didn't like being a model. And if that's so, he doesn't want to keep being reminded of it. And the best way to avoid that is to not tell anyone that he ever was a model."

"Yeah, in a town this size, if people found out he was a famous model, they'd drive him crazy, interviewing him for the paper and that kind of stuff."

"We are a little short of celebrities," she agreed.

"I guess I'd keep it a secret, too," I said.

Tom continued to walk home with me every day after school. We'd stand at the corner where we parted with Belinda and talk to her for a few minutes. After that, we'd head to my house and I'd have him all to myself. Fortunately, the weather was on my side, no rain or cold spells. I wasn't allowed to invite anyone except Belinda into my house when my folks weren't home.

That was an old rule from when I was younger, and under different circumstances I would have asked if it could be changed, but as I wasn't speaking to my father, I figured the timing wasn't right to bring it up.

On Saturday I thought up alternative possibilities to spending the day at the mall. I suggested a picnic with a group of friends at the lake. My father said a flat no. I asked if I could study at the library. He said yes, he would drive me there and pick me up again. I asked if I could have friends to our house. He said yes, I could invite Belinda over anytime.

"And Tom and Ralph?" I asked.

My father didn't argue. He said a firm no. I went back to not speaking to him.

With all that dull time on my hands by myself, I leafed through the yellow pages and phoned three hairdressers. All three told me that hair grows from two to five inches a year.

I measured the hair on the top of my head. It was five inches long. If I was a maximum-speed hair grower, it would take a year, and if I wasn't, it could be two years before I could leave the house again.

"Do you realize I'll have died of old age before I've ever had a date?" I screamed at my father.

All he said was, "Don't shout at me, Cyndi."

I slammed back into my room and spent the rest of the day trying to read, but the tears kept welling up in my eyes and I simply could not care about the problems of fictional people.

Before dinnertime I used gobs of mousse until I had all my hair combed straight up. I knew my father would hate that.

Neither of my parents mentioned my hair. They were being so adult and in control, I wanted to scream.

After supper, when my father had gone into the front room and my mother and I were alone in the kitchen for a few minutes, she said, "Your father puts restrictions on you because he feels you aren't old enough to restrict yourself. It's his way of protecting you."

"Thanks a lot," I said, in a not-very-nice tone, which made me feel worse because I knew she was trying to help me.

But like I told Belinda later on the phone, "What she's saying is that I should act older, isn't it?"

"Probably," Belinda said.

"And how can I act older? Anything I want to do isn't likely to be what they consider older."

Belinda said slowly, "Doing things that they hate is the wrong direction, so I suppose that doing things they like is the right direction."

"Yes, but if I always do exactly what they want, I won't be me, will I? I'll be a carbon copy of them."

"I don't know the answer, Cyndi. Maybe you'll have to find something halfway between and try to make them understand your side."

That would be easy for Belinda. She was any parent's delight. But I couldn't be Belinda.

I spent the rest of the weekend with a shiny face, one hundred percent makeup-free, and my hair brushed smooth, which may have thrilled my father, though he didn't mention it, but it scared me. I didn't know myself in the mirror. I felt naked.

Tom continued to walk home with me every day after school. He didn't ask again about my restrictions. He did look at me a lot and practically melt me down to my toes with the warmth in those dark gray eyes. Was he hoping to see my hair grow? I was. Every day I'd check it in the mirror.

"I'm probably the only girl in the world who wants her dark roots to start showing," I told my mother.

She laughed and said, 'Tom seems like a nice boy."

"He'll give up on me and find someone else before I ever have a chance to find out," I said.

"I'm sorry. I can't help you."

"You could talk to Dad."

"That's up to you," she said.

She wouldn't have said it if she didn't think it would help. But I knew me better than Mom did. If I marched in and told Dad I wanted to talk to him, I'd end up screaming at him and be nowhere. What I had to do was get all the anger out first. Once I read a story about a boy who worked off his anger by going out into the woods and shouting until his throat ached. Unfortunately, our backyard ran right up against the neighbor's. If I went out back and shouted, someone would figure we had a fire or burglars and call the police.

Instead I wrote down all the ways that I considered my father unfair. To my embarrassment, there weren't many. By the time I'd sat for twenty minutes trying to think up more complaints, I realized that he was a pretty nice guy, even if he was very old-fashioned.

I went hunting for him and found him in the garage with his head under the hood of the car. "Can I talk to you?" I asked.

He straightened, glanced down at his grease-covered hands, and said, "Sure."

"I want to ask you something."

"All right."

"I don't want you to get mad."

"All right."

"I don't want me to get mad, either."

"That sounds fair," he said.

"But the thing is, I don't see why bleaching my hair is such a big thing. I mean, lots of kids do it. I haven't changed my life. When I'm an old lady, I won't look back and say, gee, I wish I hadn't done that, so it isn't like it's permanent or anything. It isn't like doing something dangerous where I could get killed and it isn't like dropping out of school or something."

"That's all true," he said.

"Then why are you so mad at me?"

"I'm not mad at you." He wiped his hands off on a rag and leaned back against the car, looking at me. "And it isn't the hair. What's important is that I made a rule. I told you that the one thing you couldn't do was dye your hair."

"But why is that such a big deal?"

He smiled at me. "Listen, my darling daughter, you intentionally disobeyed. Part of becoming an adult is learning to accept responsibility for your own behavior. You broke a rule and now you want me to forget about it."

I nodded and left the garage. There wasn't anything else I could say without blowing up because I knew he was right. I sat down on the grass under a tree in the backyard to think the thing out. It was true that he'd told me the rule. It was also true that he'd told me exactly what my punishment would be if I broke the rule. So none of that should have been a surprise. How could I have been so dumb?

And then I had a couple seconds of smart. I jumped up and ran back to the garage. "Dad," I said, "you're right all the way and I'm sorry I was dumb and broke the rule."

He peered up at me from where he was bent over again, his head under the hood. "Fine."

"And I'll go to Mom's hairdresser and get my hair dyed back to its natural color, how's that?"

"I won't know until I see it, but it sounds better."

"And then after I do that, could you set a time limit on how long I'm grounded? Like maybe a month or something definite. I mean, I don't know when my sentence ends, and even criminals know when they're going to get out of jail!"

He leaned his elbows on the car and looked at me for a long minute. I was afraid he'd set my time at a year, he looked so solemn. Then he said, "Tell you what. You get the hair dyed back, and then if you promise not to tint the tips on weekends anymore, I'll drop the grounding."

"Not tint the tips? How come?"

"It's called compromise, Cyndi. You give up something and I give up something."

Put that way, it was a good deal. I ran to phone Mom's hairdresser.

CHAPTER 9

Friday afternoon was a bummer, with the hairdresser covering up all my nice bleached streaks with boring brown.

However, Friday night made up for that. Tom and I went to the movies at the mall. The fantasy he'd wanted to see was no longer on. Instead there was this crazy adventure romance about an explorer and a doctor in a jungle. When I wasn't laughing, I was covering my eyes.

Tom whispered, "Scared?"

"No," I whispered back. "I just don't like spiders."

The bad guys had tied the doctor to a tree and there were spiders crawling all over her. I spread my fingers and watched between them. The spiders went up her arms, her shoulders, into her long tangled hair, and just when I thought they were going to start across her face, which I couldn't have stood, she worked her hands free from the ropes, dashed through the jungle, and plunged into the river.

Tom whispered, "Now the crocodiles will get her."

"That's okay," I said, uncovering my eyes. "I'm not afraid of crocodiles."

Why should I be? She was the heroine. She might get covered by spiders, but she wasn't going to be devoured by crocodiles.

"How many crocodiles have you met?" Tom asked.

"That's why I'm not afraid of them."

After the doctor and the explorer found the hidden treasure, escaped a dozen or more near-death attacks, and jetted homeward, we walked from the theater across the parking lot to the mall for milkshakes at the ice-cream place. It was crowded with Friday-night couples and groups. Several people called my name and waved at me. In a town like mine a person practically had to wear a paper bag over her head to get any privacy.

"You know everyone," Tom said.

We found a small booth, the kind with a seat wide enough for one person on each side of a narrow table.

"I've lived in this boring place all my life," I said.

"Look at it this way. It doesn't have crocodiles."

"It does have spiders."

"All the same, I think it's nice to live where you know everyone."

"Would you like that?" I asked. "You wouldn't mind if everyone knew your name and no matter where you went all day long people recognized you?"

"Why not?" he said in a quick, easy way, as though it weren't a thing he'd ever worried about happening. "What flavor shake is best here?"

So he hadn't moved to a small town and kept his past career a secret in order to avoid being recognized. That wasn't it. But if it wasn't, why did he make such a secret of his past? Why did he say that the only place he'd ever worked was in a deli?

I told him my favorite milkshake flavor. We talked about anything except what I really wanted to know. But after the waiter brought our shakes, and we'd started on them, I said, "Is there some special reason your family left New York?"

"Sure," he said.

"Is it a secret?"

He gave me a look of surprise, eyebrows raised. "Secret? No. My parents were tired of living in the city. So when an opportunity came up to switch job locations, we moved."

"Oh. I thought maybe you were, well, getting away from something."

"We were. We got away from traffic and high rent and no place for the kids to play and all that kind of thing."

"It's hard to imagine anyone moving here because they want to."

Tom laughed. "I suppose we could have gone all out for change the way the people in the movie did and headed for the jungle, but how would we have kept my little brother out of the river? Just because you like crocodiles doesn't mean I want to feed my brother to them."

"At least that wouldn't be boring!"

"What a hard heart you have!"

"I didn't mean about your brother! I meant, the jungle wouldn't be boring. Did those people ever look bored? Still, you're right, it's probably not a good place for little kids."

We joked back and forth about the movie without my ever once getting any closer to learning the truth about Tom's career and why he'd left it. Was it possible that Tom had some tragic disease brought on by city pollution and his parents moved here in the hope of saving him? I studied him closely. He looked wonderful. He also looked healthy.

I'd have been smarter to forget about his career and why he dropped it, but I couldn't. The questions kept popping up in my mind. I finally decided that maybe when he knew me better he would tell me. Or when I knew him a lot better, I would ask.

We rode the bus back to our neighborhood. I'd worn my favorite T-shirt with my white jeans and my black vest because they looked terrific together. Trouble was that it left my arms bare. My mother had asked me if I needed a jacket when I'd left the house and I had assured her that I didn't because I didn't want to cover my outfit. And I'd been okay in the movies. But walking down the street, with chill night breezes rising, I shivered.

The streetlights shining through the tree branches cast moving shadows on the walk. The shrubbery whispered night sounds.

Tom said, "This is something else we couldn't do in the city, go wandering down an empty sidewalk after dark."

"Yeah, I've heard about muggers," I said.

"You say that like there's never been one around here."

"That's how dead this town is! Not even a mugger!" I teased. "Actually, there's some places I wouldn't walk at night, like round the old uptown district."

"It's nice here," he said. "Look at those stars!"

The breezes had blown away any clouds, leaving the sky a glitter of stars. I said, "All right, now, it's Friday quiz time and you're supposed to be able to identify three constellations, remember? So let's hear them, Tom Dalton, and no excuses."

"I forgot about that! You're right, you did assign me three constellations."

"Forgetting an assignment is no excuse."

"Yes, teacher," he said.

We stopped in the shadow of the hedge at the end of my front walk to look up at the stars.

"All right, I'll give you one more chance, but you'd better be ready by next quiz time."

"Wait, I think I know one," he said and caught my elbow to stop me when I started toward the house. "Hey, you're cold! Why didn't you say so?"

"I'm not cold," I said, and then I shivered. Not on purpose. Maybe it was being told I was cold that made me shiver.

Before I could protest, Tom pulled off his jacket and wrapped it around my shoulders.

"Now you'll be cold," I said.

"I'm okay."

"No, you'll catch pneumonia and then your parents will tell you that you must never again go out with that terrible girl who took your jacket so that you caught pneumonia."

"And what will your parents say if you get pneumonia?"

"They'll say, 'Cyndi, you dummy, why didn't you wear your jacket?' and they'll probably ground me again."

He did that quick laugh that made me catch my breath. His hands were still on my shoulders. The silky lining of his jacket enclosed my bare arms and it was almost as though Tom himself, and not mere fabric, was touching me.

"I have to babysit for my parents tomorrow, but will I see you Sunday?" he asked.

"We're going over to my grandparents' house for dinner. We'll be home about three."

"I'll be over about three. If that's okay." He said it in that questioning way.

In the dark his eyes looked as though they were full of stars. I meant to say that of course it was okay for him to come over at three on Sunday, but I looked up into his eyes and I couldn't say a word.

Maybe he couldn't manage to say anything, either, because what he did next was kiss me.

I think it kind of surprised us both.

His hands dropped from my shoulders and he stepped back and started to turn away.

My voice came out thin and high, not sounding like me at all. "You forgot your jacket!"

"Oh!"

I handed it to him. We stared at each other in the dark.

"You'd better go in. It's getting colder," he said.

"Yes. Right. You, too."

"I think I'm supposed to wait until you're in the house, or something like that," he said.

"Oh! Yes! All right. Goodnight." I turned and ran up onto my porch and opened the door.

"Goodnight, Cyndi, see you Sunday afternoon," he called.

All night I kept waking up and thinking about Tom and remembering the way his eyes looked and the way his kiss felt. Night went on and on until I thought it would never be morning. I wanted to phone Belinda because my life was so wonderful I had to share it with somebody.

Over breakfast, with the sun shining in the kitchen window through the white ruffled curtains and reflecting on the yellow walls, I had second thoughts. Would Belinda really want to be overloaded with my happiness when her own life had bottomed out?

What I had to do was find a way to solve Belinda's woes. And all that required was Louis Turner.

Hadn't I been faced with practically monumental roadblocks to happiness three days ago? And now, here shone Saturday.

How had my life gone from the pits to perfection? All I'd done was to single out my problem, figure out what I had to say, and go straight to the one person who could solve it. I'd had a direct confrontation.

Louis Turner couldn't possibly be as difficult to confront as my father.

Inspired, I looked up his phone number in the directory.

I think it must have been his father who answered the phone. The voice was very deep and adult. I almost hung up.

"Uh, is Louis there?" I said, and then added quickly, "I want to ask him something about the debate team."

The deep, polite voice said, "If you'll wait one moment, I'll call him."

It was more than a moment. Louis must have still been in bed. When he answered, he sounded as though he was talking around a yawn. "Hello, who is it?"

"This is Cyndi Carlisle. I don't know if you know me, but I had this question I wanted to ask you and I hope I didn't wake you. It's almost noon," I rattled.

Why hadn't I thought ahead about who would answer the phone? Or whether Louis would be awake? Maybe I should have waited until Monday to corner him at school.

After what seemed like a very long silence, he said, "Cyndi Carlisle? Oh yeah, I know who you are."

"You do?"

"What do you want, Cyndi?"

I almost said I wanted to know how he knew me. But that wasn't why I'd phoned him. "Uh, Louis, I heard that you didn't have a debate partner for next year, see, and I was wondering, could I meet you sometime to talk about that?"

"Meet me?"

"Like maybe after school?"

"I didn't know you debated."

"No, well, see I have this friend, she's very smart, practically straight A, and see, I thought if maybe you talked to her-listen, this is very hard to explain over the phone."

"Uh-huh. Okay, sure, we can meet." He sounded wide awake now. "Let's meet and talk about your friend. How about tonight? I could meet you at the mall tonight."

"The mall?" Belinda and I never hung around the mall at night. It was open until eleven on Friday and Saturday nights, but the crowds were either adults or people on dates or with groups. "I'll be out there this afternoon," I said.

"No, I'm tied up this afternoon, but how about meeting me around seven?"

Unless we had definite plans to go to the movies with friends, Belinda and I had to be home by suppertime. "I can't," I said.

"You can't?" He sounded surprised. "How about Sunday?"

Sunday Tom was coming to see me. At three. If I could wait that long without bursting.

To Louis, I said, "Sorry, I'm busy Sunday. Look, couldn't we get together Monday after school?"

After another long pause, he said, 'Tell you what. You know the drive-in?"

"I know it." It was about three blocks from school. We never went there because the food was lousy and the shakes were worse.

"Want to meet me there Monday around four?"

I said yes quickly, afraid to make any more plan changes. He might decide not to meet me at all. After I hung up, I thought through what we'd said. To meet him there at four, I'd have to wait around for almost an hour after school. I'd also have to arrange with my parents about getting home late. And I'd have to explain to Tom why I wasn't walking home.

And then it all fell together in my head. Simple. Tom could go with

Belinda and me to talk to Louis, which was a good idea and looked better the more I thought it out. Tom was a good talker. With the three of us there, we'd easily convince Louis that Belinda was the perfect person to be his debate partner next year.

After I explained it to my mother, she said, "I hope it works."

"The worst he can do is say no," I pointed out. "And if he does, Belinda won't be any worse off than she is now. But I think the three of us can convince Louis."

A few minutes later Belinda phoned to say she couldn't go to the mall because she had a sore throat. I almost said that it was lucky I hadn't arranged to meet Louis but then I decided to keep the whole thing a surprise.

The thing about Belinda was that although she always managed to look calm, she could work herself right to the edge of collapse worrying about anything, given enough time. If I told her over the phone, she would rewrite and rehearse a speech to give Louis, going over what to say from now until Monday afternoon.

Instead I told her about my date with Tom. I didn't mention the stars or the kiss, but I told her everything else.

"Lucky you. I'm glad somebody's life is going right."

"You'll feel better on Monday."

"Easy for you to say," she said sadly.

That was true. It was easy for me to say because I knew what wonderful thing was going to happen on Monday for Belinda.

In the meantime I had the choice of staying home alone or going to the mall, where neither Belinda nor Tom would be, which would leave me the thrilling company of Ralph.

While I thought that one over, I went out to get the mail from the box. There was the usual pile of stuff for my parents.

And there was a letter addressed to 'Tommy, the model on the cover," care of the publisher, and marked PLEASE FORWARD.

My return address was in the corner.

I stared at it. It didn't make sense. Why had it come back to me?

And then I saw the stamped arrow pointing to my address. It had words printed on it that read, "Addressee Unknown. Return to Sender."

Addressee unknown? What did that mean?

I phoned Belinda again. Her voice sounded worse. "I'm not supposed to talk."

"Okay, sorry, but I have to ask you one question and then I won't call you anymore."

"Call me," she said. "I'm so bored. But you've got to do the talking."

"Right." I explained about the envelope.

"Means what it says, Cyndi. Means they don't know any Tommy. Or maybe he went by a stage name."

"Or are they covering up for their models?"

"What for? They could have sent it on to him. It's a letter. He wouldn't have had to answer."

"But they must know him! They hired him!"

"Maybe they don't know where he is."

That figured. His family must have moved from New York without leaving a forwarding address. But why would they do that? They wouldn't. That was crazy.

"You think they're hiding out? With four kids?"

"Some kind of criminals?" Belinda said. "Don't be dumb. Any other addresses on the letter?"

"Just the arrow."

"Okay. The publisher would have sent the letter to Tom's home address, wouldn't they? Or to his agent. Or to the photographer. And then, if his family were hiding, you'd have got it sent back. But if there's no other address, it means they didn't try to forward it. So Tom must have told them not to forward any mail."

"Why would he do that?"

"Only one way to find out," Belinda said. "Ask him."

I explained my decision to wait until I knew him better before asking him anything, in the hope that he'd tell me without being asked. Belinda thought that was an even better idea.

And that's what I meant to do. I put the letter in my dresser drawer. It would stay there until I either threw it away or decided how to handle it. Right after I'd first met Tom, I'd had some awful days imagining that letter going straight to his mailbox. It would have tipped him off that I was following him. I'd even thought of cutting school to avoid any bad scene. Looking back, I had to laugh. Because after all, he'd been following me. And everything had turned out fine. And now the letter had come back to me instead of to him, and I could throw it away.

Or would he think it was funny? Tom had a super sense of humor. He laughed at everything. That was one of the best things about being with him, how easily we laughed together.

He phoned me after supper.

"Cyndi? No matter what you're doing, I wish I was with you."

"I'm ironing my clothes."

"Fabulous! Sounds wonderful!"

"Ironing clothes?"

"Compared to what I've been doing," he said.

"What have you been doing?"

"Playing Monopoly. Since three o'clock this afternoon."

"And you haven't won?"

"My sisters cheat. They pool their money against me."

"What about your brother?"

"He can't count past twenty. Listen, can you talk for a while?"

"Fifteen minutes exactly," I said, reaching over to switch off the iron.

"Okay. They finally got interested in a TV show, but that's about as long as I've got, too. Then they'll come hollering for me."

"Do you have to keep them entertained the whole time your parents are out?"

"That's the deal," he said. "At least I'm allowed to feed us frozen dinners."

"Wouldn't they be better heated?"

"Oh, is that what you're supposed to do with them? I wondered why they were so hard to cut."

We went on like that, talking nonsense, until his little brother got tired of the TV. I could hear him saying, "Come on, Tommy, play with me."

"Does your family always call you Tommy?" I asked.

"I'm old enough to babysit but too young to be called Tom," he said solemnly.

"They might be more impressed with how old and wise you are if you'd learn to heat the frozen dinners," I said.

"Is it only fifteen minutes? I feel as though you've been abusing me for hours."

"It's exactly fifteen minutes. My Mom is shouting at me to get off the phone," I said.

"Tomorrow," he said, and hung up.

I hugged myself, I was so happy. With Cyndi Superstar singing away on my stereo, I whipped through my ironing. After that I stripped my nails and redid them in curved lines of color, turning each fingertip into a rainbow.

CHAPTER 10

"Sunday at three, Sunday at three," I hummed to myself throughout the evening.

I felt so good I even wore matching earrings when we went over to my grandparents' house for dinner. And Grandmother was so pleased she didn't mention my rainbow fingernails. Possibly my happiness was contagious.

Anything that powerful should have lasted indefinitely.

Instead, what it did was make me too lightheaded to think. Oh, I thought all right, but it was dumb thinking. What I thought was, Tom was so wonderful, the reason he kept his modeling career secret was because he didn't want to brag.

I figured that he was afraid he would sound conceited, moving from a sophisticated city to our nothing town, if he went around telling people that back in New York he was famous.

That made more sense than any of my earlier ideas about him moving away because of his health or some other secret. Probably what he'd said was true. The family moved because of his parents' jobs and for the sake of the younger children. And Tom, being such a darling person, put on the sunshine act and made the best of what must have been a painful decision for him.

Therefore, I reasoned, still in my bubble headed state, although he might prefer to keep his past private, he wouldn't mind if I knew.

Because of all the above crazy reasoning, when he came over Sunday afternoon and we settled in our usual places on the front porch steps, along with our cans of soda, I brought out the letter I'd sent to him and the book with his picture on the cover.

I'd switched back into my white jeans and a star-spangled shirt, taken out the matching gold hoops and replaced them with an enameled heart and an icicle-drop, and brushed my hair forward and up, in Cyndi Superstar's best style.

Tom looked gorgeous in a plain striped shirt and jeans, but then he didn't have to do anything to make himself better except maybe smile. He was already perfect. The smile was almost too much, the way it lifted the corners of his dark eyes.

I handed him the letter and the book.

"What's this?" he asked, turning them over in his hands.

"I wrote to you, back when I thought you were only here for a weekend. Remember how I bumped into you at the mall? I heard your father call you Tommy. That's all I knew. Just Tommy. But I knew who you were as soon as I saw you, and where you worked and all that."

As I talked, his eyes widened. His mouth opened in that puzzled way. He tilted his head slightly. He said, "Huh?"

"How could I know you'd move here?" I explained. "It was the most fantastic coincidence! Do you realize I'd been trying to get in touch with you for almost the past month, and that I'd actually written three letters, or maybe it was four, all in one week, which is more than I usually write in a year! So when I actually saw you, I couldn't believe it!"

"Cyndi, what are you talking about?"

"That book cover! That's you!"

Tom stared at the cover. He turned the book over, read the back, turned it up again, looked at the picture. "You think that's me?"

"Of course that's you!" I said.

"And that's why you wanted to meet me, because you saw this picture?"

"I knew, as soon as I saw your picture, that I'd like you."

He looked up and met my gaze. "And that's why you like me, because of a picture on a book?"

"Uh, no," I said. "Not exactly."

"You have a thing about dating models?" He wasn't smiling. This conversation sounded all wrong. I wished I hadn't started it.

"No, of course not! It's only, well," I said, and then couldn't think what else to say.

He waited, looking at me.

When I didn't go on, he said, "You went out with me because you thought I was someone famous."

"I don't care about famous," I said.

"You're like the girls who date guys because they're on the football team."

"That's not so," I stammered.

"It's exactly the same thing. It's like guys who date cheerleaders. And that's lousy. You should go out with someone because you like him, not because he's somebody everybody else knows about. What were you going to do, show this book around school and tell everybody you were going out with a famous model?"

"Of course not! I wouldn't do that! That's all wrong!"

"I'll say it's wrong!" He jumped up, dropping the book and the letter. He was shouting and he looked as though he hated to hear himself shouting. He clenched his fists. He practically clenched his mouth.

'Tom, don't be mad!"

He turn   ed and stalked down the walk, stopped by the hedge, stood there a few seconds, swung around, and stared at me. Then he walked back, stood over me, and said, in a tight, angry voice, "I'm not that guy on the cover. I'm not anybody famous. I'm nobody and I like being nobody and so maybe you'd better go find yourself some genuinely famous guy."

He hurried away, his hands jammed in his pockets, his head bent forward.

I was so stunned it took me a minute to even consider running after him.

Dashing to the hedge, I called his name.

He had already reached the corner. He didn't look back. If I ran after him, he'd run faster. He didn't want to talk to me.

Returning to the house, I picked up my letter and book and went inside to my room. I sat down on the edge of my bed, staring at the boy on the cover, trying to figure out why Tom blew up. Why didn't he want to admit that he was the boy on the cover?

I didn't like him only because he was on a book cover. I liked him because he was nice. And now that didn't matter. Because he no longer liked me. I'd ruined everything.

My whole life had been going right straight toward perfect, all my problems solved. I'd been floating around in the clouds.

So how had I managed such a total crash?

Then it hit me. He wasn't the boy on the cover. I'd been fooling myself, and Tom had been telling the truth all along.

Tom was so much better-looking than the boy on the cover. Tossing the book across the room, I threw myself on the bed and sobbed into my pillow.

I'd thrown away the best thing that had ever happened to me. I'd thrown away Tom.

When I calmed down enough to blow my nose and breathe without choking on my tears, I knew that what I needed was someone calmer than me to tell me what to do.

I phoned Belinda.

"He isn't the boy on the cover," I said. "I can see that now. They do look a lot alike, though."

"If he says it isn't him, it isn't," she said.

"I know that. I wish I'd found it out a day earlier."

"Can't you phone him and explain?"

"What can I explain? He thinks I liked him because I thought he was somebody famous."

"You did," she pointed out.

"Not really. I mean, it just happened that I saw him first on a book cover. If I'd met him first, I'd have liked him anyway."

"Would you have followed him around like you did?"

"I don't know."

"You've seen lots of cute boys at school. You've never followed any of them before, tailed them all the way home and checked their names on mailboxes," she pointed out.

"Belinda, you're supposed to be making me feel better. You're not doing that."

"I'm sorry."

"And I've been helping you."

"You have?"

Even if I'd made a total mess of my own life, at least I could credit myself with straightening out Belinda's. Sniffing back my tears, I explained to her that I'd solved all her problems about debate. She would be thrilled, I thought.

So when I told her and she shrieked, I almost went into shock.

"You did what!"

"I phoned Louis Turner Saturday. He'll meet us after school on Monday. It's all set, Belinda."

"It's all nothing! Have you lost your brain in outer space? How could you do such a thing!"

"But, Belinda, all I did was phone him. And he was perfectly nice."

"What did you tell him?"

"That I wanted to talk to him about this friend of mine-"

"Did you mention my name?"

"Of course I didn't mention your name. I thought it would be better to wait to introduce you face-to-face. He could see how smart you are."

"He could what?"

"Anybody can tell by looking at you that you're smart. They can! You look smart. You look like somebody who makes straight A's."

"Okay, wise and observant one, tell me what Louis Turner looks like," she sputtered. "Have you ever taken a really good close look at Louis?"

"Sure," I said. "He's blond and nice-looking."

"That's all? That's all you've noticed?"

"What am I supposed to notice?" Belinda drove me crazy when she got like this. She didn't do it often, but like any best friends, we'd had arguments, and then she'd go all sarcastic, spitting out questions.

'Try looking past the surface, Cyndi. Tell me his personality."

"I'm no good at that."

"Come on, try!" she demanded.

"All right, let's see, he walks with a kind of, oh, a swagger."

"Now I am relieved. For a minute there, I thought you had a vision problem."

"Belinda, don't be like this! I don't know why you're mad at me. And I don't need anyone mad at me."

I must have sounded as upset as I felt. Belinda said, in a kinder tone, "Cyndi, Louis not only swaggers, he also always has at least one girl, sometimes two girls, trailing after him, smiling up at him, hanging on his every utterance. Haven't you noticed that?"

"I guess so," I said slowly.

"Louis expects every girl to fall madly in love with him at first glance and the awful thing is that they do. Don't you see? I can't go up to him and tell him I want to be his debate partner. He'll think I have a crush on him. He'll think I'm one of his devoted subjects. And that won't work. Debate partners have to be businesslike."

"I suppose so," I said, not quite sure what she meant.

She explained. "Listen, Cyndi, it is not possible to keep one's mind on evidence files while fending off passes from one's teammate."

"He makes passes?"

"At anything female."

After we hung up, I tried to phone Louis to break our appointment. No one answered.

Monday at school I looked for him. Our paths didn't cross.

I did cross paths with Tom. Twice. Both times he pretended he didn't see me.

After school I met Belinda on the front steps. She asked me if I'd thought of a way to solve my problem with Tom. I told her that I didn't have a problem because as nearly as I could figure, Tom and I were over. Done. Past history.

And then, to change the subject, because that was the only way I could keep from crying, I said, "If you aren't going to talk to Louis, how will you get him for a partner?"

"I won't," she said slowly. "I figured what I had to do was talk to the debate coach and get us assigned as partners. That would have worked. So today I stopped by the coach's office. I talked to Ms. Frazier. And she said she wasn't going to assign partners yet. She said she'd wait and let people make up their own teams, and then assign anyone who didn't have a partner."

"What'll you do?" I asked.

"Get stuck with the same partner I had this year."

Until that moment, I'd meant to walk home with Belinda. From my house I could phone the drive-in, have Louis paged, and explain to him that I couldn't keep our appointment.

That's what I'd planned to do.

But there were tears in Belinda's eyes. She had on her solemn face, carefully looking away from me so that I wouldn't notice. And I almost didn't. Because Belinda never cried, at least not when anyone was around and might see her.

Inside she must be hurting as much as I am, I thought. And I was hurting so much, I couldn't bear to think of anyone else in all that much pain.

Quickly, I said, "Oh, hey, I can't go home yet. I've got some stuff to do in the library. You go on. I'll phone you later."

She didn't even look surprised at the idea of me going to the library, that's how miserable she was. Her brain had gone sloppy. She nodded, waved good-bye, and headed away from me.

I took off for the drive-in.

I had absolutely no idea what I would say to Louis Turner, but I was diehard determined to have a try.

Maybe part of my stubbornness resulted from the awful mess I'd made with Tom. I couldn't let my whole life be a failure. I had to succeed somewhere.

When I made that appointment with Louis, I pictured myself with fast-talking Tom and cool-talking Belinda at my side. Now I was on my own. I wasn't happy about it. On the other hand, I wasn't happy at all about anything, so how could things get worse?

Louis had draped himself charmingly in a back booth, his head tilted toward the window to catch the light and brighten that blond hair. Why had I never noticed before how conceited he was?

He waved and smiled.

My mind did a turnabout. Honestly, wasn't I being unfair? He'd agreed to meet me. There he was. Maybe Belinda had him figured wrong. Probably he was a very nice guy and it wasn't his fault that he had the kind of looks that attracted girls.

"Hi, Cyndi," he said.

"Hi, Louis."

He straightened up to make room for me next to him on the seat, even holding out a hand toward me. That should have given me a clue.

Determined to be open-minded, I slid into the booth across the table from him. "I wasn't sure you knew who I was."

Leaning his elbows on the table, he bent toward me and gave me a slow smile, his eyes narrowing. "I've seen you around."

"Oh, that's good. That makes it easier. Easier to talk to you. I have to talk to you."

"Can I order something for you?" he asked, beckoning to the waitress.

"No, I'm okay."

"A soda? Sure, you'll have a soda. Two Cokes," he told her. "Now, what is it I can do for you, Cyndi Carlisle?"

"I wanted to talk to you about my friend," I said.

"Would your friend be named Cyndi?"

"Huh?" I stared at him, trying to figure out what he meant. What an ego! Did he think I'd made up a story about a friend just as an excuse to talk to him?

"Go on, tell me about your friend."

"My friend is real and her name is Belinda," I snapped. "She's a debater."

"Is she? I don't know any Belinda."

"You should," I said. "She's on the junior debate team, but she'll be a senior debater next year, and she's very good."

The waitress brought our drinks. Louis paid her. He gave her one of his glossy smiles along with his money.

I felt my nerve deserting me. I said quickly, "Belinda is a straight A student. She's the smartest person in the whole sophomore class practically, and with the right partner, she would probably win every debate."

What I needed was Tom and Belinda to do the talking. I'd never been good at arguments. What was I doing trying to prove a point to a senior debater?

"She sounds terrific," Louis said. "And what about you, Cyndi? Are you planning to go out for debate?"

"Me?"

"You were at the last tournament. Watching me. What were you there for? To listen to the debate or to listen to me?"

"I was there with some friends," I mumbled. I'd never thought he might remember that I'd been in the back of the room when he was debating.

"Doing what?" he asked.

I tried a subject change. "I wouldn't have thought you saw me, you were so serious about the debate. You're very good at debate, I could tell that."

If he leaned toward me any farther across the table, he'd be lying on it. His hand covered mine before I could back away. He said, "Certainly I saw you. You're not the sort of girl I'd miss. Or forget."

With that remark he hit the outer limits of dumb come-ons.

I pulled away my hand. "Look, Louis, I came here to tell you about Belinda because if you need a good debate partner for next year, she's the best. But if you've already got a debate partner, I might as well leave."

He sat back and gave me a long stare from under half-closed eyes. "What's her name?"

"Belinda Gray. She's a sophomore in junior debate. Next year she'll be in senior debate. She's very smart and she could be a terrific debater but she hasn't had a good partner and she really wants to find somebody who is serious about winning because that is what she is serious about."

"You really came to tell me about your friend?"

"I really did. Are you sure you don't know her?"

He shrugged. "I've heard that name. Does she have straight hair that kind of turns under at her shoulders?"

"You do know her!"

"I've seen her."

"You'd make a fantastic debate team," I said.

All he said was, "I'll think about it."

I thanked him for the soda and got out of there fast, while he was still on the opposite side of the table. Belinda was right about the guy. He made passes at everyone. Why she would want him for a debate partner, I couldn't figure. He'd be a pain to handle. However, I didn't think he'd think about me or my friend any longer than it took him to find some other girl to flirt with. By tomorrow he'd forget all about me and Belinda. And probably that was best, even if Belinda had to put up with another year of a dud debate partner.

I was so convinced that Louis had a fast fade-out memory for girls, I put him out of mind.

CHAPTER 11

When Belinda met me at noon the next day, neither of us mentioned Louis. It went like that all week. I didn't tell her I'd actually kept my appointment with him. She didn't mention that she'd given up her dream of becoming a champion debater.

But we both knew I'd forced her to make a choice about facing Louis. So there we were, with a topic we wouldn't discuss. That had never happened before. It strained our friendship. We made empty conversation about everything else. We avoided looking each other in the eye.

I hated that. I missed my best friend. I felt so separated from her, I couldn't even tell her how terribly broken up I was over Tom.

Life went from rotten to wretched. I might as well have remained grounded.

And then, on Friday night, right after suppertime, Belinda phoned.

"Can I come over? I've got to talk to you," she said. She sounded almost too excited to talk, which was weird for Belinda.

A few minutes later she pounded on the door. Bright spots of color flamed in her cheeks. Her hair was tangled. She gasped for breath.

Running had never been a Belinda thing.

She waved a quick hi to my parents as we hurried through the front room to my room, Belinda in the lead.

Slamming the door shut after us, she threw herself on my bed. "Cyndi, you won't believe what happened!"

"The Martians have landed."

"No, truly! More than that! Louis phoned!"

All those exclamations from my calm friend left me speechless.

"He did! He phoned! Don't you believe me?" she asked.

"Oh sure! Gosh! What did he say?"

"He said that he'd talked to the senior debate coach about me and she thought we'd make a good team!"

I jumped up and down and clapped my hands and tried not to scream too loudly.

"He actually wants to be my partner next year!" Belinda leapt from the bed and went dancing around my room. "Can you believe that!"

"That's fantastic!"

"Isn't it!" She stopped suddenly, looked at me, then threw her arms around me. "You did it, Cyndi! He told me you talked to him Monday. Why didn't you tell me?"

When she calmed down enough to listen, we sat cross-legged on my bed and I told her all about Monday afternoon. "I didn't mention it," I explained, "because it was so weird. I mean, there I was, explaining how brilliant you are, and there he was, making stupid passes."

Belinda giggled. "You had guts to go meet him alone."

"I hadn't planned to go alone! I'd thought you would be with me."

"And I let you down," she said slowly. "I'm sorry, Cyndi. You set that all up for me and all I did was get mad at you. Next time I'm such a stinker, tell me so."

I shrugged. "I hope he works out as a partner. Personally, I think he's a creep."

"Sure he's a creep," she laughed, "but he's a great debater."

"What if he starts making passes at you?"

"Oh that." Belinda shrugged and gave me a funny sideways glance. "He came on real strong with some line about getting started at knowing each other better tomorrow night. Tomorrow night! No time-waster, that one. So I said, sure, great, I'd bring my boyfriend and we could all get acquainted. You should have heard the dead silence that followed."

"Boyfriend? Yeah, that's a great line, but what happens when you have to produce one?"

Belinda picked at my bedspread, staring down at her hands. "No problem," she mumbled, "he remembered he had something else to do tomorrow and put off getting together until later."

"Sooner or later you're going to have to produce a boyfriend, or at least a name."

She didn't answer.

"Aren't you?" I insisted. "Won't he ask?"

She muttered something that sounded as though she said she had told him a name. Since when did debaters mutter?

"What's that?" I demanded.

"I did!" She looked up, her face all determination, daring me to argue. "I told him Ralph was my boyfriend!"

"Ralph?" Ralph was a friend. A child. A nut. He was also kind of sweet and I was fond of him, the same way I was fond of my cats. I didn't want him hurt. "What if Ralph hears that? He'll know you're using him."

"No, I'm not. I like Ralph."

"Sure, so do I, but that's not the same as dating him."

"I wouldn't mind dating him, if he asked me."

I practically fell off the bed. But I kept my amazement to myself. Just in time, I saw the expression in her eyes. She wasn't joking. She really did like Ralph, and not as an old kindergarten pal, either. How long had she been thinking like that? I wondered. But I didn't ask. A best friend, I figured, was somebody you didn't have to explain things to unless that's what you wanted to do.

It wasn't until after Belinda had gone home that I started thinking about my part in the whole setup. For the second time in my life, I had made up my mind to confront a person and talk a problem all the way through no matter what the outcome. I'd done that with my father and I'd done it with Louis.

What could I lose by giving it a try with Tom?

Everything. I could look like one of those dumb girls who couldn't let go. Maybe by now he had a new girlfriend.

All right, so what if he did?

What I had to make clear was that all I wanted to do was be

friends. I lay awake most of the night, staring at the ceiling, trying to figure out exactly what to say. I never did come up with a great idea.

Saturday morning I took off early, right after breakfast. Halfway to his house, I stopped and picked leaves off a shrub and listened to the birds doing their morning chatter. A screen door slammed. A car whizzed by. The world did its Saturday-morning thing. The only person out of order was Cyndi Carlisle, standing at the corner of Park Street, trying to decide which way to go.

What if his mother answered the door? Wouldn't she think I was weird, showing up practically at daybreak? What if Tom was still asleep? Or had already gone out? What if I stood at the corner all day, trying to make up my mind?

A lilac bloomed near a front walk. I picked up a spray and stuck it behind my ear.

When I couldn't think of any more excuses, I made myself head toward Tom's house.

A couple of girls answered. They were junior high age, and they gave me very careful looks, head-to-toe inspection, before darting back into the shadows of the house to shout for Tom.

A few minutes later he appeared and opened the screen door. "My dumb sisters. You'd think they'd know enough to ask you in," he apologized.

"As long as I stand out here, I can run away," I said.

He came outside and stood on the steps with me. An old bridal wreath bush sprawled around the corner of the newly painted house. The morning was blossom-scented.

"You came over to run away?" he asked.

"I came over to explain. I don't want you mad at me."

"I'm not mad at you."

"You are too. You don't even speak to me at school."

"I'm sorry," he said. "I didn't mean it that way."

"We can still be friends," I said.

"Sure."

"Because whether you believe it or not, I do like you for yourself and not because of a dumb picture." This lump rose in my throat. I was having a hard time talking around it. Next I'd be crying and then I'd really be miserable. I said quickly, "So that's all I want to say and now I've said it, so I'll leave."

He said, "As long as you're here, come on in."

I backed away. "I think I better go."

"I want to show you our recreation room in the basement. We've got it all fixed up. I've got a big CD collection."

"I'm not sure," I said, wondering if I could trust myself not to cry or do something equally dumb that would give away how much I was hurting inside.

"Come on. For a minute." He went inside. I could have left but that would have looked strange.

The entry hall was for a split-level, with stairs going up to the living room and down to a daylight basement. Upstairs there were crowd sounds like a TV show, with kids shouting and an adult telling them to quiet down. I followed Tom downstairs.

Their recreation room was carpeted, with sliding glass doors leading to a back patio and walls covered with bookshelves and shelves for CDs and beneath the shelves a counter that held a terrific stereo set.

"You've got a lot of space," I said, not sure what to say. I didn't really feel like a house tour.

"That's not what I wanted to show you," he said. "Look there."

He pointed behind me. I looked around and saw a sofa. Above it, tacked to the wall, was a collection of posters.

I was speechless.

They were all of Cyndi Superstar.

"She's my favorite rock star," he said. "I've got every album and single she's ever done."

"But-but-but-" I couldn't put my jumbled thoughts into words.

"Yeah, I know." He gave that quick laugh. "That's why I followed you around school. I couldn't believe it, the first time I saw you, you look so much like her."

"So why did you get mad at me about that book cover?" I sputtered.

"It wasn't the same. I knew you weren't Cyndi Superstar. But you thought I was that guy on the cover. Only you're right, in another way, it was the same, and I knew that as soon as I got mad at you and came home and walked past those posters. And I felt so stupid. I didn't know how to tell you."

He moved so close to me I could see the shadow line of freckles beneath his dark-lashed eyes.

My brain went into orbit. I could even imagine moonlight in those eyes. On a sunny Saturday morning. Some imagination!

He started to speak, stopped, and kissed me instead.

Surprised, I blurted, "Okay, I'll accept that as an apology."

Tom smiled. "Can you stay a while? We could play some of her albums."

I said quickly, trying to sound casual, "Sure, as long as you don't expect me to sing along."

"I won't ask you to sing if you won't ask me to pose," he said.

"Pose?"

"I don't do book covers."

END

What I Know About Boys

First published as a Silhouette First Love
Phoebe Matthews

CHAPTER 1

Let me tell you about boys. They are handsome and clever and exciting and thoughtful and sweet. That's one day. The very next day they are still handsome, but they are also bossy and cranky and thoughtless and rotten.

When I explained that to Marci, she glanced up at me over the edge of the book she was reading and said, "Had a fight with Rick?"

Marci Palmer is my roommate in Smith Hall, the oldest dormitory at the U, and also the only all-women dorm, which is why it is also almost all freshmen. We freshmen get last choice on housing.

"He makes me crazy!" I said. "We had a date to go see that movie I'
ve been waiting for all year, and now he says he's got other plans!"

"Other plans?"

"And he waited until this morning at breakfast to tell me in the cafeteria!"

"What sort of other plans?" she asked.

"He said he needed to work in the library so he can use the WiFi connection! Can you believe that!"

"Maybe he has a paper due," Marci said. That's Marci. She's always sensible, and she always thinks of things like assignments first.

"Marci," I said, trying to keep my voice calm, because, honestly, I did not need my roommate and best friend taking the side of my rotten boyfriend, "the point is, he promised. And today he said he didn't remember promising."

Marci said, "If you still want to go to the movie, I'll go with you, Greta."

"I don't care about the movie!"

"Then why are you upset?"

"I'm not upset!" I shouted.

Marci is pretty, with high cheekbones and very dark eyes and wavy dark brown hair. If she would wear makeup, she'd look like a model, but she's more interested in getting good grades than she is in being beautiful. If I didn't like her so much, she'd drive me crazy, the way she sees right through me.

She said, "Then why are you collecting all your shower stuff?"

I hadn't even noticed that I was, but while I'd been talking, I'd been gathering my towel and robe and shampoo and soap and moisturizer and conditioner and washcloth and sponge and back brush and some other stuff. Looking down at what I was holding in my hands, I said, "I'm going to take a shower."

"You took a shower before you went to breakfast. That was only two hours ago."

Our eyes met and I started to giggle. Marci grinned. She was right, as usual. Whenever I'm upset, I go stand in a hot shower until I feel better, and considering how often I've been upset since I started dating Rick, it's a miracle my skin hasn't dried up and washed away down the drain.

Grabbing her backpack and hanging it over her shoulder, Marci headed for the door. "Gotta run, or I'll be late for my nine o'clock."

"See you later," I said.

She paused outside the door to turn and say, "Greta, don't get too upset about Rick. you know he'll be in a better mood in a day or two."

"I know," I said.

She closed the door and left me alone with my armload of shower stuff that I didn't need because, although I was upset, I wasn't going to let that rotten Rick Blair drive me to taking showers every two hours.

It is important, no, more than that, it is imperative that a girl not let a boy's behavior cloud her judgment. I read that in a magazine and as soon as I saw it, I knew it was a piece of advice meant especially for me, so I cut it out and pinned it to the bulletin board above my desk. And I reread it every now and then, and believed it so completely I often repeated the advice to the other girls in the dorm.

So why did I let Rick Blair absolutely blot out every bit of common sense I'd ever had?

Let me tell you about Rick. He is tall and dark, with thick hair and sharp bones that would photograph beautifully, like some TV star, complete with an arched nose and wide brows and incredible black eyes, and when he wants, he has a fabulous smile, but he doesn't smile all that much. Everybody says we look terrific together, because I am tall and blond. Now that is a terrible reason to date a boy, and I'd be the first one to say so to anyone, and it is definitely not why I date Rick.

I date Rick because the first time I saw him I thought he was the most gorgeous guy I'd ever met, and I couldn't believe it when he noticed me, too, and that also is a rotten reason for dating a guy and not one I recommend to anyone, but I give better advice than I follow.

So there it is. The reason I date Rick is because I am crazy about him. And when he wants to be, he can be as sweet as he is handsome.

When I left home last fall to come to the U and live in a dorm, it was the first time I'd ever been away from home for more than a week or so at a time. Though I wouldn't have admitted it to anyone, ever, I was shaking hard after my parents helped me unload my gear and hugged me goodbye. When they left me standing alone on the front steps of the dorm, waving as their car pulled away from the curb, I had to grit my teeth and dig my nails into my palms to keep from running after them, shouting for them to come back for me.

Not that I didn't want to go away to college. Of course I did. But wanting to do something and feeling completely confident about it are not the same thing. I was only seventeen last fall when I started college.

It occurred to me, way back home in my small town last summer, that although I'd done a fair amount of dating in high school, college boys were going to be different. They'd probably all be sophisticated, much too adult to notice me. So I spent the summer reading all the fashion magazines, especially the ones written for college girls, and I devoured all their advice articles and columns.

I learned all the tricks for using makeup and hair stuff, gels and hot oil conditioners and color touch-ups. I won't even tell you how many days I spent scrubbing off my face and starting over again or how many times I changed my hair color. And I used only half my clothing allowance to buy my school clothes and saved the other half so that I'd have money to buy whatever was the right thing to wear at the U, in case it turned out that my clothes were not what everyone was wearing, which one of the articles said to do. I made lists of how to judge a boy's character from his behavior. I made more lists of how to handle various dating situations.

If I'd ever put that much effort into my homework, I probably would have been a valedictorian or something.

By September I was superconfident and ready to shine, and then on the trip my confidence started to shrivel, and the more my folks chattered away about what a wonderful opportunity college was, the less sure I felt. But I think I'd have been all right if my mother hadn't surprised me by opening a box that I hadn't remembered packing, and pulling out my old Holly Hobbie spread, and making up my bed in my new room in the dorm. And then she arranged my desk.

Who would have believed that my mom still had my Dumbo elephant bookends, which I think someone gave me when I was eight years old and that I'd tossed in the attic by the time I was twelve? And worse yet, why should anything so silly make me feel eight years old again?

So there I stood on the steps, with my lip quivering, almost feeling as though I'd just been dropped off for my first day of kindergarten, when this darling guy rushed up the stairs toward the dorm, paused in front of me, gave me a wide grin of gorgeous white teeth and said, "Hi, there," before continuing on his way.

I started to turn and stare at him, which would have been so juvenile, but I caught myself in time and did a casual study of the view. Not the boy view, the campus view.

A walkway stretched across the campus, bordered on both sides by tree-shaded lawns and proper ivy-covered brick buildings with stone statues of historic and legendary people tucked into niches below the rooflines. It ended at a fountain set in a wide, shallow pool that didn't have any water in it. Behind it was the Student Union Building, a large meandering of brick and Gothic arches and those narrow, small-paned windows. Wide steps led up to the bank of three double doors.

If a building's age can be determined by its ivy, Smith Hall was the granddaddy of the campus. The windows were covered by the glossy-leaved vines. When I was sure the smiling boy was gone, I turned and pulled open the heavy door.

The corridor stretched away, a length of gray shadows, past closed doors, because the lower floor was reserved for seniors who wouldn't arrive until the following week.

Upstairs on my floor, the hallway was piled with luggage and boxes and strung across the archway leading to the corridor was a paper and poster-paint sign that read, Welcome, Frosh! All the room doors stood open and girls raced in and out, grabbing suitcases and wheelie trunks and dragging them into their rooms. The rooms were all similar, with two beds, two desks, two dressers, two bookcases, two closets, plus windows and closets.

My room was 217, and that very first day, a few minutes after I arrived, Marci walked in, said, "Hi, roommate! I'm Marci Palmer," and we've been best friends ever since.

She tossed her sleeping bag on top of the bare mattress, went back out in the hall and grabbed a backpack and a small trunk and dragged them in, then sat down on the trunk and said. "I am not taking another step. Oh my gosh, is that your stuff?

My desk held a neat row of paperbacks wedged between my cutesy Disney elephant bookends and my bed was covered with the Holly Hobbie bedspread, all neatly arranged by my Mother.

"My mom likes to decorate," I said. "Is that all you've got, a sleeping bag and a trunk?"

Marci laughed. "That's all this trip. My folks are coming back next weekend with the rest of my stuff."

"You're lucky your folks live that close. And I'm lucky mine don't."

When she asked me why, I opened one of my suitcases and pulled out my collection of vintage Frazetta posters from the 1980s, practically antiques. "I'll get these up as soon as I can get to a store for tacks and right after that, I am going shopping for a bedspread," I told her.

And I did. Took me a couple weeks, but by the time we were through orientation and into classes, the ruffled stuff was gone and I had a leopard-spotted sheet that I used as a bedspread. Gone, too, were the Disney bookends, which Marci's little cousin Joanne told me was a good thing because she thought Disney clashed badly with the Frazetta posters. Couldn't argue with that.

Marci and I figured out closet space, agreed that she was a morning person and I wasn't and we could work that out, and then we went looking for the cafeteria because, honestly, when you first get to college do the first things first. Find out where the food is and you will find the boys.

We grabbed our billfolds and went searching, heading out across campus.

And before I could turn around or blink or anything, a fantastic guy glanced at me as he walked by across the lawn and gave me a wink.

I couldn't believe it. I stood there like a mindless robot and slowly turned my head, taking it all in. The green lawns ran from the dorm to the street, and were crisscrossed with paths and walkways and overhung with shining trees, and sunlight glittered off every bright surface. Behind me the ivy rustled in a light breeze against the brick walls, and all around me stretched a new world of grass-scented air, and shiny cars and honking horns and shouting, waving people.

My jeans and T-shirt and hairstyle were exactly right, fit in perfectly with the way all the girls I saw were dressed. and more than that, the whole place swarmed with guys, cute guys, plain guys, fabulous guys, some smiling, some waving, and I realized that I was not going to be some horrible misfit, after all.

What a way to start college, great roommate, great room, and after searching a bit, we found the Student Union and the cafeteria and all the other important stuff.

Right after that I met Rick. He was at an orientation meeting. He slid into the seat next to mine in the theater-auditorium on the top floor of the Union building. I was in a back row because I'd taken the wrong turn and gone into the ballroom by mistake and had to go down the curved staircase and run the whole length of the main corridor to find the back stairs that led to the theater, which was why I was late. Rick was late because he never bothered hurrying for anyone, but I found that out later.

That first time I saw him I was so aware of him, after just one glance, that I was afraid he'd hear my heart pounding. I looked away fast, but he was so handsome my eyes kept straying back to his hand, which was resting on the chair arm between us, and I didn't hear a word the speaker said.

After the meeting was dismissed, but before I had a chance to move, this deep, sexy voice said in my ear, "you a freshman?"

I nodded.

"Must be all freshmen here."

I looked up at him and straight into his eyes and I almost drowned in them, they were that deep and gorgeous.

"Let's get out of here," he said, and caught my elbow.

I sort of floated along beside him, unable to believe that anyone like him could be an ordinary mortal male freshman.

Actually, he wasn't a freshman, and definitely not ordinary. He explained over coffee in the coffee shop on the main floor of the Union building that he was a junior. He'd transferred to the U, which was why he had to go to the orientation meeting. He also told me he hated his major and he was planning to switch, and probably he told me lots more, but I had trouble remembering it, what with trying to remember to smile and nod and be a good listener and also trying to keep my heart from pounding faster every time our eyes met.

It is important not to let a boy know how you feel about him until you know how he feels about you, I knew that without checking back to my magazine articles.

So when he said, "I wonder what there is to do around here at night. Want to come along with me and find out?" I knew I shouldn't sound eager.

I said, "I'm not sure. I think I have a dorm meeting."

Instead of asking for my phone number, he shrugged, stood up and walked off, leaving me alone with my half-empty coffee cup and my memorized dating guidelines.

About the time I figured I had the rules wrong, he reappeared, pulled out the chair across from me, swung his leg over the back, sat down, leaned his elbows on the formica table top, stared me in the eyes and said, "What's your phone number?"

As you can see, I started out in full control of the situation, saying the right things at the right time. I think I lost control about six hours later, when Rick pulled me into his arms for the first time, to dance, and I'm not sure I ever regained control again, though, honestly, I kept trying.

Throughout the autumn semester Rick and I had this on-off relationship. We'd have a couple of fabulous times together and then we'd have a big fight.

When I went home for Christmas break, I made up my mind to start my New Year's resolutions with swearing off thinking about

Rick, that's how far apart we were.

So I came back to the U in January with all my priorities straight in my mind. I went out on a couple of dates with Jon Austin, this big teddy bear of a guy, the sort who never says a mean word. I had my life under control. I was even getting my class assignments in on time.

And then Rick popped back into my life. He hung around, phoned, told me how marvelous I looked and how much he'd missed me and I ended up going to the Valentine Dance with him and having a dream of a time.

So with all that going on in my life, why was I sitting at my desk by the window on a bright March morning, staring down through the curtain of ivy at the people hurrying past on the walkways? I should have been working on laundry or doing my aerobics or even studying history for tomorrow's test, but there I sat, daydreaming, trying to figure out how my relationship with Rick kept getting so confused.

I thought back over everything he'd said to me that morning, trying to think of a better answer than the one I'd given him, my mind a blur but my half-focused gaze still on the lawn, when I finally realized someone was waving at me. I shook my head to clear my thoughts.

Then I waved back.

Jon grinned and beckoned me to come outside.

After bossy old Rick, Jon was exactly what I needed. I did a quick touch-up of my makeup, fluffed my hair, popped a breath mint in my mouth and ran out of my room and down the stairs, past the front desk, through the heavy outer door and down the steps, just fast enough to look as though I was hurrying and not intentionally keeping him waiting, but not so fast as to mess up my hair.

Maybe that sounds unbelievably conceited, but honestly, I'm not, just the opposite. I know for sure that without my hair I am nothing. I have this thick mass of blond hair that is thick because I shampoo and condition and blow-dry it every day. I do not backcomb. That can cause split ends. My hair is my best feature by miles, and I can't imagine anyone ever noticing me for any other reason, so sure, I worry about it.

Early March rains had washed away the last snow. Now the sun shone down through the bare branches of the maples that lined the main walks, making a perfect day, too warm for coats but cold enough for my favorite sweater and my jeans.

Jon said, "I thought you had a class now."

"I cut my nine o'clock today," I said.

"Want to go for coffee?" he asked.

I'd had breakfast with Rick, but I'd been so upset, when he broke our date, that I hadn't eaten much. I said sure and we headed across the lawns and through the small clump of woods to the Student Union building, another ivy-draped brick building, but a lot larger than the dorms. It was fronted by an enormous round fountain that I'd never seen turned on, and stone stairs that ran the width of the building, and a row of three sets of double doors set in stone arches. Gothic, I think, which is historic and isn't the same as Goth or vampires or that stuff. Jon held open the door for me. We hurried to the coffee shop, went through the line picking up donuts and coffee and found an empty table among all the crowded ones.

Jon is big, built solid, a hunk type but not a jock. Strong but not competitive. He has a wide, friendly, honest face, covered with freckles. He couldn't lie if he tried. For sure he's an exact opposite from Rick and for sure that's exactly what I needed.

He leaned toward me across the table and smiled. "Now what's this about cutting classes? Having trouble with a course?"

I ran my fingertip around the rim of my coffee cup for something to do with my hands. Not looking at him, I said, "No, the class is okay."

"So then what's the problem?"

"What problem?" I asked, still keeping my gaze on my cup.

"Come on, Greta, this is Jon. I can tell you're upset."

His voice was so kind and understanding I practically burst into tears. I said, "It's nothing. I'll be okay."

"Rick giving you a bad time?" he said.

"Oh, Jon!" I looked up at him and tried to put on a big, shiny smile, to convince him I was okay, but I guess my smile kind of quivered.

"Don't let him push you around," Jon said. "You could have any guy on campus. Why waste your time with Rick?"

"I can't help it," I said.

"Uh-huh," he said, and his voice sounded almost as sad as mine.

It wasn't fair. Jon was so nice. Why couldn't I love him instead of Rick? There were times when I got so mad at myself, being so crazy about Rick and suspecting that was how Jon felt about me. But at least I wasn't ever mean to Jon. I didn't lead him on one day and dump him the next.

I said, "First he's nice and then he's horrid."

"What's he done this time?"

I blinked because I could feel the tears behind my lids and I didn't want Jon to catch me crying. "Nothing important. He said he'd take me to something tonight and then this morning he said he had to study tonight, and it isn't important, and I don't care that much, but the thing is, when I mentioned that he'd promised to take me out, he said he hadn't, and then he got mad and said I was making stuff up."

"You and Rick don't communicate very well."

"Huh?"

"Greta, maybe he does have to study. Maybe he has a test tomorrow."

"Maybe. He didn't say anything about a test."

"Did you ask?"

"No," I admitted.

Jon gazed at me with this really serious expression. "Ask him, Greta. Find out what he's thinking. You two will never get along until you start being more open with each other."

Jon was such a sweetie. And what he said made sense. But if I went chasing after Rick now, telling him I was sorry I'd been upset that he broke a date because I realized his school work came first,

Rick would think I was chasing him. He would. He wasn't reasonable and understanding the way Jon was. But I didn't bother saying any of that to Jon. There he was, trying so hard to be supportive, I didn't want to hurt his feelings.

I said, "Hey, that's what I should do. I should ask him. you're right."

As we left the coffee shop, Jon gave me a quick hug, which he always does, and I hugged him back, which I always do, and he said, "Feel better now?"

"I always feel better after I talk to you."

"Then don't cut any more classes or you'll be the one with problems," he said.

"Yes, sir!" I said, and snapped him a salute before heading away from him across campus for my next class.

My eleven o'clock was tennis. I'll admit that I don't like tennis much. I've never been very good at sports, though heaven knows, I try. I fling myself into any game anyone asks me to join, including soccer and Frisbee and canoeing, but I am invariably the one who kicks the ball toward the wrong goal or tips over the canoe.

However, tennis is different. For some reason, people expect doubles to be played correctly. They get upset when I dash into my partner's territory. I don't know why, but I have a terrible time remembering to stay on my own side. And then there's the scoring, which has nothing to do with logical counting, and I seem to always forget the score. And also there are very fussy restrictions about whether a ball is in or out. Now if I am close enough to the ball to actually hit it, I hit it, because I am so amazed to be there at all, but if the ball is going out, a player is supposed to know that and not hit it, just stand there and watch it go out, only I never do, so then my partner shouts at me.

As a result, I love to hit the ball back and forth with friends who don't care about rules, but I hate taking tennis as a class. In a class, people are absolutely demented on the subject of rules.

However, none of that is the reason I didn't make it to tennis class. I did not cut on purpose. What happened was that I was distracted.

I was rushing down the hill below the woods toward the athletic building where I had to change clothes and collect my gear before reporting to the outdoor courts at eleven sharp, and I wasn't sure I was going to make it. Also, I was still thinking about my problems with Rick, and Jon's advice.

As I cut across the footbridge that crosses this funny little stream that's at the bottom of the woods where it opens into the narrow meadow surrounding one of the play fields, I didn't see this guy at all.

Scrunched down, sitting on his heels, his chin on his knees, he was peering into the long grass at the far side of the bridge. He was wearing faded jeans and a khaki sweat shirt. His hair was the same sort of soft, light brown as his tan. I didn't notice all this until afterwards, but I think that's why I didn't see him. He blended in with the tall grass and the dirt path.

I ran right into him, my knee colliding with his shoulder. I couldn't even guess what I'd hit. My mind did a total blackout. All I could think to do was flail my arms, which sent my purse flying off into the undergrowth but didn't do a thing for my balance. As I doubled up, he toppled over, and we ended in a tangle of legs and arms, both of us shouting.

We weren't shouting words, more like grunts and moans. I felt as though I'd been hit by a flying tackle.

Then a voice from under me said, "Are you okay?"

As I didn't even know where to begin inventory to see if I was okay, I said, "I guess so."

"Then could you get off me?" he asked.

CHAPTER 2

Carefully, I pushed myself up, trying not to put my foot in his ribs or my elbow in his eye, but I wasn't entirely successful. As I untangled myself and stood up, he let out some groans.

"Hey, I'm sorry," I said to the back of his head. He was sprawled face down in the grass.

He rolled over slowly and squinted up at me, the sun in his eyes.

"I didn't see you. Let me give you a hand," I said, and held out my hand.

At first I thought he was going to refuse. Probably he thought that anyone clumsy enough to trip over him would also let go of him. But then he reached up, caught my hand and clambered to his feet.

"How about you? You okay?" he asked.

"Oh sure, maybe a bump or two."

"It was my fault," he said.

At that point I should have insisted that I was the klutz, should have been looking where I was going, and so forth. Only he had this funny look on his face, as though he was waiting to see what sort of line I'd come up with. His eyes crinkled at the edges. Was he secretly laughing at me?

I forgot all I knew about being charming on a first meeting and sputtered, "Yeah, it was! What were you doing, anyway, all bent down like that in the path?"

"Do you really want to know?" he asked, and before I could reply, he added, "Come here, I'll show you."

As he was still holding onto my hand, I followed him a step or two to the edge of the grass where he knelt down and I knelt beside him.

Letting go of my hand, he pushed aside the grass and pointed to a fiddlehead, which is the first curled shoot of a fern. As they grow wild everywhere, I couldn't think why he found it so interesting.

"I'm keeping a log on them," he said. "I noted the date this one first appeared, and now I'm measuring it every three days to chart its growth."

"Why?"

"For a botany class. I'll do a scale drawing of its development to turn in with my term paper."

"You a botany major?"

"Uh-uh," he said. "I'm an art major. That's why I'm doing the drawings. My reports are always so poor, I count on my illustrations to get me a decent grade."

"I wish I had a talent," I said. "I can't write and I can't draw and I'm not athletic and oh! my gosh!"

"What's wrong?"

"I'm supposed to be at tennis at eleven!" I jumped up.

He checked his watch. "It's eleven-fourteen now."

"Oh no! That's the second class I've missed today!"

He stood up and gave me a wide grin and said, "You picked a great day to cut."

He was right. The sun was shining, the sky was bright blue, the air smelled like springtime. All around me new leaves on the birch trees rustled in a light March breeze. I could even hear the stream making little gurgling noises under the wooden footbridge.

And right there in front of me, smiling at me, was this supernice guy. I could tell he was supernice because he had all the right looks for supernice, kind of like anybody's brother, average height, average build, soft wavy hair, slightly crooked teeth, a nose that was maybe a tad too short and too wide but fit perfectly in his square face, and eyes that were the same light, warm, sunshine brown as his hair.

And he definitely didn't look like the kind of guy who expected every girl he met to fall madly in love with him, like that rotten Rick.

I said, "I'm Greta."

He said, "I'm David."

"Um, I don't suppose you saw where my purse went?"

He ran over to the bridge railing and peered down into the water of the little stream. "Tell me you didn't drop it in the water."

"Why?"

"Because then I will be duty-bound to go wading into the stream to find it for you, and if you haven't noticed, that stream is kind of muddy."

Kind of was a major understatement. "If I say that is where I dropped it, you will wade into that muck?"

"Have to. If I hadn't tripped you, you wouldn't have dropped your purse. So what do you think? Do you have some idea where you dropped it or do I have to search the whole stream?"

Another thing I know about boys is this. Even the shining knight types can get really sick of a girl who plays tricks. "It went flying off into the weeds over there."

He was so relieved it showed all over his face. "Weeds, huh? Me and weeds are friends. Well, actually, they are my models and who knows, if I go searching through that patch, I may even find a new type to draw."

It took us about ten minutes of pushing aside the leaves and branches of ferns and salal and Oregon grape, me pushing, David identifying, before we both saw the purse at the same time and managed to bang our heads together when we bent over to pick it up.

Brushing leaves off my sweater, I said, "It's been nice running into you," and we both laughed. I added, "If I'm not going to make it to tennis, I better at least head back to my dorm and get my laundry done."

"Uh-huh," he said.

Now I know enough about boys to know that at that point I could have said something about going to lunch early and he probably would have said that was a good idea and tagged along with me, but honestly, no matter how cute he was, I didn't need another guy in my life. So instead I mentioned the laundry.

Another thing I know for sure about boys, they never offer to help with the laundry. They may ask girls to help them do their laundry, pretending they don't even know how to put soap in a machine, but never the other way around.

"See you," I said, waving, and turned and ran back up the path.

When I reached the top of the woods, I turned to glance toward the bridge, expecting to see him standing there watching me. He wasn't.

He was crouched down on the far side again, his notebook open, writing something and peering into the grass. Keeping a log on ferns? I'd have to remember that one to tell to Marci.

Back at the dorm I honestly did do my laundry, which was way past due. I maybe had one clean shirt left, and a couple of sweaters, but I was wearing my last pair of jeans.   Planning on catching up on my reading assignment for my afternoon lit class, I sat cross-legged on top of the washing machine while it chug-a-chugged through a load of my stuff. The laundry room was in the basement and it looked like a basement. There were pipes overhead, a few hanging lights and a couple of grimy windows at ceiling height, which was why I had to sit on top of the machine to get enough light to read.

The assignment was an abysmal bore. There were long paragraphs of descriptions of some guy's guilt complexes. What with the warm soapy smell rising around me, plus the dim light and the small print, I was battling to stay awake. So when Allison, a girl on my floor, wandered in, I was relieved to be interrupted.

"I've got three of the machines going," I said, "but those two on the end are empty and one of mine will be done in a couple of minutes. It's my light stuff and I've got it on the short cycle."

She nodded and headed for the two end machines without saying anything to me or even looking at me. Her face was bent down over her laundry basket. Her long pale hair fell in a straight curtain on either side of her face.

"Actually, this time of day is pretty good for using the laundry because everybody's in class," I said.

She opened a machine and started dumping her stuff into it.

"I should be in class, too, but I was late, so I figured I might as well get caught up on laundry," I said.

She brushed her hand across her face. I couldn't see her face, but I could see her hand. Also, she made a soft gulping sound.

I never waste time being diplomatic when somebody's crying. "What's wrong?"

She shook her head.

"Flunking something?"

She muttered, "No."

"Then it's got to be a guy."

She turned to look up at me. For sure she was crying. Tears streaked down her face. Her skin was all puffy and red. "How did you know?" she mumbled.

"Who'd know better than me? I could fill one of these washing machines with the tears I've shed over guys. Sometime when you have a week or two to do nothing but listen, I'll tell you about my rotten boyfriend."

She smiled a little at that, but it's rough smiling when you're crying and I said so, adding, "None of them are worth it."

"I know that now," she said. "It's too late."

"Too late for what?" She could always tell me it wasn't my business and she wouldn't hurt my feelings at all, but she looked to me like she wanted to talk.

She did. She started in slowly, in a mumble. Then her voice rose and she spoke faster and faster. "You know Mark, the guy I go with, or anyway, the guy I thought I went with? Umm, sure, everybody knows Mark, every girl, oh, I don't mean you, and anyway, it's not that so much, it's that he knows every girl, and he keeps saying he loves me, he tells me that, and then I see him with someone else and he says it's nothing, she's just some friend in one of his classes, and I keep believing him, and then last night he broke a date and when my roommate came in, she told me she'd seen him sitting in a back booth at the Den making out with some girl and so I phoned him this morning and asked how his studying was going, because that's what he told me he had to do last night, study, and he said he'd been at the library all night and he'd have to study again tonight and so I slammed down the phone and I hate him!"

"I know what you mean," I said.

The Den is the local off-campus hangout, a dimly lit place with high-backed booths. On weekends it's a mob scene, fun sometimes, with everyone singing along with the recorded music, but on slow nights it can be half-empty and a lot of couples use the booths to get privacy. It's not too easy finding privacy on campus. Still, the Den isn't that private, either, because even if only a half dozen other people wander through, they're bound to be from the U and at least one of them is going to be somebody who recognizes you And reports you to your steady.

Allison shrugged, as though she'd run out of words. And hope.

I said, "Same thing happened to me when I first started dating Rick. Somebody told me she'd seen him with someone else. I wanted to kill him. Or myself."

"What'd you do?"

"Told him what I thought of him. Had a big fight. Broke up. That was about a thousand fights ago."

"You kept going with him?"

"I love to suffer. Tell you what I did do, though, if you want to hear."

"Go ahead," she said. Misery really does love company.

"I made up my mind that I wasn't going to be his doormat. I told him I'd go out with him but not steady, that there were other guys I liked."

"What did he say to that?"

"You wouldn't want me to repeat his language. Oh, he was mad, and we didn't speak for a while, and then we'd go out again, and it kind of went on like that, and we're still dating."

"Do you date other guys?"

"Not exactly," I admitted, "but sort of."

"What's that mean?"

"Okay, let me tell you. What I do is this. I make friends with lots of guys, guys I meet in classes and stuff, and I go for coffee with them or study with them in the library, or meet them in the cafeteria for meals, see, but if they ask me out, I tell them I'm going with somebody. But I keep them as friends. That's the important thing. That way, Rick sees me with other guys."

"Doesn't he get mad?"

"Sure, but he can't admit it. He can't get mad about me having friends."

"What's the point?" she asked. By now she'd stopped crying.

"Allison, the point is that he knows I know lots of guys, and that I could date them if I wanted to, and that if he dates somebody else, he can be sure that I will, too."

"So you never have dated anyone else, after all?"

"A few times. When we broke up and he went out with someone else. I dated Jon Austin, who is one of my very best friends. But I don't date him now that Rick and I are back together."

She shrugged. "I don't think that would work for me."

"Why not?"

"I don't know any other guys."

"Everybody knows other guys!"

"Not any who would ask me out."

"Look," I said, "all you've got to do is be seen with them. Mark'll hear about it, believe me. Now what you do is this. Today, when you go over to lunch at the cafeteria, look around until you spot some guy who's in one of your classes and then go sit next to him and ask him something about the class, anything, just be seen talking to him, and when he leaves, get up and walk out with him, and when you get outside, walk a few feet away from him and then turn and wave at him. Somebody will see you and Mark will hear about it."

She got a sort of half smile on her face, which was a big improvement.

The washing machine came to a loud, vibrating stop and I tossed stuff in one dryer, then unloaded the other dryer, folding stuff into my laundry bag. As I was dragging the bag out of the laundry room, Allison said, "Thanks, Greta."

I said, "Good luck."

Then I went bump-bump up the stairs, dragging my laundry bag two flights, and made it down the hall to my room just in time to grab the receiver off the wall phone on the third ring.

"Greta?"

My heart did this skip-a-beat thing it always does when I hear his voice. Rick has the lowest, sexiest voice of any guy I've heard.

He said, "I've got a car this afternoon. Let's go to Azuza's and get some real food."

Azuza's was a restaurant a couple of miles from campus where they didn't have a captive clientele and had to serve decent food. They did a steak sandwich that Rick really liked.

"I have a class at two," I said.

"So cut it for once," he said.

The way my day was going, I was never going to get that chapter read before two, anyway. And as I'd already missed two classes, why not miss the third and call the whole day off? Besides, I knew he was asking me to Azuza's as an apology for not taking me to the movie, which meant he really did have to study.

We owed each other apologies. I shouldn't have blown up at him for canceling, and he shouldn't have pretended that we'd never had a date. As Rick and I had never been much good at giving each other straight-out explanations or apologies, I accepted his offer as my way of saying everything was okay between us.

"I'd love to," I said.

"Pick you up in front of your dorm in twenty minutes and don't be late."

"Make it thirty."

We both knew that no way could I freshen my makeup and steam-curl the ends of my hair that had gone limp and redo the nail polish I'd chipped in twenty minutes. And sometimes Rick was mean about waiting. But if I didn't look perfect, he wouldn't be attracted to me, right? It was better to keep him waiting than to go out looking like a mess.

This time he said, "Okay, thirty minutes," and laughed. He really was in a good mood.

I was on the curb in thirty minutes flat, having tossed myself back together, though after a morning of rushing to missed classes, falling over guys in paths and hauling laundry up from the basement, I'd have preferred a couple of hours.

Rick pulled up in somebody's old blue heap and I jumped in.

"Whose wheels?" I asked.

"Guy in my dorm," he said.

Rick was never one for long explanations.

I slid down in my seat until I could rest my head on the back and turn my face to watch him. Just looking at his profile practically knocked me out. Movie stars go to plastic surgeons to get profiles like that.

So that he wouldn't think I had nothing better to do with my life than stare at his profile, I said, "Today's been a total washout. Haven't made it to a single class. If I were in high school, they'd be sending the truant officer after me."

Rick said, "You ever seen a truant officer?"

"On TV. On a morning kiddie show. The truant officer was always collaring the naughty clown."

"Was that yesterday's episode?" he asked, straight-faced.

I snapped my fingers at him, flicking his shoulder, for implying that I still watched clown shows. "Wonder whatever happened to old Oggie Clown? He was the naughty one, and don't give me a hard time about the word naughty. That's what they called him, Oggie, the

Naughty Clown."

Rick parked in the lot. I followed him into Azuza's, a low building of brick and wide, glare-tinted windows, with an overhang of shake roof. Inside the waitress led us to a window booth with a view of the parking lot and the highway.

The booths were done in imitation brown leather. Above the tables hung Old West-style brass lanterns. Wagon wheels mounted on low walls divided the space into small dining areas. The inner walls, away from the windows, were covered with sepia photo murals of cowboys and herds of cattle.

"Ah, the real world," I sighed as I picked up my menu. I loved the U, with its ivy and Gothic, and everyone either students and wearing jeans or faculty and wearing tweed, but sometimes it was nice to get away.

"Real food," Rick said.

After we ordered, he said, "How come you missed your morning classes?"

As I wasn't about to satisfy his ego by telling him I'd been too upset by him to go to my nine o'clock, I said, "I went back to the dorm after breakfast and got to talking to Marci, and next thing I knew, it was nine-fifteen. And then I started out in time to get to my eleven o'clock, but, and you are not going to believe this, I fell over some guy."

He didn't say anything, just sat there looking at me, waiting for me to go on.

"I did. I was running down the back path to cut across that footbridge by the lower field, and this guy was all crouched down in the grass."

Rick raised his eyebrows. That pleased me. I didn't usually get that much reaction out of him.

I said, "And I ran right into him, hit him with my foot, you know, and kind of did a flip up and across him and knocked us both flat."

"What was he doing in the grass?"

"Looking for fiddleheads. He had this notebook for keeping a record of how fast they grow. For some science class, botany, that's what he said. Only he was wearing a shirt that was kind of grass-colored so he blended right in and I never saw him until I'd practically killed us both, and by the time I got up and asked him what he was doing, and checked to be sure we were both alive, well, it was too late to make it to tennis."

"So then what'd you do?"

"Went back to the dorm and spent an exciting two hours in the laundry room listening to the soapsuds slosh. It's really been a thrilling day. You can see why I was so eager to get away this afternoon."

"And here I thought it was the sandwiches." Rick gave me one of his long, gorgeous, dark-eyed looks.

We both knew perfectly well why I'd accepted his invitation. Not that I'd say so. It's no good letting boys know how much you care about them, especially boys like Rick who automatically expect total devotion.

I said, "That, too. I wouldn't have cut lit for anything less than Azuza's."

When the waitress brought our steak sandwiches and shakes, we quieted down to eat. Or at least, Rick did. He goes at his food in that steady way boys do, as though they're refueling. I pick at the edges more, and stop to look around. Azuza's wasn't too busy. We were past the lunch hour, but there was a family in another booth, a mother and father and a couple of little kids, too small for school, who acted tired, rubbing their eyes. I guessed maybe they were on a trip. And there were three women in another booth, all wearing suits but kind of frilly blouses and lots of jewelry. I couldn't decide if they were working women or shoppers.

I related all this to Rick, who ate away, glancing up at me occasionally.

I did get his attention when a Mercedes pulled into the lot and I described it as well as the two guys who climbed out of it. Rick looked out the window at the car. I looked at the guys. They were in three-piece suits.

"You think they're bankers?"

"This year's model," he said, impressed by the car. "What's one of those cost, I wonder?"

When we finished eating and headed back to the U, Rick said, "Where you want me to drop you?"

"Any place. I'll probably stop by my room and get my notebook and then I better get over to the library to do some studying."

Rick parked in the lot for student cars, near his dorm, saying he'd leave the car there for his friend. There wasn't anyone in the lot except us and a lot of empty cars. Rick slid his arms around me and pulled me into one of his wonderful, warm kisses.

"I've missed you," he whispered.

He'd seen me at breakfast, but I knew what he meant. Whenever we fought, I missed him terribly.

We walked back across the street, up a path, and stopped at the main walk that ran the length of the campus. We didn't said much, but we had our arms linked around each other, and just being together like that was like talking for hours.

It wasn't until we moved apart to go off in our separate directions that Rick said, "Watch where you're going now. Don't trip over any more muggers."

I laughed and said, "David isn't a mugger."

Rick said, "David?"

Right away I knew I shouldn't have let on that I knew David's name, because then Rick knew I had stopped to talk to him for a while. People don't exchange names when they bump, say excuse me, and immediately part company.

But I wasn't going to make any explanations. "Yeah, David."

"David who?"

I shrugged, trying to look nonchalant. "I dunno. Just David."

"You didn't tell me you knew him."

"Didn't I?" I thought about saying that when you've knocked a guy over and sprawled all over him, you're no longer strangers, but I decided that would irritate Rick more. "I don't really know him, just his name. If you get done studying early, why don't you call me?"

"Okay," he said, so I thought everything was still fine between us.

CHAPTER 3

But it wasn't. Rick didn't phone that night or the next day. When I rang his room, nobody answered. I looked for him at mealtimes in the cafeteria. He wasn't there. And I didn't see him anywhere on campus.

Three days later he still hadn't called. I was back to moping about and standing in hot showers.

Actually, standing in the dorm shower was sometimes very close to going to a psychiatrist, not that I'd ever been to a real one. But it was like going to the ones on TV, where you stretch out on a couch and tell them all your troubles.

I was rubbing shampoo in my hair, trying not to get it in my eyes, with hot water streaming down over me, when someone shouted, "That you, Greta?"

"Yeah," I shouted over the noise of the water. "Who's that?"

"Inger."

I rubbed the water out of my eyes and peered around the edge of the shower curtain.

Inger Peters stood across the room by the row of sinks, her foot propped up on the edge of one sink. She was thin and long-legged and she looked like she was doing some sort of aerobics, standing on one leg that way.

"What're you doing?"

"Shaving my legs," she said, glancing at me. She had long-lashed eyes, and her black hair was cut about an inch long all over her head. On anyone else it might have looked terrible, but on Inger it looked terrific.

I ducked back under the water and closed the curtain.

"Do you still date Rick?" she called.

"Sometimes more than other times."

"Sounds like me and Hal. One day he's talking about getting

married and the next day he's talking about hitchhiking around the world with his buddies."

"One day Rick says he'll phone, and the next three days I don't hear a word from him."

"Guys are weird," Inger agreed.

"It's not as though I told him I owned him. I try not to push. I give him lots of space. So wouldn't you think he'd keep in touch, even if he only has time to tell me he's busy?"

Inger shouted back, "Hal said he'd come to my town to meet my folks over Christmas, and I phoned home and arranged it with them and everything, and then the day before winter break, he breezes in, cheery as you please, and says he's heading for a ski lodge and won't see me till January."

I turned off the shower and stepped out, wrapped in my towel.

As I rubbed my wet hair with my other towel, I said, "You know what their trouble is? Guys want to own girls. They want to feel a girl is all theirs. But they don't want to be owned."

"That sounds very one-sided and unfair."

"It is. We shouldn't put up with it."

"What else can we do?"

"Be as independent as they are," I said. "Make other plans, be busy when they call, let them know we have our own lives and that we are not hanging around breathlessly waiting for them."

She said, "If I did that, Hal would probably quit calling."

I put on my robe and collected my shampoo, conditioners, sponge, brush, soap, towels, face cloth, and the rest of my stuff, and headed out the door. "At least I feel better, knowing someone else has the same problems."

As I reached for the door handle, my roommate, Marci, pushed it open from the hallway.

"Greta, Rick's on the phone."

"Remember to let him know you have your own life," Inger shouted after me as I raced down the hall to my room.

When I was inside, I stopped by the wall phone, its receiver dangling on its cord, and took a couple of deep breaths. I didn't want to sound as though I'd been running. Then in my calmest voice, I said, "Hello?"

"Where were you?"

"In the shower. Did you get finished?"

"Finished?"

"Studying."

"Oh that! Yeah, sure. But listen, honey, I've got a lot bigger problem and you're the only person who can help me with it."

Whatever it was, I hoped he didn't need it in the next ten minutes, as I needed at least forty minutes to put myself together.

"Honey," he said, a second time. He almost never called me honey. "I've broken the antenna on my TV, and I've got to watch a documentary tonight for notes for my anthro class, and then I've got to have a book that they don't have at the U. But I called the public library and they're holding it for me, and there's a radio shop where you can get the antenna about a block from the library."

"Me?"

"Greta, I've got a seminar this afternoon so I can't go, and I need the antenna and the book and even then, I'll be up all night doing the report and if it isn't turned in at nine o'clock tomorrow, I'm dead in anthro."

I said, "Gee, I'd like to help, but I've got a lit class at two."

"If I flunk anthro, I'm washed out! You can miss a lit class, nobody'll notice, but if I a cut seminar, there's only eight people in it, so there's no way the prof won't notice and he's been looking for an excuse to drop a bomb on me."

"But, Rick," I said.

He shouted, "Okay, if you don't care, forget it."

"Of course I care."

I tried to sound really caring. Right after that I was going to explain that I'd be glad to get his antenna and book, under any other circumstances, but as I'd already missed lit the day we went to Azuza's, and that was only three days ago, I couldn't miss it again.

But before I could launch into any of that, he said in this really sweet voice that makes me feel like my insides are hot fudge, "Honey, you're the only person I can depend on. You're a doll. Now grab a paper and I'll give you the address of the store and the model number on the antenna and the title of the book."

So I wrote it all down. He told me again how wonderful I was. I felt important and wonderful.

After I hung up, I remembered Inger repeating my own advice to let him know that I had my own life. For sure I knew all the right ways to handle boys and for sure I'd never been able to use any of them with Rick.

And I'd had my day so well organized, too. I'd made it to my morning classes, gone to lunch hoping to run into Rick in the cafeteria and treat him to a casual but friendly greeting, nothing eager. When he wasn't there, I'd consoled myself that was just as well as my hair was limp from tennis. So I'd gulped lunch and dashed back to shower, which would both drown my disappointment and give me a chance to do my hair, planning that after my two o'clock I could circle through the usual places he might be, confident of my looks if of nothing else.

Instead, there I was at two-thirty standing on the bus corner waiting for the unreliable city bus to show up. I'd thought about waiting until after lit class.

Then I'd checked the bus schedule. There was a bus at quarter to three and nothing more until four o'clock. It took twenty minutes to get uptown. From there it was twelve blocks out to the library, which I could either walk or wait for another bus, and Rick thought the library closed at five, so what else could I do but skip lit?

I stood on one foot and then the other, peering down the street in the direction from which the bus would come. Maybe it should have cheered me that the sky had cleared to a brilliant blue, and that clusters of daffodils shone like sunlight in the shrubbery beds that lined the campus walkways, but it didn't. The best I could hope for was that my lit prof would be so busy gazing out the window, she wouldn't say anything important in her lecture.

A car pulled up to the curb.

Jon leaned across the seat from the driver's side to peer out the open window at me. "Greta? Need a ride?"

I crossed my arms on the windowsill and leaned down to say, "I have to go uptown to the main library and then to a store."

"Hop in, I'll drive you."

"I have a couple of errands. It could take a while."

"I'm free," he said, and smiled.

"You're not free, you're priceless," I said and got into the car. "What's that saying? A pearl beyond price?"

"Tell me more." Still grinning, he drove me toward town.

"Wouldn't want to destroy your modesty. It's half your charm."

"What's the other half?" he asked.

I laughed and gave him a sideways glance through my eyelashes. He expected me to tease him, so I did.

"If I told you that, you wouldn't be modest anymore."

His large hands moved on the wheel, tapping out a rhythm. I watched the scenery slide by, from campus greenery to neighborhoods of neat houses with carefully tended gardens, to apartment rows, and finally to a confusion of storefronts and billboards.

"I don't know how close to the library I can park," he said.

"Drop me off and circle the block. All I've got to do is run in and grab a book."

"Won't you need to look it up and get a call number?"

"Rick's got it on hold at the desk," I said, and then could have bitten my tongue.

"You're picking up a book for Rick?"

"He has a seminar this afternoon and he needs this book to finish a report for his anthro class and it's due tomorrow."

Jon didn't say more, just dropped me at the library, circled the block and was there waiting when I came running back down the steps with the book in my hand.

The radio store was in a small shopping center with a parking lot. Jon parked and came into the store with me. I found a clerk who found the antenna model that I needed, paid for it and headed back out, and Jon still didn't say anything, but before we got in the car, he said, "Want to stop for coffee?"

I really wanted to go back to campus and take Rick his stuff. Even if he had to spend the evening studying, we could still go to supper together. But Jon had been so kind to drive me to town, and it was only quarter to four, so it seemed the least I could do.

I gave him a big smile. "I'd love that, but let me treat you because you've been such a life-saver."

There was a coffee shop in the mall, one of those small places with metal chairs and tables done in curled iron and painted white. The table top was glass. The chairs were almost too small to hold anyone the size of Jon. The waitress looked motherly and bored. Her tired expression didn't match her flowered shirt.

After she served us coffee and croissants and then went back to her own cup of coffee at a table on the far side of the otherwise empty shop, Jon said, "What happened to your two o'clock?"

It was sweet of him to remember my schedule. Rick never did. "They weren't doing anything important today."

"Not as important as running errands for Rick?"

"He's really afraid he'll flunk his anthro class."

The muscles in Jon's face tightened beneath his freckled skin. He gave me one of his searching stares that left me thinking he could see right through to my brain.

He said, "Greta, a guy is supposed to take care of his girl, not the other way around. He shouldn't be sending you off alone on a city bus to run his errands."

Now that business of a guy taking care of his girl is one I adore. I have this poster over my bed in my dorm room. It shows this gorgeous, musclebound hunk standing between a dragon-type monster and a beautiful damsel. In one upraised hand he's brandishing a sword. His other powerful arm is held out in front of the girl to protect her. You know, looking at the picture, that the only way that monster will reach that girl is by killing the hunk first. Talk about excitement, romance, drama!

Great stuff for posters, but real life isn't like that. Sometimes I wish it were, sure, and then I remind myself that those dragon-plagued princesses didn't have hair dryers. Or cars. Or TV.

I said, "Jon, I am eighteen, old enough to ride a bus alone."

"Old enough to think for yourself, too. So why do you let Rick tell you what to do?"

I tried to match his stare with what I hoped was a sincere gaze. "Jon, it's a gorgeous day, lit class is a bore and I wanted an excuse to cut."

"You cut to run Rick's errands."

Why is it that guys always tell you to think for yourself and then turn around and criticize your decisions? As I didn't want to argue with Jon, I tried to think of something clever to say to change the subject. A magazine article that I once read said that when a conversation with a boy turns tense, toss him a compliment.

I gave it my best shot, eyes wide, smile bright. "I'm glad I did cut because now I'm here with you."

Whoever wrote that article must have known Jon. He grinned and stopped lecturing me.

Jon was so much easier to figure out than Rick. For sure he was easier to get along with.

Guys come in types, and it's good to know how to tell them apart. My roommate, Marci, has a younger cousin, Joanne, who is still in high school, and as Jon sat there smiling at me, I remembered the first time I met Joanne and she asked me something about boys. Right away I could see she needed advice, so I told her what I knew.

"Joanne," I said, "boys come in three types: jocks, hunks and your average guy." I told her then to avoid the jocks because they were too tied up with sports. And the gorgeous hunks always wanted to have their own way. "Concentrate on the guy who is average cute and dresses right because he wants you to like him. He'll be sweet and dependable."

That was Jon, sweet and dependable.

And Rick was a gorgeous hunk.

After Joanne met both of them, she once said to me, "Why don't you follow your own advice? If you had good sense, you'd drop Rick and grab Jon."

Certainly she was right. Looking at Jon, who was trying so hard to impress me with his thoughtfulness, I knew how much he cared about me.

If I'd had any sense, I'd have forgotten Rick and fallen for Jon, then and there. But what does good sense have to do with love?

That's another thing I know about boys. It's hard to think about them and keep one's thoughts sensible.

That evening I met Rick in the cafeteria for supper and gave him his book and TV antenna. He was wearing a white turtleneck pullover that set off his dark coloring.

He glanced at the book and said, "This had better have the information I need, or I'm dead."

I knew he was worried about his grade, but still, he could have said thank you. I said, "I cut a class to get that for you."

He gave me one of his dark gazes. "You're a doll."

When he looked at me like that, cutting a two o'clock seemed like no bother at all.

But the next day when I sat in lit class and watched the prof pass a quiz back to the other students, I had other thoughts. To the girl at the next desk, I whispered, "I didn't know we were having a quiz."

She whispered back, "It was announced three days ago."

With this awful hollow feeling building up in my midsection, I realized that the quiz must have been announced on the day I'd cut to go to Azuza's with Rick.

Why hadn't I thought to ask someone in the class if we'd had any assignments? That had been stupid of me. Not knowing what to do, I stopped by the professor's desk after class.

My heart started beating in my throat, which was really dumb but I couldn't make it stop, I was that nervous. My voice came out ragged. "Excuse me, I think I missed a quiz yesterday."

"Yes," she said, not looking up at me.

"Is there, is there any way I can make it up?"

"If you have a form from the health office that you were ill."

"No," I mumbled.

She looked up, met my gaze and smiled. "It wasn't an important quiz. It was only twenty percent of this week's grade. The rest is the paper, so it shouldn't hurt you too much."

There was no answer at all that I could make to that, as I didn't know anything about a paper. I nodded my thanks, then turned and dashed out of the room and down the corridor and out of the building. Halfway across the lawn, disappearing down a path, was the girl who sat next to me in class. Since I didn't know anyone else in that class, I went flying after her.

By the time I caught up with her, I was panting for breath. "Wait," I gasped.

"What's wrong?" She stopped to stare at me. So did half a dozen other students who were wandering by.

"Tell me about the paper! When did she assign a paper?"

"In lit?" Her eyes widened. "Didn't you do that, either? Oh gosh, she assigned it the same day she told us about the quiz. It's due tomorrow."

"Tomorrow! What's the subject?"

"Pick any of the authors we've covered so far and take any four of their works and compare them."

"Compare four authors?" I said.

"No, compare four works of one author, four works that we haven't covered in class. Oh, and the works are supposed to be stories or essays, not poems, and the paper should be about ten pages long."

"Ten pages!"

"I've been working on mine all week." She gave me this very doubtful look.

If she felt doubtful, it was nothing compared to how I felt. In a blind panic, I took off for the library, sure I could never get four works read, much less write ten pages comparing them, before our next class. And if I turned the paper in late, I might as well not turn it in at all, because by the time the prof deducted points for being late, and twenty percent off for missing the quiz, I'd have a zero for the week. As it was, I was carrying a very weak C in lit. I felt a solid D coming on.

By a stroke of luck I found a library assistant who had taken the same lit class the previous semester and was familiar with the course. He knew right where to find a good collected-works edition of one of the authors and he also stood over me and gave me some good suggestions as I wrote rapidly in my notebook.

"Compare his use of subplots, because this guy is especially noted for his subplots, and be sure to use the third story in the book, because it's his most famous, and then I'd suggest you use the seventh one, also, because it's one of his least quoted and gives the impression you're really well read," he said, and rattled off a string of other points to include.

By the time I left the library, my hand ached from writing, and it wasn't until I was running up the steps in my dorm that I even stopped to think about that library assistant. He'd been cute, I was sure of that, but what had he actually looked like?

I couldn't remember, that's how upset I was about that paper.

As I dashed into my room, my roommate, Marci, was taking the phone off the hook and saying, "Hello?"

I threw myself across my bed and opened my book to the third story. Leafing through it, I saw it was over twenty pages long. Worse, as I checked through the rest of the book, I saw that none of the stories was much shorter.

"Phone for you, Greta."

"I can't talk to anybody," I shouted, still in shock. How was I ever going to get all those pages read, plus figure out comparisons and write a ten-page paper?

The print swam in front of my eyes. I reread the first paragraph of the story three times without understanding a word. Taking a deep breath, I willed myself to calm down.

It was then that I realized what Marci had said.

Turning over on the bed, I asked, "Who was on the phone?"

By that time Marci was back at her desk, where she was busy typing away on her laptop. "Somebody named David."

"Okay," I said, and went back to my reading. As long as it wasn't Rick, I didn't care who it was, because I didn't have time to talk to anyone else.

CHAPTER 4

It was a nightmare night. Marci, who has to be the best roommate in the world, did her best, answering the phone, talking in low whispers and tiptoeing around me while I read through eighty pages of short stories. My eyes felt like those cartoon characters' eyes, the kind that spin like pinwheels.

I heard Marci whispering into the phone, "I'll ask her tomorrow, Joanne. She's tied up now."

For a moment I wondered what Marci's cousin, wanted, and I almost turned and asked, but then I thought about flunking and getting kicked out of college, and I riveted my eyes back on that book.

Later I heard her whispering, "I know, Steve, but I think she's flunking something." Steve is Marci's steady.

And once there was a tap on the door and Marci answered and slipped outside into the hall. Somebody wailed, "But I've got to ask her," and then again I heard Marci's whisper, though I couldn't catch the words. She came back in the room and closed the door softly.

By the time I finished the reading and had my laptop open and started typing lists of comparisons, it was midnight and Marci was getting ready for bed.

I knew that if I stayed in the room with the light on, she would cover her head with her pillow and not complain, but I also knew she wouldn't get much sleep. So I packed up my laptop and headed for the door.

Marci said, "Is there anything I can do to help you?"

"No. It isn't hard and I understand it, it's just an assignment that takes time, like four days, and it's my own stupid fault I didn't know about it four days ago."

"Well, okay, but if you need me to proofread or anything, come on back and wake me up."

I gave her a weak grin, which was the best I could manage, and trudged down the hall to the swinging door that led onto the balcony. The narrow balcony ran the width of the lounge below. The lounge was a large room, two stories high, filled with couches and overstuffed chairs. Occasionally it got used for dorm parties. More often, it served as an all-night study hall for people whose roommates were sleeping. Also, as it could be entered from the first floor, it was occasionally used by couples to sit around and talk after a date.

That night its sole occupant of the lounge was a girl curled in a chair, her head bent over a book.

The total furnishings of the balcony were one wooden desk and one straight-backed chair. I spread out my computer, book and notebook, and got right to work.

An hour or so later I glanced down to the entry level and saw that the other girl had given up and left. I typed on.

An hour after that I stood up to stretch. My back and neck felt as though I'd spent the last hours lifting weights, they were that stiff. Taking a three-minute break, I returned to the hallway, dropped my coins into the soft drink machine, and chose a caffeine-loaded drink. After setting the opened can on the floor next to the desk, I got right back to typing.

Several times during the night, when I reached for the soda or went back to the machine for another, I glanced at the tall windows of the lounge below me. The lounge was almost dark, with only two heavily shaded lamps left on all night. Outside the dark windows, dark maples swayed above the walk, their branches lit on the undersides by the walkway lamps.

And then the next time I looked up, the lamps had gone out and the sky was pale gray.

By the time I finished the last page, checked it over and packed up my stuff, sunlight made a wide strip across the room from its eastern angle, zigzagging up and down over the couches, then shooting straight across the carpet to the next row of furniture. Outside, people hurried toward the cafeteria for breakfast.

I stumbled into my room just as Marci was rushing out. "Did you get it done?" she asked.

"Barely. It's probably terrible, but at least it's done. Now I need to print it out."

She gave me a long, worried look and said, "Greta, why don't you go throw yourself in the shower and I'll do a quick proofread and then get this printed?"

Like I said, she was the nicest roommate in the world. I was too zonked to turn down such a fantastic offer.

When I returned from my shower, feeling a few degrees closer to being a human being again, my printed pages were neatly stacked by my computer.

In case I didn't see her later in the day, I drew a big heart on a piece of paper, wrote 'A million thanks!' in the center, and left it on her desk.

By the time I'd dressed and dried my hair and all that, I'd missed breakfast and barely made it to my nine o'clock. After sitting through that class, holding my eyes open with my fingertips, I made a straight line for the cafeteria, grabbed coffee and a doughnut and, after gulping it down, headed for lower campus.

If there was one thing I didn't feel like, it was tennis, but this wasn't the day to cut another class. I mean, even though they don't pull pop quizzes in gym class, it's the one place where they positively do take attendance and count it into the grade.

Ever try to play tennis in your sleep? Don't. It's suicidal. I hit the showers again, this time the gym shower, hoping it would keep me going until two. Then I dashed back to my dorm to get my lit paper, gave it one last glance-over, realized I'd attributed a quote to the wrong story, a point Marci couldn't catch as she hadn't read the stories, and, letting out a shriek that should have awakened anyone who might still be sleeping, I flung myself into my desk chair to make the corrections.

The book I'd used was on reserve and had to be returned by noon, which was already past, but if I looked desperate enough maybe the librarian wouldn't cancel my library-use privileges, which they could do for four days for late returns on reserve books. So by the time I'd taken care of all that, and yes, I did look desperate enough, and ran from my dorm to the library to my two o'clock, I missed lunch.

But I had that wretched paper in on time.

I think the prof gave a lecture, in fact, I am sure she did, but afterwards, I couldn't remember a word. All I could remember was turning in the paper and then sitting stiffly upright, battling exhaustion, terrified that I would fall asleep and land on the floor. I didn't think she'd be impressed, at least, not impressed the way I wanted her to be.

At three I headed toward the Union building, hoping to grab something to eat in the coffee shop before going back to my room to sleep. But when I reached the lower path, I was shaking so hard I was honestly afraid I'd fall.

It was a case of delayed panic. My brain wouldn't work. My vision blurred. All I could see was the bridge and the little woods that edged the stream and a patch of very green spring grass shining under a very bright afternoon sun.

I crossed the bridge and sank down on the grass. Maybe if I sat in the sun for a minute I'd feel better. Until that moment, I hadn't noticed how warm the day was, how much more like summer than spring.

Closing my eyes, I slid slowly down and stretched out and rested my head on my arm. Beneath my face, the grass smelled sweet.

I was so tired I didn't even dream, though I did have a jumble of disconnected thoughts. There was Marci, looking worried, and Jon frowning, and Rick scolding, and my lit prof glaring, and a tennis ball headed right at me.

And then someone shook me and said, "Greta?"

I rolled over and found myself staring into those warm brown eyes. David was crouched down beside me, peering at me. For some reason that I couldn't figure, he looked super worried.

"I was sleeping," I mumbled.

"Here? Outside?"

"What's the matter, is this your space, nobody else can trespass?" I was too tired to be polite.

He leaned back and gave me room to sit up. "No, only I thought, uh, sorry I woke you."

It hit me why he looked worried. "Bet you thought I'd tripped over something again and this time knocked myself out."

His nice, square face went all embarrassed around his grin. "Something like that," he admitted.

"I didn't get any sleep at all last night. I had this horrendous paper to do."

"You want me to go away and let you get back to sleep?"

Laughing, I stood up. "No, I'm fine now. How are your fiddleheads growing?"

"That's what I came to check. Come on along and look. There should be skunk cabbages further up the stream."

Who could resist an invitation to visit a skunk cabbage? Maybe I'm no scientist, but I can ooh and ah over new foliage as well as anyone. I tagged along.

David held out his hand to help me down the stream's bank. His hand was like the rest of him, firm and warm. We wandered at the water's edge, picking our way through the marshes, beneath a lacy canopy of willows with their new leaves unfolding, until the water's turning path took us out of sight of the bridge.

"Think I'll wade," he said, pulling off his shoes.

"Good idea." I stood on one foot to untie the laces on my sneaker. When I leaned dangerously to one side, David put his arm around my shoulders to keep me from falling. The boy obviously had a fixation about my tendency to collapse.

When I was barefoot, and solidly standing on both feet, he moved away from me, walking in front of me into the water. It was shallow and sun warmed. The stream's bed was mossy. With each step, mud oozed around my feet.

"I haven't waded in mud since I was six years old," I told him.

"Nice, huh? Hey, here's skunk cabbages!"

Yes, they were pretty, with their wide yellow petals, and no, they did not smell pretty.

However, the spring air was so filled with sunlight on blossoming trees and meadow flowers that the skunk cabbages couldn't compete.

David pulled a small notebook from his hip pocket and did a sketch. With only a few lines, he caught the graceful newness of the plants.

"You're awfully good at that."

"Think so?" He gave me a pleased smile.

We found patches of sweet woodruff, their tight white buds promising to open at any moment, and marsh flowers in shades of pale green and yellow that neither of us could identify, and even an early violet and a wild narcissus.

We also spotted tadpoles and thrushes. Small creatures rustled through the grassy banks, keeping out of sight. And an occasional brightly colored insect hovered above the water. David watched everything, catching shadowy shapes with his pencil. He gave them personality, made each leaf and creature more interesting than I'd at first thought it could be. Watching him sketch, I forgot about being tired.

Instead, I found myself noticing details, light reflections, odd angles of branches, the way a bird cocked its head, that sort of thing.

When David finished a sketch and glanced at me to see if I was still there, I couldn't help noticing that there were gold flecks in his light brown eyes.

It's the sort of thing writers always give characters in romance books, but David was the first person I ever met who actually had gold flecks in his eyes. Maybe it was a trick of the sunlight. I was surrounded by gold flecks, glittering off the water and the marsh grass and the whispering trees.

We climbed up the bank to a dry patch of grass. While David wrote notes in the margins around his sketches, identifying plant parts with words like stamen, pistil and so forth, I braided dandelion stems into a bracelet.

When he noticed what I was doing, he laughed. "Another leftover skill from your six-year-old mud-wading days?"

"I have a very narrow range of talents."

"Okay, I'll be honest with you. You've got a talent I've always envied."

"What? Weaving dandelions?"

"Yes," he said. "I could never do that. They always break for me."

I said generously, "Make you a deal. I'll trade you this bracelet for one of your sketches."

He handed me the notebook. "Take them all."

"What, and be responsible for you flunking botany? No, fair's fair, and this bracelet is worth one sketch."

After I pulled out the page with the sketch of the skunk cabbage on it, I handed him the bracelet. He slipped it over his hand and held out his wrist to admire it.

Our eyes met and we both laughed.

And then for some funny reason I had this weird, dizzy feeling. At first I thought, come on, Greta, he's cute, but he's not Rick. And then I realized I really was dizzy. Afraid to stand, I stayed where I was, sitting on the grass.

"Are you all right?" he asked, in the same worried tone that he'd asked me earlier, when he'd found me sleeping by the bridge.

"I guess so, only I feel kind of, uh, kind of faint."

David put his hand on my shoulder. "Probably because you didn't get any sleep last night."

"Now don't give me that worried look again," I mumbled, and then I realized I was mumbling. Somehow, my mouth didn't seem to be able to work right. I felt his shoulder against my head and knew that he was holding me to keep me from falling over, and this time I was very glad he was.

David didn't say anything more, just sat there quietly hanging on to me, his arm around me, while I waited for the world to stop spinning. As my head cleared, my stomach began to ache.

I sat up straight and David's arm dropped away from me. "You know what? I think I'm hungry."

"You get faint when you get hungry?"

"I haven't had anything to eat today except a doughnut. I missed breakfast and then I missed lunch."

While I sat there with all the animation of a rag doll, David picked up one of my feet and wiped away the damp mud, using a handful of soft leaves. I couldn't figure what he was doing. And then he dried my other foot. Next he pulled my socks out of my sneakers, put them on me, and then put my sneakers on my feet and tied the laces.

"I really could do that myself," I protested, but I wasn't actually sure I could.

"Uh-huh," he said, and stood up and caught hold of my hands and pulled me to my feet. We stumbled across the meadow, David's arm around my waist and me feeling very dumb.

"This is stupid," I said. "I felt fine not twenty minutes ago."

He said, "Uh-huh," again, nothing more, and steered me across the bridge. He led me through the wooded path, or maybe he was half-carrying me, until we crossed the lawn, and he continued to hang on to me as we went up the steps onto the back patio of the Union building.

The patio was a wide concrete strip edged by a low brick wall that overlooked the woods, and it was filled with hundreds of metal deck chairs, the type with arms. I sat down in the first one I reached, or maybe what happened was that David steered me to the chair and got me into it.

I felt considerably more secure sitting in a chair with arms.

"Will you be all right for a few minutes by yourself?" he asked.

"Sure. Where are you going?"

"Be right back," he said, and dashed off.

That's the last of him, I thought, as I closed my eyes and tried to rest. He'd write me off as the campus dunce and work hard at never letting our paths cross again.

But I was wrong. While my thoughts were still drifting off in odd directions, he returned.

"Greta?"

Had I fallen asleep again? I opened my eyes. David stood in front of me, holding a cafeteria tray.

"Greta, do you feel well enough to eat?"

"That's what I need, something to eat," I made an effort to give him a cheerful smile. From the expression on his face, I'm afraid my smile was more sickly than cheerful.

David pulled around chairs, putting one between us to serve as a table, and placed the tray on it. He'd gone to the coffee shop rather than the main cafeteria. The tray contained two burgers and two milkshakes and containers of fries, coffee shop food.

"There's a huge line at the cafeteria now. I didn't want to wait," he explained, "but you can always go get a regular supper later when you feel better."

"What's supper?" I asked, as I picked up my burger.

He gave me a funny look, wrinkling his nose. "Chicken stew."

"Wow, I think I'll look you up every chicken stew night and do my fainting act." Because students had pass cards to the cafeteria but had to pay for coffee shop food, I added, "What do I owe you?"

"Nothing."

"Sure, I do." It wasn't as though he was some guy I was dating. Or even some guy I knew very well.

"No, you don't."

"If you go around buying food for every faint girl on campus, you won't have any money for tuition. Come on, what do I owe you?"

I'd had a couple of bites of the burger and several swallows of milkshake, and I was feeling much better.

"Make you a deal," he said slowly, watching me. "Next time I feel faint, I'll phone you and you can bring me supper and we'll be even."

"Do you feel faint often? You don't look like the fainting type."

"What does the fainting type look like?"

"Actually, in magazine stories, fainting types are always female, usually eighteenth century. I think it had something to do with tight corsets. Nowadays, women faint so seldom, most men don't know what to do."

Surprised, he said, "What's that supposed to mean?"

I felt much better, relaxed, expansive, talkative. My old self. I launched into one of my long explanations. "David, read any historical romance, or watch an old costume movie. There's always a girl who swoons away at some point, and when she does, she sinks slowly and gracefully, giving the hero plenty of time to catch her in his arms and carry her to some handy couch or grassy knoll where he dabs her forehead with a perfumed lace hanky until she comes round with a flutter of eyelashes."

"Sorry I don't have a lace hanky," he said.

"But nowadays, women faint so seldom, nobody even remembers what the word swoon meant. And if a woman does start to swoon, who'd rush forward? Probably some guy fresh from a first aid class, who'd tell everyone to stand back while he stretches her arms over her head and starts pumping her ribs up and down."

"And she comes to coughing."

"Uh-huh. The romance of the lace hanky is a lost art."

"At least I didn't pump your ribs," he said.

"You may be some throwback to historic man."

"Next time I'll let you fall on your face in the stream."

Finishing up my supper, I said, "Seriously, you are an absolute angel and I owe you a supper because you have probably saved my life, but now I have to get back to my room because I still have a couple hours' worth of studying and I'm not even sure I can stay awake that long."

As I began to gather up paper cups and napkins and pile them on the tray to return to the clearing counter, he said, "Let that go, I'll get it."

"Next time the whole works are on me, serving, paying, clearing."

"See you around," he said.

I gave him a wink, which is one of those things I am always doing even though my mother says girls shouldn't wink.

He stood there with his hands full of our trash, and grinned back at me. "Are you going to be all right? Maybe I should walk you back to your dorm."

And come in with me and then I'd have to figure a way to tell him to go away and I was up to winking but I wasn't up to explaining I had a boyfriend, so I assured him I felt one hundred percent. He looked kind of disappointed.

It wasn't until I was all the way back at Smith Hall and upstairs and rushing along the corridor to my room that I remembered that he had phoned me sometime the previous night.

I distinctly remembered Marci saying that David had phoned. I'd been too busy to think about it at the time, but now that I had time, I thought. I didn't know any other David on campus. It had to be that David. But I didn't even know his last name.

And I hadn't told him mine.

How had he known my phone number?

I very nearly U-turned to go back and ask. Then I decided that if I did, he'd figure I was leading him on, interested in him, and of course I was, but only as a friend, because for sure I didn't need another guy complicating my life. So I didn't go back.

But I did still wonder.

CHAPTER 5

A few days later, after I'd totally put David out of my mind and stopped wondering why he'd phoned, he popped back into my life.

My relationship with Rick was on again. We spent two evenings in a row together, and he was reasonably apologetic when I told him how I'd missed a test and almost missed an important assignment the day I cut to pick up his book and antenna.

After I met him at three in the coffee shop, he walked back to my room with me.

"If Marci's gone, maybe I'll come in and study for a while," he said. He did that sometimes, stretched out on my bed and read while I worked at my desk.

He climbed the stairs ahead of me. I reached up and jabbed him in the ribs with my finger. "Okay, but you can't smoke."

"Says who?"

"Says me. The last time you smoked in our room, Marci could smell the smoke in her closet."

"Did she complain?"

"She didn't cheer. Anyhow, it's against dorm rules and you'll get us both in trouble."

"Quit nagging," he said.

We turned down the corridor past the open doors into other rooms. The rooms started out being identical in the fall, each one with a bare linoleum floor, walls painted pale nothing colors. Carefully planned blah.

During the year all the rooms underwent a metamorphosis. They grew decorations. The original bare furnishings were like naked trees that sprouted leaves, hidden beneath their finery. Each room was now an individual collection of bright spreads and throw pillows, the linoleum hidden beneath rugs and carpets, the walls papered with posters. Kites and Chinese lanterns and mobiles and wind chimes and a variety of other colorful decorations hung from the ceilings.

I'd packed away the Holly Hobbie spread and replaced it with this terrific leopard-spotted sheet. And then I covered my half of the walls with my posters and Marci covered her half with movie posters.

There were hooks in the ceiling, a half dozen of them, that some former tenant had used for hanging mobiles or something, but we used them to hang up sweaters and shirts to dry.

When I opened the door, the first thing Rick did was walk in and get slapped in the face by the tails of a wet shirt.

"Jeez, don't you ever pick up this room!" he exclaimed.

As I had to stand on a chair to loop the clothes hanger over the ceiling hook, the shirt was high enough for Marci and me to walk under without brushing it.

"So it's my fault you're too tall?"

I meant it as a joke.

Rick didn't laugh. He sat down on my bed, scowling, and picked up one of my magazines. When he was annoyed, he went dead silent. I let him pout it out. If there's one thing I know about boys, it's that there's no use arguing with them when they've got attitude showing.

I flipped on my stereo, stuck in one of my favorite CDs, and hummed along with it while I straightened out my nail polish bottles on my dresser top. I loved lining up bottles of cologne and cosmetics in front of the dresser mirror, so that they reflected themselves into a double row of colored glass. It made me feel as though I owned a department store's whole cosmetics counter. Everybody's allowed a favorite fantasy, and that's mine.

Allison poked her head in the open doorway. "Anybody here? Oh, there you are!" she said, and then she spotted Rick sitting on my bed. "Sorry, didn't know you were busy."

"Come on in," I said, because I could see at a quick glance that she was upset about something. She was finger combing her pale hair back from her forehead and her hand was shaking. There were red blotches around her eyes.

The last time I'd talked with her, beyond saying hi as we passed in the hallway, was that day in the laundry room when she'd been so upset about her boyfriend, Mark.

"I don't want to bother you," she said.

"That's okay." As she wouldn't tell me her problem in front of Rick, if the problem was Mark, I added, "Rick was about to go down the hall and get me a soda. You want one?"

For sure I was taking a chance on irritating Rick, but usually he behaved himself when anyone else was around. At worst, he'd walk out without saying a word.

Instead he did his best, sweetest Rick, and said, "Okay, three sodas, huh?" and headed down the hall.

Obviously he saw that Allison was crying.

She flung herself onto my bed, right where Rick had been, and wailed, "I came by a few nights ago to talk to you but your roommate said you couldn't be disturbed, and every time since you've been out and I've got to talk to someone!"

"Sure, honey. Is it Mark?"

"He's dating some girl who lives in Dorrance Hall. I've seen them together. He hasn't called me in a week, and I'm flunking biology and I think my parents are going to get a divorce and my hair's turning green." Her voice faded away into a soft sobbing.

"I know what you mean." Because that's another thing I know. Problems never come one at a time, especially if there's a boy in the mix. I sat down on my bed beside her and put my arm around her shoulders. "Look, let's go through it slowly. Mark's done this before, right?"

Allison nodded.

"Okay, for sure it's lousy on you, but you can't change him. Did you try talking to other guys?"

She whispered, "There's a boy in my economics class who keeps following me around, but, Greta, I don't want more problems."

"He doesn't have to be a problem. Go to coffee with him. Talk to him. But don't date him. It'll give you something to think about besides Mark."

"Oh, I don't know."

"Yeah, it's rough. About your parents. you can't do anything about them except keep your fingers crossed. Maybe they'll change their minds. And about biology, I can't help you at all. I've got the same problem in lit. I guess all we can do is keep studying."

"Maybe I should give up and drop out of school and go home."

I gave her a hard look to see how much she meant that. I didn't think that was what she wanted to do at all. But what else I noticed was that she was right, her hair was turning green.

Jumping up, I said, "Know what makes your hair turn green? It's copper, it comes off the water pipes in swimming pools or something like that. My aunt's a hair stylist. If you use a shampoo and conditioner every time after you swim, that helps."

"Or I could dye it blue and be done with it," she said, but although that didn't sound too positive, her voice was steadier.

"Tell you what, that's one problem I can solve. Most of the green is in the tips. Why don't I trim your hair for you?"

"Do you really know how to trim hair?" She was almost smiling.

"Do I ever." I may be very short on talent and not all that big on academic skills, if there's one thing I know, it's hair. Between my beautician aunt, and my beauty magazines, I'd learned hundreds of tricks.

Grabbing up an old school newspaper, I spread it around on the floor, then plunked my desk chair in the middle. With a sweeping bow and wide arm gesture, I said, "Voila! Madame Greta's Hairstyling Salon! Have a seat, miss!"

"Are you sure you know what you're doing?"

"I do my own hair and Marci's hair and I've done haircuts for lots of the girls here," I said.

"Honest?" If Allison still looked worried, at least now she was worrying about what I'd do to her hair and not about Mark. That was a big improvement for her mental health, I figured.

I had my combs and brushes and scissors lined up on my dresser top, and a towel tucked around Allison's shoulders by the time Rick returned with our three drinks.

"Now what are you up to?" he asked.

"Trimming Allison's hair." I took my soda can from him and set it on the dresser.

"Oh yeah?" He didn't sound especially confident, but he also didn't sound as doubtful as Allison had. I think what he was was curious, because he sat back down on my bed to watch. He knew I could cut hair. I'd told him so lots of times. On the other hand, I was better at listening to him than he was at listening to me.

"I don't want it short," Allison said.

Handing her my makeup mirror, I said, "Here, you watch and see what I'm doing, though personally I believe you will be surprised and delighted."

She giggled nervously. Putting the mirror in her lap, she folded her hands on top of it. "I don't really want to watch. I'd rather trust you."

Rick snorted.

I grabbed my glass water jar from the dresser and held it out to him. "Go fill this."

"Huh? Where?"

"There's a drinking fountain in the hall."

"Fill a jar in a drinking fountain?"

"Or there's the girls' bathroom. Just knock and shout before you open the door."

He didn't bother answering. We both knew he'd fill the jar at the fountain.

After he left, Allison said, "I didn't mean to cause your boyfriend a lot of bother."

"You aren't. I'm sending him on errands on purpose. It's important to keep guys busy. Let them sit around too long with nothing to do and they get bored and start arguments for the fun of it."

After fluffing out her hair with my hands, I pushed it around to get the feel, then combed it into sections, pinning it out of the way, so that I could unpin one section at a time to trim. Rick returned with the water, handed it to me, and returned to his spectator's spot on the bed, all without a word.

I said, "Thanks so much. Did you go in the girls' bathroom?"

He didn't bother to nod. We both knew he hadn't.

I combed water through the first section of Allison's hair and then positioned the hair on the comb and snipped off the green tips, letting them fall onto the spread newspapers.

She glanced down and saw that I'd cut off less than an inch. She let her shoulders drop, relaxed.

I combed away, snipping only fractions of an inch at a time and stepping back to be sure I liked the effect, humming as I worked. I love cutting hair. When I'm doing it, I can't worry about anything else.

From the doorway, Inger said, "What's going on?"

"Giving her a trim."

"Mind if I watch?"

I said I didn't mind and Inger leaned against the doorframe while I continued to comb and snip.

"Some collection you have."

"What?"

"On your door," she said.

The outside of the door was covered with scraps of paper taped to the wood, half mine and half Marci's, a collection of cartoons and newspaper articles and postcards, anything either of us liked and wanted to share with the other girls on the hall.

While Inger read our cartoons and Rick leafed through a magazine, I finished up Allison's hair.

After the last snip, I combed through her hair again with water, then used my dryer to shape it in place.

At that point I wished I had one of those swivel chairs, like my aunt has in her shop, so that I could swing Allison around to face a large mirror, but the best I could do was pick up the hand mirror and hold it in front of her.

"Oh my!" she said, and jumped up and ran over to my dresser, where she stared at her reflection in the larger glass. "Oh, that's wonderful! I love it! Greta, you're a marvel."

"I wish my professors thought so."

"You really do have talent," Inger said, her head tilted, her eyes narrowed, as she appraised Allison's haircut.

"Sure, but it's my one and only."

"Not if that's a self-portrait on the door," she said. "You should be an art major."

As all of the papers on my door were clippings, I didn't know what she was talking about. I'd have asked, except that Allison started saying she should pay me for the trim, and since I'd done it to cheer her, I had to think of some nice way to say no, and then Rick asked when we were going to supper and Allison asked Inger if she was ready to go to supper and they both remembered things they had to do first.

Shouting "See you later," and "Thanks again," they dashed off.

Rick stood up, dropped the magazine on the bed and said, "Ready to go, now?"

"As soon as I pick up these papers."

"Do that later."

"No, I can't leave hair all over the floor. Marci isn't fussy, but that's too much." I knelt down to fold the hair trimmings into the newspapers I'd spread out. While I worked, Rick wandered to the door and stood in the opening reading the cartoons.

I brushed past him and carried the rolled papers down the hallway to the incinerator chute. When I returned, he said, "Who did this?"

He pointed to a drawing taped to my door. I hadn't noticed it earlier, probably because I was so used to our clipping collection, I never looked at it except when I had something new to add.

"Who did what?"

But as soon as I saw where he was pointing, I knew.

A half sheet of sketch-pad paper was taped among our clippings. On it was a pencil drawing of me, definitely me, done in a cartoon style but leaving no doubt about who it was. It was my shape, my face, my hair, all collapsed against a mountain of school books.

And the sketching style was the neat, crisp lines that I'd watched David produce in his drawings of insects and birds and fiddlehead ferns.

"I guess it's me," I said.

"I can see that. But who drew it?"

"I don't know. One of the girls, maybe."

Rick swung around and glared at me. "So you have a girl named David in your dorm?" He stalked off, leaving me standing in the hallway with my mouth open, while he disappeared around the archway and down the stairs.

I started to run after him. Then I wondered where he'd come up with David's name. Returning to my door, I looked more closely at the sketch.

In very tiny lettering up the spine of one of the books was printed, "David."

David must have dropped by to see me when I was out.

Looked like he knew my room number as well as my phone number.

Thinking of Rick, I almost grabbed the sketch from the door to wad it up and throw it away. But then I looked at it again. It really was clever. In the sketch the little cartoon Greta looked exactly the way I'd felt the last time I'd seen David, overwhelmed by my assignments.

It was such a funny sketch, I couldn't help laughing. David really was a clever artist.

Then I noticed more printing on the other books' spines. One said Cole Hall, another said Langford, and another book spine contained a line of numbers. A phone number.

The meaning was obvious. His name was David Langford and he lived in Cole Hall and he expected me to phone him. Maybe I'm no detective, but I know enough about boys to figure out that simple a message.

I untaped the sketch from the door, working it loose carefully to avoid tearing it. If I left it on the door, Rick would think David was somebody I cared about. The sketch was too good to throw away. I put in the drawer of my desk to save it, so I could show it to Marci, and then I ran after Rick.

By the time I caught up with him, he'd picked up his tray in the cafeteria and found a seat at one of the long tables. I sat down beside him.

He didn't bother looking at me. I didn't bother speaking to him. We ate in a total silence that was so thick it practically blocked out all the cafeteria noise, the voices and the scraping sounds of chairs and trays and dishes. Sometimes I could actually imagine a gray cloud surrounding Rick, he could be that horrid.

I gave him until he finished eating to work through his grumpy mood. Then I said, "Can I help it who sticks cartoons on my door?"

"Why did you lie about it?"

"I didn't! Rick! I didn't even see it until you asked about it, and I didn't see David's name on it until after you left, so how was I supposed to know who drew it?"

"Gonna tell me who David is?"

In a very casual voice, as though it were the most unimportant comment in the world, I said, "Um, I expect it's that guy I bumped into one day, remember, I told you, he was sketching some ferns down by the bridge. At least, he's the only person I know who sketches and is named David."

"Why should he make a sketch of you?"

"I don't know. Maybe he goes around sketching everyone he meets."

"How did he know your room number?"

I could be absolutely honest and look Rick straight in the eye when I said, "I don't know. I didn't even tell him my last name, so that is odd, isn't it? Still, I suppose he could have seen me going into Smith Hall and asked somebody which room was mine."

"How come he's hanging around Smith?" Rick gave me this really cold stare, like he was looking through me and didn't believe me.

"How should I know?" I said, then added quickly, before he could start seriously arguing about David, "Listen, they're showing movies upstairs tonight. If we get up there fast, we can get good seats."

Rick shrugged and I didn't know if that meant yes, he wanted to go to the movie or no, he didn't, but I pretended I thought it meant yes. As we'd first met in the auditorium-theater, I considered it a lucky place.

Jumping up, I said, "Come on, it's one of those spy films, but I can't remember the name," and rushed out.

If there is one thing I know about boys, it's that there is no point waiting around giving them time to continue arguments, because if you do, they will.

So there I was, managing this touchy situation with Rick, rushing along the crowded corridors of the Union building toward the back staircase, when a voice shouted, "Hi, Greta!"

And there by the wall, about ten people away from me, was David the Artist, waving like mad, a big grin on his face.

Rick muttered, "Who's that?" in my ear.

I rushed on by without turning my head, but I did raise my arm to wave over my shoulder, which Rick couldn't see as he was slightly ahead of me. I said, "How should I know?"

"He knows you."

As we headed up the stairs I said, "Listen, Rick, he's probably in one of my classes, but I do not know the name of every guy on campus."

"Yeah, well, they sure all know your name."

What? He was jealous? Hmm, sort of nice. And as I couldn't think of any answer to what he'd said that wouldn't lead to a worse argument, I kept my mouth shut and hoped Rick would love the movie.

Luckily for me, he did.

By the time the film ended, he'd forgotten all about David and the sketch. We walked back to Smith with our arms around each other, on the best of terms.

CHAPTER 6

The last week of March started out with that "This is the first day of the rest of my life" feeling. I was in tune with my world. My lit assignments were up to date, my laundry was caught up, my skin was clear and Rick hadn't said a cross word to me in three days. If I mention Rick last, it's because he was so much more important to me than anything else that it scared me. Sometimes our relationship seemed so fragile, I felt as though I had to tiptoe through it to keep it from shattering.

Maybe that's why I was just this little bit nervous when I came swinging up the path at noon from my tennis class and bumped into David.

This time I didn't physically bump into him, not again, but there he was, standing on the bridge, leaning with his back against the railing, very obviously waiting for me.

Sure, he said casually, "Oh, hi, Greta," as though I were the last person he expected to see.

And sure, I said, "Oh, hi, David," as though I believed our meeting was a coincidence.

But I knew he was waiting for me and he knew I knew it.

Most times, I'd have been flattered because having a darling boy stand around waiting to accidentally meet me is a huge compliment, but that particular day my life was humming along so well, I didn't want to chance anything that might upset Rick.

"Going to lunch?" he asked.

It crossed my mind to say that I had laundry to do, but he had this funny look on his face that made me think he was in a mood to willingly agree to tag along and help me with anything I mentioned. And as I didn't have so much as a dirty sweater left in my laundry bag, I didn't think I'd better take a chance on that excuse.

Definitely if I said I was going to the library to study, he would follow me.

Instead I silently prayed that Rick had gone to lunch early, which he often did, and was by now well on his way out of the cafeteria.

To David, I said, "Sure."

Honestly, it was not a wildly encouraging sort of reply, and I didn't give him a big smile or bat my eyelashes, or anything, but his already happy-shiny face lit up like a light bulb.

It was impossible not to smile back at a grin like that.

As we walked up the path to the Union building, I said, "I liked the cartoon you left on my door. How'd you know my room number?"

"Looked it up in the student directory. I was going to give the cartoon to you, but when I knocked on your door, nobody answered, and I saw all those other cartoons on your door, so I decided to just leave it."

"But how could you look me up in the directory? You don't know my last name."

"I do, too. Your last name is Greenley."

"How did you know that?"

David stopped walking, faced me and gave me this teasing grin. "What, you're a secret undercover agent and by learning your name I've broken your code?"

"Right," I said quickly, "so now I'll have to inform the bureau that our passwords have been rendered inoperative."

"I think my stomach is going to be rendered inoperative if I don't get some food in it soon," David said.

We hurried to the cafeteria, joked over the food choices as we went through the line, found a table with a couple of side-by-side empty places, and said our hellos to familiar faces before settling down to our lunches.

David was easy to talk to, I mean, he actually listened to me. I chattered away at top speed, which for me can be very rapid-fire.

Yes, I had one nervous moment, when we first entered the

cafeteria. I saw a dark head across the room that I thought was Rick. My breath kind of choked up in my throat, which was dumb, because, honestly, if it had been Rick, why should he give any thought to who was standing next to me in line? But then it wasn't Rick, and I let my breath out slowly and scanned the huge room and satisfied myself that he wasn't there and relaxed.

"Guess I owe you another dandelion bracelet."

"What for?" David raised his eyebrows and watched me, waiting for me to answer.

"Although that's maybe not fair. You give me something I can keep and I pay you with a bracelet that's not much good an hour later."

"I put the one you gave me under my pillow and it's still there."

Oops. He was going romantic on me. Nothing but problems in that direction, and so I switched subjects. "What are you planning on doing with an art major?"

"Something in commercial art. My first choice is illustrating science fiction books or posters, but that takes a long time. So I plan to minor in programming and maybe do web design."

"A plan is good."

"What about you? What's your major, Greta?"

Hmm. I almost said, boys, because that's what my roommate told her cousin. On the other hand, I was trying to keep a distance between myself and David.

"That's why I think a plan is good. I don't have one. I don't know what I want to do."

"Going to college is a plan. Whatever you decide to do, an education will help."

"Oh that's so sweet!"

"I'm sweet? Hold onto that thought, woman." A grin kept twitching at the edges of his mouth.

What I learned about David was that he was as good as me at talking, and when he wasn't talking, he listened, which kept me talking, and so it wasn't until after lunch and after he waved good-bye and I headed over to my lit class that I realized he never had told me how he learned my last name.

I had supper with Rick. Afterwards, he had to study, so I went back to my room because I probably needed to study more than he did. But I never quite made it to my books.

Allison was waiting for me, sitting on my bed leafing through one of my magazines, her wet blond hair hanging dead straight.

Marci was at her desk, typing.

Allison said, "You told me to come back next time I washed my hair."

"Right." I put my fingertips under her chin to tilt up her face and then I squinted and peered at the shape of her cut. "Uh-huh, it needs a little more trimming. I missed a place."

I also noticed that Allison's eyes were red and figured she'd been crying and wanted to talk to me, as much as anything. "Going to bother you if we talk?" I asked Marci.

My nice roommate must also have noticed Allison's eyes, because she said, "Not at all, you go right ahead," and she snapped on her iPod headset.

I spread out the papers and settled Allison in the chair, and figured that I'd spend twenty minutes doing a two-minute touch-up trim, to give her time to talk out whatever she wanted to say.

She said, "The haircut is terrific. It's the only terrific thing about me. Everything else is blah."

"That's not true."

"Yes, it is. I look like every other freshman in the world. My mother couldn't find me in a crowd. Probably I should make a career of bank robbery, because I could go in without a mask and nobody'd ever remember what I looked like."

"You're underrating yourself, but still, I know what you mean. We all feel that way about ourselves, sometimes."

"I'll bet you never do."

On an up day when everything went well and Rick told me how

much he hated having to go study and how much he'd rather be with me, it was hard to remember my down days, but I thought about it. "The thing is, we're each different. We have to figure out how and then make that special."

"Give me an example," she said.

I was spinning my wheels because the girl desperately needed someone to talk to. Showed all over her. "Umm, okay. Listen, take color. We each have our own color types, see, and when we wear the right colors, we feel better, and when we wear the wrong colors, we get the depressed."

"I've heard that, but I am a nothing color."

From the doorway, Inger said, "Define nothing color."

She leaned against the doorframe, one hand on a hip, relaxed, as though she'd been there for a minute or two. She was dressed in jeans that clung to her long legs, and a red sweater that set off her cropped black hair.

Allison said, "Greige."

"You are not greige," I said. "You are sunny colors, rose or peach shades."

"Terrific, I am a sweet little pink nothing," Allison said.

"Yeah," I admitted, "I used to think that, too. We blondes always get dressed in pastels and hair ribbons by our parents, so we grow up feeling like half-melted sherbet cones. What I did was, I switched from baby pastels to adult pastels, you know, well, here, take a look."

I leaned past her and pushed open my closet door. There hung my row of pastel colors on hangers, all beige and ivory and shades of light yellow through gold. "I call them the jungle pastels."

"Jungle! Oh, sure, like your leopard bedspread, beige and gold, and oh my gosh, so are your posters!" Inger said, coming into the room to peer more closely at my Frazetta poster collection. They were all in tawny, jungle colors, probably because some were of illustrations Frazetta once did for Tarzan book covers.

After I finished with Allison's trim, we went back to Inger's room to watch a movie on TV. Marci needed some silence in which to work. I thought about studying and then I thought about what I'd told David, that I didn't really know what I wanted to do with my life and I decided maybe instead of staring at a book, I should watch a movie. Maybe I'd see a role model, some woman with her life all figured out.

About halfway through a movie that wasn't much good, and definitely didn't include any role models, Marci came running down the hall to tell me I had a phone call.

"Who is it?" I asked as I followed her back to our room.

"It isn't Rick. Some other guy."

Jon, I figured, and picked up the receiver and said, "Hi."

"Hi, Greta Greenley," David's voice said. Not that I'd been with him all that much, but David's voice sounded the way David looked, warm and cheerful and not quite like anyone else.

"Hi, David."

"I just remembered that I owed you an answer, and as I didn't want you to sit up all night worrying about it, I thought I should call and tell you."

"Owed me an answer?"

"Thing is," he went on, "in case you do wake in the night and remember that you asked me a question that I never got around to answering, I don't want you to have some nightmare idea that I'm a double agent and really did break your cover--"

"Oh!" I shrieked, and Marci, who had returned to her desk and was working quietly, swung around, startled, to stare at me. "You didn't tell me how you knew my name!"

"Jackpot! Truth is more boring than fiction, but I'll tell you anyway. I was sitting in my dorm lounge doing that cartoon of you and one of the guys walked by and said, 'What's that?' and I said, 'My friend Greta,' and he said, 'Oh, I know her! That's Greta Greenley!' So that's the answer I owed you."

"Ah hah," I said. "And who was the stool pigeon?"

"I think his name is Pete."

I knew a couple of guys named Pete. "Well, it goes to prove what good likenesses you do."

"Anything from skunk cabbages to a beautiful woman," he said. "See ya."

And before I could reply to that comment, he hung up.

"Beautiful woman, huh?" I said more to myself than to Marci, which was just as well because she didn't hear me over her iPod, anyway.

Now it is always nice to be referred to as a beautiful woman, and who am I to throw away compliments, but it's also one of those things college boys love to go around saying without meaning a word of it. What I liked better was the easy way David had referred to me as "my friend Greta." He hadn't said it to impress me. He'd only been repeating what he'd told Pete, and I don't think he even thought about what he was saying to me. So I liked that, that David thought of me as his friend.

Marci glanced up at me. "Now what are you daydreaming about?"

She was right. There I stood in the middle of the room staring at nothing. I opened my desk drawer and slid papers around until I found the one I wanted. Setting in next to Marci on her desk, I tapped it with my fingernail so she'd look at it. "That was David on the phone. The one who did this sketch of me."

"Clever. Really looks like you. What's he like?"

I started to describe him from a mental picture I had of him standing by the bridge in his jeans, his light brown hair and skin and sunny eyes all blending with his clothes, and I had to laugh. "He looks like my wardrobe," I pointed at my closet with its open door. "He's a blend of jungle pastels."

"Don't tell me you color code your boyfriends. Do it if you want to, just don't tell me about it."

And that is how my up day ended, with a phone call from David. The next day my bubble burst.

After my first morning class, I stopped back at Smith Hall to check my mail, in case my dad had sent me a check which I'd sort of hinted I could use in my last email to him, because my allowance had somehow run out.

Anyway, I opened my mailbox, hoping for money, and instead what I got was an official university envelope. Inside was a notice, one of those horrid computer printout things, that I was flunking lit.

They might as well have sprung open a trapdoor under my feet because that's what I felt like. My mind did a total blank and my heart pounded. I stumbled out of the building, automatically heading over to tennis, but not really thinking about where I was going.

Jon must have said hello to me three times before I realized he was walking beside me.

"Greta? Greta, is something wrong?"

Fighting back tears, I blurted, "I'm flunking lit! It says so right here!"

He took the slip of paper from my hand, studied it and said, "It's a warning notice but it doesn't mean you will positively fail."

"It doesn't?"

"No, it means you are on the edge at midterm."

"But what can I do?" I wailed.

Jon put his arm around my shoulders and gave me one of his warm hugs. "Come on, Greta, the world hasn't ended. Now calm down. What you do is you go talk to your lit prof after class, and have her go over your grades, and see exactly how far behind you are."

"Far enough to be flunking!"

"Sure, but if that's only for the first half of the semester, and you are simply borderline, find out what sort of grades you need to get yourself back to passing."

What Jon said made perfectly good sense, Jon always did, and by the time we finished talking, I was calm enough to go to tennis and anyway, if I was flunking lit, I didn't want to take any chances with any other classes.

As it turned out, I had my best day ever in tennis, because I was so upset I hit that stupid ball as though I was trying to annihilate it, and wound up with some terrific shots.

Afterwards I showered at the gym, I was that hot and steamy, and then headed back to the upper campus to grab lunch before facing my lit class. As I approached the bridge I wondered if David would be waiting for me again. If so, he'd certainly see me in one of my worst moods.

As I wasn't looking for a boyfriend, that was okay. I didn't want to impress him. I wanted him to listen to me complain and then say something funny. Or sympathetic. Or just stand there and grin. Any of the above would be better than being stuck with myself for company.

But he wasn't there.

I went on up to the Union building and through the main hallway and had almost reached the cafeteria when Rick hurried over to me, saying, "You're late."

As he hadn't said anything about meeting me for lunch, I couldn't figure what he was talking about.

"I've been waiting for you," he said, and then he gave me a close look and added, "What did you do to your hair?"

What I'd done was I'd stood under the gym shower and let it run over my head, and then I was so upset, still, about the lit notice that I'd forgotten to dry my hair. Until he mentioned it, I hadn't realized the ends were dripping all over my shirt.

"What am I late for?" If I sounded apologetic, it was because my self-confidence, like Samson's strength, was in my hair. When it was a mess, so was my personality, my intelligence, everything. All I could think about was how horrible I must look.

"I was expecting you earlier, that's all. We've got to hurry now so come on," Rick said, grabbing my arm.

"Where are we going?"

"We've got to go to the city library. I need some stuff."

"What's the we about? I can't go."

"Will you quit arguing and come on?" he said, pulling on me. His voice was low, so that only I could hear him, but I caught the impatience. There we stood in the middle of the corridor with waves of students pushing past us in both directions, and I suspected we looked weird, this wild-eyed guy glaring at this dripping girl.

"Rick, I have a class at two and I've barely got time to grab some lunch and I don't want to go without eating because I've got to think straight, I've got to talk to the prof after class--"

"Greta, cut your two o'clock. We'll get something to eat later."

"I can't cut my two o'clock!"

Rick glanced around, suddenly aware that we were in the middle of a crowd.

"Come on outside and I'll explain," he said.

I followed him out onto the long steps above the fountain, to a spot where we could across the length of the campus and see hundreds of people hurrying along the walkways, but we were out of earshot of any of them.

Rick gave me one of his gorgeous smiles, which only made me more aware of how awful I looked. "Honey, the thing is, I lost one of their stupid books, so now they won't let me check out anything until the book is returned, and I can't find it. But you can check books out, so I need you to come along and let me use your card."

"All right," I said, "I can go at four. I should be done talking to the prof by then."

"Greta, I need to get this stuff now."

"Yes, but Rick I got this notice--"

"And you're wasting time standing here arguing."

"Let me explain--"

"Greta, unless we get going I am not going to get done in time," he shouted, drowning me out, and I stood there staring at him, my mouth open, realizing that there was no way he was going to listen to my problems or care about them, even though he expected me to turn my world upside down for his, and maybe there were times when I'd have shrugged and said that's how guys are but this time I was already falling apart. I could not pull myself together enough to shrug off a snowflake, much less six feet of shouting male.

All I could manage was to shout back, "No!" and turn and run away from him and down the path to Smith and up the stairs to my room, all in a red-faced, sobbing blur.

When I reached my door I was crying so hard I couldn't find my key. I sank to the floor and sat with my back against the door and put my face down on my knees and let it all pour out. Fortunately, I was alone in the corridor. Anybody hearing me would have thought I was dying. Matter of fact, that's what I felt like.

Over and over in my mind I replayed that scene on the front steps, with Rick looking furious, his eyes narrowed, his hand gripping my arm so tightly that I felt bruised.

We'd had our fights, sure, but not like that. Before when we disagreed, he clammed up after a few angry words, then went off to sulk. But he'd never shouted like that, screaming me down, drowning out my replies, not giving me a chance to explain.

And he'd never grabbed me. Did he know how his fingers had dug into my flesh? Did he know he was hurting me?

I couldn't believe that he did.

He wouldn't hurt me, not on purpose.

When he calmed down, and he would in an hour or two, I would show him my failing notice. And then he would understand, wouldn't he?

Through the closed door, I heard the phone ringing. Fumbling through my pockets, I finally found my key, unlocked the door and grabbed the receiver off the wall hook, sure that it would be Rick, telling me how sorry he was.

Instead, it was Jon, and what he said was, "I've been thinking about that lit class. Are you feeling any better?"

"Oh sure," I said, but my voice wouldn't stay steady.

"Are you crying?"

"It's not just that, it's everything, I've had a big fight with Rick and oh-" My voice broke again. I stopped talking and rubbed at my eyes, trying to push away the tears.

Jon said, "Don't cry, it'll work out. Listen, I've been thinking, maybe you ought to drop that class and take it over next year."

I tried to think through the pounding in my head. "I'd lose all that time, five credits, and then, too, I've already paid for that class and it's too late to switch to something else."

"Yes, but if you're this upset about it, it isn't worth it."

"Oh, I don't know what to do!" I wailed. "But I can't drop a class, not without trying to pass it!"

"All right, there now, tell you what, if you want to go ahead, why don't you meet me and I'll go to the class with you and afterwards we can talk to your prof and there's bound to be a way to work this out."

When Jon said that, I had this weird flash memory of a time in second grade when I'd gotten in a fight on the playground. I'd hit another little girl in the face. She burst into tears and told the teacher. And the teacher said I couldn't go out on the playground at lunch hour anymore and I was so upset I cried all the way home. The next day my mother took me back to school and went in to talk to the teacher.

But I'd been six years old then.

I was eighteen now.

And yet Jon sounded exactly like my mother when she'd said, "Now, Greta, I'll go to school with you and we'll talk to the teacher and we'll work this out."

I bit my lip to stop it from quivering. Then I took a deep breath. And then I said into the phone, "Jon, you are a sweetheart, but I'm okay, really. I'll talk to you tomorrow."

And I said good-bye and hung up.

"Okay, Greta," I told myself, "glue your drippy self together." I washed my face, reapplied eye makeup, did a quick steam-curl of my hair ends, and though I still looked like Dracula's bride, I figured at least I looked like her on one of her better days.

That lit prof was going to be more interested in how well I could discuss my assignments than in how I looked. As I only had thirty more minutes until class, I decided I better run get some lunch because passing out while I talked to the prof probably wouldn't help my cause. Not with a woman prof.

I dashed back to my room from the bathroom, grabbed my notebook, pulled my door shut, locked it, and then saw the new addition to the door display.

With only a few lines, David had done his own unmistakable likeness sitting at a coffee shop booth under a clock that read four o'clock.

Underneath the cartoon was penciled, "If you're free."

CHAPTER 7

A horrible half an afternoon later, with my life still verging on the brink of disaster, I headed for the coffee shop. It was four-fifteen.

My lit prof had said that if I could do B level work for the rest of the semester, I could pull a low C.

Rick wasn't speaking to me.

The March sunshine had faded into a cold gray drizzle.

And the only smiling face in my life had probably given up and gone home fifteen minutes ago.

But no. Although the daffodils were bent double under the rain, and the fountain's basin was a shallow swamp of dead leaves, and the Union building's wide steps were deserted, and the corridors were slick with tracked-in mud, David Langford's smile remained sunshine bright.

As soon as I rounded the corner into the coffee shop, breathless with running, I saw him across the room at a far table, waving.

I filled a coffee cup from the machine, dropped my change at the cash register and headed for his table. Coffee sloshed over the rim onto my fingers. I let out a yelp.

David took the cup from me, set it on the table and said, "Hi."

"I'm sorry I'm late," I gasped. "I had to stop and talk to my lit prof, I am flunking that stupid course, and she says if I make a straight B for the rest of term I'll pass, but if I'm flunking now, how am I supposed to do that? Still, she could have said I didn't have any chance at all."

"That's true. So what will you do?"

"Well, I could drop the class."

"Uh-huh."

"And then I wouldn't have that failing grade on my record."

"Sure."

"Only I can't get my tuition back, so that's five hours I'd lose in money, and also, I'd be behind next year."

"That's a lot," he said.

"So what should I do?"

David leaned his chin on his fist and gazed thoughtfully at me. His eyes were the soft brown of coffee with cream in it and they really did have gold flecks. "I don't know, Greta. I think it's one of those things you have to decide for yourself."

"What would you do if you were me?"

"Oh. That's hard to say. I guess I'd figure out how much time I'd need to get the B, and then see if I really had that much time, and if I didn't, I'd drop it, and if I did have the time, I'd go for it."

"Is that what you'd do?"

"That's not what I said." He laughed, and his face lit up in that funny way. "You asked what I'd do if I were Greta. Greta is a sensible person, so if I were sensible Greta, that's what I'd do. Being me, I'd never think through all that stuff about the cost or being credits behind or keeping a failing grade off my record. I'd just muddle through and either pass or fail."

Let me tell you, boys have said many things to me. They've told me that I am pretty, funny, dumb, clever, sweet, spoiled, graceful, klutzy and lots more, but that was the first time one had ever said I was sensible.

It really went to my head.

I sat there in a state of numbness, staring back at him. He didn't seem to mind. He just kept gazing into my eyes.

When I found my wits, I blurted, "I never thought of myself as sensible!"

"How do you think of yourself?"

"I-I don't know!"

"I guess that's one of the most important purposes of college," he said, nodding. "I mean, not to lecture, or anything, but I've thought about that, sometimes wondered what I'm doing here, anyway, especially when I botch up a quiz."

"And what have you decided?"

"Are you sure you want to hear all this?"

"Sure, I do."

"See, I figure I'm here to learn about the world, and when I've done that, I'll be better able to know who I am and how I fit into the world."

"But you're so talented! You're an artist!"

"Maybe. I've drawn pictures for my family and friends and for school projects. So that makes me an artistic son, brother, friend and student. But none of that tells me what I'm supposed to do with my life as an adult."

"What do you want to do?" I asked.

"That's what I'm here to find out. And it isn't just what I want to do, because I know I want to do something with art, but it's who I want to be. Some days I feel really ambitious, like I want to charge into the commercial world and make a fortune, and other days I feel like I want to hide away on some island and create the sort of stuff nobody buys."

"Wasn't there some painter who did that, went off to an island?"

"Gauguin," he said.

"And he became very famous."

"All that solitude, he could concentrate on his art."

I had this sudden memory of color slides of Gauguin's work that an art teacher had shown us in high school. I exclaimed, "Solitude! His models were beautiful half naked island women!"

David sat back and let out a yelp of laughter. "Oh, Greta, I hadn't even thought about that!"

"Uh-huh, sure, tell me again about how you are going to spend your life on a deserted island painting skunk cabbages."

For the next hour we sat over our empty coffee cups, trying to sort out our identities and the meaning of life and a whole lot of other serious questions, which always turned into jokes, and by the time either of us thought of checking our watches to see what time it was, the cafeteria was opening for dinner.

We went through the line together, sat at a table with friends, finished and left together. Without really planning it, we wandered downstairs to the game room area, where there are pinball machines and video games and a couple of pool tables.

We emptied our pockets of change. I had two quarters and David had three. It took us about ten minutes to lose our whole combined fortunes in a game machine, that's how talented we both were.

We could hear music from the sound system blaring through the open arch to the rec room, a space at the end of the lower corridor with a dance floor surrounded by booths. It was sort of the on-campus hangout, and anybody who was bored drifted through it at least once an evening to try to spot friends.

Not that we were bored, we weren't, or at least, I wasn't. We wandered through the archway and melted into the group of dancers. I don't think either of us said a word about dancing to the other. It just happened.

David did some quick dance steps. I imitated him, arm-shrugs and all. He saw that I was imitating and laughed. And then we faced each other and started doing our own interpretations of the music.

At first we were moving fast, swinging around each other, really going. Sometimes we were hardly together at all, then we'd spin and face each other, and occasionally we'd grasp hands in a fast turn. But then the music did a skidding stop and switched to a slow, moody beat and I just naturally moved into David's arms.

Right away I liked the way he held me. Some guys kind of grab and hang on, as though they're afraid you'll fall down without their support, their arms rigid, their hands tight. And some barely touch you, so that you have to guess what step they're doing, because they don't give any lead.

With David, his arms felt just right. I knew what he was doing. We were perfectly in step and when I looked at him he was looking at me and smiling back.

If anybody had asked me at that moment whether or not I could ace that lit course, I'd have said, "Of course I can." That's how comfortable and happy I felt inside.

And then David said, "I hate to say this, but I've still got to hit the books tonight."

"Aargh. You're right. I am not going to raise my lit grades by hanging around here."

We picked up our notebooks from where we'd dropped them on the table by the door and headed outdoors into the shimmering curtains of spring rain. The sky was dark and the rain formed silver halos around every walkway lamp. We ducked our heads and made a dash for Smith Hall.

At the entrance, David said, "Tomorrow?"

And I said, "Same everything?"

And he grinned, waved, then turned and ran toward his own dorm building, across campus. We both knew we meant we'd meet at four in the coffee shop.

I hummed my way upstairs, wandered through the open door of my room, said hi to Marci who was busy working at her desk and then got a look at myself in the mirror.

If I'd looked like Dracula's bride when I left the room around noon, now I looked even worse. I let out a shriek.

Marci asked, "What's wrong?"

"Look at me! My hair's flunked! My makeup's expired!"

"There's a wastebasket in the corner, if you want to throw yourself away," she said.

"I've been like this all afternoon!"

"No wonder no talent scout spotted you."

"Marci, this is no joke," I wailed. "I have been like this the whole entire time I was with David!"

"How long were you with David?" She looked up from her books to study me.

"Since four o'clock! All through supper! And after, at the rec room!

And I looked like this!"

"Did you have him on a leash?"

"Huh?"

"Presumably he could leave, if he was too shocked by your appearance. Is this the David who did that drawing?"

I sighed and sank down on my bed, unable to look at my reflection any longer. When I am a mess, my ego collapses and so does my backbone.

I tried to think of how to explain that to Marci, but I couldn't. Marci looked the same all the time, neat, pretty, with naturally wavy hair and big dark eyes, and though she could look like a model if she wanted to spend the time on fixing up, she was perfectly happy going around with her basic self showing. There's no way to explain to people like that what it's like to become less than nobody every time your hair goes limp.

Besides, she was right. It didn't seem to matter to David how I looked. And as I wasn't trying to impress David, it shouldn't matter to me. It wasn't as though I'd been with Rick.

I said, "I don't suppose Rick phoned?"

"Not since I've been here."

I shrugged and collapsed back on my bed, swinging my legs up against the wall, which is supposed to send blood rushing to the head and improve the complexion, or something like that. "He'll probably never call again."

"Oh? Had a fight?"

"I think it was more like a war."

"You two will make up. You always do."

"Do we? I guess so. Only, I've never seen him this mad. Maybe I ought to call him and tell him I'm sorry."

"Was it your fault?" Marci asked.

"I didn't think so at the time, but I suppose maybe it was. I was so busy worrying about my problems, I couldn't help him with his."

"You can't always help everybody."

"But I could have explained why I couldn't help."

Marci stopped working on her computer and swung around in her chair to look at me. I stared back upside down, from where my head was hanging over the edge of the bed. "Greta, if you are going to fret over it all night, why don't you simply phone Rick now and get it over with?"

I couldn't think of any argument for that suggestion, short of admitting that I was a coward.

The worst that could happen would be that Rick was still in a shouting mood. And that's not so bad, over the phone. I could always hold the phone at arm's length.

Getting up from the bed, I said okay to Marci, took the wall phone off the hook and punched in his room number. When his roommate answered, I asked for Rick. The roommate said just a sec, and I ended up waiting eons.

As it is embarrassing to have your roommate know how long your boyfriend keeps you waiting, I rounded the corner of our door and sat down on the floor of the hallway, which was as far as the phone cord reached, and which we both did occasionally when we didn't want to disturb each other with talking. We didn't do it much for privacy. After six months of sharing a room, we didn't have secrets.

Rick finally answered.

"It's me," I said. "I've been worrying about if you were able to get that book all right that you needed."

"I got it."

"Oh, because otherwise I could get it for you tomorrow, only, see, today I had to talk to my lit prof. It was really important. I got this notice in the mail." I wasn't explaining myself well. Somehow, when I talked to Rick, my words jumbled and I had an awful time saying what I meant. He made me that nervous. Even as I was talking, my fingers tightened around the receiver until my knuckles whitened.

"It doesn't matter now," he said. "Leanne Chase went with me and checked out the stuff I needed."

Leanne Chase was this gorgeous girl with blue-black hair and a fabulous figure, a tiny girl who barely came up to Rick's chin. Her room was on the third floor of Smith.

"I didn't know you knew Leanne," I said.

"I know her."

"Oh. Well, that was nice of her. Checking out the books for you, I mean."

"Greta, I've got a lot of studying to do. Did you want something?"

After a put-down like that, there wasn't much I could say except, "No, I guess not."

He hung up. Flat. No good-bye, nothing.

I stared at the phone, considered smashing it against the wall, remembered that it was university property and also was used by my roommate.

As I hung the receiver back on its hook, Marci said, "They're showing a sci-fi movie in the lounge in about three minutes. Want to go?"

"No." I stared at the wall so that she couldn't see the tears I could feel burning at my eyes. "I've got some reading to do."

"Everything okay with Rick?"

"Sure, fine." I did this award-winning job of keeping my voice cheerful. "It's all straightened out."

"That's good. See you later."

I held in the tears until she was gone. Then I closed our room door, dived for my bed and pulled my blanket over my head. Huddled beneath the covers, with the world shut out, I prepared for my second major crying jag in one day.

My head ached, my throat ached, my heart ached, but the tears wouldn't come. Mixed in with all my misery over Rick was this expanding fury. I mean, it was rising inside me like milk in a pan on the stove when the heat's set too high. It went right through simmer to scald to boiling over, I was that furious, and two minutes earlier I hadn't even known I was angry.

Throwing off the covers, I paced around my room like some crazy person. I wanted everything out of there that reminded me of Rick. He was not going to put me down that way. I was not going to let him ruin my life.

Digging through my sweater drawer, I found the ribbon from the corsage he gave me for the Valentine Dance. I crumpled it up, pretending it was Rick himself, and tossed it in the wastebasket.

Taped to my mirror was a heart he once drew on a piece of notebook paper. In its center he'd written our initials. Wham, into the basket with the ribbon.

In my desk drawer were some candy wrappers from one rainy afternoon when he'd come over to study with me. Crumple! Wham!

And a dried-up ballpoint that he'd left behind and I'd kept because it was his, and the empty plastic case from a CD he'd loaned me, and ticket stubs from a movie, and a paper napkin from a restaurant, and even an empty paper tube from a drinking straw.

How could I ever have been stupid enough to treasure such junk?

I'd even stuck into my wall a couple of thumb tacks that he'd emptied out of his pocket once, muttering something about having used them on a bulletin board. I'd treasured them because Rick's very own thumb had pressed against them.

Was there another girl in the whole world as stupid as me?

Why would anyone make such a fool of herself over a guy for no other reason than because he looked like a TV star?

And he did.

He not only looked like a TV star, with his marvelous profile and his deep dark eyes and his thick hair and his hunk build, he even sounded like one. All he had to do was say my name and I was head-to-toe goosebumps.

For one awful moment, I very nearly dug all that junk out of the wastebasket.

Now let me tell you what friends are for. Friends are for showing up when you most need them, even though they don't know that's what they're doing. And that's what happened.

They banged on my door and shouted for me.

I wiped at my hot, dry eyes, pushed my limp hair around to no purpose as it would take far more than a push to make it presentable, and opened the door to Allison and Inger.

Inger said, "Hey, Greta, want to be on the decorating committee for the April Fool Party?"

"Oh, I don't know." My mind was on Rick.

"Too bad," Inger said, "because we already volunteered you."

"Lynne Belmont set up the committee assignments, and freshmen are in charge of painting a mural," Allison added.

Lynne was hospitality hostess for Smith Hall. She was a senior, lived on first floor and took her job very seriously.

"What sort of mural?" I asked.

"The party theme is an Hawaiian luau, so there's supposed to be a big paper mural on the back wall of the lounge that looks Hawaiian. Palm trees, sunshine, like that."

"I can't draw."

"Who can? It doesn't have to be a masterpiece, just a big splash of color," Inger explained. "Come on, say you'll help. At least come on down to the lounge now. We're having a committee meeting to plan the mural."

I followed them down the hallway, through the second-floor door to the balcony. From there we could see the far side of the room with the screen backed up to the window and the circle of couches filled with people watching a noisy space-odyssey show. Clumping down the stairs, we stood beneath the balcony, staring at the empty wall, waiting for someone else in the crowd of volunteers to come up with a brilliant suggestion for a mural.

"Maybe we should measure the wall and figure out how much paper it takes to cover it," Allison said.

"Do we paint the paper before we hang it or after?" Inger asked.

"Unless we've got an artist in the crowd, it probably won't make much difference."

Someone else said, "Anyone can paint a palm tree."

"Yeah, but can anyone else tell it's a palm tree?" Inger asked.

We joked back and forth about the design, not getting much accomplished other than to agree that the wall needed color. The meeting reminded me of committees I'd been on in high school. We'd talk for days without getting anything done, and then the day of the party, everyone would wander around staring at the place where the project was supposed to be, argue over who was supposed to have done what and then start in working at the last possible moment and somehow put it all together, finishing up as the first guest arrived.

"Are you wearing a costume?" someone asked.

And the conversation broke into parts, with Allison and Inger talking wall design, several people discussing what to wear and, behind me, a couple of girls talking about who they planned to ask.

The party was a week off. By then Rick would be speaking to me again. Maybe by then I'd be speaking to him. I was so torn up over the way he behaved, I kept going back and forth in my mind, one minute thinking I never wanted to see him again, the next hoping he'd phone in the morning and say everything was okay.

One of the voices behind me said, "He keeps following me around, so I suppose I could ask him, but if I do, then he'll think I like him and I'll never get rid of him, will I?"

"Do you want to get rid of him?" the other voice asked.

"What if Harry calls? Then I'd be in a mess, if he was hanging around."

"Do you think Harry will call?"

"I don't know. He said he would. And if he does, I'd want to ask him to the party, but if he doesn't, I don't want to be stuck without a date. What about you?"

"I sort of thought, well, there's this guy I like, only I thought he was going with someone else. But then today he asked me to go someplace with him."

"He asked you out?"

"Not a date, really, he wanted me to do him a favor, which was okay, but I figured that's all it was, only then this evening he phoned. He didn't ask me out exactly, but he asked about my class schedule and said he'd see me at lunch."

"Sounds like he's trying to work up to asking you out."

Would you believe that at that point, I almost turned around and told that girl that of course the boy wanted to ask her out, that he was probably shy and that's how shy boys acted. I almost did because that's what a big know-it-all I am about guys, Greta the Expert, forever passing out advice, asked-for or not.

And then she said, "Maybe you're right. I guess I will ask Rick. The worst that can happen..." she went on saying, but I didn't hear the rest.

I was too busy turning very slowly to catch a glimpse over my shoulder without letting her know I was looking to see who she was, and the whole time I was doing this spy maneuver, I was thinking, there must be a million guys named Rick.

That's what I was thinking. I was also thinking, because, unfortunately, the human brain is capable of multitasking, that I knew without looking who she was.

Which meant that I also knew that although every third boy on campus might be named Rick, she was talking about my Rick.

And I was right.

Behind me, talking away to her friend, her face ducked forward so that her blue-black hair half hid it, was Leanne Chase.

And my Rick was planning to meet her for lunch the very next day.

Oh, he was a great one for memorizing schedules and meeting girls for lunch, I wanted to say out loud. Cheap date, that, meeting at the cafeteria, and a sure way to keep track so that she'd be handy whenever he needed an errand run for him and why had it taken me so long to figure him out?

Who knew him better than me? But I didn't dare open my mouth.

I'd never be able to keep my voice friendly and controlled. Instead, I melted my way through the crowd and did my silent disappearing act until I was safely in my room with the door closed where I could kick the wall.

CHAPTER 8

Smith Hall's April Fool Party was a campus tradition. It had the reputation of being one of the best dorm parties of the year. To attend, you had to be invited as the guest of a Smith Hall resident, and as Smith was a women's dorm, it was a girls-ask-the-guys party.

All of the dorms gave parties at one time or other during the year. And all of the parties were popular, but many of them were little more than open houses, with refreshments set up in students' rooms, as well as games and dancing and movies. People wandered through the corridors from room to room. Very informal and unplanned.

None of that stuff for Smith Hall, probably the best-organized dorm on campus, maybe because it was the women's dorm. We had officers and committees and subcommittees and planning councils, and when a committee wasn't putting up decorations, they were taking them down.

I'm not sure if this was always Smith Hall's style, but certainly the hall had never missed decorating for a season or holiday since Lynne Belmont, our current hall president, moved in, and she'd been living in Smith since her freshman year. This was her senior year.

Lynne Belmont wasn't one of my favorite people. Sure, I tried to like everyone, but some people were harder to like than others.

Marci said I was unfair about Lynne and probably Marci was right, but to explain my side I need to describe what happened the morning after I overheard that rotten conversation between Leanne and her friend.

After a wretched, sleepless night, I knocked my radio alarm clock on the floor turning it off. As I grabbed to catch it, I was so entangled in my sheets that I fell out of bed.

From under her covers, Marci mumbled, "You okay?"

I mumbled back that I was. Then I lay on the floor until I could rouse myself enough to unwind from the blankets. Staggering to my feet, I tried to right the radio, dropped it a second time and decided to let that go until later. Grabbing my towel and washcloth and soap and toothpaste and toothbrush, which I did by feeling my way around the room and jamming the smaller items into the pocket of my pajama top, I fumbled my way through the door and groped along the hall toward the bathroom.

My eyes were narrow slits, through which I could barely make out shapes of light and shadow, and that's all the way they would open.

My mind remained asleep.

Into all this bleakness soared a cheerful, bright voice, singing out, "Greta, I am so pleased you agreed to be on the decorating committee! I know you've been too busy to do committee assignments before, but I do think everyone should work on at least one committee, just for the experience, and I know you will be wonderful!"

Uh-huh, it was Lynne Belmont.

I tilted my head to improve my vision through the slits. Lynne looked as perfect as she sounded. She had all her makeup done, her hair curled and she was neatly dressed in a knockout outfit by six-thirty in the morning.

I managed to croak, "Sure, right."

She said, "You're in a hurry so I won't keep you now, but I did want to tell you how delighted I am to have you on our party committee."

Maybe I would have been more receptive to Lynne's enthusiasm if I'd had any reason to look forward to the party. Instead, I'd spent a night drifting through confused nightmares of myself crouched on the balcony peering down through the banister at Rick and Leanne, standing below me in a dimly lit lounge, their arms wrapped around each other.

Was she really going to ask Rick to the dance?

My head ached at the thought. Stepping into the shower, I let it go full blast. For sure it woke me up. And as soon as I was awake, I realized I'd forgotten to bring my robe, which meant I had to put my pajamas back on to return to my room, which put me a couple more minutes behind schedule.

Back in the room, I dressed and set to work on my hair. Sometimes that's my best thinking time, staring at myself in the mirror while I hold the dryer. Today all I could see was tall, skinny me, too pale to notice, with huge pores and invisible eyelashes. Leanne was my opposite, small and dark and curvy, with huge eyes and invisible pores.

Maybe I should phone Rick immediately and ask him to the party before Leanne could.

But then, if she asked him later in the day, would he be sorry he'd accepted my invitation?

Or would he say no to me to start with, counting on Leanne asking him? What I knew about that boy for certain was that he never doubted his own killer charm.

I wanted to die or scream or kick something. Instead, I kept right on putting myself together. And my thoughts went right on stirring through every remembered conversation, trying to sort things out.

Leanne said that Rick was waiting around for her. That meant he was interested in her. So even if he went to the party with me, he'd be wishing he was with her.

Or was I being foolish in my jealousy? Maybe he wasn't the least bit attracted to her and had only used her to get those dumb library books checked out.

By the time I headed over to the Union building for breakfast, I hadn't solved a thing. I still was totally confused.

Inger waved me over to her table as I went through the cafeteria line, pointing to an empty chair. The cafeteria was always quiet at breakfast. It was more than half-empty, and the people who did make it to breakfast didn't look awake.

Inger leaned toward me and said, "Where did you disappear to last night?"

"Sorry, I had to leave."

"Greta, you won't drop off the committee?"

"Too late for that." I told her about my morning encounter with Lynne.

Inger said, "It'll be a great party and you'll be glad you helped."

"I don't mind helping. But I'm not sure if I'll go to the party."

"How come?"

If she hadn't asked, I wouldn't have said a word, but as she had, I blurted out what I'd heard Leanne say.

Inger said, "That's not like you! Where's the girl who isn't going to let a guy push her around?"

"He's not pushing me. He's ignoring me."

"So you have to let him know you have your own life and that you don't care!"

"I hate it when people give me back my own advice and I can't follow it."

"Why can't you?"

"What am I supposed to do? If I ask him and he turns me down, I'll feel rotten, and if I ask and he says yes, I'll worry that he'd rather go with her."

"Why not ask someone else to the party?"

"And then what if he's really waiting for me to ask him and has no intention of going with Leanne? That'd end us for sure."

Inger frowned, a deep crease forming between her eyebrows. "Sorry. Wish I could help you."

"Don't you let it wreck your day. Mine's already shot, so I might as well keep it my problem."

"Wait a minute, tell you what I could do," she said slowly. "I'll see Leanne sometime today, or if I don't, I'll make it a point to find her this evening, and I'll ask her who she's invited to the party. Then I'll let you know."

We finished breakfast, carried our trays to the clean-up counter, said so long and headed for our morning classes. As I walked toward my nine o'clock, Jon fell into step beside me. I smiled up at him. It wouldn't do to let Jon see that I was worried. He'd feel required to give me a long pep talk and I didn't have time for that.

"Have you made a decision about your lit class?" he asked.

"I talked to the prof like you suggested and I think I can pass if I really work at it."

"Good," he said. "Now what you need to do is set up a regular study schedule. Allow a set time every day. I'm pretty good at lit. I can drill you for quizzes. And I know a couple of guys who are English majors. They can go over your papers."

Why did Jon remind me more and more of my mother? I said, "You're an angel, you really are. But there are some lit majors in my dorm. They'll help me."

"All right, but you know you can call me. Any time."

"I will if I need to," I said, blew him a kiss and turned and fled toward my classroom building before Jon could organize me any further.

At noon I ran into Marci and Allison in the cafeteria lunch line. Allison said, "I don't have anything Hawaiian to wear to the party."

"What! No grass skirt in your wardrobe?"

"How about beach gear?" Marci said, ever practical. "I figure I'll wear a bright T-shirt, white shorts, sandals."

"That sounds okay," Allison said, adding, "I guess we know what Greta will wear?"

"What?" I asked, having no idea what she had in mind as I hadn't given it a thought. I was too busy wondering if I was even going to be attending the party and with whom.

"Jungle pastels," she said and giggled.

"Maybe you could wear a bikini, clunky jewelry, back-comb your hair into a mop and go as a Frazetta poster," Marci said.

"I could take my tray and go eat my lunch alone in a corner. Then you two would be free to continue making hilarious jokes at my expense."

"You don't have to leave. We'll make jokes about you in front of you," Allison said.

"What else are friends for?" Marci added.

And then Allison said, "Mark wants us to wear matching outfits for the party. Would that be all right?" which explained her cheerful mood.

Even though my own love life was in tatters, I was happy for Allison. Besides, maybe I was wrong. Maybe Inger would find out that Leanne had asked Rick and he'd turned her down, never having had any intention of going with anyone but me.

I hung onto that positive thought right through lunch.

Inger hailed me on the way to my two o'clock, standing above me on the upper path. When I turned back and started up the slope, she ran toward me.

Out of breath, she gasped, "Can't stop, I'm late, but I did ask Leanne when I saw her this morning and I hate to tell you this but I might as well get it over with. She phoned Rick last night. Must have done it right after you heard her."

From Inger's expression I knew what it was she didn't want to tell me. "So he's going with her."

Hands on hips, Inger put on her determined expression. "Now, Greta, it's no good throwing your heart after some guy who's not worth it."

"Maybe he's worth it," I blurted.

"Stop that! Shape up! Shoulders back! Go ask someone else!" she shouted.

At least we were outdoors on a side path, shielded from the main walkways by the shrubberies. I could have run into her in the cafeteria and had her straighten out my life at the top of her lungs in front of the whole student body.

I mumbled, "Yeah, well, thanks for finding out."

As I headed away from her toward my lit class, she called after me,

"It's what you'd tell me to do!"

True. And that's the whole trouble with advice. It's easier to hand out than to follow.

I'd have gone off somewhere alone to feel sorry for myself if my next class hadn't been lit. Flunking lit would not only not get Rick back for me, it would remove me from college and from any hope of seeing him again.

After lit class I remained at my desk, copying some authors and titles the prof had written on the blackboard. By the time I finished, I was alone in the room. Flipping through my notebook, I began to see what Jon meant about putting things in order. My lecture notes were a jumble, having no chronology. Authors' names were scattered. If I went over each name with my highlighter, I could then go back and organize my notes. Highlighting away, I was surprised when a janitor came into the room.

"Hi," I said in answer to his nod. Glancing at my watch, I saw that it was four-ten. And then I remembered that I'd promised to meet David at four.

Once again I'd totally forgotten I'd made plans to meet David, which is one of those things I am always telling girls not to do. Guys have a lot of attitude when it comes to being forgotten.

And only a day ago I'd had such a wonderful time with him.

Yes, but that was back when Rick was my boyfriend and I thought our fight was temporary like all the others. That was back when David was simply a friend to get me through a difficult afternoon.

And that's what he'd done. For a few hours I'd forgotten about Rick and had a good time. Standing David up now was hardly the way to treat a friend.

Gathering up my books, I raced across the campus to the Union building's coffee shop. If he'd given up and gone off without me, I wouldn't have been surprised.

But he hadn't. He was waiting.

I slid into the chair across from him, propped my elbows on the formica table top, waited a second for my breathing to slow and blurted out, "I'm sorry, honestly, I stayed to take some notes and I'm really going to have to spend the rest of today studying, I'm so much behind."

David did a slow smile, like I was the best thing in his day. Even his eyes smiled. "Hi, Greta."

"Hi, David," I said. I'd meant to apologize further for keeping him waiting. It wasn't necessary. Without his saying anything else, I knew that. He understood why I was late.

He said, "I should be working on my botany charts. It's nice out. You want to go down to the bridge with me? Can you study there?"

"That's maybe the quietest place on campus," I said.

On the dash from my classroom to the coffee shop I'd had time to think about David.

What I'd thought was this: I was letting David become more than just another guy to be seen eating lunch with. I was letting him think of me as a possible girlfriend rather than just a friend. In no time he'd be like Jon, waiting for me, following me around, telling me how to run my life. I didn't need another guy waiting around for me to change my mind about Rick.

So why did I agree to study with David? I wish I knew. Tossing away my good intentions, I picked up my books, went by the service counter with him to pick up a couple of milkshakes in cartons, and then headed down the path to the grassy area on the far side of the bridge.

David was right. It was nice out. I hadn't even noticed what the day was like, I'd been so busy with my other worries, until we wandered along the stream's edge for a few yards, out of sight from the path, and found a soft patch of sun-warmed grass beneath an alder. The tree trunk shone dappled silver in the sunlight that filtered through its shimmering new leaves.

"How's this? Quiet enough? Go ahead and study. I won't bother you," he said.

That wasn't exactly true.

I spread out my papers around me, poked the straw through the hole in the milkshake container lid, and settled to the job of organizing my notes. Beside me David stretched out on his stomach, propped himself up on his elbows, and concentrated on his open notebook of botany charts.

Sorry, but it was not easy to sit next to a guy who was all stretched out with sun and shadows shifting across his jeans and shirt, and then there was that golden brown hair and most guys don't use conditioners and they don't backcomb and being a hair freak, I kept wanting to touch his hair to find out if it was as soft as it looked.

The sun warmed the top of my head.

David shifted position beside me. I didn't need to look at him to know that. Even though there was space between us, I could feel him moving.

The authors' names overlapped each other in a confused chronology. I frowned at them and kept working.

David rolled over onto his back and gazed up at me, the sun in his face. He raised his arm to shield his eyes and squinted through the narrow shadow. "Have you ever taken any botany classes?"

"No. Hit a problem?"

"Have I ever!"

"Sorry," I said. "I don't suppose you've taken Lit 103?"

"Nope. We're equally useless to each other as tutors."

Having determined that, David sat up, pulled his notebook onto his knees, and bent over it, his forehead drawn into frown lines of concentration.

"How are your other classes going?" I asked.

"Shh," he said, not really at me, but at the whole world, staring at his book. Something had begun to make sense to him and he didn't want to lose the thought.

I returned to my own confusing notes, rearranging pages and recopying information that was out of order. And at about the point that I was sure it would never make sense, something snapped into place and I saw how the chronology affected the writers' works and why that was important.

And I think David said something and I know I said shhh at him and twenty minutes later I looked at him and laughed and shouted, "I've got it!"

"Got what?"

"The whole point of the lectures! Now I see what I was doing wrong on the quizzes and on my last paper!"

"That's great."

"This place must be inspirational!" I cried, waving my arms at the marvelous bright blue sky.

"In that case, I'd better do all my studying here," he said.

"I'm sure you're on the verge of inspiration."

"Know what? Glimmers of comprehension work up terrible appetites and the cafeteria opened for dinner a half hour ago."

"Why didn't you say so?"

"I did, half an hour ago, but you were wavering on that verge you mentioned and I didn't want to interrupt."

How had I gone from wanting to touch his hair to getting so lost in my reading I forgot he was next to me?

As we gathered up our books and headed for the cafeteria, I said, "That's sweet, a guy who'll silently suffer through hunger pangs for me."

"That's my How-to-Attract-a-Woman Technique Number Three," he said.

"What is?" I stopped in the path to stare at him.

"Suffering through hunger pangs. Creates a real martyr image."

"Martyr? Were martyrs interested in women? Weren't martyrs a bunch of guys for died for their beliefs?"

"Cross that out. Let's see, would suffering bring out the mother instinct in a woman?"

"It might in my mother. Not in me."

"Maybe I'd do best to toss out Technique Three altogether."

"Well," I said slowly, "I do find it attractive so it must have some value."

"Care to analyze that?"

"All right, I guess what I appreciate is your patience rather than your hunger."

"Ah! So that's the secret! Maybe that should be my Technique One, display inordinate amounts of patience!"

Realizing how accurately that rule applied to any guy who wanted to impress me, I giggled. "Definitely Technique One with girls who are always late."

"Are you always late?"

"I don't mean to be. Do you always conduct your relationships according to a list of techniques?"

I had another peculiar flash of insight. Was it possible he was a male version of me? Because I was always figuring ways for the girls in the dorm to attract boyfriends, even though my methods hadn't been completely successful for myself.

"You're my trial run," he said.

"What! I'm some sort of experiment?"

He stopped dead still. "No, of course not!"

I'd been teasing but David looked honestly worried, as though he really believed I thought he was using me to practice his attracting-women techniques.

Continuing up the path, I left David behind. A few seconds later, he ran to catch up with me.

Then I said, "I understand perfectly, Mr. Langford. I am your late afternoon guinea pig. No doubt you also have a morning subject and a late evening subject and maybe even a noon subject."

"Greta!" he tried to interrupt.

"What did you say your university major is?" I continued. "Psychology? Women's Studies? Or just women?"

"Greta," he said, flatly, no question mark, no explanation point.

"Greta what?" I stopped walking, because he'd put his hand on my arm to stop me.

"That's what I'd like to major in. You."

A comment like that is very hard to answer, especially when it is said in a low, serious voice. Add to that this nice, solemn face, with warm brown eyes gazing at me in a terribly sincere manner. What could I do?

If I made another joke, I was afraid he'd be hurt and it would show all over his face and I'd feel about two inches high.

So instead I gazed right back and said, "David, would you like to go to the Smith Hall April Fool Party with me?"

CHAPTER 9

It took me the next three days to decide what to wear to the April Fool Party. I don't mean that I actually stood in front of my closet grabbing out handfuls of clothes and spreading them on my bed, trying to decide. That's my thirty-minutes-before-time-to-go approach.

I went to my classes and did my assignments and carried out all the other routines of my life.

But nagging at the back of my mind, and popping into the front of it whenever I wasn't actively thinking of something else, was the question, What to wear?

And so naturally it became the main conversation topic with the other girls in the dorm. They brought it up as often as I did.

Inger, who is clever with her hands, put together a grass skirt of crepe paper streamers and made a lei to match.

When she showed it to us, standing in her room and wearing it over shorts and a red halter top, Allison wailed, "If I made one of those things, about halfway through the party the streamers would fall out."

"That's one way to hold Mark's attention," Inger said. She turned in front of her mirror, checking the effect. The skirt did a super job of showing off her long legs.

Unhooking the grass skirt, she held it out to me. "Let's see how it looks on you, Greta."

I fastened it on over my shorts. The effect was not the same. I said, "Inger, if I had your legs, I'd stay up all night putting one of these things together. But face it, the way it looks on me, it's not worth the bother."

After I'd removed the skirt, I held it out to Allison. She shook her head and pushed nervously at her pale hair with her fingers. "No, I don't think so. What I'd like is a sarong. you think I could wrap a peasant skirt into a sarong?"

"Get your skirt and let's see," Inger said.

When Allison left to run down the hall to her room, Inger said to me, "I'm glad you asked another guy. No way should you let Rick think you'll wait around for him while he dates other girls."

"I didn't ask David to make Rick jealous."

"Didn't you?"

"No. Honestly. David's nice, I enjoy being with him and I figure he'll like the party."

"That the only reason?"

I said firmly, "He is not my type because as you and I both know, I am only attracted to bums and creeps."

Allison came back dragging her skirt, which could not be turned into a sarong, so then Inger pulled the navy blue sheet off Marci's bed and wrapped that around Allison.

Standing in front of the mirror, looking at herself, Allison said, "A sarong might work."

Inger said, "Try it on Greta."

The two of them draped the sheet around me. It did about as much for me as the grass skirt had done.

"This isn't right, either. I never wear navy," I said.

"Oh, you!" Inger laughed. We already know what you'll wear. Some combination of jungle pastels!"

So of course my subconscious kept nagging at me to think of something different to wear.

By the Friday before the party I still hadn't made any decision. And Friday night, I didn't have time. Allison and Inger and Marci and I spent the first half of the night standing around listening to everyone argue about what to paint on the backdrop and the other half of the night hanging the paper and painting, naturally, palm trees and a sunset.

But at least everyone had their say.

We trudged off to bed at three A.M., stiff and paint-covered. We did manage to pull off our stained shirts and jeans before getting into our beds, but that was all.

"If we don't wash our faces, they'll fall off," I muttered to Marci.

From her bed across the room, she muttered back, "Let them fall."

I spent a good half minute seriously thinking about getting up and going down the hall to the showers, and wondering how much permanent damage my complexion would suffer from missing one night's washing. My face lost. Shutting out my terribly guilty conscience, I pulled my covers over my head and went to sleep.

But I made up for it Saturday. I spent most of the morning in the shower. Actually, that's an exaggeration, but it was what Marci said when I finally returned to our room in my bathrobe, my hair dripping.

"You've been in the shower all morning," she said.

"It takes some of us longer to get beautiful," I said.

"Have you decided what to wear tonight?"

Shaking my head, I stood in front of my open closet door. Nothing looked Hawaiian. I pulled clothes from their hangers and spread them around the room, trying to match up something. I must have done a lot of mumbling, because Marci finally said, "Really, you can wear anything casual. It's not a costume party."

"Everyone else will be going Hawaiian. I'll be going plain Greta."

"You need a confidence boost? You want me to tell you that you never look plain?"

Staring at my freshly scrubbed, unmade-up face and my straight wet hair in the mirror, I said, "Please do. Nobody will hold a white lie against you."

What I finally did, after spending most of the day setting my hair and doing my nails and taking a boring study break to review for Monday's quiz, was dress Greta style. Maybe not plain Greta, but definitely Greta. I decided that if I didn't look good in a Hawaiian costume, I might as well wear something in which I did look good, otherwise it would be a monumental waste of all that hair spray and nail polish and lip gloss.

Not that the decision was easy. First I pulled on jeans and a T-shirt and my leather jacket with the studs.

Marci said, "You'll pass out from the heat in that."

I dropped the jacket and shirt on the floor and pulled on a sweatshirt that has a big lion's face printed on the front of it.

Marci'd disappeared so I stepped out into the hallway to find her.

Somebody let out a shriek, but then, people were always shrieking so I didn't think too much of it, and then Inger dashed toward me shouting, "Greta, help, come on!" and dragged me back into my room.

"What's the matter?"

"My eyebrows won't work! I want them thick and dark, to look really good, and I have these false eyelashes but I can't make them stick!"

"Let me see them."

"Wait here, I'll get them."

"Listen, what do you think of this shirt?"

"Lions in Hawaii?" she said, and dashed out.

I changed to a flowered shirt while she found her eyelashes. When she returned, I put them on for her and did her eyebrows.

"That shirt is better," she said.

"Think so? I dunno, my mother sent it to me and I guess it's okay but I've never worn it because I'm not real crazy about it." I started to follow Inger into the corridor.

She practically knocked me over, spinning around and shoving me back into my room, saying, "You're right! You are! I can see that now! That shirt is not you! Find something else."

Next I tried on a yellow cotton knit top with my tan shorts. Turning in front of the mirror, I thought maybe that combination was too casual for a party. Totally confused, I headed out of my room again to look for Marci. When I couldn't see her in the hall, I thought she might be in Allison's room.

I knocked on Allison's door. Allison started to throw it open, then pushed it closed, practically catching me in it, and peered at me through the crack.

"What do you want?" she said, which made me feel like I might be carrying some plague.

"I just wanted to ask what you thought of this outfit."

"Oh!" She looked really startled, almost guilty, as though she were hiding something in her room. She blurted, "Uh, yeah, no, looks like you're going to play tennis."

"Umm, that's what I was afraid of."

"Find something else," she said, and closed her door.

Heading back to my room, I bumped into Inger dragging a laundry bag down the hall.

"Why are you doing laundry now?" I asked. "There isn't time."

"Oh, I'm in no hurry, I don't have a date for the party, anyway, so it doesn't matter if I'm late."

And then Marci popped out of Inger's room, said, "Greta, you'll never be ready if you don't hurry up," and practically dragged me back to our room.

So I went back and changed one more time.

I wore my favorite khakis, the ones with the brass snaps on the pockets plus heavy ankle zippers. And my beige mesh shirt. And my pale gold silk scarf. And my extra-long bead-and-copper earrings.

Marci said, "I hope you're completely satisfied with that outfit now."

I spun to face her, my atomizer of gardenia cologne in my hand. "Is it too terrible?"

"It is wonderful," she said.

"You're the one who looks wonderful." She did in her red shirt and white shorts. They showed off her great legs.

She assured me, "You look fine. And if you take one more thing out, I won't be able to find the door."

Half the contents of my closet and drawers were strewn across both beds and chairs. I let out a shriek of shock, because, honestly, I hadn't realized I'd pulled out that much of my stuff. Racing around the room,

I jammed stuff back into drawers and onto wall hooks, and kicked several odd shoes under my bed.

"Let it go till tomorrow," she said. "The guys are probably already in the lounge."

"What time is it?"

"Five-thirty."

"I told David I'd meet him at five!"

"That's going to be hard to do," she said in her ever-calm Marci tone as I raced past her and down the hallway.

The dorm looked like the ticket line for a rock concert, there were that many people milling around. Everyone was shouting to someone else, usually someone half a room away. They were dressed in an assortment of outfits, from shorts and jeans with tops, to serious Hawaiian costumes, to a totally formal couple who showed up with the guy in a white tux and the girl in a long, flowing, very gorgeous muu-muu.

Colored crepe paper streamers tied from the balcony to the far wall of the lounge formed a rainbow ceiling. All the couches were draped with flowered print bedsheets. By the far doors that led to a patio area behind the dorm, there were enormous plastic palm trees. And out on the patio was a real sailboat, ten or twelve feet long, its sail rustling in the warm evening breeze. The boat itself was filled with ice and canned drinks. Next to it were the barbecues, the portable metal kind, giving off fantastic clouds of charcoal and hamburger aromas.

And standing on the far side of one of the barbecues, spatula in hand, turning hamburger patties above the flames, was David. He was wearing shorts and a sweat shirt, with the sleeves pushed up above his elbows. His face was flushed from the heat.

I shouted his name.

He looked up, saw me, grinned.

Beside him, Inger said, "Keep working!" I was surprised to see her. She must have changed her mind about doing laundry.

He gave her his nice smile, but he also handed her the spatula and left to walk around the barbecues and join me.

"Quitter!" she shouted after him.

"I'll be back," he said to her, and then to me he said, "Hi."

"I'm sorry I'm late."

"I was early," he said.

We circled the room, saying hi to friends. Remembering that Marci had never actually met David, I led him through the crowd toward her. She was standing in front of our mural, pointing at it and saying something to Steve, her steady.

Now I want to make it clear that I have nothing against Steve. In fact, I would highly recommend him to anyone but Marci. He was exactly the sort of boy a girl should look for, nice-looking in a neat, well-groomed way, except for Steve's hair, which was so straight it continually slid into his eyes no matter how often he combed it back. Average tall and average smart, or maybe above average on that one, Steve had an average charming personality. Because he was not a hunk, he didn't expect girls to swoon at his feet. He was just naturally polite and thoughtful. A perfect guy in every way except one small flaw.

He and Marci went to high school together. They came from the same home town.

Now, honestly, as I've said to Marci a thousand times, what's the point of going away to college if you then date a guy you could have stayed home and dated?

After I introduced everyone, Steve said, "Which part of the mural did you paint, Greta?"

"The rose and lavender stripes in the rainbow."

"Best rose and lavender stripes I've ever seen," he said, proving what a nice guy he was.

David asked, "How many rose and lavender stripes have you seen?" proving that my methods of evaluating guys were not infallible.

"I expected you to be at least as polite a liar as Steve," I told him.

Marci said, "No art major could look at that mural and say something nice."

As even I, who was not artistic, could see that although the mural was large and bright, it displayed the quality level of kindergarten work, I forgave David.

Returning to the patio, we picked up plates and went down the food tables, helping ourselves to pineapple baked beans, spiced applesauce cake, a half dozen different kinds of salads and then, from the barbecue, hamburgers piled with barbecue sauce, pickles, mustard, onions and lettuce.

Some people piled their hamburgers higher than others of us, as I pointed out to David.

"That's the best part, the pickles and stuff," he said. "I only eat hamburgers to give me something to put the garnish on."

We sat on the lawn, crushed in among everyone else, with people on the outside getting the drinks from the sailboat and passing the cold, wet cans through the crowd to those of us in the center.

We were packed so tightly together that as we sat cross-legged on the grass, David's knee overlapped mine and our elbows kept tangling. I bumped him and knocked the beans off his fork.

"Here," he said, holding out a forkful of salad toward me. "Maybe it would be easier if I fed you first, and then you can feed me."

"Or we could feed each other at the same time."

"Impossible."

"Is that a challenge?"

Ever try to eat off a fork someone else is holding while holding out a forkful of food to him? It was a good thing we started with the salad instead of the beans.

"Your aim is terrible!" David sputtered, brushing lettuce from his bare knee.

I reached out and wiped salad dressing off his chin. "This would be easier if you'd stop laughing."

"Reminds me of the games we played at birthday parties when I was little."

"Funny, I never think of boys as going to birthday parties," I said.

"Only girls have birthday parties?"

"I guess I was thinking of the kind of parties my mother gave for me. She'd dress me in ruffles and a huge hair bow, and she'd fix up the table like a ladies' luncheon, with paper lace decorations, and invite four or five other ruffled little girls."

"On your next birthday I'll give you a proper party, with tug-of-war and water pistol fights and arm-wrestling and egg-on-a-spoon races..."

"Wow! You sound like a guy who really knows how to celebrate a birthday!"

He leaned his shoulder against mine. "I'm a guy who knows how to party. Even without a birthday."

As people finished eating, they divided into a variety of activities. On the patio Tim Canfield, a senior and one of those guys everyone knew, was organizing a game of charades.

I shouted, "Hey, Canfield, making up new rules for the game?"

He looked through the crowd, saw me, waved and shouted back, "I'll play by your rules any time, gorgeous!" which was a truly Canfield reply.

David and I picked our way through the crowd to return to the lounge where a dance band began strumming Hawaiian melodies. They wore white pants, flowered shirts and paper leis, and their instruments included three guitars, a ukelele and drums. One of the guitarists also played piano. And they all sang, even the drummer, being typical multitalented music majors.

Marci and Steve and Inger were in a noisy discussion group on the balcony. In a corner of the lounge Allison and Mark were deep in a private conversation. I couldn't tell how that was going, but for her sake, I hoped it was romantic.

We moved into the growing crowd of dancers, David leading to open a path, doing dance steps and swinging his shoulders in time with the beat. I followed, imitating him. When he found an open place, he turned to me and we circled each other, picking up the rhythm. He was a terrific dancer.

Some guys dance because they think it is one of those things they have to do as part of dating girls, and some guys dance because they love to dance. Anybody watching David could see he was that second kind of guy.

His smile lit his face. His eyes sparkled. And although we weren't touching each other, so he wasn't actually leading me, I felt as though I was dancing better than I'd ever done. Just by watching him, I became a better dancer.

The major problem with fast dancing is that it makes conversation impossible. I mean, there we'd be, face-to-face, our noses almost touching, and I'd start to say something, and then the next step would bounce us in opposite directions and I'd find myself shouting into the startled face of some other guy.

Laughing, David leaned toward me and put his hands on my shoulders to keep us in line with each other. "Hard place to carry on an intimate conversation."

"How intimate you want to get?" I teased.

His eyebrows shot up with such surprise that without giving my action any thought, I stretched forward and gave him a quick kiss on the cheek.

His grin widened and so did his eyes.

As David's hands dropped from my shoulders and we swung shoulder to shoulder facing the same direction, there I was staring straight into Rick's scowl.

His glance raked over both of us. In a low voice that we could both hear clearly but that did not carry beyond us, Rick said, "Two can play that game, my girl."

Then he turned away to pull Leanne into his arms.

I felt stunned.

David kept on dancing, as though nothing had happened, leading me through the crowd away from Rick. We circled each other a few times before he again put his hand on my shoulder and leaned over to say, "Who was that?"

"Just a dumb guy I used to date."

Until I said it, I'd thought of Rick as the love of my life. But when I put it into words, I realized that he was no such thing, he was simply a person I'd once been stupid about and no longer cared for at all.

Rick was exactly what my friends had been telling me he was. He was selfish and bad-tempered. Maybe with some other girl who didn't treat him like a TV star he would be a nicer person, but I'd been so in love with his looks, I'd never thought about him as a real person.

As all these thoughts dashed around in my head, I went right on dancing and smiling at David.

And then I couldn't think about anything but David. I watched the way he moved and the way he laughed and the way his face lit up when he looked at me. And I wished I'd met him my first day at the U, so that we would have had all these past months together.

And then, guess what? I was glad I hadn't met him back in September, because now it was spring and spring was the perfect time to fall in love and the more I watched David and listened to David, the more I knew that was exactly what was happening, I was falling crazy in love with this darling guy.

During a break in the music, when we were standing in the crowd, not talking, just looking at each other, because all of a sudden that's all I wanted to do, just look at David, someone said very clearly, "Good for you, Greta."

For a minute I didn't hear, but when I did realize what he'd said, I looked around and saw Jon walking past.

David glanced at Jon and then back at me, but he didn't ask me who Jon was.

The crepe paper ceiling trembled above us in the fading evening light. As the lounge darkened, the lamps were turned on low.

"It's kind of warm in here," David said.

"Uh-huh," I said, knowing exactly what he wanted to do.

As I followed him across the dance floor to the patio doors, we passed Inger, dancing with some guy I didn't know.

She peered over his shoulder at me and said, "Way to go, Greta."

I winked back.

David turned to see if I was still behind him. He gave Inger a vague smile, caught my hand and led me outside. I didn't know what he thought Inger meant and I hoped he wouldn't ask. She was referring to me taking her advice, bringing someone new to the dance, but I certainly didn't want to explain that to David.

Outside the air was all April lovely, like the touch of velvet, with stars everywhere in the night sky. We wandered across the patio and beyond, onto the grass, and David continued his quick, light dance steps and I continued to imitate him.

We danced our way all around Smith Hall, up the path to the main walk, past the grove of alders, right up to the Student Union, until we couldn't hear the April Fool Party band anymore.

We danced around the fountain, with its empty pool, and circled the walk lamps, and even danced up the wide stone steps to the main entrance, and at that point we could hear the music from the rec room, very faintly, but enough to pick up its beat.

We held onto each other's hands and danced around each other from one end of the wide landing to the other, until we were both so out of breath, we slowed down, leaned into each other's arms and started laughing. Trying to laugh and catch my breath at the same time wasn't easy, so it was a good thing we were hanging on to each other. Otherwise we might have fallen over.

I must admit that wasn't the main reason I was glad we were hanging on to each other. One thing I know about guys, if you want one to kiss you, he's a lot more apt to do that if he already has his arms around you. And I really wanted David to kiss me.

I could have kissed him first, but as I'd already given him a quick kiss in the lounge, and I didn't want him to think I was chasing him, though by that time, I was, I waited.

I had this panicky moment when I thought he was going to step away from me and suggest we get back to the party.

And then he settled all my worries by going ahead and kissing me. The way his heart was pounding against me, I knew he wasn't kissing me simply because he thought I expected him to, either. For sure he'd been wanting to kiss me for quite a while before he finally got around to it. I could tell that by the way he kissed.

It was the perfect way to fall in love, under a starlit sky on a warm spring night. I knew that. I knew it because I'd read it in dozens of novels and I knew it because it's another one of those things I know about boys. And I knew it because right then, right there, at that exact moment, I was as happy as I'd ever been in my whole life.

CHAPTER 10

The party never had a formal ending.

It kind of dwindled down. The food ran out. And then the soft drinks. And then the band packed up and left.

But as everyone lived on campus and no one had to be home by any time, Lynne Belmont and her boyfriend, Scotty, set up the sound system, playing people's favorite songs. Couples wandered in and out of the lounge, some dancing on the patio, others gathering in groups with friends.

And then people began to drift off and disappear, until there were only a few of us left. Finally, though I hated to say it, I whispered to David, "Do you suppose the party is over?"

We were dancing on the grass at the edge of the patio. I had my arms around David's neck and he had his arms around my waist.

He whispered back, his mouth against my ear, "The music stopped about ten minutes ago. Is that a sign?"

"Did it really?"

"Uh-huh."

"I hate for parties to end."

David said, "Don't look at this as an end. Think of it as intermission."

"How long an intermission?"

"Umm, I don't suppose I'll be up too early tomorrow, so say, until tomorrow afternoon?"

"I think we're supposed to clean up the lounge tomorrow afternoon," I said.

"What time?"

"I don't know."

"Well, when you find out, call me. I can come help."

We let it go there, definitely agreeing to meet at some vague future time. There were no doubts in my mind. None at all. I was in love with this guy. And if he wasn't in love yet, he soon would be. And then we'd be happily ever after. Who knew more about boys than me? And David had "falling in love" written all over him.

After we said our good-byes for the fifth time, I floated up the stairs and drifted down the hallway to my room, daydreaming about David. And what we'd do together tomorrow and the next day and so on after that.

The hallway was quiet and empty.

When I opened the door to my room, I could see that Marci was already in bed asleep. Reaching around the door without turning on the lights, I grabbed my robe and towel and headed for the bathroom. When I returned, I dropped my clothes in a corner and tiptoed through the dark to my bed.

I didn't notice the time. But it must have been late. As excited as I was, I thought I'd never fall asleep. And then the next thing I knew, there was light filtering in around the window blinds.

Pulling my covers over my head, I went back to sleep. Later, I woke, not enough to open my eyes, but enough to tune into the dorm's hall noises. People were running up and down, slamming doors, shouting good mornings, shushing the shouters. I spent a long time wondering whether it was still early or way past time to get up. Should I push back the covers and check my clock? If Marci was awake, she would see me. She wouldn't actually say I should get up, but she might ask if I was ever planning to, and there I'd be, faced with a decision.

With my head under the covers, I felt like I was smiling inside and out, all warm and happy and remembering David kissing me. This was the way I always thought love should be.

I stopped thinking about him long enough to listen. I couldn't hear so much as an indrawn breath. Slowly I opened my eyes and even more slowly I pushed back the covers and started to sit up to look at the clock.

And then this terrible thing happened. Maybe terrible isn't the right word. But I don't know the right word.

What happened was I woke up in the wrong room.

It wasn't even a room I'd ever seen. It wasn't the room of one of my friends. Certainly it was in Smith Hall, I knew that from the hall sounds and the familiar molding around the ceiling and the shape of the windows and the closet doors. But where in Smith?

It would not do any good to pinch myself to see if I was dreaming. I knew I was awake. And I did not blink in some wild hope that the strange room would go away. I simply stared.

Above me the wall was pink, baby pink, and hanging on it were posters on pink mats. The pictures on the posters were as un-Frazetta as was possible, glossy prints of roses and other pink flowers.

I looked down at the covers around which my curled fingers were now frozen.

The bedspread was chenille. Pink chenille. The sort of thing my Great-Aunt Millie had in her guest room. The sheet was flowered pink. With a lace edge.

I sat up slowly. I was really terrified as well as unbelieving. How could I possibly have gone to bed in the wrong room?

Thinking back over the night, I remembered reaching into my room and getting my robe and then going down to the showers to change. I'd done all my bedtime stuff, my head full of thoughts of David, and then I'd come back to my room and felt my way to bed in the dark, so as not to wake Marci.

Oh. I hadn't looked at anything. Not even the outside of the door. I'd been way to happy and way too tired.

Now I looked. Carefully. There were some things about the room that weren't wrong. It was the right size, the window blinds were torn in exactly the same place as my blinds. The furniture was arranged the same. But of course, all the rooms were about the same size and had the same kind of furniture. But the tear in the blind? What had happened to me last night? Had falling in love left me brain dead?

The empty bed on the opposite wall, which should have been covered with Marci's dark quilt, was hidden beneath a pink quilt with a ruffled flounce. And above it, on the pink wall, hung posters of kittens instead of Marci's theater posters.

I almost flung back the covers and dashed into the hall in my pajamas. Almost, but not quite.

As I swung my feet to the floor, I glanced up and saw the dresser top. My dresser top.

Reflected neatly in the mirror was my row of glass bottles of cologne and nail polish and bath oil and shampoo. Nobody could have a row of bottles exactly like mine, could they?

Either I was having a nightmare, or I was having a breakdown. Its no secret that I don't think clearly first thing in the morning before my shower. Add a very late party date with a dream of a guy, and I considered crawling back under the covers because this was way too crazy. But I hung in there, looking slowly around. The clock was mine. The notebook on the desk was mine. And I was pretty sure that was Marci's computer on the other desk, and oh yeah, that was Marci's row of books plus one cactus in a clay pot on the shelf above the desk.

And then I saw my open closet door. If I'd been in shock before, now I almost died. The whole length of the rod was filled with neatly hung pink clothes. All pink. One hundred percent pink. I jumped up and ran to the closet and started pulling them out, examining them, looking for labels, wondering what size they were and what they were doing in my closet.

Freaking out is one of those things people forever say they're doing when all they're doing is feeling a little crazy, but this time, believe me, I was way past crazy and practically to basket case and on the brink of a personal demonstration of freaking out.

And then it hit me.

I went over to the walls and ran my hand across all that pink. It wasn't wall at all, not painted plaster wall. It was pink bed sheets, carefully tacked up to cover my walls.

I stumbled back to sit down on the bed before I fell down. And then I started pulling apart the bed. Between the pink spread and the flowered sheet was my own gold blanket. And inside the flowered case was my pillow.

I let out a shriek and jumped up and threw open the hall door.

The whole dormitory wing must have been waiting since sunrise for me to wake up. As soon as I opened the door, they burst into laughter.

I stared at them, my mouth hanging open.

In chorus, they shouted, "April Fool!"

And then it all fell in place, the way Inger and Allison teased me about my jungle pastels. The way Marci had hurried me to get down to the party. The running and whispering in the hall the previous day. The way Allison had slammed her door practically in my face.

They must have been collecting pink stuff all week, getting ready to pull off this joke.

And they must have had quite a crew, to completely redo our room in such a short time, because they'd all been at the party.

I looked at them and then I looked back at my room and then I started to laugh, and the more I thought about them racing back and forth, lugging sheets and clothes and posters, probably stationing someone to watch for me to be sure I didn't return to my room during the evening, the funnier it got. And I couldn't stop laughing.

I leaned against the wall, slid down it, sat on the floor and laughed until my sides ached and the tears ran down my face.

And so did everyone else.

If a stranger had walked into the hall, she'd have thought we were a genuine case of mass hysteria.

When we could breathe and talk and move again, which was a long time later, the girls removed all the pink stuff collected from everyone's rooms, and returned my things.

"How could you do that and keep so quiet about it?" I asked Marci after the others left.

She giggled, which was very un-Marci. "I didn't know if I could, but as soon as Inger told me about it, I knew it was worth a try."

"So this was Inger's bright idea."

"She started it. We all thought up stuff."

"Did David know about it?" I asked, wondering if they'd told him to keep me busy and away from my room. I had this sinking feeling that maybe all that dancing around the fountain was part of Inger's plan.

"David? No. None of us had met David until last night. He seems like a really nice guy."

"He is and I can hardly wait to tell him," I said. "About the joke, I mean. He'll love it."

Marci nodded and asked if I was going to brunch at the cafeteria. I told her I was, but probably with David and that I wanted to phone him first. She said fine, she'd see me later. Grabbing her billfold, she jammed it in the back pocket of her jeans, and left to go to the cafeteria.

She was barely out the door when the phone rang. I grabbed it off the hook and almost said, Hi, David, but didn't quite because Marci had stopped in the hallway and was looking at me and I realized she might be expecting Steve to call.

So all I said was hello and then Rick's voice said, "Morning, darling."

Once I would have fallen apart at that deep voice calling me darling. Now all I felt was annoyance that it wasn't David. I wanted Rick off the line so that David could phone.

Shaking my head at Marci so that she'd know it wasn't for her, I said a flat, "Good morning."

Marci waved and left.

Rick said, "Have a big time last night?"

I said, "Yes."

He laughed in that slow way of his. "Good for you. And now are you done playing games?"

"What's that mean?"

"Meet me at the cafeteria and I'll tell you."

"Sorry, I'm busy," I said.

"Still mad about Leanne?"

"Leanne has nothing to do with it."

"No, she doesn't," he agreed. "You know I only went out with her for the same reason you were with that guy."

I waited for him to explain further, but being Rick, he stopped there, expecting me to rush in with understanding and apologies. And once I would have done that. But now I didn't. Sure, I knew what he was trying to say, only I didn't care.

Finally he said, "Greta, I don't want to play a lot of dumb games to make each other jealous."

I knew from that he'd lost interest in Leanne and wanted me back. I also knew him well enough to know he'd keep calling unless I made very clear my feelings about him.

That's why I said bluntly, even though blunt isn't usually my style with guys, "Rick, it's over."

"What's over?"

"You and me."

"Still mad, huh?"

"No," I said slowly, "I am not mad at you. I like you. You're a nice guy when you want to be. But you're not right for me. I don't want to go out with you anymore."

I'd never burned my bridges that way in my life. I mean, keeping ex-boyfriends as friends is one of those things I believe in because who knows when I might need a friend?

I held my breath, half expecting him to start shouting at me.

Instead there was this long, awful silence, and then he hung up. Didn't say goodbye or anything, just hung up.

I had this fantastic it's-over-and-I-made-it feeling, like I'd aced a major exam, only more so. I let out my breath. My shoulders relaxed.

I felt like inviting the whole world to a party to celebrate.

Instead I phoned David. He'd love the April Fool joke. I could hardly wait to tell him about all those pink sheets tacked to my walls. In my imagination I could see his grin widen and his face light up.

He answered and said hi and I said hi and then I said, "Want to meet me for brunch?"

Instead of saying yes, he didn't say anything for a minute. And then he said slowly, "I'm sorry, I guess not today."

"Not today?"

"No, I, uh, I forgot, I've got something I have to do."

There wasn't any sunshine in his voice. The flat tone came through to me. But I didn't want to believe it.

"You're busy all day?"

"Uh, I think so."

"Well, shall I call you later?" If I hadn't been so sure of how he felt about me, I'd have thought he was trying to get rid of me.

"I don't think I'll be here."

He was trying to get rid of me! Now I knew how Rick felt. Rick was as sure of me as I was of David. No wonder he had trouble believing me when I said I didn't want to see him again. I couldn't believe that was what David meant. And yet, that's what his tone of voice and his evasive answers were saying.

Had he gone home and thought about me and decided that the whole evening had been a mistake, that I wasn't his kind of girl after all?

Or had I misread him completely? Was he really a guy who naturally poured on the charm with any girl, without meaning a word of it?

Could I be that wrong about guys?

My voice stuck in my throat. I forced it out and to me it sounded more like croaking than speaking, but I managed to say, "See you around later, then," which meant nothing at all.

And David said, "Okay," in that quiet tone and then we hung up.

Why had I ever thought I knew anything about boys?

I knew nothing! I was the dumbest girl at the U! Marci's cousin Joanne, who was still in high school, knew more about boys than I did! She at least knew when a guy wasn't interested in her. I didn't have that much common sense. I'd been spinning around in my daydreams thinking this darling boy was either madly in love with me or well on the way in that direction and definitely past any point of changing his mind. I'd thought I'd finally found the perfect guy for me.

I'd seen all the signs in his words, his actions, his face. It was like going step by step through one of those magazine articles on dating and falling in love, and we'd progressed from A to B to C as neatly as the examples in the articles.

Could all those experts be wrong?

Could my heart be wrong?

Biting back tears, I rummaged through my desk searching for David's sketches.

By the time I found them, my nose was running as well as my eyes. I pushed up the window and leaned out, planning to rip the pictures into tiny bits and let them flutter like blossoms through the air. I needed something symbolic to convince myself that love is a rotten lie. I wanted to make a farewell gesture.

The April morning lifted my hair with light breezes, swirling it into my wet eyes. The trees and grass shimmered in the sunlight. People strolled by on the paths, laughing.

I drew back into my room and took a last look at those sketches. The skunk cabbage was as pretty as the morning. The picture of me, overwhelmed by books, was done with such care, I couldn't believe it had been drawn by someone who thought of me as nothing special, just another girl.

And the picture of David, well, that one about tore me apart. It was done quickly, carelessly, in contrast to the one of me, done as though he'd dashed it off in place of writing a note and had only accidentally drawn that funny line that so perfectly captured his wide smile.

I couldn't tear them up, those three sketches. Maybe sometime when I was an old lady and my heart had healed, but not now.

After putting them carefully back in my desk, I wiped my eyes dry on the hem of my T-shirt and headed out of Smith Hall.

What I wanted to avoid was running into any of my friends. They'd ask what I'd thought of the party and if I'd had a nice time. Everyone of them would say something like, "Who was your date? Really cute."

And then I would fall apart and burst into tears. And they wouldn't know what to say because everybody knows I'm the one with all the answers.

The cafeteria would be as bad, full of people I knew. Not that I could possibly eat anything.

Or my friends might be in the library or sitting on the lawns or wandering down any of the paths.

I had to find someplace where none of them hung out.

And then I thought of the clearing past the bridge and above the stream, the patch of grass by the tree that couldn't be seen from the paths. Maybe if I sat there by myself I could sort out what had happened to my life. Not that I expected to make sense of it, but at least maybe I could get myself calmed down to the point where I could accept the idea that David really did not care for me.

I ran across the bridge, my shoes pounding on the wood slats. On the other side, I turned off and down the slope toward the water and pushed through the ferns. At the stream's edge, I slipped out of my shoes and walked slowly along the stream's mossy bank.

The cold dampness oozed through my toes.

The sun shone in my eyes, half blinding me.

I turned up the bank toward the clearing and I almost fell over him before I saw him.

David was sitting there, his sketchbook in his hand, looking as startled as I felt.

I stood with my mouth open.

He recovered first and said, "Hi."

I blurted, "You want me to go away?"

"Should I?"

He said it as pleasantly as if we were either on the best of terms or were strangers who had no reason to be rude to each other. I didn't know which.

And I couldn't think. My mind was so muddled. Probably there were dozens of answers to give him that would have been right. Probably I could have told Allison exactly what to say in a similar situation. Probably tomorrow I'd know what I should have said.

But right then, I forgot about tact and charm and snapped, "I don't want your nice lies!"

His eyes widened and he sort of looked like I felt. He looked like he wasn't sure what to say. "Lies? What lies?"

His behavior had been a lie, but how could I explain that? He'd say it was my fault if I misunderstood the way he acted, wouldn't he? Wouldn't any guy?

The sun felt burning hot on my face. Or maybe it was my face that was burning hot, all by itself with no help from the sun.

I didn't know how to explain, so I blurted, "Maybe you didn't lie, but you weren't exactly honest!"

"When?"

"Last night."

"Last night?" He looked at me for this long, uncomfortable moment. "You want honesty? All right. Honesty is that I don't like to be used to make someone else jealous."

"What!"

"I guess I'm pretty stupid but I'm not deaf. This morning I heard some people in the coffee shop talking about the party last night. I wasn't paying any attention, really, because I was just having coffee and doughnuts to kill time. I woke up really early, see, and so then I was afraid you'd be asleep still and I couldn't think what else to do until it was late enough to phone you. And then while I was thinking about you, somebody said your name."

What was he talking about? It was like we'd never looked into each others eyes and hearts. It was like I was wrong and I'd never seen his face light up. It was like we'd never kissed.

He went on, "So of course I listened and they said who was the guy you'd been with and someone else said probably some guy to make Rick jealous and someone else said you two were always doing that to each other."

"And you believed that?" Dumb question. I was past thinking up smart questions.

"I remembered a guy last night saying something about two could play games, and another one who said 'Good for you' and then your friend Inger making some remark about 'Way to go' and it all made sense."

"You believed it," I said, accusing him with my voice, because I wanted David to be perfect and perfect people don't believe rumors.

And people in love don't pay attention to what anyone else says.

He looked down at his sketch pad and rubbed at something with an eraser. "I wish you'd told me you have a boyfriend."

He was not perfect. He had a rotten flaw. Because of that flaw, he'd come here by himself, probably feeling as unhappy as I did. And I had a flaw, too. His was that he didn't trust his own heart. Mine was that, more than anything in the world, I wanted him to love me.

I couldn't stand to see David unhappy.

Now if there was one thing I knew about boys, and I was beginning to doubt that there was, but if there was, it was that they don't like to be rushed. They like to do the rushing. They want to be the first to fall in love, because if it happens the other way around, they feel trapped. Telling a boy you're crazy about him before he's told you is the sure way to scare him off. Everyone knows that.

But I couldn't stop myself. I blurted out, "You want honesty? Honesty is that I am not absolutely sure how I feel about you, David, but I have this growing suspicion that I am falling madly in love with you."

At that point, according to all I've ever read, David should have told me that I was a nice girl and he valued my friendship but that he wasn't ready for any serious commitment.

Instead he stood up and walked down the slope to me and kept getting nearer and nearer while I stood there with my heart pounding away in my ears and finally he was right there in front of me.

"Are you saying you don't have a boyfriend?"

"I hope I have a boyfriend. I hope he's you."

He started to smile and then he put his arms around me and then he said the only thing that mattered to me.

He said, "I love you, too, Greta."

Which all goes to prove that when it comes right down to basic facts, I don't know the first thing about boys.

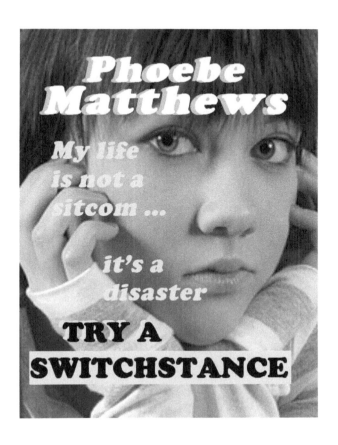

TRY A SWITCHSTANCE

First published as an Avon Flare book
by **Phoebe Matthews**.

CHAPTER 1

The dumbest thing I ever did was cut off my hair. Well, no, maybe that wasn't the dumbest. Maybe the water tower was the all-time dumbest. But if I had to list, one to ten, all the stupidities of my life, haircutting would be right up there in the top five.

It's not that I have anything against short hair, because I don't, but the trouble with homemade cuts, done at boiling point fury, is that they come out too jagged to be tolerated when the anger is over and too short to be corrected by even the most talented beautician.

Before I cut it off, I had terrific hair, long and black and naturally curly, a sort of cloudy mop that bounced around my shoulders and half-hid my not-that-terrific face. My father, when he wasn't busy chasing illusions and was still trying to play the parent role, liked to call me Curlylocks and said that my hair was my Crowning Glory.

The day I cut my hair was the day Mom hung my clothes in Gran's spare bedroom, piled boxes of my belongings on the floor between the bed and the dresser, and said, "I've got to run or I'll miss my plane."

That was my first day at Gran's house. My father had moved out of our used-to-be home two months earlier. I'd missed him, but still, I'd learned in two months to think of myself and Mom as a family. I kept thinking it, even while she packed up all our belongings into boxes. I kidded myself that my parents would change their minds, that he'd come back any minute and we'd be ourselves again, a real family. I never believed in the divorce.

That day I had to believe.

Mom looked like a stranger, dressed in a dark blue tailored suit, her curly black hair combed back into a neat French knot. She'd always worn sweatshirts and faded jeans and wandered around our house barefoot, leaving in her wake books overturned to the page she'd been reading. The laundry was always spread out unfolded on the couch, the mail torn open and dropped on the nearest chair. And always there was a wet painting, never quite finished, leaning against a wall at an angle to catch daylight from a window.

"You won't have time to paint, now that you have a job," I said, unable to think what else to say.

"Maybe later," she said.

I wished she wasn't wearing a suit. My father always wore suits, three-piece sometimes, and hung all of his clothes facing the same way in his closet, and we'd teased him about being such a neatnik. But I'd really thought he looked nice. He belonged in a suit. Mom didn't. It made her someone else, someone who could leave me behind.

"I could live in New York with you," I said.

New York City was a whole continent away from Seattle, Washington, our home, and from Eastside, a suburb twenty miles outside Seattle, where Gran lived. I didn't want to believe that my mother would go a continent away and leave me behind.

"New York is no place for you. I don't even know what my apartment is like. It's just a sublet a friend found for me and I think it's very small. And I won't have time to do anything with you. I don't want you wandering alone in the city."

"Can I come to the airport with you?" I asked. I give up hard.

Mom looked away. Maybe she was crying. I couldn't tell. My own eyes brimmed with tears.

She said, "I can't leave you at the airport, darling, that would break my heart." She grabbed her purse, gave me a quick hug, and ran out of the house and down the walk to the waiting taxi without once looking back.

If she could do that, I figured, her heart wasn't broken at all and probably not even dented.

After that last door closed, I slammed into Gran's bathroom for a screaming cry, stuffed a washcloth between my teeth so that Gran wouldn't come knocking at the door, had my tantrum, then stared at myself in the mirror trying to figure out who I was now.

I was no longer the fifteen-year-old daughter of Marie and Randall Block, because there no longer existed a couple with those names. I was no longer part of a family. There wasn't any Block family.

And the first thing that stared back at me from the mirror was that big mass of hair that looked so much like my mother's hair, though hers wasn't as curly, and that my father loved so much. Or had said he did.

I pulled open the drawer by the sink, rummaged around until I found a manicure scissors, and started cutting.

It took a long time, probably about as long as it would take to shear a sheep with a toenail clipper, but I had nothing else to do.

A half hour later I was someone else. My face, which had seemed small beneath all that hair, looked larger. Under the black slash of heavy eyebrows, my eyes appeared wider and darker, their corners tilted down. My nose looked wider, my cheeks more rounded. Only my mouth appeared smaller. It had always been small, with thin lips, but now a frown tightened it into a short line, which was probably how it would remain permanently. I doubted that I would ever laugh again.

My hair stuck out in jagged peaks all over my head. I tried to slick it down with water. With most of the weight removed, the curls bounced right back up like springs.

When I walked into the kitchen, my grandmother said, "Where did you leave your hair, Elvy?"

"On the bathroom floor," I said, ready for an argument.

"Go sweep it up," Gran said.

So much for arguments. I banged around in the cleaning closet, digging out the broom and dustpan. When I found them, I gave Gran another glance, thinking that surely now she would say more.

She poured herself another cup of coffee, lit another cigarette, and began to brush magenta polish on her long fingernails. So much for grandmotherly grandmothers, the cookie-baking kind that wander through TV commercials.

I said, "Grandmothers on TV sitcoms don't smoke."

Gran didn't bother to look up. Squinting at her nails through the spiral of smoke that rose from the cigarette she had clenched in her teeth, she said, "Life is not a sitcom."

"That's for sure," I snapped, which wasn't fair and I knew it.

It wasn't Gran's fault that her daughter and son-in-law decided marriage and parenthood were mere childhood mistakes that now stifled their creative personality growth, or some such explanation which I'd at first tried to understand. All their wordy explanations meant the same thing, that they were bored with each other and no longer had time for me.

But that was no reason to take out my anger on my grandmother. Whether Gran wanted me or not, she had at least offered me a home. Despite the cigarettes and the nail polish, she had an old-fashioned sense of obligation, and that was more than my parents had.

I was sweeping up the last of the hair from the floor when Gran came to the bathroom door and said, "Elvy, would you like me to take you to my beautician and get your hair shaped up a bit?"

My grandmother was a tall, thin woman, pretty, really, for somebody in her late fifties. Her hair gleamed dark blonde with a few streaks of silver. She wore it the way she wore her clothes. Her outfits were very tailored, with everything matching and nothing wrinkled, and that was the way her hair was, too, curled up into a beehive with all the ends tucked in and never a stray wisp anywhere.

I decided that any beautician who could do that to hair wasn't going to touch my head.

I said, "No, thanks. If she cuts off any more, I'll be bald."

"Then I'd better be leaving," Gran said. "See you later, Elvy."

It was Saturday, Gran's busiest day because she sold real estate and most people looking for houses had to look on weekends when they weren't working. I listened to the high heels click across the front room away from me. After the front door closed, I spent another ten minutes staring at the mirror.

What was I supposed to do with myself all day? There I was, in the home of Dorothea Holden, realtor, who had lived alone since my grandfather's death ten years ago. Her house was one of those in which everything had a place and was in its place. There were no clutters of photos, souvenirs, or whatnots on the tables, no rows of plants on the sills, no piles of books or magazines in the chairs, nothing to indicate that children might be welcome. I couldn't remember what the house had been like before my grandfather died. I'd been five years old then. My memories of the house were since that time, as it was now, an office away from the office, a living space for an efficient, hardworking business woman.

As I couldn't think of anything to do inside, I dug through my boxes, found my skateboard, and went outside. Gran lived on a street sort of like the one where I'd lived with my parents in Seattle, except that here in Eastside the houses were newer, smaller, and farther apart, with wider lawns. The Saturday sounds mingled barking, shouting, and power mower roars. The Saturday air smelled of trash-burner smoke, cut grass, and gas fumes.

Skating slowly around the block, tracing a zigzag pattern on the sidewalk, I checked out the neighborhood, peering up driveways into backyards. Besides losing my parents, I'd lost my whole world, all my school friends, and everything. I felt like a TV space explorer dropped into an alien world. As I had never spent much time at my grandmother's, not even the occasional Sunday dinner because Sunday was a working day for Gran, I had never known who lived near her.

I sailed arcs up and down driveways, cutting back and forth across the empty street, and even did a curb hop at one corner, with a perfect landing, but without friends it wasn't much fun. I headed back.

Two doors short of my grandmother's place I spotted a boy I didn't know, but at least he was a teenager. He was tall, blond, on the thin side, one of those honor student types, wearing cords, a neatly pressed plaid shirt, and glasses. Maybe a brain wasn't what I'd choose for a boyfriend, not being much of a brain myself, but he might be okay to know. His type didn't think they had to forever pop up with smart answers. And what I wanted was some straight information.

Doing a wheelie in his drive, followed by a switchstance, which means jumping straight up in the air, doing a spin and coming down facing the other way with my feet reversed on my board, I came to a quick stop and jumped off my skateboard. The boy had been staring into the open hood of an old car, as though he expected something to happen, like maybe the engine to fall out.

His head jerked up but his expression didn't change when he saw me. He wore a sort of half-smile.

"Do you go to Eastside High?" I asked.

He said, "Yes."

Nobody said yes. They said yeah or sure or uh-huh, but never yes.

"Um, well, I've moved in a couple doors down, with my grandmother. Mrs. Holden. Today."

He stared at me, unblinking, through his glasses, smiling that smile that didn't give me a clue to his thoughts.

I stood with one foot on my skateboard, my thumbs hooked through the belt loops of my jeans, trying to look casual. "I, uh, I wonder, could you tell me where the school bus stop is? And what time?"

"Yes. It stops across the street in front of that yellow house at the corner at seven thirty-four."

So maybe I hadn't discovered a friend in the neighborhood. At least I'd certainly found a reliable information source.

"Thanks," I said.

He said, "You're welcome," which seemed to close the conversation.

Remembering Gran's empty house, I made one last try. After all, he lived there. He must know who else lived in the neighborhood. If we chatted for a few minutes, maybe he'd help me meet some of the other kids.

"Is that your car?"

"Yes."

All right, that meant he was older than me because I was fifteen, a year too young to have a driver's license. It might also mean that he either had a job or had generous parents, but that was as much as I could do with a one-word answer.

"Is something wrong with it?" I asked, thinking that if I asked a boy about his car, certainly that would start a conversation.

He said, "No."

Okay, I'd run into a brick wall, to use one of Pop's clichés. I shrugged, muttered, "Bye," and swung into a one-foot spiral takeoff.

Unfortunately, I hadn't paid much attention to his driveway. It curved toward me, so that where I'd expected pavement, there was a gravel edging.

My skateboard flipped onto the hedge.

I flipped the other way, headlong into the cement.

I sprawled across the driveway with my sweatshirt twisted up around my ribs and my bedspring hair dangling into my eyes. It wasn't fair. The day had already been too miserable. And I couldn't even cry. I was cried out.

From above me I heard him say, "Are you all right?"

I rolled over slowly. My ankle had that wretched dull ache that meant a wrench. My hand burned. I didn't have to look at it to know I'd scraped off a huge patch of skin. When I was on my back, stretched out flat, I squinted up at him and the bright sky above him and gave him one of his efficient one-word answers. "No."

Crouching down beside me, his knees sticking out at sharp angles, he said, "Did you break something?"

"No."

"Should I call a doctor?" He looked frightened.

I tried to smile, which was hard to manage through throbbing pain. But I hadn't learned to curb hop a skateboard without a few falls. I didn't want him to think I was a beginner. "I twisted my ankle and skinned my hand, but I guess I'll survive."

His half-smile returned. "Come on, I'll help you."

He held out his hands and I caught them, but when I started to pull myself into a sitting position, he lost his balance and slipped off his heels, sitting hard on the concrete. I scrambled to my feet without his help. Standing above him, my weight on my good ankle, I turned my hand over and stared at the bleeding palm. I tried not to stare at him.

He did the clumsiest job of getting to his feet I'd ever seen.

"I'll get you some ice," he said.

"What for?"

"To put on your ankle. To keep it from swelling. And you ought to wash that hand off."

"Sure, well, I will, as soon as I get home."

In some way that I couldn't explain to him, I almost enjoyed my injuries. They were real pains, the kind I could complain about, unlike the pain that had been tearing me apart these past months.

"Look, uh, tell you what, why not come inside? Uh, my mom's inside."

With a shrug, I followed him into his house, through the laundry room to a sunny yellow kitchen where his mother was repotting violet plants on the sink counter amid a clutter of stacked dishes. She was blonde, like the boy, but short and plump, and her hair had gray streaks, like Gran's. She looked much older than my mother.

She smiled at me and said, "Paul, dear, who's your friend?"

"She, uh, she cut her hand," he said and then, to my surprise, he blushed.

I said, "I'm Elvy Block. I just moved in with my grandmother, Mrs. Holden, down the street."

"Yes, of course. I know your grandmother," his mother said. "How nice to meet you, dear. Now you sit right down over there and Paul will take care of you. He is very good at first aid. Did he tell you that he helps the football trainer? But you must know that. Are you in Paul's class?"

Paul muttered something about getting the antiseptic and rushed out of the room, bumping into the door frame on his way.

"I'm a sophomore," I said. "And I haven't been to Eastside High yet. Monday will be my first day."

"That's nice," she said. "You'll like it fine."

Oh sure, I'd love starting a new school and not knowing a soul. But I didn't say that.

There were cut flowers on the kitchen table, tucked between stacks of folded laundry, and a magazine open to an article on gardening.

"Paul's a junior. He'll be glad to show you around school," his mother said.

Returning, Paul set the antiseptic on the counter, crouched in front of the lower cabinet, pulled out a dishpan, and almost fell over again as he stood up. His mother chattered away about who the neighbors were, giving me strings of names, while Paul took two ice cube trays from the freezer section of the refrigerator and dropped them on the floor. His mother didn't seem to notice. After scrambling around on his hands and knees retrieving the ice cubes, he dumped them into the dishpan.

Kneeling in front of me, he said, "Want to take off your shoe?"

"She can't, dear, with that torn hand," his mother said, continuing, "And beyond the O'Briens' is the Dayton place and then, let's see, across the street..."

"Right," Paul muttered and untied my shoe. He eased my foot gently out of the shoe, then peeled away my sock, all of which I found somewhat embarrassing, but I knew that if I insisted on doing it myself, his mother would insist that Paul do it, so I said nothing. He turned up a neat cuff in my jeans, lifted my foot, slid the dishpan under it, and piled the ice cubes around my ankle.

While my foot froze and Paul's mother moved around the corner to the next street with her identifications, Paul sponged my hand with warm water.

At the first touch, I winced and tried to pull away, but although his grip was light, it was also firm.

"I'm sorry, but it's got to be washed," he said, which made me feel about six years old.

"I know it," I hissed.

He hissed back, "Look the other way, if that's better."

"That's worse. I can stand pain if I can see it coming."

"That's a psychologically sound decision."

"Are you taking psychology?" I knew that it was one of the junior electives.

"No, I learned that in an Emergency Aid class."

His mother returned to her violet pots, chatting over her shoulder at me about the neighborhood, while Paul and I muttered at each other. After he finished bandaging my hand, he served me a Coke, a courtesy prompted by his mother, had one himself, checked my ankle by touching it with his fingertips, and decided that I could take it out of the ice.

I decided that I could put on my shoe and sock by myself.

Paul's mother decided that I could not walk home by myself.

"You better see Elvy to her door, dear. She might stumble again on that ankle," she said, then added, "So nice to meet you, dear, I hope you'll come visit again."

When we were outside, I said, "You don't need to walk with me. It's only two houses away."

"I'll carry your skateboard," he said.

"You think your mother is watching from the window?"

The half-smile didn't waver. "No, I think that if you go alone, you'll try to ride your skateboard and fall off again."

Here was this kid who could get A-plus for Awkward inferring that I, who could do a curb hop followed by three wheelies, was clumsy.

Speechless, I hurried to match his long steps with lunging skips to avoid putting all my weight on my sore ankle. At my front walk he stopped. He handed me the skateboard.

"Thanks for bandaging my hand," I said grudgingly.

"Yes."

I felt like smacking him. How could he be so kind one minute, so horrid the next? But until I met someone else, he was the only person I knew in Eastside.

"What time did you say the school bus stopped?"

"Seven thirty-four."

"Across the street?"

"Yes."

As he turned away to walk home, I shouted after him, "Hey, Paul, what's your last name?"

Over his shoulder, he shouted, "Macintosh."

I shouted back, "Like Apple?"

He stopped dead, turned around to stare at me, and the half-smile turned up into a wide grin. Without saying anything, he swung around again and headed home. He had shiny, soft blond hair that had no weight to it, and as he strode up the street, hands in pockets, shoulders squared, his hair bounced around his head.

Clapping my hands to my head, I remembered my own dustmop haircut. If Paul had thought it strange, he hadn't let his thoughts show.

On the other hand, who could guess the thoughts of a boy who gave one word answers?

CHAPTER 2

Sunday wasn't any better. After breakfast I turned on the small TV set that my mother had left behind.

"You might as well have it, darling," she'd said. "Gran may not always want to watch the same things you do."

A year earlier I would have considered a TV of my own a tremendous gift, even if it was an old one. Now it seemed more like a bribe meant to convince me how much my mother loved me.

Sitting on the bed, watching the TV, which I'd centered on my dressing table, it was easy for me to ignore the boxes that needed to be unpacked. Unpacking was right next door to admitting that the move was permanent.

Although I knew there wasn't a chance that my parents would decide to reclaim me before their sixty days ran out and I was sold at auction, the way it said on the sign at the dry cleaners, I was not going to give them the satisfaction of thinking I had accepted the move happily. I didn't want my grandmother to write to my mother, "Elvy's unpacked all her things and seems to be settling in nicely, so don't worry."

At noon my grandmother poked her head around the door of my room and said, "I'll try to be home by six, Elvy."

"Sure, Gran," I said.

"Do you like pizza? I could pick one up on the way home for your supper."

"What are you going to have?"

"A salad and maybe a cup of soup is all I ever have for supper, Elvy."

"Okay, I'd like a pizza."

"Fine. I can't stop now. I have a client waiting. But I wanted to tell you to go ahead and help yourself to anything in the refrigerator for lunch."

She didn't suggest that I unpack the boxes, as I had expected her to do. With a hurried wave, Gran withdrew her head from the doorway and clicked across the hardwood floors, out the front door, headed for whatever it was she did in her exciting world and leaving me behind.

I didn't care. If people wanted to leave me behind, all right. I wasn't going to ever care about anyone again. I was cried dry. Loving people just meant sticking your chin out and letting people sock you.

The Sunday morning cartoons ran out on every station, although I flipped channels chasing them, until finally there was nothing left but a discussion panel on world finances, two Westerns, and a choice between sports coverage of ski runs in Switzerland or a golf match in Hawaii.

The refrigerator was even less exciting, containing the makings of a lettuce salad plus a new jar of peanut butter and an unopened pack of bologna. I wondered if someone had told my grandmother that teenagers liked bologna and peanut butter. Certainly it hadn't been my mother who bothered, because my mother knew that although I liked peanut butter, I wouldn't touch bologna on a challenge bet.

After a quick lunch of milk and a peanut butter sandwich, I flipped through the TV channels once more to be sure I hadn't missed something, then collected my skateboard and did my round-the-neighborhood routine. Sunday was worse than Saturday. There was nobody anywhere except adults working in their gardens or small children chasing dogs. Paul's car wasn't in his drive.

There was no one to say hi to, unless I wanted to greet strangers. When I returned home, I tried to phone Melissa, my best friend in Seattle, but no one answered. So then I tried two other friends. Not even a busy signal, just ring, ring, ring. Probably they were all off together somewhere having fun, I thought.

My grandmother returned at eight o'clock looking exhausted, but she hadn't forgotten the pizza. Saturday it had been chicken from the drive-in. Sunday it was pizza from another drive-in.

Along with my departing family, I apparently lost home cooking. Not that my mother had ever been a terrific cook, but at least she had tried. And so had my father. He'd been a good cook, sometimes almost inspired and occasionally, when someone gave him a new, complicated recipe, a little too inspired for my tastes. I preferred hamburgers and fries to dishes with foreign names. It was a pity, I thought, that he hadn't put the same effort into being a husband and father.

What would Gran say if I took up cooking? It couldn't be too hard. Probably I could find some beginner cookbooks in the library. Or would that be too much like unpacking, one more way of admitting that this move was forever?

Did Gran understand why my parents had left? I almost asked, hesitated, and wondered if I could ask without crying. Maybe my grandmother was thinking about the same question. Maybe together we could figure it out.

Gran said, "Elvy, you're welcome to eat whatever you can find, but would you please be sure the lids are tight on the jars before you put them back in the refrigerator?"

We weren't thinking about the same things at all. I said, "Sure, Gran. Sorry."

On Monday I discovered what Monday morning was like with no mother to wake, feed, and push me out the door in time to catch my bus. Gran had told me to set my alarm, and I had, but I hadn't realized that when I tottered bleary-eyed into the kitchen I would face morning alone.

A cereal bowl, spoon, glass, and box of cereal were set out on the otherwise bare Formica tabletop. They must have been set out the previous night, I realized, when I wandered back down the hallway to peek in my grandmother's door and saw that she was asleep with the covers pulled over her head.

After racing through a bowl of cereal and a glass of orange juice, which I found in the refrigerator in a plastic container set in front of the milk carton where I wouldn't miss it when I reached for the milk for my cereal, I raced through dressing. That was more difficult, requiring some deep digs into my unpacked boxes. Everything I didn't need was on top of clean jeans and the red T-shirt that I did need.

With no time to comb my hair in front of a mirror, I dashed out of the house running my fingers through my short curls, my purse swinging from its shoulder strap, my notebook clutched in my other hand. I was down the walkway and across the street to the bus corner before I realized I was the only person in sight.

Was I possibly at the wrong corner? It certainly contained the yellow house pointed out by the sort of boy who never confused his facts. I stood in the gutter, kicking the curb, wondering what to do.

A car pulled up, stopped in the middle of the street, and Paul leaned out. The morning sun reflected off his light hair and his glasses.

"Did you miss the bus?" he called.

"I don't know. Did I?"

"Yes."

I glared at him. Having answered his own question, might he possibly drive off? It wasn't a chance worth taking, pride or no.

"You going to school?" I asked.

"Yes."

"Can I have a ride?"

"Yes," he said, and waited for me. I walked around his car and got in.

At least he wasn't going to wear me out with small talk. I had dated a boy the previous autumn who followed me around school from September through November asking me out. It had taken me that long to make up my mind. I hadn't dated before that and didn't know if I wanted to start. When I finally did go out with him, he spent the whole evening telling me every thought he ever had. His thoughts only covered baseball and video games, but were in such depth that he could talk hours on either subject without noticing that he never gave me a chance to talk. After the third horrendous evening I spent with him, I told him I'd flunked a history test and that my parents had grounded me.

Maybe a boy who didn't talk too much would be an improvement.

Paul said, "How's your ankle?"

"I can walk on it."

"Stay off your skateboard until it doesn't hurt at all or you'll wrench it again."

I didn't tell him that I had been skateboarding on Sunday. I was tired of everyone telling me what to do without asking me what I wanted to do. Certainly nobody ever asked me where I wanted to live.

I said, "You're awfully bossy."

When he didn't answer, I looked at his profile. He stared ahead through the windshield, his hands gripped on the steering wheel, wearing that half-smile that I couldn't read. But I did notice that he had a very determined jaw. His whole face was strong, with bones that showed in the firm brow line, the straight nose, the square chin. Take away the neatly pressed plaid shirt, replace the clear glasses with mirror shades, muss up the neatly combed hair, add an earring maybe and dress him in a tank top and jeans, and he would look as good as a rock star.

When we entered school, Paul asked, "What's your first class?"

I pulled out the schedule the counselor had given me the previous Friday when my mother had brought me to the high school to register.

"Sophomore health, Byquist," I read.

"Mr. Byquist's room? Down that corridor, third door," he said, pointing.

Then he said so long or good-bye or something like that and left me standing alone in a corridor full of strangers. I wanted to run after him and grab his sleeve and ask him to take me along to his class with him, like a first grader might do, I felt that awful. But I wasn't a first grader. I was a sophomore in high school. So I squared my shoulders and hurried to my first class.

And right away I discovered that some things are always the same. There's always a smart guy in class who sits with his legs stuck out in the aisle, hoping somebody will trip over him. Sure, I could have gone down another aisle, but he was watching me, daring me. If I backed out now, I'd set myself up as a target for teasing.

I considered stepping over his feet or maybe even hurdling them, but what if he moved his feet to catch mine? Sprawling in the aisle was not my idea of how to start out at a new school.

Walking up to him, I said, "Excuse me, please," in a firm tone.

He surprised me by grinning and swinging his feet out of the way.

That, I hoped, would be my first and last encounter with the class joker.

I was wrong. When I went to the teacher's desk and introduced myself, Mr. Byquist pointed to the seat directly across the aisle from the joker and said, "That seat is empty, Elvy. You can sit there."

As soon as I slid into the seat and put my books on the desk, the boy stuck his legs back in the aisle, leaned toward me and said, "Hi, you new here?"

I said yes without looking at him.

"What's your name?"

He'd find out, anyway. I said, "Elvy Block."

"I'm Harry Snider."

Behind us a girl said, "Move your feet, stupid," and out of my side vision I saw Harry give the girl one of his wide-eyed innocent smiles.

"Are my feet in your way? Golly gee, I'm sorry," he said with sticky sweetness, but he didn't move his feet.

What the girl replied wasn't "golly gee," as she aimed a kick at his legs. Harry, who was small and quick, pivoted in his seat, at the same time tucking his feet neatly under his chair and folding his hands on his desk.

The teacher, Mr. Byquist, swung around from the chalkboard in time to see the girl kick air and stumble. And there was Harry, in praying position, his square face an expression of sleepy inattention, his eyes half-closed so that only someone sitting next to him, like me, could see the black glitter beneath the dark eyelashes.

To the girl in the aisle, Mr. Byquist said, "Sit down, Carolyn, the bell has rung." He had a voice that meant business.

As Carolyn hurried to her seat, she blushed with embarrassment. It was easy to see that Harry had wrecked her morning.

Mr. Byquist pulled down an abysmal chart that was mounted on the wall above the chalkboard. It pictured a sexless person, stripped down to the muscle structure. Despite the curriculum guide given to my mother by the counselor, which assured her that sex ed was part of health, the whole health program managed to be either unisex or sexless, I couldn't decide which, including Mr. Byquist, whose shape was well-concealed beneath an oversized lab coat that hung to his knees. He had stringy hair that caught in his white collar, no hint of facial hair, tinted, wide-rimmed glasses that hid his eyes, and beneath the coat hem, faded jeans and worn jogging shoes.

Mr. Byquist extended his pointer toward the chart, saying, "I will spell out the muscles for you. Write them down. We'll have a test on Friday and I will expect you to be able to identify each muscle by location and name."

After the class had taken notes for fifteen long minutes, he said, "You will find a similar chart in your books, in Chapter Seven. Now I would like you to get out your books and read that CHAPTER carefully. We will discuss it tomorrow."

A muffled rustling of papers and books blended with muttered complaints and foot shuffling noises until Mr. Byquist rapped a pencil against the chalkboard and said sharply, "That's enough, I want everyone reading."

I waited until he settled behind his desk and started correcting a stack of papers. The class was using the same book I'd used in Seattle, and my class there had already covered the CHAPTER. I was bored enough the first time. No reason to be bored twice.

With a quick reach into my purse, I pulled out a paperback and opened it inside my open health book. My paperback was a story about a girl training to be an Olympic skater.

Even though I knew the book would end with the girl winning, I still enjoyed reading all the details of the training. It was hard to imagine a mother who devoted her whole life to her daughter's skating career, which was what the mother in the book did. I wondered if there really were mothers like that.

Harry cleared his throat loudly. Then he did a short pencil-drumming thing. I ignored him, figuring he was a dumb showoff.

He made a hissing noise between his teeth which I also ignored. I thought if I looked at him, he would probably make a face or toss a spitball.

What happened next happened so quickly that it took me a while to sort it out. While Harry's left elbow knocked all his own books on the aisle floor between our desks, his right hand streaked across my desk in a blur that carried my paperback to the floor to join the mess.

I stiffened and stared at him, wordless.

Harry stood in the aisle muttering, "Oh, golly gee whiz," in a silly little boy voice while Mr. Byquist, whom I hadn't heard approach, stood over us, glaring down at Harry.

Harry spread on innocence like peanut butter, but why it didn't stick his voice to the top of his mouth I couldn't guess.

"I was trying to turn my book around to get a better look at that chart. That is a wonderful chart. I want to make a copy of that chart," Harry said, as he dropped to his haunches and gathered up his books, sliding my paperback somewhere out of sight in the pile.

A terrible silence followed. Everyone except Harry held his breath. There should have been popping sounds from all the tensed spines.

Harry gave Mr. Byquist one of his wide-eyed smiles. "Sorry about the noise."

Mr. Byquist's pale face was as tense as the students' spines. He didn't say a word. He waited while Harry sat down, arranged his books on his desk and opened his health book. Then Mr. Byquist turned and walked back up the aisle to the front of the room.

When I glanced at Harry he was leaning his face on his fist, his elbow on his desk, with his head tilted back and his chin thrust forward, his eyelids lowered as though he were reading his book. The black glitter moved back and forth beneath the curtain of lashes. He was either watching everyone or planning another disturbance.

I didn't like that. He had gone through that whole routine to protect me because he didn't wanted the teacher to catch me reading a paperback. Did he think that put me in his debt? I didn't want to be in anyone's debt. What would I say when he gave back my book? And who was this guy, anyway?

Maybe he deserved a thank you for saving me from a detention, but saying thanks was a tricky business. If he was a friend, I would say thanks without a thought, because he'd know that I would do the same for him. Or if he was the Paul Macintosh type, I would figure he had had an attack of Sir Galahad, and I would thank him and he'd say uh-huh and that would be that.

But this guy looked like a troublemaker to me. Maybe he planned to blackmail me. Or return the book with some loud, embarrassing remark.

I was in misery for the rest of the class.

When the bell rang, Harry shot out of his seat and the room before I could say, "Hey," which left me puzzled. Certainly he didn't want my book. It wasn't the sort of thing a guy would read.

On my bus ride home I saw no one I'd seen in any of my classes. No one waved or helloed or in any way hinted that they recognized me. I sat silently next to two freshmen who chattered to each other without once glancing at me.

After a supper of a heated-up frozen dinner, during which my grandmother tried to make conversation and I worried about my school day and answered with nods without hearing what she said, I cleared the dishes and went to my room.

My friend Melissa phoned from Seattle. At first I was excited to hear from her.

"I can't talk long. I am way over my limit," she said.

"Sure, I know," I said. Between texting and time limits on calls, we all had the same problem. Our parents didn't ground us. They grounded our phones.

"It's good to hear your voice, Elvy. I miss you."

"Quick, tell me what everybody's doing. I haven't figured out the buses yet, but maybe we could meet on Saturday at one of the malls. Bellevue Square or Southcenter? I think I'm closer to Southcenter," I said.

"I wish I could, honestly, but I've got this stupid report for history. I'll be in the library all Saturday. What a pit."

"Oh." I tried to keep my voice cheerful. "Well, maybe the next weekend."

"Sure, maybe. Listen, Elvy, Mom says she'd like to have you, that is, you're to feel welcome any time you'd like to have Sunday dinner with us."

"Thanks," I said and tried to make it sound as vague as one word could. I would not go be any family's Sunday charity case.

And that's what I would be if I clung to my Seattle friends. They all knew about the divorce. They all were upset about it. I needed new friends. Here. Here in Eastside where I wasn't known as the kid whose parents split and left her behind.

The next morning when I went flying out of the front door with plenty of time to get to the bus stop, I found Paul's car pulled into the driveway. For an awful moment I panicked, thinking he'd been sent by his mom, who probably knew about my parents. So maybe I'd get overdoses of sympathy here, too. I wasn't sure I could handle that.

"Want a ride?" he called.

I walked over to the car. "I can take the bus."

"Yes." No flicker of expression, nothing but that irritating smile.

I thought of the way all school buses smell in the morning, of bologna and squashed bananas and wet sneakers. I said, "But I don't like to."

"Nobody does."

I walked around the car and climbed in beside him.

Halfway to school, he said, "Why are you living with your grandmother?"

"My parents got a divorce." So he hadn't known. Pull out the umbrella, Elvy girl, I thought. Prepare for the sympathy drench.

"Yes? So why aren't you living with one of them?"

"My father is remarrying some young thing and my mother is searching for the bright lights."

"Where's that?"

"New York, New York, what a wonderful catchall."

"You mad because she didn't take you with her?" he asked.

"None of your business," I snapped. It felt really good to snap at someone.

Paul said, "Yes."

I liked that. He'd do as a friend. He had a clean approach to information-gathering that I respected. He could accept shut up for an answer.

When we reached school and headed across the parking lot, I asked, "Isn't there a door around that side of the building? Wouldn't it be closer to my class?"

"Yes. I'm not sure you want to go that way."

"Why not?"

"It's across from the football field bleachers."

"What does that matter?"

"That's where all the smokers hang out before school," Paul explained.

He was right, I didn't want to enter with the smoking crowd because everyone pegs smokers as poor students or troublemakers. But the warning bell was ringing and I knew the corridors would be crowded.

"I'd better try it today or I'll be late," I said and ran across the lot toward the back door, while Paul headed for the main door.

I had a clear run until I reached the door and met the crowd who were cutting across from the bleachers.

I didn't see Hany Snider until he pushed up against me, his shoulder nudging mine.

"Want your book back?"

He looked the type to turn a yes answer into an opportunity to tease and I suspected he could tease mean.

Very nonchalantly I said, "Sure, if you've got it."

"And if I don't?"

"Doesn't matter. I'd about finished it."

If I wanted to look him in the eye, I could do so on the level. We were about the same height. But I knew better than to look at him at all. First, he'd be watching me with his head tilted back and his lids lowered, and second, if I so much as blinked, he would know he had succeeded in irritating me.

I kept walking.

At the classroom door, as I turned away from him, Harry pulled my book from his hip pocket and tossed it on top of the pile of books I carried in my crossed arms.

I didn't thank him.

He followed me into the room, sliding quickly into his seat so he could stretch out his legs in time to trip Carolyn. Carolyn muttered some very bad language at him and Harry laughed.

I ignored both of them. I wasn't going to give Harry an audience. But several times during class, when I caught him as a blur in my side vision, he was staring at me. It made me uncomfortable. Was he planning some stupid joke with me as the victim?

After class I thought I was free of him for the day. But at noon, when I managed to find a space at a table in the cafeteria, Harry slid his tray next to mine.

All I did was glance up to see who was swinging a leg over the back of the next chair. Our eyes met.

I didn't speak but before I could look away, Harry said, "Hi, Curly."

Nobody answers that sort of salutation. Digging into my macaroni and cheese, I ignored him.

"I like your haircut," Harry said.

It didn't surprise me that he had rotten taste.

We sat at a long table, one of fifty or more that filled the cafeteria. Surrounding me were conversations about motorcycles and how drunk Suzy Somebody had been at last night's party. These were not people I wanted to join.

Rather than look at them, I turned to Harry and said, "Thanks about the book."

"So you owe me one," Harry said, not to my surprise.

"No, I don't."

"Why not?"

"I didn't ask you. If you want to go knocking books on the floor, that's up to you."

"You'd have got detention," Harry said.

"I'd rather get detention than owe you anything."

Although I didn't look at him, I could feel him staring at me. Finally he said, "I didn't mean it like that."

"Like what?"

"Like whatever you think I meant."

I nodded and filled my mouth with macaroni. It tasted flat but at least it was hot.

"You always mad?" Harry asked.

Around the macaroni, I mumbled, "I'm not mad."

"You've got chips on both shoulders."

"That's me, chip off the old Block."

"How come?"

"My last name is Block," I said and Harry laughed.

"That's right, I forgot."

"No reason for you to remember."

"There you go again, talking mad," he said.

"Listen, Harry," I said, deciding that I might as well look at him, talk directly to him, and get it over with, "I am not mad at you. It was nice of you to help me out. Sometime if I see the teacher watching you, I'll warn you."

Harry's eyes narrowed. "Don't worry about Byquist. I'll get him."

"Okay," I said, hoping to close the conversation.

As I tried to slide my chair back to get out, I found that Harry had his foot firmly planted on a rung. He didn't lean toward me. If anything, he leaned away, so I didn't feel threatened. The impression I got was that Harry wanted to keep me there to talk without antagonizing me.

He said, "Me and a couple of friends have got this idea, Elvy. You know that lab coat old Byquist wears?"

"Uh-huh." I couldn't figure out how to get Harry's foot off my chair without asking him to move it and I didn't want to ask anything of him. I sat quietly and listened.

"We're going to make one of those dummy things you hang up, like at a rally, what are they called, efly or something?"

"Effigies?"

"Yeah. We're going to make one. I found some old big glasses frames like he wears. We're going to put his lab coat on the dummy and hang it. We've got it all figured out. You want to hear how?"

"Not especially."

"We're going to do it tonight. You want to come with us? It'll be fun and can you imagine old man Byquist when he sees that thing hanging up?"

Playing practical jokes wasn't my idea of fun. I told Harry no at about the same time the bell rang. He took his foot off of my chair and let me out. While I headed down the corridor toward my next class, he kept in step beside me.

"It'll serve him right," he said. "He's given me three detentions already this quarter. He's got it coming."

"What if you get caught?"

"I don't get caught. Listen, my friend's got a car. He could pick you up if you want to go with us."

I kept walking and didn't bother answering.

Harry said, "Okay, but if you change your mind, be at the back corridor at midnight."

"Midnight!" I exclaimed.

When I turned to look at him, he was gone, heading off toward his next class. I saw his back and then he darted into the crowd.

What an odd guy, I thought. Really kind of nice looking, with his dark hair waving neatly around his square face. And he was well built for a short boy, with everything in proportion so that he moved very gracefully. We had that in common, being well-coordinated. And he hadn't actually been rude at lunch.

As I walked toward my next class, Carolyn, the girl from health class, fell into step beside me. Without bothering to say hello, she said, "What were you doing, sitting with Harry Snider?"

"He had something to tell me."

"You mean you were with him?"

"And twenty other people. It's a big table."

"Oh," she said, sounding relieved. "That's what I thought, only, I saw you talking to him, so I thought maybe that, uh, you'd sat over at that table because you didn't know, I mean, because you're new here."

"Know what?"

"Harry Snider has a terrible reputation!"

"Does he? What's he done?"

"Oh, he's the kind who makes bad grades and cuts class and gets detention and stuff like that."

"Grades? Cutting? How about real trouble? Like pushing drugs or stealing?"

"N-n-no," Carolyn said, dragging out the word out slowly. "I guess not. Why, are you missing something? I wouldn't put it past him."

"No, I'm not missing anything. I just wondered, that's all," I said.

The bell rang.

Carolyn said quickly, "I wanted to warn you. Because you're new," and rushed off.

CHAPTER 3

I went home mad. What difference did it make whether I sat next to Harry in health class or in the cafeteria? And who was this Carolyn to tell me what to do?

"One thing I don't need is another mother, substitute, teenage, friend's mom, or whatever," I muttered angrily to myself that evening.

Gran had gone to bed. I sat at the kitchen table, my notebooks spread out, working on an assignment. I thought it was kind of neat that Gran always said, "Good night, Elvy," without adding any parental junk like, "Don't stay up too late."

When the kitchen phone rang, it was half past eleven. I grabbed it quickly, to keep the ringing from disturbing Gran. I thought it might be Melissa. She sometimes phoned late at night.

"Elvy? Hi, darling. How are you?" It was my mother's voice but high and strained.

"Mom? Okay . . . what time is it there? Hey, did you get the job?"

"Yes. Yes, I did. It's not quite what I thought, I mean, it's working out, I'm sure."

"Working out? What's wrong?"

"Nothing, only, it's hard going back to work. I'm not always sure what they expect of me. But it's a nice office. Really nice. Light, and I have a desk by a window, Elvy."

"How's your apartment?"

"It's nice. Small. The kitchen is kind of at one end of the living room and the bedroom is barely big enough for the bed, but from my front window I can see the park."

"Central Park?"

"No, it's a neighborhood park. The trees are getting buds on them."

"When can I come live with you?"

There. I said it. I had told myself I would not ask because it seemed to me I should never have to ask my own parents if I could live with them. But when I heard my mother's voice, I wanted so badly to be with her, I asked.

"Oh, darling. I wish you could. But the apartment is so small, and there isn't any very good school in this neighborhood, and it's not the sort of place where you'd have anything to do, and I have to bring home a lot of work at night."

A lump pressed against the inside of my throat. While I could still talk without crying, I said, "So does Gran."

"I know." My mother's voice rose higher and her words came faster. "But at least you're in a good school and in a town that's safe for you. How is Gran?"

"Asleep," I said, not trusting my voice to more than one word answers. I would soon be in tears.

"I'm sorry about calling so late but I had a lot of things to do. I'll try to call earlier next time. Say hello to Gran, will you, darling?"

"Uh-huh."

"Elvy?"

"Huh?"

"Has your father phoned?"

"No."

"Has he written to you?"

"No."

After a long pause, my mother said, "Darling, I have to hang up now, it costs so much. Listen, try to help Gran, will you, and take care of yourself."

I'll have to, won't I, as there is no one else to take care of me, I thought. But all I said into the phone was, "Bye, Mom."

I couldn't keep my mind on studying after the phone call. Closing my books, I went into my bedroom. I made a face at the mirror, then turned on my TV with the sound low so it would not wake Gran. The screen flashed its colors and shadow shapes at me. The picture was a blur through my tears.

Why had my mother bothered to phone at all if she didn't want me to join her in New York? She didn't seem like a mother anymore, not the mother I remembered. It was as though she'd been an actress playing a mother role and now she'd run off to New York and run out of script. She hadn't asked me how school was or what I was doing. There hadn't been time to tell her that I'd cut my hair. Or to talk to her about classes. I would have liked to tell her about Harry knocking the books on the floor.

It was the sort of story I used to tell her when I got home each afternoon from school and we sat together at the kitchen table peeling oranges. We would talk, around mouthfuls of orange slices, and we'd laugh together.

My face burned under the paths of my tears. I had never been one to cry. Not until this year. Perhaps if I sat outside on the front steps, I thought, the cool night air would clear out my brain. What I really wanted to do was ride my skateboard, but I was afraid the noise would wake the neighbors.

Still, it couldn't hurt to take it along. I dug the skateboard out of my closet, flipped off the TV, and tiptoed out of the house, quietly pulling the front door closed behind me.

From the steps I could see the dark, symmetrical shadow shapes of the surrounding houses, with their garages added to their sides like a load of books under a person's arm, and their neat gardens of matching trees, fences, and foundation plantings. Everything was so neat, neat, neat. If the neighborhood had been a sheet of paper, I would have torn it into tiny pieces and scattered it in the darkness.

Instead I walked out to the middle of the street and slowly began to weave my way along on my skateboard. I had never gone out on the board at night before, with only the stars awake, plus an occasional lighted window, but not a car or person moving. At the corner I felt removed from anyone who might care. Pushing off, I flew down the block, following as straight a line as possible, picking up speed, block after block, while the breeze I created lifted my heavy curls from my forehead and dried my tear-soaked face.

Maybe there was no one else awake in the whole town, now that it was nearly midnight.

And then I thought of Harry. He had said he would be at the school at midnight.

He hadn't told me that I should or shouldn't be there. He had left it up to me.

And he hadn't invited me out of any sense of neighborliness or pity or duty. He invited me because he wanted to, and as far as I could figure out, that was his only reason. Maybe he didn't know anyone else to invite. Okay, I didn't know anyone else who would want to be with me at midnight, either. It couldn't hurt to at least go see what he was up to.

During the day, when cars clogged the streets, I would have had to travel slowly, winding my way around pedestrians on the sidewalks. But now, with the town turned off for the night, I flew along the street's center line, covering the four miles to school in no time. At the edge of the school yard I hopped off my skateboard, flipped it up, and tucked it under my arm.

The high school was a complex of one-story buildings connected by covered walkways. As I moved away from the streetlights and into the shadows of the front walkway, a police car cruised slowly past. My heart stopped.

But when the red taillights disappeared around the corner, I decided it must have been covering a night route, not looking for anything in particular.

At the back corridor door, where Harry had said to meet him at midnight, I tossed my skateboard behind the shrubbery that edged the building. I could have been the only person alive in the whole town for all I could tell. There was no one in sight. No sound. I sat on the step outside the door, my knees tucked up under my chin, making myself as small as possible in the shadows. I wasn't sure of the time, but knew it must be close to midnight. If Harry didn't show up in ten or fifteen minutes, I would go home.

When I had headed toward the school I hadn't thought much about what I was going to do, or why. Sitting alone, I had time to wonder. Harry wasn't someone I wanted to get mixed up with. And I never liked practical jokes.

Maybe I should leave. Hanging around with Harry was bound to mean trouble.

About the time I had decided Harry wasn't going to show and hurrah for that, I heard footsteps. It sounded like more than one person.

What if it was the principal? Or a policeman? That rotten Harry, what had he set me up for?

And then I saw their shapes. There was a large boy walking beside a girl who barely came up to his shoulder.

I wedged myself tighter into the corner of the entry way.

They didn't see me in the darkness. They stopped on the walk, so close to me that I could have reached out a hand and touched them.

The girl said, "You sure he'll be here?"

The boy said, "Yeah, sure he will."

She said, "I wish he'd hurry. It's weird here."

From nearby in the darkness, Harry's voice said, "Okay, let's go."

"Lisa didn't think you'd show," the boy said.

"I didn't say that."

"You did, too."

Harry said, "Come on, get a move on before somebody hears us."

That's when I said, "Harry?"

The girl let out a strangled squeak.

Harry said, "Elvy?" He didn't sound at all surprised.

"Who's there?" the other boy demanded.

"It's me, Elvy Block." I stood up and stepped out of the corner.

A car went past, its headlight beams playing across the lawns and casting shadow shapes on the walkways. The boy and girl rushed toward the bushes. Harry reached out, caught my arm, and pulled me after them. We ran around the corner of the building toward the football field.

"Who are they?" I asked and he knew what I meant.

"Tom and Lisa."

"Where are we going?"

"Out to the goal posts."

"What for?"

"Wait and see."

As we hurried through oblongs of light cast by the streetlights between the buildings, I could see Tom and Lisa more clearly and remembered her from health class. Lisa was a thin, blonde girl with wispy hair who sat near the back of the room and stared into space. When Mr. Byquist called on her, she looked surprised, as though she had suddenly wakened, then ducked her head, shaking it slightly, until he called on someone else.

Tom was big, large-featured, with woolly hair. I couldn't see more than that. He stayed so close to Lisa, he could have been her shadow.

They both had their arms filled with large, shapeless bundles. Harry wore a bookbag on his back.

We walked through blackness, knowing the way from memory. At the edge of the football field Harry moved in front of us and pushed open the gate in the chain link fence.

"I thought that was locked at night," Tom said.

Harry laughed and bowed us toward the field with a sweep of his arm. Moonlight cast gray paths across the grass.

"How'd you get that gate open?" Tom asked.

Harry shrugged. There was no point in asking again. He wasn't going to tell. He said, "You bring all the stuff?"

"Sure."

The shapeless bundles that Tom and Lisa carried turned out to be plastic garbage bags filled with newspaper. Harry swung his bookbag off his shoulders and to the ground. Kneeling beside it on the grass, he pulled out a scissors and masking tape. He worked quickly, cutting and taping the bags while I crumpled papers the way that Lisa showed me. Lisa and Tom stuffed the paper into the bags again, under Harry's direction. When they finished, Harry stood up beside the project. It was a shiny plastic dummy that was a little taller than Harry.

"That's weird," Lisa said.

Harry handed me a flashlight. "Here, turn it on so I can see what I'm doing, but keep it aimed low."

Pointing the beam at the ground, I cupped my hand above the lens to make it less visible from a distance.

Harry covered the front of the head with masking

tape, making a bump for the nose, then added a wig and glasses.

"You gonna draw eyes and mouth?" Tom asked.

"No, it looks more like Byquist this way," Harry said.

He was right. The tape glowed in the flashlight beam almost the color of sallow skin, and Mr. Byquist had one of those faces where the features didn't seem to show much.

"Where did you get the wig?" I asked.

"Thrift Shop. They have boxes of them. Same as the glasses and shoes."

"You cut the hair like that?"

"Yup."

He'd found exactly the right color wig and then combed and trimmed it to match Mr. Byquist's hair. And the glasses' frames were exactly the right style, as were the sneakers. Harry tied twine around the dummy to form a loop for hanging it.

Next he pulled Mr. Byquist's lab coat from his bookbag.

"How'd you get that?" Lisa and Tom and I said in unison.

Ignoring our question, Harry said, "Ever see any other teacher wearing a lab coat when there's nothing to protect?"

When Harry said it, I thought about it and knew Harry was right.

Mr. Byquist didn't need a lab coat. He taught health and math. Both classes were the sort where the teacher stood in front of a classroom equipped only with desks and chalkboards. Nobody worked with chemicals or paints or anything that could splatter.

"Why does he wear it?" I asked.

"Probably wants people to think he's like a doctor or somebody," Tom said.

Harry snickered. "Or he only owns one shirt and one pair of pants."

He held up the effigy, now buttoned into its coat, with a twine loop protruding above the back of its collar.

"Hurry up, let's hang it and get out of here," Tom said.

Harry climbed on Tom's shoulders to reach the goal post. He lit a couple of matches for light while he figured out how to fasten the twine. He did the actual tying in the dark by feel. We didn't dare shine the flashlight upward. The glow might be seen by a passing car on the street.

When it was done, Harry lit one more match and held it up to show off the dangling dummy. It did look like Mr. Byquist.

That time, when Lisa said, "That's weird," I agreed.

After Harry carefully picked up all the burned matches and stuck them in his pocket, we left.

Tom drove us home in his car, with Lisa practically sitting in his lap and Harry and I in the backseat. Harry reached over and started playing with my hair, winding my short curls around his fingers. While I was trying to decide whether or not I wanted Harry playing with my hair, and if not, what to do about it, he said, "I'm glad you showed up tonight."

"I didn't have anything else to do."

"That the only reason?"

"It was a nice night out."

"Still is." He ran his fingertips along the back of my neck and then out through my hair as though he were combing it. It felt odd but pleasant.

I thought about telling him to stop. I thought about sliding further away from him on the seat. But when I opened my mouth, all that came out was, "Uh-huh."

Although I had been totally sure that I didn't want Harry to kiss me, when he leaned over and did just that, moving slowly to give me time to move away if I wanted to, I didn't move away. To my surprise, I found out that being kissed by Harry Snider was kind of fun.

From the front seat, Tom asked, "This where you live?"

Pulling away from Harry, I looked out the car window. I was embarrassed to realize that I hadn't known that the car had stopped until Tom spoke. But then, I didn't think Harry had noticed, either.

"You have to go in now?" Harry asked.

"I'd better. It's late."

"See you tomorrow before school. In the back alley. With a good view of the goal posts," he said.

I didn't answer. Okay, so I was lonely and Harry was nice to me. That didn't make me stupid. I knew Hany and his friends weren't my type. I'd get in trouble if I hung around with them. I wouldn't go out with him again.

Quietly, I hurried up the walk to the front door. If the door made any noise opening, it might wake my grandmother. I didn't want to have to explain where I'd been.

After grasping the knob firmly, I turned it slowly. Nothing happened. I pushed harder.

It took a few minutes of slushy thinking before I realized the door was locked.

Had I locked it when I came outside? Of course not. I didn't even know how to lock my grandmother's doors.

Deciding that perhaps I had bumped an inside catch that made the door lock automatically when it closed, I headed around the house to try the back door. A fine tracing of moonlight marked the edges of the house and path, turning the lawn into a pattern of silver and shadow. I went softly up the cement steps to the back door, eased open the screen door and tried to turn the handle. Locked.

Why? Gran's doors were always open when I came home from school. I went in and out afternoons and weekends. Had Gran heard me leave and purposely locked me out? Would she do that? She had never said a word to me about being in at any time or not going out at night.

Still, this was the first time I had left the house at night since I'd moved in with my grandmother. I didn't know all of her routines. Perhaps Gran always locked the doors before she went to bed.

Probably she did, a woman living alone. Even though she left them open in the day, she probably locked up at night and hadn't thought to mention it to me.

Wandering slowly around the house, I tried to think what to do. The nasty little evergreen shrubs caught at my jeans. I bumped into a garbage can set out in the driveway for the next morning's pickup. It went over with a crash. It's metal lid hit the pavement with a twang and rolled away into the street, continuing its rhythmic clatter.

I ran after the lid, grabbed it, stood breathless in the middle of the street. I expected lights to flip on in all the houses. From the distance I heard a dog howl. After that the only sound was a slight stirring of the maple leaves overhead.

When I could breathe again, I righted the garbage can, returned its lid, and backed away from it toward the house. Remembering that I had left my bedroom window open, I hurried to check it.

The window was covered by a screen. It's lowest edge was six feet above the ground. If Gran owned a ladder, I didn't know where it was.

That left two choices. I could either sit on the back steps until morning or I could ring the doorbell and wake Gran. And after I woke Gran, what would I say? "Gran, sorry to wake you, but I've been out vandalizing my new school."

Sitting on the doorstep wouldn't be much better. When Gran found me there in the morning, I would still have to explain.

Why I thought of Paul I wasn't sure, but as he was my only contact in the whole sleeping neighborhood and what could possibly be classified as a Last Ditch Far Out Chance, I headed for his house.

He would hate me, which I could handle. What mattered was that he was clever and probably knew how to get into a locked house.

His house was a reverse plan of my grandmother's house. That meant that the master bedroom was on the side and the two small bedrooms in the back. Paul could be in either one. Maybe he had a sister or brother in the other room. I didn't know. But I'd have to chance that.

Figuring if I picked the middle window, the one between the kitchen and the corner bedroom, I would be less likely to be heard on the master bedroom side, I made my decision.

With a handful of gravel scraped up from the driveway edging, I stood under what I hoped was Paul's window and began tossing gravel, a piece at a time. I paused a few seconds between tosses, creating a steady tap, tap, tap on the screen.

After a few minutes, Paul's voice called through the screen, "Who's there?"

I moved close to the house and whispered, "It's me. Elvy."

"What time is it?"

"I don't know. Late, I guess."

"So what do you want?"

"I'm locked out of my house."

Paul could have asked what he was supposed to do about that or even told me to get lost. I was prepared for a long whispered argument.

Instead, after a pause he said, "Wait there."

"As though I have any place else to wait," I whispered. He didn't reply.

I heard him coming out of his house before I saw him. He rattled the handle on his kitchen door, let the screen slam behind him, then bumped into something on the back steps that fell, possibly a flowerpot from the sound of the crash. He moved out of the shadow of the house, limping toward me, wearing only his glasses and his jeans.

"I think I've broken my toe," he muttered.

"Where are your shoes?"

"Couldn't find them. How did you know which window was mine?"

"Lucky guess. My room is the back middle window, too."

"How did you get locked out?"

"I don't know. I came home and all the doors were locked. Gran must lock up before she goes to bed."

"She didn't know you were out?"

"No. I sort of went out to get some fresh air and I sat on the steps."

"At three in the morning?" His voice showed definite signs of stress, as though he were furious but trying to remain calm.

"Is that the time?"

"Yes."

"Oh. Uh, no, see, then I decided to skateboard for a while and, oh blast!"

"Now what?"

"I left my skateboard at school! I tossed it behind the bushes by the door and I forgot it!"

"What were you doing at school?" he said in such a firm, level tone that I answered without thinking.

"I was meeting Harry Snider. He had this idea, and it was kind of funny-"

Paul cut me off. "Don't tell me."

"But it won't hurt anyone."

"I don't want to hear about it." Although it was too dark to see him, I knew he was clenching his teeth, the muscles in that stubborn jaw tightened, to keep from saying more.

"Sorry I woke you," I grumbled. "I thought maybe you could help me get in my bedroom window."

Paul didn't answer. Instead, he strode away from me, across the lawn, marched onto the driveway, across the intervening neighbors' lawns, bumped into something, and gasped. I followed. He hopped ahead of me, one foot raised as though it hurt too much to walk on. It was the same foot he'd smacked against whatever had fallen off his back porch.

Beneath my window he stopped and stared up.

"How do I get up there?" I asked.

"Got a ladder?"

"Maybe in the garage. It's too dark to see." Remembering the way Harry had scrambled up onto Tom's shoulders, I added, "Could I reach the window if I stood on your shoulders?"

"You can't do that!"

He thought I couldn't climb. I knew I was as agile as Harry. However, I didn't know if Paul could keep his balance with my weight on his shoulders.

"Sure I can," I said.

"You'll fall."

"If I do, it will be on the grass. Only, the thing is, what if the screen is locked?"

"You've got the same kind of screen I do. It's got a pin latch on the left side. If you poke a screwdriver through the screen, you can catch the latch and move it toward the center to release it."

"And where do I get a screwdriver?"

"That's the easy part," he said softly. He pulled one out of his back pocket. Some weird guy, as Lisa would say. He came outside without his shirt or shoes, but he brought his screwdriver.

He asked, "Do you really think you can stand on my shoulders?"

"Sure I can."

"I guess I could kneel and you could sit on my shoulders and then I could stand up," he said uncertainly.

He was right to be uncertain. He could barely stand up himself without falling over. But I didn't want to mention that.

I said, "Tell you what. If you face the wall and lean against it, I can climb up."

"You can what?"

I kicked off my shoes. "Try it, huh? That way we can hang onto the wall for support."

"You ever done this before?"

"I got A in gymnastics."

"Yes, but did you ever climb on anyone's shoulders?"

"If you keep arguing, we'll be here at dawn and we'll both have a lot of explaining to do."

"Yes," he said in the most resigned tone I had ever heard him use. He faced the wall and braced his hands against it.

After digging my fingers into his shoulders for a firm hold, I planted the instep of my foot on the waistband of his jeans, just above his hipbone, and hoisted myself up. When I settled my other knee on his shoulder and clutched the top of his head for balance, he shuddered. I froze.

"You okay?" I whispered.

I thought he might collapse. But he didn't. He muttered, "Yes, go on."

Grabbing at the windowsill, I caught my hands around solid wood and pulled myself to a standing position, my bare feet planted on his bare shoulders. He shuddered again. I waited while he steadied himself.

"Now where is the screwdriver?" I asked.

"In my right hand."

He started to lift his hand away from the wall, lurched, and fell forward against the house while I clung to the sill.

"Don't move," I said. "I'll lean down and get it."

The only answer was a kind of grunting sound.

I leaned to the side and down, moving extremely slowly, my hand searching space. I was afraid to look down in case I threw us off balance. My fingers finally touched metal. I caught the screwdriver's tip and pulled it free of his raised hand.

Peering through the screen, I located the latch in the dark, poked a small hole in the screen and freed the latch.

"I've got it open."

I braced myself to one side of the window, throwing all my weight on one foot, which was a mistake but the only way I could swing out the screen on its top hinges. Paul's shoulder sagged beneath my weight. I tossed up the screen and dove for the sill, looping my arms over it.

The screen banged down against my back. Paul fell forward against the wall. By the time he straightened, I had managed to pull myself up and over the sill.

"Elvy?" he whispered.

"I'm inside. Hand me up my shoes, will you?"

Pushing out the screen, I held it open with one hand and reached down with the other to take my shoes from his outstretched hands.

I said softly, "I know you're going to hate me forever, but thanks, anyway."

All he said was, "Yes," which I guessed meant that he was going to hate me forever. Then he headed home.

CHAPTER 4

To my amazement, the next morning there was Paul waiting in Gran's driveway in his car. The morning gleamed springtime under a bright sky and smelled of grass lawns. Paul showered me with all the friendliness of a school bus driver, not so much as looking at me but waiting to hear the click of the door on my side before backing out of the driveway.

"Good morning," I said, hoping I sounded cheerful.

He said, "Your skateboard is behind the seat."

"My skateboard?" I spun around and peered into the rear of the car. "Where'd you get that?"

"Where you left it."

"You went over to school this morning?"

"Last night."

"Why?"

"You want it or don't you?"

"Of course, thanks, that was really nice of you, Paul."

He ignored my gushing. "I'll leave it in my car. You can come over after school. Probably I won't be around. You can get it yourself and take it home."

There were all sorts of hidden messages in his tone of voice that anyone could pick up. Clearly he wanted me to take my skateboard, not bother him anymore, move to another neighborhood if possible, and, in general, keep out of his life.

I shrugged and kept my mouth shut for the rest of the ride.

In the school parking lot, I said, "See you later."

He didn't answer. I guessed that he was hoping fervently that he wouldn't see me later, or ever.

Harry bumped against me as I rushed into the building. He asked, "Where have you been? Hurry up, you'll miss everything."

"Like what?"

"Like Byquist."

Beneath the usual outer-limit sound level of screams, the corridor hummed with whispers. "Did you see it?" "Where?" "On the goal post." "What is it?" "Who did it?"

Harry pushed his way through the crowds, leading me to our first period class. We were both in our seats before the bell rang, with books open and feet tucked neatly beneath our desks.

At the front of the room, Mr. Byquist bent over the open drawer of his desk, rummaging through it. Beneath the stringy hair and oversized glasses, his face was its usual expressionless blob, but a shade paler than yesterday. He wore one of those pup-tent-green raincoats. As the bell rang, he straightened up, looked slowly around the room as though he were taking a mental roll call, and turned to the blackboard. In foot high letters he wrote, "153-167."

His voice sounded higher than usual. "Open your books and read those pages. I will quiz you on them at the end of the period."

Several people asked, "Since when do we get pop quizzes?"

With no further explanation and not a glance at the waving hands, he hurried out of the room.

While everyone else turned in their seats to talk to their neighbors, Harry gave me a quick grin and then bent over his book, as though all he ever did in school was study. We were the only two people in the room who knew that Mr. Byquist had gone to his closet to hang up his raincoat and put on his lab coat, and that its absence was what had upset him. The rest whispered about the dummy on the goal post, thinking he knew about it and that was the cause for his behavior.

The girl in the seat in front of me swung around to ask, "Did you see it?"

"See what?"

"The dummy of Byquist."

"A what?"

"It was terrific. Looked just like him."

"Really?" I said, and decided I would be wise to imitate Harry and concentrate on my book before I said something that gave me away.

The class period was about half over when Mr. Byquist returned, wearing his lab coat. There was a lot of muffled giggling until he said, "You've had enough time to finish the assignment. Put away your books and take out pencil and paper."

Harry and I earned the highest grades on the quiz. We were the only ones in class who actually read the assignment. Although I usually did well on quizzes, I suspected it was a first for Harry.

After school, I took the bus to my corner and then walked to Paul's house. He wasn't around outside, but his old car was parked in its usual place in the driveway. It was making inroads into my affections, like a neighborhood pup. I patted its hood. A layer of yellow maple tree pollen coated the car and stuck to my hand.

After I retrieved my skateboard from the back seat, I traced a message in large block letters in the pollen dust.

THANK YOU, PAUL.

As I added an exclamation mark, I heard Paul's mother's voice from inside the house.

"Paul, dear, isn't that your little friend in the driveway?"

I waited. He had two options. He could either say that I was no way his friend, was the neighborhood plague, and he intended to avoid me, which would shock his mother, or he could go outside and say hello to me.

The screen door swung shut behind him as he hurried down the back steps.

"Hi, Paul," I called in a loud cheery voice for his mother to hear.

He nodded.

When he was within hissing distance, I hissed, "So why did you bother collecting my skateboard for me if you're so mad at me?"

"I'm not mad."

"You do a good imitation."

He didn't answer.

"You don't have to be nice to me just because your mother told you to," I said.

The corners of his mouth turned up in that irritating grin. He was very good-looking when he grinned, but he was also unreadable.

He said, "Yes, I do."

"Your mother wouldn't know about my skateboard."

"No."

"And she wouldn't know whether or not you gave me rides to school. So you can't be doing that to please her."

"I go by your house," he said, looking over my head, avoiding my eyes. "Would you rather I didn't stop?"

I hadn't a clue to his thoughts. If I said yes, I'd be stuck with riding the bus. If I said no, he'd think I was asking for a ride. I didn't want to ask for anything from anyone.

Finally I said, "It's up to you."

He said, "I don't mind giving you rides. But if you're going to run around with Harry Snider and his friends at night, carry a key."

"I won't wake you up again. Next time I'll sleep on the lawn, even if the temperature is below freezing." I meant that as a joke.

He didn't smile. "Is Harry worth that? The effigy wasn't funny."

So Paul knew enough of Harry Snider to know what we'd been doing together. I shrugged. "At least it got Harry to study. He was so busy acting innocent in Byquist's class that he read the whole chapter and aced the quiz."

His eyes narrowed and the muscles of his jaw tightened. He turned and started back toward his house. As he passed his car, he stopped, read my note in the pollen dust, hesitated, then turned back to face me.

"Do you want a Coke?"

"Did your mother tell you to ask me?"

He said, "Forget it," and turned away.

I ran after him, caught his elbow and said, "I'm sorry. I didn't mean that the way it sounded."

"How did you mean it?"

"As a joke. It was a dumb joke. I really would like a Coke if the offer is still open."

I waited on the back steps while he went into the house. The Macintosh garden was a large square of grass edged by flower borders.

Paul brought out two cans, sat down beside me on the step, and handed me one.

I said, "Listen, I owe you a favor. For last night. You want me to wash your car? I could do that."

"Then where would you write notes?"

"On the windshield with soap?" I suggested.

"Wonderful. I can see that you're going to be a popular addition to this neighborhood."

"Your mother likes me."

He laughed at that. "My mother likes anybody."

"Come on, let me wash your car and then I won't feel guilty about waking you up last night."

Paul rummaged in the garage and brought out buckets and rags while I walked around the car tracing my name in the pollen on all the windows and doors and across the hood. We washed the car together, occasionally reaching past each other and dripping soapy water on our jeans.

"I'm not sure if it looks better clean," I said, standing back to examine a fender for missed spots.

"What's wrong with it?" he asked.

"The dust at least hid some of the dents. And look at those scratches."

"Don't belittle my car, woman. The only thing holding it together is its faith in itself. If you hurt its feelings, it will fall apart."

"Oh, don't do that," I said to the car, patting its hood. "You're beautiful, really you are."

"That's laying it on a little thick."

"Maybe your car isn't Queen of the Parking Lot, but it beats a yellow school bus any day."

"Okay, okay, that's enough. You don't need to thank me any more."

We were friends again. To play it safe, in the following days I didn't mention to Paul what I did with Harry, or vice versa. It was odd about that, because I didn't care what Harry thought, so I wasn't covering up to protect myself. I just had this funny nagging feeling that I'd as soon keep my friendship with Paul a secret from Harry. I didn't think Harry would be jealous and play tricks on Paul, or would he? I couldn't figure Harry.

Life fell into a pattern of evasions. Mornings I rode to school with Paul. Afternoons I went home on the bus. Evenings, after Gran was in bed, I went cruising with Harry and Tom and Lisa. Sure, I know that after that first night I'd made up my mind to avoid Harry and his friends. And I'd meant to. The trouble was, no one else seemed to want me for a friend.

The other kids at school said hi to me and acted nice enough, but no one actually invited me to join anything and no one phoned me at home. I had lived in the same neighborhood all my life before I moved to Eastside and I guess I didn't know where to start when it came to making new friends.

Besides, I didn't care. I didn't. Not having special friends was okay. That way I couldn't get hurt again. It wouldn't matter if I had to move again. There wouldn't be anyone I'd miss.

So when Harry kept asking me out, I kept saying okay.

But now I checked the lock on the back door and left it open so that I could get back in.

If I asked my grandmother for a key, she might give me one, but I didn't want to ask and have to explain about where I wanted to go.

There wasn't anyone anymore to whom I could talk. Once I'd shared my thoughts with Melissa and her friends, and what I couldn't tell them, I told my mother. Now I had to keep everything inside myself. I couldn't talk about my parents, I couldn't talk about Harry, I couldn't talk about Paul, I couldn't talk about how mixed up I felt inside. There simply wasn't anyone to listen.

A few days after the Byquist effigy incident, I received a letter from my mother.

Mom wrote about her job and her apartment and asked me to write, then signed it, "My love to you, darling."

I thought about writing a long letter, telling my mother all my thoughts. And would my mother care? Did anyone? And how would I begin to explain the changes in my life?

At dinner Gran said, "I saw a letter for you from your mother. How is she?"

"Okay."

"How is her job working out?"

"Didn't say much, just that it's okay."

"It's hard for her, going back to work."

"Uh-huh."

Gran picked at her salad while I ate a TV dinner. "I expect it will take your mother a while to find out whether there's any future in that office."

"What's that mean?"

"Starting a career is a shaky business. After your grandfather died, I tried three different jobs, none of which worked out for me, before I found my place in real estate."

"How long did that take?"

"About a year, I think."

"Uh-huh." I tried to sound noncommittal, but even though my grandmother wasn't a TV sitcom see-your-thoughts grandmother, she could surprise me with her insight.

"Sometimes we don't get our druthers and we have to plug along with what we get," Gran said quietly. She leaned back in her chair and lit a cigarette, her eyes on my face the whole time so that I could feel her watching.

"It was different with you," I said. "You didn't plan to be alone.

Grampa died."

"Right. So all I could be mad at was God."

"What's that mean?"

"I didn't have to feel guilty. I couldn't do anything to prevent him from dying, and I knew that."

It was the longest conversation we'd had about anything personal. I felt uncomfortable. I also suspected it wasn't any easier for Gran, bringing up a conversation about the family. I liked my grandmother. She was easy to live with, not bossy or snoopy, but she wasn't a cozy person, not like my Mom had been when things were right. Gran wasn't the kind of person I wanted to rush home to and share my day.

I said, "Do you think Mom feels guilty? Why should she? I mean, I think they both wanted to, uh, to split." I didn't like the word divorce.

"Yes, well, sometimes you learn to want what you can't change," Gran said, "though I refuse to learn to like wet towels on the bathroom floor, so please remember to hang up your towel, Elvy."

"Sure, okay."

I cleared away my glass and plate while my grandmother washed out her coffee cup. I even remembered to wash off the table with the cloth, the way Gran had asked me to do it, and dry it. I concentrated on rubbing every last streak from the Formica top because concentration seemed an effective escape route from thinking about my parents.

"I'll be busy for a couple of hours," Gran said. "Then I think I'll try to turn in a little earlier tonight. Do you have something to do?"

"Yeah, there's a movie on TV."

Gran paused in the kitchen doorway, watching me clean the table, until I looked up and met her gaze.

"Am I doing this wrong?"

"The table? No, Cinderella, you can go to the Ball," she said and we both laughed. "By the way, if it's not too snoopy of me to ask, who's the boy you ride to school with?"

"Paul Macintosh. He lives down the street."

"Ah. I thought he looked familiar," she said, and left without telling me how she knew that I rode to school with Paul.

She left me wondering how much else she noticed. Still, would Gran have asked about a morning ride to school if she had heard me coming home at midnight?

That night, after Gran went to bed and the movie ended, I let myself out of the back door quietly, making sure to set the lock, and went cruising again.

It wasn't the big thrill that it looked in the movies, with wild crowds and gang fights and police sirens, not in our small town, but it was something a notch above utter boredom. We drove past the movie complex and watched the crowds coming out, then swung through a few parking lots, where Tom honked his horn and surprised a few parkers so that their heads popped up above the tops of the seat backs. We ended up at a drive-in for milkshakes.

Harry made a big deal of smoking, trying to talk me into learning.

I told him, "Why learn to do that when I know it causes cancer?" It was a popular excuse, but it wasn't my real reason. Gran smoked. I didn't like the yellow stains on Gran's fingers.

"And you just washed your hair," Harry teased.

"Right, and smoke makes it go straight," I teased back.

"I wouldn't like that," he said. "Golly gee whiz, no."

"Stop that." The golly gee whiz line sounded like baby talk.

Lisa swung around in the front seat. "What's he doing?"

"Nosy," Harry said. "Must be pretty dull in the front seat, huh? Want to come back here with us?"

"That'll be the day, when I get in a backseat with you," Lisa said.

"Goodness gracious me! What a cutesy thing to say."

Harry's baby line drove Lisa right past the limits of her vocabulary. Lisa opened and shut her mouth a couple of times, gave it up, and turned back to talk to Tom.

The drive-in was a glare of orange walls in a black parking lot, with high, harsh lights on poles that bounced odd reflections into the car. Harry's face was a white square under his dark hair, except for the glitter of his black eyes. He stuck out his tongue at Lisa's back, then grinned at me.

Leaning toward me, he whispered, "Lisa in the backseat sounds about as exciting as old man Byquist in the backseat."

"I thought Lisa is your friend."

"Yeah, sure." He shrugged. I wondered if Harry really considered anyone his friend.

Lisa turned around again and Harry moved away from me. "Harry," she said, "you know what that rotten Spanish teacher did? She flunked me on my last quiz. I'll probably flunk the class."

"Is Spanish hard?" I asked.

I was thinking of taking Spanish the next semester. Harry gave one of his mean laughs that sounded like a small explosive noise deep in his throat.

"I'll bet that's not why Lisa flunked."

Lisa said, "Bug off."

"Tell the truth, Lisa."

"It wasn't my fault." Lisa's voice rose to a whine.

"Caught you cheating, didn't she?" Harry said.

"Did she?" Tom asked, surprised.

"Forget it," Lisa said.

She did that thing she did in health class, ducked her head to hide her face. I was surprised when I heard Lisa sniff and realized she was crying.

The boys realized it, too.

Harry said softly, "Hey, Lisa."

Tom said, "Lay off her, Snider."

"I didn't mean anything."

"Yeah, that's what you always say."

Harry gave it one more try. "It was only a quiz. You won't flunk the class."

Lisa's answer was another sniff. She rubbed at her eyes with her fists. Tom leaned toward her, muttering something like, "Aw, honey."

Lisa whispered, "She's been out to get me. Right from the start. She watches me all the time. It wasn't my fault."

"Don't worry, we'll get her," Harry said.

Lisa raised her tear-streaked face from her hands to look at him over the backseat. "How?"

Harry said, "Lisa, stop crying and I promise I'll get even with your Spanish teacher, okay?"

After Lisa calmed down, we headed home. Harry slid across the seat toward me, wrapped his arms around me, and began to kiss me.

"Wait, I gotta breathe," I said.

"Uh-huh."

"Really."

He moved his face away a half inch or so. "How come you have to breathe if I don't?"

"I'm built different," I said, trying to make a joke, then immediately realized what I had said and regretted it.

Harry snickered. "That's for sure."

To change the subject, I said, "What are you planning to do about Lisa's Spanish teacher?"

"I'll think of something."

I didn't find out until the next day what Harry had planned. When he told me, it struck me as so funny I wished I could tell someone else. But that was one of the drawbacks of helping Harry with his jokes. While everyone else in school laughed, I had to play dumb.

I wished I could at least tell Melissa and Tami, the way I used to tell them everything. I really missed my old friends. And my mom. And even Pop.

No, I didn't. I wasn't going to sit around feeling sorry for myself. I didn't need any of them.

Besides, they wouldn't have laughed at Harry's idea. They would have disapproved. It was just as well I couldn't tell them.

Still, it would have been fun to tell Paul. He was smart enough to appreciate the amount of stealth involved. Even though I had never liked practical jokes before, I did admire Harry's ability to come up with jokes that weren't harmful but were on target. However, as Paul had made it clear he preferred to pretend Harry did not exist, I couldn't tell him.

I was leading a double life, divided between Straight-Arrow Paul and Banana-Peel Harry.

CHAPTER 5

"It's the Spanish teacher's free period and I saw her heading into the copier room, so we've got at least five minutes," Harry told me the next day when he caught up with me in the school corridor.

He spoke so softly, I had trouble hearing him over the hall noises.

"Who's where?"

Harry muttered, stiff-lipped, "The Spanish teacher. She's out of her room. Walk over to her door, stand in front of it like you're waiting for somebody, and if anyone starts to go in the room past you, just say something in a loud voice, okay?"

"I'll be late to my next class."

"You won't. All I need is twenty seconds."

Harry managed to shoulder me across the corridor. By the time he stopped talking, we were standing at the door to the Spanish classroom.

I felt like a lookout in a bank robbery even though I didn't know what Harry was up to. Slipping past me, he did a quick circle of the empty room and disappeared into the closet behind the teacher's desk. I swung around and stared into the corridor, trying to look nonchalant, per instructions.

Hard to do, with Paul staring back at me from six inches away. I did a rapid blink.

Paul said, "Hi, Elvy," and smiled.

"Hi." I said it loud, startled.

"I didn't know you were taking Spanish."

"Who, me? Spanish? I don't take Spanish. Why?"

"This is the Spanish room," he said, always sensible.

"Is it? You have a class here?"

Remembering that I was supposed to be standing lookout for Harry, I could barely think of what to say. If Paul's next class was

Spanish, he'd walk into the room and see Harry.

Paul said calmly, "No, next room. But I've never seen you here before."

"What do you take next door?" I heard myself shout, my voice rising to match my taut nerves.

Paul didn't answer. I could do nose-to-tail wheelies around him on a skateboard, but he could circle me mentally with quicker grace. His jaw went hard, his eyes narrowed. I knew what he saw without turning to look.

Harry brushed by, not giving us a glance. Harry didn't know Paul and didn't guess that I knew him.

Afterwards I realized that what I should have done, when Paul first walked up, was shout one loud hello to Paul and then walk away with him before he could see Harry.

That was afterwards. At the moment all I could do was stammer, "I think I'd better run. I'll be late."

In that flat tone that I hated, Paul said, "Yes."

I tried not to care. It didn't matter what Paul thought, did it? He had no right to judge me.

Harry cut school for the rest of that day. That night he showed me what he had done.

We were sitting in the back of Tom's car while Tom and Lisa went up to the drive-in window to pick up milkshakes.

He had swiped the Spanish teacher's grade book as well as a blank grade book. He had then, to my amazement, copied out every name in every class roll on every page, matching page for page with every name, date, and notation. He had even matched the color of the ink, and as for the Spanish teacher's printing, if the Feds ever saw Harry's counterfeiting skill, they'd start a file on him right away.

"You're wasted in a backwater like this," I said as I studied the grade book. "You should be in a city running a syndicate."

Harry had even scraped and rubbed the cover of the counterfeit grade book and the page edges until they matched the original, looking like a book that had been in use all year.

All he left out were the grades. Every column was blank.

"She'll never remember who flunked what," I admitted. "If that doesn't even the score for Lisa, I don't know what could."

"She may know but she can't prove it," Harry said. "It'll drive her nuts. She'll have to start everybody over with a clean slate."

"There's a lot of people who'd vote you class president for that one," I said.

"Now if stupid Lisa can keep her cheat notes out of sight, she can still pass."

"You think she'll cheat again?"

Harry laughed. "She always does."

"So what will you do if she gets caught again?"

"That's her lookout," Harry said. "I owed her one and now it's paid. Speaking of lookouts, you were a noisy one."

"You told me to be."

"Who was the guy?"

"What guy?"

"The one you were talking to?"

"I don't know. Nobody," I said, not wanting to involve Paul.

At the time I didn't know what Paul would do, but whatever he did, report us or not, I didn't want Harry to know about him.

"You made so much noise, I thought it was a hall monitor."

"Sorry if I lack finesse, but I'm not your experienced criminal."

"Lack what?" Harry asked.

"Finesse. My dad says, oh! Never mind."

I didn't want to think about my father. I hadn't heard from him at all, other than a couple of postcards.

I slid over next to Harry. At least when he hugged me I could enjoy being hugged without getting my heart broken.

How Harry returned the fake grade book the next day I didn't know and didn't ask, but he did it without being detected. By noon the whole school knew about it.

To Lisa's disappointment, the Spanish teacher didn't scream or faint in front of the class when she looked in her grade book and saw that all the grades were missing. But what she did do was take the grade book to the office, where the student assistants heard her discussing it in distressed tones with the principal, the vice principal, and the counselor, none of whom were sure what had happened. Possibly they thought she had lost her mind and had never posted any grades in her grade book.

At noon the story spread from the whisperers to the town criers, so that even the likes of Paul, who didn't intentionally listen to gossip, heard it. If the faculty doubted the Spanish teacher's sanity, the students didn't. They knew exactly what had happened. They didn't know who but they knew what.

Paul went back to silence for the rest of the week. I got a "Hi," and a "See ya," and in between I had to settle for the hardened jaw and nary a sideways glance. I hated that, but not enough to turn down rides and take the bus.

After I floundered badly on a few pop quizzes, I decided it was time to cool it a bit with Harry. I told him that I needed to stay home and study.

"What, you'd rather study than see me?" he argued.

"I live with an old-fashioned grandmother. She thinks I should pass my classes."

Harry assumed I was grounded. Grounding was something he understood, so I let him think so.

Of course Gran didn't grounded me. She never asked about my grades. During the past week Gran had been so tied up with a couple who had cash but hadn't found the right house to buy that I had seen very little of her.

"Cash," Gran explained, leaning into the kitchen to give me a quick wave, "gets rarer all the time. If I don't find this couple a house fast, some other realtor will."

I looked up from my notebook. I didn't have to understand the world of finance to know that Gran meant she'd be busy.

"Sorry to leave you alone so much," Gran added. "But if I land this one, we'll go out someplace for a fancy dinner, I promise."

"That's okay, Gran," I said and gave a weak smile.

For the next two nights I warmed up a frozen dinner and ate alone, then spent the evening studying.

With no Gran and no Harry, and no phone calls from my mother, by Saturday I was bored. Rummaging through my dresser drawer, I found Paul's screwdriver.

He still wasn't talking to me, but it was worth a try.

I skateboarded up Paul's drive, left my board by the steps, and knocked on the kitchen door. I expected Paul to answer, say, "Yes, it's mine," take the screwdriver, and close the door.

I did not expect a thank you.

Still, any conversation would be better than my silent house.

Mrs. Macintosh opened the door. "I was separating my violets when I saw you through the window, dear. Come on in. Paul's around somewhere."

"Why do you have to separate violets?" I asked, following Paul's mother into the kitchen. I didn't know anything about plants and had never been interested, but I was desperate for conversation.

"They become root-bound, dear. I'll have some extra plants if you'd like one."

"Oh, you're digging them up and separating the roots!" I exclaimed, examining the row of pots on the kitchen counter.

"Yes, what did you think?"

"I don't know anything about plants. I thought you meant you were putting them around the room so that they wouldn't be near each other, like maybe one of them had an infection or something."

Paul's mother had a warm laugh that made me feel comfortable rather than stupid. Her eyes were like Paul's, blue-gray, but rounder, and she had the same sort of flyaway blond hair except that hers was streaked with gray. Otherwise, they weren't at all alike. She was short and round while Paul was tall and lean.

Stepping into the hallway, she called, "Paul, Elvy is here."

I heard a scraping noise overhead, as though a chair were pushed back, and then footsteps pounding down a staircase.

"I didn't know that you had an upstairs. My grandmother's house doesn't."

"It's an attic space with headroom in the center. Paul keeps his hobbies up there," Mrs. Macintosh said and returned to her violets.

Paul filled the doorway, or seemed to. I had never felt intimidated by his height before. Now I was aware that he wasn't pleased to see me and it made him seem taller.

I waited for him to say hi.

When he didn't, I said, "I brought back your screwdriver that I borrowed from you."

He nodded.

His mother said, "Paul, why don't you take Elvy upstairs and show her your hobbies while I start lunch. Now we've more than enough, so you stay to lunch with us, dear."

"Thank you," I said, staring at Paul.

He turned silently and headed back to the hall and up the stairs.

I followed.

The attic was unfinished, with exposed rafters and a ceiling too low to allow Paul to stand up except under the center. There was a window at each end. The floor was covered with faded carpeting. Under the far window was an enormous train set, mounted on a board, complete with tunnels and bridges and dust-covered villages. Under the roof slopes were stacks of books. Pillows were piled beneath the other window to form a reading nook, and a book lay open to a diagram that looked like a car engine.

"Does the train work?" I asked.

"I suppose so."

"It's yours, isn't it?"

"Yes."

"Then you ought to know if it runs."

"It runs."

I almost wished I had the nerve to give him a fast kick and then march down the stairs to show him I didn't need his friendship if he didn't want to give it. And maybe I would have if he hadn't chosen that moment to put his hand flat on the top of my head.

"Watch out, you'll hit the rafters."

"You wouldn't care," I snapped.

"You think I want bloody rafters?" he snapped back.

I laughed and he had to laugh, too.

"Listen, if you don't want me to stay for lunch, I'll tell your mother I can't, and I'll go home and try to find something in our refrigerator and then I'll sit all by myself at our table and eat a plain piece of bread and peanut butter, if there's any peanut butter."

"Wow, you can lay on some guilt trip," he said.

"You want me to go home?"

"No."

"Then show me your train. I never had a train."

"All right. Watch your head." Leading the way, he ducked beneath the low ceiling and knelt by the train. Kneeling beside him, I brushed at the dust with my palms.

"You haven't used this for a long time," I said.

"I guess I graduated from trains to cars."

"I always wanted a train. I kept saying so in letters to Santa Claus, but I never got one."

"So what did Santa give you?"

"Oh, dumb stuff. Like dollhouses and tea sets."

"And a skateboard," he said.

"No, I bought that myself."

Paul ducked again to reach the electrical outlet, but bumped his head twice before he got the cord plugged in. He set his jaw and wouldn't wince. I winced for him.

When the train was running, he explained the switches. The engine made a grand, chugging sound that went from ka-thum to a whine as I increased its speed, until finally it hopped over a sharp curve in the track, flipped on its back, and lay there clicking.

"Shut off the switch," Paul yelled.

I was so startled, I pushed the wrong switch. He leaned across me to flip off the main control.

"You're too old to take up trains," he said, glaring at me. "This is a skill that you have to learn young or not at all."

"I've never heard you shout."

That stopped him cold. He gave me one of his long stares, then grinned. "Keep messing around with my train and you'll hear me shout plenty."

"Go ahead. I can't say I like to be shouted at, but it's better than the old macho silent treatment."

"Say that again?"

"A little conversation would make the ride to school a lot pleasanter. It's not fair to blame me for making you an accessory, if that's the word, to Harry's pranks. How was I supposed to know you'd come walking by the Spanish room?"

"Yes," he said, in that maddening, noncommittal tone.

"Paul Apple, you make me so mad! If your conscience is killing you, go ahead and tell on Harry and on me, too. I never asked you not to!"

"That's not the point."

"Not that I'd tell on you, if it were you," I added.

"It wouldn't be."

"No, because you're perfect. And so anybody who doesn't behave like you is wrong!"

He ignored my comment. "I'm not going to tell. Why should I? Give Harry enough time and he'll trip himself up."

"Is that what you want?"

"No." He concentrated on righting the engine.

"Don't do that! I can't talk to you when all you give me is one word answers."

Paul flipped on the train set. Over the clatter, he said, "Elvy, I'll talk to you about anything you want except Harry. I don't know why you like him, but you do, and that's your business, and I hope you know what you're doing. So if you want to be friends with me, you do what you want, but don't tell me about it if it involves Harry."

We spent the next half hour racing the train. Paul dug out another engine from a storage box and showed me how to hook on the cars, time the crossings, control the speed, and put everything back in order after a pile-up. He crouched down over his knees, his elbows out at angles. I scooted around the track on all fours, grabbing at overturned cabooses.

Every so often Paul would forget where he was, start to rise to take a step, bang his head on the rafters, and make a face. I continued to wince for him.

When Mrs. Macintosh called up the stairwell, I had forgotten all about lunch. Paul and I looked at each other and laughed. We were both covered with dust.

"It's been a couple of years since I played with my trains," Paul said. "Come on, we'd better wash up."

He went down the stairs in front of me. Following, I brushed my palms across his shoulders. He looked back at me, startled.

"You've got cobwebs on your shirt," I said.

"I guess that beats having spiders."

"Gross."

We washed at the kitchen sink but there was a limit to what we could do. Our clothes were dirt-streaked. "After I go home, your mother will tell you to find a cleaner little friend to play with," I whispered.

"I didn't realize the train was that dusty. I never go in that end of the attic anymore."

When Paul's father came into the kitchen from the outside door and took the fourth chair at the table, I had an urge to bolt. Something inside me rebelled against the whole Happy Family scene.

It wasn't that Mr. Macintosh looked like my father in any way. He was a nice, ordinary man, tall and thin, with gray-brown hair. But there they all sat around a table covered with a flowered cloth, passing salad, dipping into steaming bowls of soup, asking each other what they'd done during the morning, and treating me as though I were a regular part of their lunch hour. When their eyes met, any of the Macintoshes, they smiled at each other, as though they never doubted that they would go on together forever.

I once thought that about my family, too.

Mr. Macintosh said, "You're Mrs. Holden's granddaughter? Didn't your mother move to New York recently?"

"She's working there."

"I was talking to your grandmother the other day and I thought that's what she said. Lucky for you that you could stay here. You couldn't pay me enough to go to New York and get in all that traffic. No, I'm a country boy."

Paul and his mother smiled as though the phrase about being a country boy was one Mr. Macintosh often used, a family joke.

I saw the quick smiles and almost burst into tears. We'd had jokes like that, the three of us, me and my mother and my father.

Mrs. Macintosh said, "Trouble is, there's no finding a job around here now, times what they are."

"That's what Gran says," I said and concentrated on my soup.

"Did I hear your train running?" Paul's mother asked him.

"Elvy's never run a train before."

After lunch and a long discussion about electric trains by the three Macintoshes, I said a hurried good-bye and rushed home to my grandmother's empty house.

Seeing the Macintoshes together, belonging so much to each other, I knew I wasn't the stuff of which successful foster daughters were made. As much as I wanted my own family to be the way it had been, I couldn't slip into a substitute family. I felt miserable around people who had what I'd lost.

So when Harry phoned and asked, "Can you go out tonight?" I said yes.

CHAPTER 6

My double life continued. I felt like a character in a soap opera. My only two friends at my new school were two boys, neither of them madly in love with me, so I wasn't faced with a jealousy problem. That might have been fun. But no, my problem was that one disapproved of the other and the other was the sort who liked to even scores with people who disapproved of him.

You'd have thought I was afraid of jealous lovers, the way I ducked around.

Once, when I was walking down the hall with Harry, I saw Paul through the crowd coming our way. He hadn't yet seen me.

I said a quick, "Oops, forgot a book!" to Harry, did an about-face, and dashed off in the opposite direction.

A day later I was walking across the parking lot with Paul and I spotted Harry, his back to me, standing at the far corner of the lot, talking to some guys.

To Paul I said, "Oops, I left my papers in the gym!" and dashed toward the other side of the school.

Okay, so that's not as dramatic as the soap situations, but as Gran says, life is not a sitcom. In life, small things can be a lot more serious than they'd be on TV.

On the other hand, my oops dashes were pretty mild compared to Harry's way of avoiding a confrontation.

The first time he pulled his cigarette trick on me, I almost shouted, "Fire!"

What happened was, we were standing in back of the school near the bleachers, a place where I didn't usually go, but he'd cut the morning classes and I had to tell him I couldn't go out that night.

First thing he said when I walked up was, "Wanta drag?" and held out his cigarette.

"Where were you this morning?" I asked, ignoring the cigarette.

"Oh, did you miss me? Golly gee, that's sweet."

"Harry, stop that."

"Stop what?" He gave me his big innocent smile.

"I just want to tell you, I can't go out tonight."

"How come?"

"History paper due tomorrow."

"Big deal."

I shrugged and said the one thing that I knew would carry weight with Harry. "Not to me, but if I flunk it I'll get a bad grade and then Gran will ground me again."

"Geez, what a pain. Hey, get it done tonight, okay, because I've got a great idea."

"Like what?" I said. And then I looked past Harry and saw the vice principal heading around the building. Dropping my voice, I said, "Mrs. Kline is coming this way from the side door, Harry."

What I thought Harry would do was walk nonchalantly away, his cigarette hidden in his palm, like I'd seen other kids do when they spotted a teacher. It never occurred to me that he'd jam the thing into the pocket of his jeans. But he did. Then he slapped his pocket to extinguish the cigarette.

"What are you doing?" I gasped.

Harry made a shushing noise. He turned to face the building, said, "Hurry up, we'll be late," in a loud voice, and walked me right by the vice principal and into the school.

He even had the nerve to grin at her and say hi as we passed.

"You're crazy," I told him, when we were safely through the door and headed down the hall. "You'll set yourself on fire."

"Nah, jeans don't burn," he said. He edged behind an open classroom door, glanced around, decided no one could see him, and pulled that cigarette from his pocket and dropped it. Then he kept walking as though he hadn't done anything odd.

And he got away with it.

So of course he continued to smoke on school grounds. Three days later he didn't see the vice principal approach him.

I heard about it that night.

He picked me up on the corner, where we always met, but this time there was only Harry in the car, driving.

I stood by the open car door, looking in. "Where are Tom and Lisa?"

"Over at Lisa's. Tom loaned me his car. Come on. Hurry up. You're late."

No Harry grin or dumb joke or anything. Which was not like Harry. He was rude to other people but not to me. If he was going to start bossing me, I could do without him.

"I can walk back home," I said.

He gave me a long look and then he shrugged and said, "Sorry. I'm not mad at you, Elvy. It's that stinking vice principal. She saw me smoking and gave me detention. A whole week."

"Oh." I got in the car then. As long as he wasn't mad at me, I didn't care how he felt about anyone else.

"So don't give me any goodie talk about not smoking," he said.

"Hey, I thought you said you weren't mad at me."

"You ever get detention?"

"No. What's it like?"

"Try sitting in the office after school some day."

"Just sit there? That's all?"

"What did you think? That they make me do push-ups?" Harry glared at me. His eyes were narrow slits and shone like black mirrors in the darkness.

I was not cheering him up. I said, "I guess the school office isn't a very exciting place. Empty. Nothing going on." My voice trailed off. I didn't know what else to say.

Still he didn't answer. He kept staring, and it made me nervous. He had that look he got when he was thinking up trouble. Then he laughed that low, mean laugh, deep in his throat, that sounded like a small explosion.

"What's funny?" I asked.

"Empty. Nothing going on. That what you said? Maybe it's time to change that. Yeah. I think so."

"What are you going to do?"

Probably I shouldn't have asked. But then, probably I shouldn't have been out with Harry at all. But I was. And his idea was funny. So I helped him with it.

The next morning I went into the office and asked the secretary if my transcripts had arrived from my old school. She was busy on the phone, but as soon as she finished, she went to the file cabinet and found my file.

"Can I take a look at my file?"

From where I stood, I could see Harry just outside the office door, beyond the secretary's view. Lisa stood beside him, nervously twisting her blond hair around her fingers.

"Is there a problem?" the secretary asked.

"Uh-huh. I've got a list of the classes I took, but I can't remember all my grades, and I want to have a record."

She put the file in front of me and waited while I copied my grades. I read aloud, saying things like, "Oh yeah, ancient history, that's right, I forgot about that completely, and I thought I had an A in English last year but then I wasn't sure. Um, algebra, that was rough, but I did better than I thought I would." Stuff like that.

The phone rang and she stood at her desk, talking, but also facing me because I continued to talk as I copied. Several teachers and students wandered through, leaving papers on the counter or picking up materials or walking past her desk to the counselors' offices.

With the traffic and my distracting chatter, she didn't see Lisa walk quickly past her and slide a typed piece of paper into a pile beside her computer.

I didn't know how Harry knew which pile, but Harry knew, the way he always did. And he'd told Lisa what to do.

As soon as Lisa was out of the office, I closed the file folder, said, "Thanks so much," and left.

At the beginning of first period, while Harry sat bent over his book like an honor student and I doodled in my notebook to keep from laughing, a hall monitor came in and handed Mr. Byquist the morning bulletin from the principal's office, same as every day. He picked it up and started reading it out to us.

He read, "Photography club will meet in the lab after school.

"Anyone interested in helping with the spring fund raiser, please contact Mrs. Carradine.

"Park department schedules are available in the office now and contain the pool schedules.

"Will all students who drive their own cars to school please report to the vice principal's office immediately?

"Bulletin notices must be turned in by three p.m. daily."

As soon as Mr. Byquist stopped reading, several students said, "What was that about cars?"

He picked up the bulletin again and read, "Will all students who drive their own cars to school please report to the vice principal's office immediately."

"Like right now?" they asked.

Mr. Byquist must have read the bulletin more slowly than some of the other teachers because when the first student from our class opened the door to the corridor, we could hear people running down the hall.

"Yes, it appears so," Mr. Byquist said. "What a nuisance. All right, class, while they are gone, you can work on your assignments. This is very disruptive. I do wish the office would let us know when they plan to call people out of class this way."

He continued to complain while Harry and I studiously bent over our homework and all around us people whispered, "What's all that about? Somebody get their car wrecked?"

Five minutes later the students who had left class returned. They were all talking at the same time, saying things like, "We go all the way down there and Mrs. Kline says she doesn't want to see us and to all get back to our classes. Must have been two hundred people trying to get into her office."

It sounded like more than that, scuffling along in the corridors, shouting to each other, asking what was going on.

And everyone in our class asked, but no one knew. Except Harry and me.

By the time Mr. Byquist banged his pencil on his desk for the hundredth time and finally restored order, first period was half over.

So that was that, I thought, and Harry had his revenge, and now we could all stay out of trouble for a while.

The next morning on the way to school, Paul said, "Good morning, Elvy, and thanks for messing up my first class yesterday. I'd stayed up late studying for a test and then we didn't have time to take it so I had to do the reviewing all over."

I didn't try to pretend to be innocent.

I said, "Sorry," and slid down in the seat, raising my shoulders up to my ears, expecting a big lecture.

"Yes."

"It seemed funny at the time."

"Yes."

"Okay, so it wasn't that funny."

"No."

For once I was glad that Paul stuck to one word answers. I had a feeling that if he said more, I wouldn't like hearing it. He would either give me a lecture on my behavior or on my friendship with Harry, and both subjects were off-limits as far as I was concerned.

On the other hand, I didn't want to go back to silent rides. Silent suppers, with Gran off working, and silent breakfasts, with Gran still asleep, were getting to me. To change the subject and keep up some sort of conversation, I said, "I don't suppose you know how to cook."

"Cook? Like what?"

"Anything besides TV dinners."

"Is that what you eat for supper, TV dinners?"

"Or pizza or chicken from the drive-in. Gets dull, you know?"

"Yes."

"So maybe I should learn to cook. I could start with something easy. Do you know anything easy?"

"You want to learn to cook?" he asked again, as though I'd requested something really weird, like flying lessons.

"Yeah. What would be easiest? To start with?"

"I'm not that good at it, but I can make spaghetti. And eggs any way. And hamburgers, but anybody can make hamburgers."

"Can they? I can't. Could you teach me how?"

"Oh." He sounded surprised but at least he didn't say no.

I waited, not wanting to push it, but hoping he'd agree. He parked and we left the car and walked toward school and still he didn't say anything.

"I could teach you how to skateboard," I offered. "In exchange for cooking lessons."

He laughed at that but he didn't say no. He also didn't say yes.

When we reached the corridor, where we both went in opposite directions, I thanked him like I did everyday and he nodded goodbye like he did everyday and that was all.

So I figured he figured that teaching me to cook was a dumb idea. I couldn't blame him. Who would want to come to my house to scramble eggs when he had a mother at home who made him wonderful suppers? Besides, Paul never came to my house, except when I woke him in the middle of the night to ask for a boost through a window. Giving me rides to school was his limit, his good deed for a new neighbor.

I really only brought it up to get him to talk to me again.

I didn't care if he didn't want to teach me to cook.

I could get along without Paul Macintosh's help.

Besides, I hadn't offered much in return. When I tried to visualize

Paul on a skateboard, all I could come up with was a cartoon picture of Paul landing on his head. Maybe that's why he'd laughed. Maybe he figured I'd be about as good at cooking as he'd be at skateboarding.

Having decided that, I put the whole conversation about cooking lessons out of my mind. Sometimes I think I think too much.

Also, when I returned home that afternoon, there was a postcard in the mailbox for me.

It was from Pop.

The picture was of a beach and the ocean waves, shimmering in sunshine. There was a headland in the background and a couple of palm trees. Across the bottom margin was printed GREETINGS FROM CALIFORNIA.

The message said, "You'd love the beach. Wish you were here. Love, Pop."

Never mind about the beach. What mattered was that he'd written, "Wish you were here."

I read it over a dozen times.

There was no mistake. That was what he said. He said he wished I were there in California with him. That sounded to me like he wanted me with him and that was more than Mom did.

CHAPTER 7

"I'm going to take the bus to California," I told Gran.

Gran was sitting at the kitchen table, a cup of coffee in her hand, a lit cigarette balanced on the edge of the saucer. Late afternoon sunlight shimmered off the kitchen walls and brought out the silver streaks in her smooth blonde hair. Her face was as controlled as her tailored suit.

She put down her coffee cup and picked up the postcard. Turning it over slowly, she first studied the photo of the beach scene, then the scribbled message from my father. I waited, chewing on my lower lip, my throat tight with agony. Would she forbid me to go?

She tapped the message on the postcard with one hard, rose-enameled fingernail.

"That's not exactly an invitation," she said.

I didn't expected her to understand. But my mind was made up. I wasn't going to get angry and shout or do anything childish. I wouldn't make it easy for her to forbid me to go.

Although I tried to tell myself that I didn't need Gran's permission, I wasn't sure I had the nerve to go without it. I didn't want to hurt Gran.

"Pop's like that," I said. "Very vague. But he does say he wishes I was there."

"People write that on postcards."

"I have enough money. I checked the bus fare."

It would wipe out every penny I had, but I didn't tell her that.

She looked up at me, her eyes narrowed, as though she was thinking very carefully about what to say. I held my breath.

"What about school?" she said finally.

"Oh, school. Well, I'll only be gone a week or so. I can make that up."

I didn't want to come right out and say that I wasn't planning to return. That would be like saying I didn't appreciate that she let me live with her. I did appreciate it. It's just that I wanted to be with my own parents, and if I could only be with one of them, that would have to do.

What I'd figured, sitting alone all afternoon working it out in my head, was that I'd tell Gran I was going for a visit. And then later, when I was all settled into Pop's home in California, I'd phone and tell her that he wanted me to stay and that I'd decided to do that.

She wouldn't mind, really. Probably she would be relieved to have me gone and her house to herself, everything neat and in place again.

"Have you phoned your father?" she asked.

"I phoned the bus company and got the schedule. I'll phone him tonight. I figure he won't be home during the day."

"What about your mother?"

"She won't care," I said. I didn't mean to sound angry, but it was hard to keep my voice low.

Gran looked at me, not saying anything, until I turned away. I didn't want to say anything against my mother. Neither did Gran. I knew that much. Neither of us liked what had happened, so there we were, left with loving Mom but not liking it that she went away and left me behind, and not able to talk about her to each other.

I rummaged through the refrigerator, taking a long time finding the milk carton.

At least Gran didn't tell me I had to have my mother's permission to visit my father. I'd been afraid she might do that. Or had I? Maybe I would have expected it of any other grandmother. But maybe not Gran. I was never sure how she felt about anything.

That evening, while Gran was in the shower, I dialed information and got my father's phone number. Then I took a deep breath and put the receiver back in the cradle.

What if I called and he said no, he didn't want me?

Wasn't that what my mother had said?

I had his address. I could find him.

And he said he wished I was with him. He said it right in the postcard. I had it in writing.

I could imagine myself knocking on his door. He'd open the door and see me and grin and grab me in a hug. I could imagine his arms around me, my face pressed into his shoulder. He'd smell of wool suit and shaving lotion. He'd say, "My gosh, Elvy! What a surprise! What a wonderful surprise!"

He would. I knew he would. By now he must be terribly lonely, the same as I was, and maybe seeing me, he'd even want to come back to Seattle and phone Mom and we'd all be together.

Or maybe that would happen later. When I'd been with him a while and he'd start remembering how good it was when we were all together.

But over the phone it would be too easy for him to say no, don't come yet.

He was like that, Pop was. He wasn't very good at making decisions. He was better at putting things off. So I'd make the decision. Sometimes I felt as though my parents were the children and I was the adult.

When Gran came out of the shower, I was still standing in the hall, next to the phone.

She asked, "What did he say?"

I nodded my head and said, "It's okay."

I couldn't lie, not if she asked anything more, not if she asked how was he and what exactly had he said and would he meet me and all that sort of thing. Then I'd have to tell her that I hadn't talked to him.

But she didn't ask. All she said was, "Do you want me to drive you to the bus station tomorrow?"

The next day was Saturday, her busy day. I knew she had appointments. And I didn't want any more questions.

"No, that's all right, I can get the city bus."

The next morning, while I was in my room tossing a few clothes into my backpack, she stopped in my doorway and said, "When will you be back?"

"Next weekend? I'll probably only stay a week."

"Elvy, phone me when you get there, will you? Phone me from your father's place."

For the first time I saw something about her that looked like Mom. I'd never thought they looked anything alike. But I could see it now, a kind of tightness around her eyes, and I knew what it meant because I knew Mom's expressions so well. She was worried about me.

"I will," I promised. "I'll be okay, Gran, honest. I won't get on the wrong bus or talk to strangers or anything like that."

She smiled then and held out her hand with a couple of twenty dollar bills in it and said, "All right. Here, you better take a little extra. If your father doesn't meet you at the bus station, take a taxi to his place. Don't go wandering around a strange city by yourself."

An hour later, when I was settled in a window seat on the bus to California, my backpack on the empty seat next to me, I tried to watch the scenery and think about anything other than what I was doing. What if Pop was out of town? What if he'd gone to New York to find Mom? What if he was headed for Seattle to see me? What was a postcard, anyway? Did it mean anything?

I had his address. I could go to his place. I could wait there for him.

Did he live in a house or an apartment?

I didn't have a key.

Would a landlord let me into an apartment?

If I tried to climb through a window into a house, would a neighbor phone the police?

Was I crazy?

Why hadn't I phoned him last night?

He wouldn't say no. He wouldn't tell me to stay away. He'd certainly invite me to visit, even if it was only for a week. And then I'd talk him into letting me stay forever.

Sure, I should have phoned him. Because if he knew I was on my way, he'd meet me at the bus station. Or tell me how to get to his place.

I didn't know where he lived. Not really. What if he lived a long way from the bus station, miles away? I'd have to depend on strangers to tell me how to get there.

The more I thought about it, the more afraid I felt.

When the bus reached Portland, Oregon, the driver said, "We'll be here for forty minutes. Anyone who wants to get off can leave their bags on the bus."

Almost everyone got off.

In the bus station, I saw the row of pay phones. Maybe I should phone right now. If I said I was in Portland, he wouldn't tell me to go back. He'd never been very firm about anything, not Pop. He always let me have my way. He would now. I was sure he would.

I stood in line at a ticket counter to get change. Then I stood in line and waited for a phone. All the booths were full. The longer I waited, the more nervous I felt.

After I dialed his number, I listened to the ringing tone. Ring, ring, ring, was he gone? It was Saturday. Why didn't he answer?

I couldn't hang up. I let the phone keep ringing.

Maybe he had gone away. What would I do?

And then I heard the receiver click and then a woman said, "Hello?"

"Hello. Is this Randall Block's number?"

"Yeah."

"Oh. Is he there?"

"Randy? No. Who's calling?"

"This is his daughter. Elvy."

"Oh, yeah," she said. "I'm sorry, he's not here. You want him to call you back? He'll be home in a couple of hours."

A couple of hours. I clung to the receiver, trying to think what to say. "Uh, no, I'm in a bus station. I want to come stay with him. For a while. Could you tell him that?"

"Stay here?" Her voice was a surprised squeak. "Here? Gee, I don't know. We haven't got much room. We've just got a one bedroom apartment, see, but, oh, I guess you could sleep on the couch. For a night or two. Does Randy know you're visiting?"

I'd forgotten about the girlfriend. I'd made myself forget her. Or maybe they were married now.

If she was still there, he wouldn't leave and go to New York with me to get Mom.

With the girlfriend there, would I even have a chance to talk to him alone?

I said, "Never mind. I'd better talk to him first. Before I make any plans."

"Yeah, maybe so," she said.

"I'll call another time. I'm kind of busy now."

She said, "Okay."

Would he phone Gran as soon as he heard I'd phoned? I didn't want him to do that. "Tell him I only called to say hello," I said.

She said she would.

I went back into the bus station and sat on one of the benches until they announced that my bus was leaving.

I didn't care. I wasn't going to get back on.

And then I remembered my backpack.

Running out of the station, bumping into people, trying not to panic, I raced to the loading area and saw the bus start to move out. I ran alongside of it, shouting, banging with my fist against the metal.

The driver braked and opened the door.

"You almost missed it," he grumbled as I rushed up the steps.

"I'm not going," I said. "I changed my plans. But I left my backpack."

"You're not going?"

I hurried down the aisle, grabbed my backpack, and hurried back to the door.

"Your ticket is to San Jose, isn't it?" he asked.

I didn't bother answering, just jumped off the bus and headed back to the bus station.

Randy. That's what was wrong. No one ever called my father Randy. His name was Randall.

What sort of a dummy would call a man in a three-piece suit Randy?

Or wasn't he like that anymore?

She said they lived in a one bedroom apartment. Maybe they lived in one of those complexes that looked like a motel, like I'd seen on TV, with outside staircases and a swimming pool between the buildings.

Maybe he spent his free time lying around on a lounge chair by the pool, wearing shorts and a shirt covered with brightly colored pictures of palm trees.

Maybe he wasn't anybody I'd recognize anymore.

My mother always called him Randall.

CHAPTER 8

The bus station smelled of disinfectant. I noticed that, finally, after I'd sat on the bench for I don't know how long, staring at my hands, trying not to cry, thinking about my parents. When I noticed the disinfectant smell, I looked around and realized the station was full of strangers, not just to me, but to each other. Nobody acted like they knew anybody. Everyone was busy reading or staring at the ceiling or rearranging things in their suitcases or walking to the glass doors to peer out.

I was in Portland, which wasn't near anything, and unless I wanted to spend the night sitting on a bench in the bus station, I'd better find out how to get back to Seattle.

At the ticket counter I learned that I would have to wait two hours for a bus to Seattle. But at least the ticket seller agreed to trade in my unused miles to San Jose for a return ticket to Seattle. She did ask why I wanted to go back so soon and I tried not to cry when I told her the people I planned to visit weren't going to be in California and so I was going back home to my grandmother's house.

She nodded and said that was a good idea and I should phone my grandmother and tell her what time my bus would arrive. I said I would.

Returning to the bench, I settled down to wait, my elbows on my knees, my head in my hands.

"You look a long way from home," a soft voice said.

A guy sat down next to me. He looked maybe eighteen or nineteen, but I wasn't sure. He was dressed neatly and had a nice smile.

I said, "Uh-huh."

"You have any friends here in Portland?"

I didn't answer. I didn't know why he wanted to know and it made me uncomfortable, the way he was looking at me so closely.

As though he sensed that, he leaned back against the bench and looked away from me. He said, "Nothing worse than a strange city. It's rough when you don't know anyone. I know what that's like. I came here by myself a couple of years ago and it was real hard until I met some people and found a job."

I didn't answer. He seemed nice enough, and probably he was just looking for someone to talk to, but I wasn't in a talking mood.

"Listen," he said, "if you're looking for a place to stay, I've got a girlfriend who'd put you up for a few days. Maybe she could help you look for a job. You looking for a job?"

I shook my head.

"No? Oh well, then, if you're okay I won't bother you. Just thought you looked like you might need a little help. I'd be glad to help you. I could call my girlfriend and she'd come down here if you want to meet her."

That was nice of him I thought, and I started to say that I wasn't staying in Portland, but I didn't get a chance.

An elderly woman beckoned to me from a bench across the way and at the same time she said, "Girlie, come here."

"Me?" I asked, looking at her.

"Yes, you. Come here. I need some help."

She rubbed her head as though she felt faint. I stood and started toward her.

"Bring your luggage," she said.

Puzzled, I picked up my backpack and walked over to her. She was older than Gran, bent, with frizzy gray hair and a lined face. She had on a flowered dress and a heavy coat, even though it wasn't cold, and a small hat. Her hands appeared to be twisted. She was grasping a large purse.

"Sit down next to me," she said softly. I had to lean close to hear her.

I sat next to her and she said, "Now you look in my purse and see if you can find a bottle of aspirin. That's right, look in it. Now you just get that out and open it for me. I can't turn the lids on these bottles.

That's a help."

She looked across at the opposite bench at the young man. He sat there pretending not to look at us. I knew that from the way his head was turned.

"Do you know that boy?" she asked.

I said, "No."

"Are you a runaway?" she asked.

"No! I'm waiting for my bus. Back to Seattle."

"Do you have family in Seattle?"

"My grandmother. I live with my grandmother."

"That's all right then," she said. "You stay right here with me until your bus comes."

"Yes, sure, if you're not well. Maybe I should get you some help," I said. Did she have a bad heart? Was she going to faint? I didn't know what to do, but I figured I could go to the ticket counter and ask somebody there what to do.

"Nothing like that. I'm fine," she said, and I realized that she had dropped the aspirins back in her purse without taking any. "But I want you to stay right here."

"Okay," I said. Maybe she was crazy. How had I gotten into this anyway, alone in a strange city with a crazy woman?

Very softly she said, "Do you know what that boy is?"

"What he is?" I didn't understand.

"Do you know what a pimp is?" she asked.

I said, "I think so. Sort of."

I'd seen pimps on TV shows. They were older and looked mean, like criminals. She must have figured I didn't really know because she kept talking in that low voice that only I could hear. "Pimps hang around bus stations looking for runaway girls. Young girls like you. Girls who haven't any friends or any money. Then they pretend to be their friends. They give a girl a place to stay and feed her and act nice for a while. And then they make her be a prostitute."

"How can they make her do that?" I asked. "If she doesn't want to?"

"Lots of ways. Trick her. Pretend to love her. Get her on drugs. By the time the girl figures out what happened, it's too late, she's got herself in so deep she doesn't know how to get out."

"Why are you telling me this?" I asked. Like her, I was whispering.

"Because that pimp was trying to pick you up. Now I want you to tell me the truth. Are you really going home to Seattle?"

When the bus finally arrived, I climbed on and found a seat and huddled against the window. I wasn't any of the things I'd been that morning, not nervous, not excited. I was tired. I didn't know what Gran would say or how I would explain why I'd returned. And I didn't care, not just then. I was too tired to think. I wasn't tired from the riding or the waiting, none of that had been physically difficult, but my brain was tired. I'd thought and thought and none of my ideas made sense and I didn't know what I was doing, riding a bus to Portland and then back.

All I knew was that I didn't know how to make my life the way I wanted it to be.

And then after I got off the bus in Seattle, I had to wait another hour for the city bus to Eastside. By the time I reached Gran's house, it was almost midnight. I walked up the steps, my backpack hanging heavily from my shoulders. Tonight I rang the bell.

After a long wait, I heard Gran moving through the house. The porch light came on.

She opened the door and peered out at me. Her hair was covered by a net. Her face was scrubbed clean of makeup. She clutched her bathrobe closed with one hand. Only the bright fingernails looked like my glamorous grandmother.

"Elvy?" Even her voice sagged with sleep.

"I'm sorry about waking you up," I said.

"Come in," she said, and led the way into the kitchen, where she flipped on a light. "Had any supper?"

"No. I'm okay."

"Better fix yourself a sandwich," she said.

No "Where have you been?" or "What's going on?" or "Explain yourself." In that moment I liked my grandmother more than I had ever liked anyone. Of course I'd always loved her, she was my grandmother, after all. But right then, I liked her the way I'd like a friend. A lot more than I liked my father.

She poured herself a glass of wine, sat down at the table, and lit a cigarette. Her health habits were terrible. She needed someone to take care of her.

She needed someone but that someone probably wasn't me. I couldn't take care of myself very well.

I spread peanut butter on bread while she watched, silent.

Finally I said, "When I got to Portland, I thought I'd better phone and see if Pop could meet me. At the bus station. In San Jose. Or tell me how to get to his place. But he wasn't there." Her eyebrows rose but still she didn't say anything.

"His girlfriend was. She answered."

Gran nodded and said, "Uh-huh."

"I'd forgotten about her."

"Oh."

"I'd forgotten all about her. I didn't want to see her." My voice rose, even though I tried to keep it down. "Maybe they're married! I don't know! Nobody tells me anything! I don't even know her name!"

"Cheryl."

"What?"

Gran said, "I think her name is Cheryl."

"Are they married?"

Gran shrugged. "I heard her name once. That's all. I don't know anything else."

"They live in an apartment. She said I could sleep on the couch. For a night. Maybe two nights. That's not what I wanted! She'd be there! I'd never get to talk to him alone!"

I was crying, rubbing at my tears with my fists, my throat so tight I could hardly breathe, and yet somehow I was forcing myself to take little bites of the sandwich.

"Anything I can do to help you?" Gran asked.

I shook my head. "Maybe I'll watch the late movie on TV. I don't think I can sleep now."

Gran washed out her wine glass and put it back in the cupboard. I carried my sandwich and a glass of milk into the living room and turned on the TV, keeping the sound low.

Gran stood looking down at me, as I settled myself in the armchair. I thought she was going to question me further, or give me a big lecture. Having me around must be rough. I didn't expect her to remain patient forever.

But all she said, before she left and went into her bedroom, was, "Apartment couches are always lumpy. You wouldn't have been comfortable."

About an hour later, after I'd eaten my sandwich and finished my milk and watched half the movie, I thought about what she'd said.

"Apartment couches are always lumpy."

She was a very strange person.

But nice. Not like some people.

She didn't expect me to sleep on a lumpy couch. Which I wouldn't have minded. Or tell me I could only visit for a day or two. Which I did mind. Very much.

The movie ended and I didn't know what had happened, my mind was so full of so many mixed up thoughts. I kept hearing Gran saying apartment couches were lumpy and That Girl saying I could sleep on the couch for a night or two and Mom saying her apartment was too small.

CHAPTER 9

And then as though I didn't have enough trouble in my life, I had a fight with Harry.

I don't know what Harry actually did in the library. According to

Harry, he was reading a book and not bothering anyone. However, Harry never read except when he was trying to look busy to cover up some other activity, so I knew that wasn't the whole story.

And none of that mattered. I didn't really want to know what Harry had done. Whatever it was, it got him expelled from the library.

"I was minding my own business, studying, not doing anything!" Harry complained that night. We were in the backseat of Tom's car, parked at the drive-in and drinking milkshakes, as usual.

"Sure you were," Tom said.

"I was! Anyway, it wasn't any of his business and it wasn't my fault and I'm gonna get that creep," Harry said, and we all knew he was talking about the librarian, Mr. Moore.

It did seem to me that if Harry spent half the energy studying that he spent getting even with people, he'd get straight As, but there was no point telling that to Harry.

"What are you going to do?" Lisa asked.

"Don't worry, I've got it figured."

"You gonna tell us?" Tom asked.

"Yeah, maybe," Harry said.

He was like that when he was angry, spreading his anger at Mr. Moore around at all of us. I knew he'd sulk until he'd played his prank, whatever it was, and then he'd be cheerful until his next fight.

"So don't tell us," Lisa said. "But don't expect us to help, either."

"I don't need your help. I'm doing this one alone."

Something about the way he said that made me uneasy. Harry could be stupid. And he could be mean. And if he did something really awful, like paint insults on the school walls, Paul would think I helped him.

"You could at least tell us," I said. "Or don't you trust us?"

"I don't have to tell you guys everything."

"No, and we don't ever have to help you again."

At that point I wouldn't have been surprised if he'd jumped out of the car and left us, but he didn't. He gave me one of his long, slow looks, his eyes glittering beneath half-closed lids, his mouth a tight line. He seemed to be making some decision. I couldn't figure what.

Then he said, "Okay, I'll tell you. I've got some fireworks. I can set them up in his desk drawer. When he opens the drawer, they'll go off."

"You've got what!" Lisa screeched.

"How you gonna make that work?" Tom asked.

"Fireworks!" I said. "You mean like firecrackers or like explosives?"

"What's it matter?" he said, and the tone of his voice dared us to question him further.

"It matters a lot," I said. "Someone could get hurt."

"Yeah, I knew I shouldn't have told you."

"Harry, listen, a joke is a joke, and the grade book was funny and so was the school bulletin, but explosives! Somebody could loose a hand or an eye or something and that is not funny."

"Nobody gets hurt. It makes a big noise, that's all, and scares the hell out of him, that's all."

"That's not all," I argued. "You can't be sure he won't put his hand too close. And anyway, you can't trust fireworks. They can misfire. They can start fires. They can shoot off in weird directions and hit somebody."

"I didn't want to tell you! I knew you'd start yelling! I didn't ask you to butt in!" Harry shouted.

"Right! And I am butting out right now!"

Jokes were one thing, but fireworks! I'd been crazy to ever go around with Harry. Without waiting for any more of his arguments, I opened the car door, got out, and marched away from them across the parking lot.

"Where are you going?" Lisa called after me.

"Home," I shouted back over my shoulder.

Home was only a mile away. I could walk it easily and hardly notice, I was so angry. Harry didn't run after me or try to stop me, which didn't surprise me. Harry was as stubborn as I was, and I didn't go around running after people, either.

At first I was boiling mad at that stupid boy. Imagine anything so dumb as putting explosives in a desk! He could kill someone. Probably himself. I wasn't going to be any part of it. If Harry wanted to blow himself up, wiring up a desk, that was his business. I didn't care. I'd had it with caring about other people. All around me people messed up their lives and mine and then expected me to get myself out. This time I'd stay clear. I didn't care about Harry. He wasn't anyone special. I didn't care about anyone. Not anyone. Nothing that happened to anyone else was ever going to hurt me again.

As I walked, I cooled down. By the time I turned in my street, my thoughts were changing. I was pretty sure that the person most likely to get blown up by Harry's explosives was Harry. No telling what he had hold of, or thought he could get hold of. But whatever it was, he could get hurt. And I really didn't want that to happen. Not because he meant anything to me. He didn't. Already I wished I'd never started going around with Harry. But still, I'd helped him with his other pranks, so maybe if he blew himself up, in some way I'd be responsible.

But how could I stop him?

It wouldn't do any good to tell on him. What was there to tell?

If I went to the principal and said, "Harry Snider has explosives that he's going to put in the librarian's desk," then what? They'd call in Harry and he'd deny it.

At some later time, he'd use them someplace else.

I'd only be delaying trouble.

I walked slowly around Gran's house in the dark and sat down on the back step. What I had to do was think of a way to stop Harry.

How could I do that?

I stared into the dark garden. In the starlight the branches of a conical bush glowed, little tips of branches reflecting light, and it looked a bit like a Christmas tree.

I wasn't really thinking about the bush. My mind was on Harry. But something kept pushing at my thoughts. There were night noises around me, leaves rustling, insects chirping, then a car going by on a nearby street and a dog barking.

And then I thought of it. I thought of a trick that would make Harry forget his stupid explosives.

CHAPTER 10

The next day, on the way to school, I was so busy thinking about my idea and how I'd sell Harry on the idea, I hardly spoke to Paul at all. He said a few of the usual things about having a test and how were my classes, but if he said anything else, it missed me.

Later, thinking back, I did remember him asking, "Do you like chocolate chip cookies?"

"Now? For breakfast?"

"No, of course not now for breakfast. Or maybe so? Why? Do you?" he asked.

"Do I what?"

"Do you eat cookies for breakfast?"

"I eat whatever I can find in the refrigerator," I said and went back to worrying about Harry. I mean, it wasn't the sort of question that I needed to remember or even spend any extra time pondering.

In first period I slid Harry a piece of paper on which I'd sketched my idea. At first he didn't look at it, just put it under his book to let me know that nothing from me could interest him. What if he crumpled it up without looking? What if he wouldn't speak to me?

Harry wasn't the sort of person anyone could walk up to and say, "Let's talk." If he was in a mean mood, he might say anything, and he'd say it loudly so that everyone would hear, and he'd make it something embarrassing.

That left me no choice but to put my idea in a sketch and hope he liked it. If he turned it down, I would be back to last night, trying to find another way to keep him from doing something dangerous.

While I kept my book open and pretended to study, I watched Harry. He sat slumped in his chair, his head back, his lids lowered, those dark eyes moving steadily, seeing everything in the room including me watching him.

I was glad I hadn't written a dumb note saying I was sorry or something like that. The way he looked, he might have held it up, cried, "What's this, oh, my!" and read it aloud.

Maybe he would do that with the picture.

Still, the picture wouldn't mean much to anyone else. It wasn't something that needed explaining.

Finally he slid it out from under his book.

I chewed my lip.

He unfolded it so slowly I felt like shouting at him.

With both palms, he spread it smooth on top of his open book.

He took another slow look at me.

And then he looked down at the drawing.

For half a minute his expression remained the same. I was afraid he wouldn't figure out what I'd drawn. Or he wouldn't connect it to his library prank. But then the corners of his mouth turned up. And very slowly he sat up straight, bent his head forward on his neck and turned his face halfway toward me. Then he winked.

I'd been holding my breath. After I winked back, I started breathing again.

So that was that. Harry would use my idea and nobody would get hurt. Just shocked.

He sat with me at lunch and we figured out exactly how to pull it off.

"It's going to take a long time," he said.

"Yes, well, it will, but it will be worth it. I don't think we can do it alone. Will Tom and Lisa help?"

"They'd better. We'll pick you up at your corner at midnight."

"Tonight?"

"As good as any night."

Really, I would have been as happy to make it never. It wasn't as though I thought up the prank because I wanted to do it. And the longer it was postponed, the longer until Harry began something else. And where did it end? Still, it was exciting, going out with Harry and Tom and Lisa, the kind of excitement that comes on a roller coaster, scary, awful, mind-numbing.

I liked my mind numb. Then I couldn't remember that I hadn't heard from my mother since a week ago Sunday and that I no longer could even bring myself to ask on the phone if I could come live with her. I couldn't set myself up to be hurt every time she phoned.

That afternoon after school, while I was sitting in Gran's empty living room playing with the TV remote control, flipping through commercials and talk shows, the doorbell rang. I wasn't expecting anyone.

When I opened the door, there stood Paul, tall and blond and solemn, with a large grocery bag held in the curve of one arm. He peered at me through his glasses and it seemed to me that his eyes were brighter than usual, but maybe it was just a reflection on the lenses.

"Time for your cooking lesson," he said, his face deadpan. I must have looked shocked, because suddenly he grinned.

Paul wasn't a grinner. Having him look at me that way, his eyes shining, his mouth turned up with a teasing expression on his face, well, with no warning I felt funny inside. Something fluttered right in my middle and I couldn't think of a single word to say to him. For once, he did the talking.

Brushing past me, not even waiting to be invited in, very un-Paul, he said, "I decided to start you on chocolate chip cookies. You do like chocolate chip cookies, don't you?"

"Of course I like chocolate chip cookies. Everybody does. Don't they?" I followed him into Gran's spotless kitchen.

"Everybody may like to eat them, but not everybody knows how to make them. Let me tell you, Elvy Block, chocolate chip cookies are what I know how to make best. That's why I'm starting with them."

I helped him unload boxes of flour and sugar and chips and spices onto Gran's counter. He'd even brought the eggs and a recipe card from his mother's file.

"Where do I find the mixing bowl and the cookie tins?" he asked.

"I don't know. Maybe we don't own any."

"Oh, come on, Elvy, everybody owns mixing bowls." He opened cupboard drawers and began a search. The kitchen had never sounded like that before. Gran always moved quietly. Now doors banged and drawers squeaked and flatware and pans clattered against each other as he dug through them.

"Here, we need this!" he exclaimed and then, "Yes, this, too!" He piled the table with bowls and baking tins.

He also knocked a number of small items to the floor, spoons and a cooling rack, and I followed him around the kitchen, picking up after him.

I was amazed that Gran had all the supplies for baking.

"Gran never bakes cookies. In fact, she never bakes anything."

"Maybe she used to bake. When her husband was alive."

"Maybe. I can't remember."

"We'll surprise her," he said, and dropped a measuring cup filled with flour on the floor. Right away he was down on his hands and knees, trying to scrape it up in his palms. The flour slid between his fingers like beach sand, spreading further across the clean linoleum.

He looked so funny, his face suddenly gone serious, his forehead lined with worry, and his knees and elbows sticking out at awkward angles, that I had to laugh.

"Let's not surprise her that way," I said and got the broom.

"Right," he said and swung around and bumped the empty pans with his elbow, knocking them off the table.

I made my voice very firm, kind but firm, and said, "Paul, sit down in that chair and read me the recipe. Tell me what to do, step by step, and I'll do it."

He said a meek, "Yes," sat in the kitchen chair and read to me. The yes was meek. That's all. As soon as he started telling me what to do, he became even firmer than I'd been, even borderline bossy.

"Half a cup of sugar. No, that's too much, take out a spoonful, careful, hold it up to the light, yes, that's it, okay, now mix it into the eggs, don't dump it! Mix it."

"I am mixing! This is mixing!" I protested.

"You don't mix by shaking the bowl. Use a fork."

"Oh. A fork. Why didn't you tell me that?" I found a fork.

"Sort of fold the eggs under. Gently. Don't slosh."

"I am not sloshing!" I shouted. "Any fool can see that I am folding!"

"Do you want me to teach you cooking, or not?"

"You remind me of the gym teacher giving directions. All you lack is a whistle."

"Next time I'll bring my whistle."

"You own a whistle?"

"I'll purchase one especially. If I'm to teach you, I obviously need to be properly equipped," Paul said.

"What's that mean?"

"It means that you're a difficult pupil."

"Maybe you're a rotten teacher!"

We were arguing on the surface but it wasn't real arguing. It was teasing, thinking up silly things to say, the way we'd done when we played with Paul's trains.

It was fun doing things with him. Mom had never been much of one for cooking, but sometimes during the holidays she'd go on a baking binge, whipping out fruitcakes to give to friends, and she'd put me to work chopping up nuts and candied fruit. "I'm the captain here," she'd say, "and you're my team."

It was nice to be part of a team again.

And we made a good team, Paul and I, if the cookies were any proof. They were terrific.

"Look out, they're hot, you'll burn your mouth!" Paul warned too late.

I'd already bitten into a warm cookie and hit a fiery-hot chocolate chip.

With a howl, I dashed to the sink and leaned over it and drank straight from the faucet.

"Are you all right?"

"Of course not!" I screamed. "How can I be all right with a burned tongue?"

"Then you better not eat any more," he said.

"I'm not that burned! Besides, I need another cookie to console myself."

"That's sound reasoning," he agreed.

When Gran came home, the house smelled of baking. She walked in, looked at the racks of cooling cookies, then at Paul and me washing off the counters.

"I feel like the shoemaker who got surprise visits from the elves," she said.

At that moment, nibbling on warm cookies and making jokes with my grandmother and Paul, my life really did feel more like a sitcom than it had in ages. Or than it would again for a long time.

If I could have stopped time right then, I would have.

And just when things were humming along, Paul said, "I better head home now. It's dinner time."

As I walked with him to the door, I tried to keep my voice bright. "Probably we've wrecked your appetite."

"Probably."

"Don't tell your mother it was me or she won't let you come play with me anymore."

"I keep telling you, my mom likes everybody."

"Okay. I owe you a skateboarding lesson."

"You don't owe me anything," he said.

"Yes, I do! That was the deal! I said that if you taught me to cook,

I'd teach you to skateboard! Don't you want to know what a wheelie is?"

"Without knowing what a wheelie is, I am sure it is something I don't want to do."

"How can you say that? You might love wheelies!"

In a solemn voice he said, "I will give you more cooking lessons only on the condition that you never, as long as we both may live, expect me to get on a skateboard."

"Oh, all right, you'll probably live longer that way," I agreed.

"You didn't have to say that. You could have made up some polite lie," he said. "See you tomorrow."

I wished he didn't have to leave. But then, I'd wished that about other people and in the end, they always did leave me. So I didn't say anything else except goodbye.

Gran had work to do after we finished a quick supper of soup and salad. Then the evening fell into the usual dull pattern of homework, watching a few TV shows, then pretending to go to bed.

At midnight I was on the corner, waiting for Harry.

CHAPTER 11

Getting into the school building was the easy part. Harry knew his way past any lock. In the school library we turned on our flashlights and put them on the floor where there would be no chance of their light showing through the windows. The flashlights sent thin, weak lines of light crisscrossing each other. The windows were large squares dimly glowing from the distant streetlights. The room was as dark as a moonlit night. We couldn't see colors, but we could see shapes, and that was all we needed.

First we moved all the tables, carrying them from the center of the room and lining them up against the wall. Then we started on the books.

Shelf after shelf, we emptied the books and set them on end to form a large circle in the center of the library floor. We filled it in, a solid circle of books, not just a perimeter. On top of that, set in six inches from the edge, we built another solid circle. We emptied all the shelves in one row.

Lisa moaned, "This is killing me. My arms are falling off. I'm quitting."

Harry knelt beneath the window level and shone the flashlight on his watch.

"We've already been here an hour and we've only got two layers. We gotta keep moving."

"I can't," Lisa whined. "My back hurts."

Tom said, "Sit down a minute, honey."

Harry said something and it was just as well that he mumbled it, because if we'd heard what he said, we all might have walked out.

Instead, Tom, Harry, and I kept walking back and forth to the shelves, lugging armloads of books. Whenever I felt as though I couldn't lift one more stack, I worked on the encyclopedias. They had dark red covers with gold trim, and though I couldn't see the color in the darkness, I knew how they would look in daylight. Walking around the circle, I used the ledges formed by the inset of each row. I placed an encyclopedia, face out, every ten book widths, to make a pattern.

When Lisa grew bored with sitting, she went back to lugging books.

"I hope you think up something easier next time," she said.

"Quit grousing and keep working," Harry said.

"Something where we don't have to lift anything."

"Yeah, sure."

"Maybe someplace besides in the school. I don't like it in here at night. I don't even like it in here in the day."

Hany laughed. "That's about the smartest thing I've ever heard you say."

"What's that supposed to mean?" Because she was tired, Lisa was whining again. We all knew that sound. She could go from there to tears in seconds.

Harry said quickly, "It means you're right. Next time we do something outside. Hey!"

He stopped, silhouetted in front of the window. "Hey, Lisa! How would you like to climb the water tower?"

There was a water tower on the land behind the school, a storage tank of some kind, that rose more than one hundred feet in the air. It stood on a steel framework and its base was surrounded by a chain link fence. I had a vague memory of a barbed wire top, but I wasn't sure. I hadn't paid that much attention to it.

Lisa said, "Are you crazy? Who'd want to do that?"

Harry said, "If a person climbed that thing, he could paint his initials on it with spray paint, you know?"

"Leave your initials? What for? Then they'd know it was you."

"So what?" Harry said. "It's not like breaking into school. What's anybody going to do? Besides, unless they caught me, how could they know I did it? I could say I was somewhere else."

"Oh, sure, who'd believe that?"

"Okay, so what if I climb it and then paint 'Hi, Lisa' on it? Anybody knows you wouldn't climb it."

"That's really crazy," Lisa said, but she sounded happier, as though she liked the idea of her name on the water tower.

"Yeah, well, maybe I will," Harry said. "How about you, Elvy. You game?"

I wasn't about to commit myself to anything. I said, "By the time we finish this, I may never move again."

We'd been at it for three hours. I couldn't actually see the sky getting lighter yet, but I knew it would soon. I ached all over. Would I be able to make it out of bed in the morning? Would I even get a chance to go to bed before morning?

While we worked, Harry kept talking about how we could climb the tower. He and Tom lugged tables close to the tree, stood on them and kept stacking books.

The circles of books reached almost to the ceiling now, each one a bit smaller. We stood back and took it in.

It looked like my drawing, a Christmas tree shape of books more than ten feet tall, decorated with a pattern of matching encyclopedias. It was ready for the star.

Tom put the big table dictionary on the top shelf of the nearest bookcase. The case was empty now. He and Harry slid it as close to the tree as they could get it.

"Look out, don't push any farther, we're against the bottom row. If we put any weight on that tree, it might start collapsing," Harry warned.

Tom grunted his agreement. He held the bookcase steady while Harry climbed up it. Then Harry lay flat on his stomach on the top shelf and inched his way toward the tree. Tom stood behind him on a table and held Harry's ankles.

Harry leaned out like one of those actors who wears shoes that are attached to the stage. I held my breath. I really wasn't sure he could do it.

He held the large dictionary in his hands. Its weight made Harry top-heavy. I could see his arms shaking. I could feel perspiration popping out on my own forehead.

And then the edge of the dictionary touched the top circle of the tree.

Harry slid it slowly, slowly into place.

Tom clung to Harry's legs, rooting him to the top shelf.

Harry said, "One more minute."

He opened the dictionary flat, so that its pages stood up in a fan, making a decoration on the very top of the book tree.

Until Harry climbed down and was firmly on the floor, I held my breath. Then I applauded, very softly. It really was a sight, that book tree.

"Can we go now?" Lisa asked.

Harry glanced around and saw two shelves of books. Only two shelves left in that whole library. But Harry was a perfectionist in his peculiar way.

He insisted that we unload those shelves and stack the last books in neat little piles around the tree, like packages.

Then we left.

It was three thirty in the morning and I was ready to drop. All I wanted to do was get home to bed. We let ourselves out of the school, carefully closed all doors behind us, and headed down the walk.

We all heard the car turn the corner, saw the headlight beams cut across the school lawn. It happened so fast, we didn't have time to duck. The lights caught us, shone in our eyes, then swept on, but we heard the brakes, the tire squeals.

"Cops!" Harry hissed. "Run!"

I took off at top speed, not stopping to see where anyone else was going, cutting across the lawn and ducking between buildings, running faster than I'd ever known I could. I plunged into darkness.

A hand reached out of nowhere and grabbed me, a long hand, the fingers completely circling my wrist. The hold didn't stop me. The person raced along with me.

I almost screamed.

"Elvy! This way!"

It was Paul's voice, barely above a whisper.

He turned toward the back of the gymnasium, still holding onto my wrist. I could hear our feet pounding on the ground. My heart pounded even more loudly.

We'd only gone a few steps when Paul stumbled. I wrenched my wrist free from his grip just in time to stop him from pulling me down on top of him, then grabbed his arm to help steady him.

He continued to run in a half-crouch, limping awkwardly, banging against me. I was afraid he would sprawl flat and there we'd be, waiting for the police to catch us.

"Let's go, let's go!" I whispered, as though I was cheering on a team.

We raced across a brightly lit patch of paving, rushing toward the shadows.

A few steps more and we were at the dumpsters.

We wedged ourselves in between those tall metal trash containers and the side of the building. In that narrow space the air seemed suddenly cold and it smelled of garbage. I almost dashed back out.

A flashlight's beam played across the alley, running up the building walls, casting deeper shadows where we hid. I held my breath.

Paul's hands gripped mine, our fingers digging into each other's palms, sending each other messages to be quiet, not move, not breathe.

Footsteps pounded past on the blacktop driveway that circled the back of the building. Someone said, "You go left, I'll take the right."

Was it a trick to draw us out? Did they guess we were there, almost in touching distance? Was it a cop game where they talked as though they were leaving and one left while the other remained in the shadows, waiting?

I was too terrified to move, sure they would hear the slightest noise.

The footsteps faded away into the distance. It sounded like two people running, not one.

I let out my breath slowly.

"Are they gone?" I whispered.

"I think so."

"Paul, what are you doing here?"

"I could ask the same of you." He sounded angry.

"Paul, did you follow me tonight?"

"Hush. Listen. That's their car."

I listened but I didn't hear anything. "Whose car?"

"The police car."

"I don't hear it. What are they doing?"

"Driving away. Or circling the block."

"What'll we do?"

"Get out of here. Come on now, I'll take you home. I'm parked over in the next block."

"I can get home," I said, not one bit pleased to have Paul tagging after me, acting like my keeper.

He pulled me out from behind the dumpsters, where the pale light of the streetlamps shone on us.

He stood over me, staring down, and he opened and closed his mouth twice, as though he wanted to say things that he could not bring himself to say. Maybe he wanted to shout at me.

Finally he spoke in that tight, controlled voice that I'd begun to recognize.

"Yes. You can start to walk home. And the police will pick you up and take you there. That would be a nice surprise for your grandmother."

"Listen here, Paul Apple..."

"Shut up," he said, so firmly that I did.

Besides, I was too mad to speak softly and I didn't think that shouting at him, there in the back alley behind the gymnasium with policemen popping up unexpectedly, was a good idea. So I held it in until we reached his car.

After we were in, with the doors closed, I said, "Get this straight. You are not my big brother."

"Thank God for that."

"So just quit trying to run my life."

As he drove, the dashboard lights outlined his face. His jaw had that hard, square look, like he was clamping his teeth together, which he wasn't because actually, he was yelling now. Not loud, not like I yell, but it was yelling for Paul, his voice strained with fury.

"You get dumber and dumber, Elvy Block. For a smart girl, you're ignoring your brain. You've got your path set on self-destruct. And what for? Because you're mad at your parents, that's what!"

"That's none of your business!" I shouted, and my shouting was real shouting, loud and sharp.

"Nothing you do is ever anybody's business! You think you're your own world and that what you do doesn't matter to anyone else. But sure as you keep this up, somebody is going to get hurt or something is going to get wrecked and you'll wind up in the police station or the hospital, and how do you think your grandmother will feel then? Or your mother? Or is that what you want? Do you want to hurt everyone around you?"

"You're like everybody else, you know that, Paul? You want to be my friend only as long as I behave by your rules. Let me be the least bit of bother and you're not my friend any more. You want to know about my parents? I'll tell you about my parents. They loved me just fine as long as it wasn't any trouble. But when they thought of better things to do, they forgot I existed. So there it is and I hope you're happy with it." I was fighting back tears. I was determined not to cry in front of him.

"And what about your grandmother? Did she desert you?"

"Leave Gran out of this!"

"No! I won't! I like your grandmother. She's a nice person. She doesn't deserve you. Or maybe I mean that the other way around. Anyway, it's time you thought about her."

"Gran took me in like she'd accept any obligation! She's one of those people who does what she thinks she has to do. She didn't ask for me. She got stuck with me. And we both know it. She would probably dump me in the garbage if she thought she could!"

"That's not fair, Elvy," he said. "Your grandmother isn't like that at all." His voice was low. So in control. So know-it-all.

I knew I wasn't being fair and I really didn't mean what I was saying about Gran, but I couldn't bear listening to Paul criticize me.

"Don't tell me about my life! It's my life, not yours! I can do what I want!"

We'd reached my house. He pulled up to the curb. He said, "Don't be stupid."

I opened the door softly because although I was so furious with Paul that I wanted to pound him with my fists, I was not so mad that I forgot about Gran.

I hissed, "Stay out of my life, Paul. Just leave me alone!"

And I didn't wait to hear his answer. It would be another dumb lecture. Who needed that?

CHAPTER 12

The tree of books wasn't as much fun as we'd thought it would be. Mainly because nobody got to see it. When we arrived at school the next morning, the library door had a "closed" sign that covered the glass. No one could see in. Also, all of the window blinds were drawn. And that's the way things remained all week, with no explanation to the student body.

The following Monday the library was open as usual, all of the books shelved in the regular places.

Oh, sure, everyone heard rumors, but that wasn't the same.

Harry was furious. So were Tom and Lisa. It wasn't just that the stunt had been covered up so well. It was more than that.

"I wrecked my best jeans and tore my hands climbing over the fence," Lisa whined when we all met at lunchtime the following day. "And Tom tore his shirt."

"What fence?" I asked.

"The fence around the football field. The gate was locked. And we could see those cops. We could see their flashlights."

"Big deal," Harry grumbled. "Anybody could get over that fence okay."

"Look at my hands!" Lisa held her hands out, palms up. They were bruised, with deep red cuts. It made me wince just to look. But not Harry.

"Yeah, well, if you weren't so clumsy. Wish I'd been close to the fence. Instead I got cornered by the bus shed and I ended up hiding in there all night."

"Serves you right!" Lisa said.

"All night?" I said.

"Yeah, the door opens right by that side road and those cops kept cruising by, shining their lights along there. I couldn't get out."

"It was your dumb idea. You made us work too long. I was too tired to run," Lisa said.

"So don't do me favors. Get lost," Harry said.

"Hey, that's enough," Tom said.

"I won't anymore," Lisa said. "Do your stupid tricks by yourself."

"Hey, Lisa," Harry said, his voice softer, but he was too late.

She pointed a finger at him. "I don't want to do anything more with you."

When she turned and marched away, Tom gave a shrug and followed her.

"What's she mad about? I'm the one who got stuck all night in the shed," Harry said. "Hey, where did you go, Elvy?"

"Down the alley behind the gym."

"And you didn't get caught? Wouldn't you know it. You're the one who thought up that stupid tree and you're the only one who got away easily."

I said, "Thanks, Harry, thanks a lot for nothing," before I walked away.

Now neither Harry nor Paul were my friends, which made me one hundred percent friendless in my new school. Not that I minded so much about Harry. Or Lisa and Tom. I never much liked them, anyway. They were just people to talk to and go out with.

I wouldn't have minded losing them if I still had Paul as a friend.

I didn't. I didn't even have him as a silent driver. That last blowup was too much. Well, I told him to stay out of my life, didn't I, so I couldn't blame him when he did just that. Now I rode the bus to school like everyone else. The difference was I didn't know the other people on the bus. None of them were in my classes and no one said hello to me.

And Mom didn't phone that weekend and Gran was home late every night.

I wished I was somebody else.

By the middle of the next week I was so bored and lonely, I would have welcomed a goldfish as a best friend.

That was Wednesday. What is it the poem says? Wednesday's child is filled with woe. Something like that. And it could have been a prophecy.

On Wednesday I walked across the parking lot at school during noon hour. That may seem an odd place to walk, but what happened was this. I couldn't face one more lunch hour sitting at a table full of kids in the cafeteria and having nobody say anything more to me than, "Would you mind moving over so my friend can sit next to me?"

So I picked up a sandwich and a carton of milk and headed out to the parking lot to eat alone. Actually I sat on the hood of Paul's car. His car was the only friend I had left. It didn't mind me being there and it never told me what to do. Also, it was once again covered with a thin film of yellow pollen from the trees, almost as though it was expecting me to write notes on it.

Reaching up from my perch on the hood, I wrote in the pollen on the car's roof, "Miss America of the Parking Lot."

So there I was, sitting on Paul's car, writing notes, and probably given another few minutes I would be talking to the car.

Instead I heard Harry call my name.

He was standing on the far side of the building, where all the smokers stood, and waving at me.

If I had ignored him, and let over be over, none of what happened would have happened, or at least, I don't think so. So in a way, it was my fault.

What I did was, I went to talk to him. I should have known he hadn't called to me just to say hello. Not Harry. He had something else in mind. Back to trouble.

"Look," he said, sticking his hand in his jeans pocket and pulling out a handful of little firecrackers. They were all strung together, so if one end of the string was set on fire, they'd go off one after another, bang, bang, bang.

I hate those things. And I told him so.

"What are you doing with those at school? Trying to get more detention?"

Harry scowled at me. "Okay, be like that, I won't tell you."

"You don't have to. I can guess. You're going to toss them into a restroom or the shower room or maybe even light a long fuse and leave them in the principal's desk. Something stupid. And get yourself in a lot of trouble and maybe hurt somebody."

"Golly gee whiz, I'm sure glad I saw you," Harry said and stuffed the firecrackers back in his pocket.

As I couldn't think of anything else to say to him without getting into a shouting match, I walked away, back to Paul's car, where I climbed up on the hood and finished eating my sandwich.

Across the lot, I could see Harry. He had a cigarette in his mouth.

His head was bent down over his cupped hands. After he lit the cigarette, he shook out the match.

That's when I happened to look toward school and saw the vice principal come out of the side door.

It was like watching a slow motion shot of a disaster, one of those films where a car careens toward the edge of a cliff and then floats out into space, or a cop-killer circles behind the cop and slowly raises his gun. One of those scenes.

Where you want to scream a warning.

But screaming won't change a thing. You're already too late. The bad thing is happening.

I saw Harry look up. That must have taken half a second. It felt like half an hour. Because I knew exactly what he would do and I couldn't stop him.

Even if I shouted, he would do it. Maybe faster.

Maybe given a few seconds to think, he'd remember what he had in his pocket, I prayed, but if I shouted, he wouldn't think, he'd just catch the warning about the vice principal approaching.

That thought went through my mind.

I didn't do anything and it didn't matter.

Hany never once remembered that string of firecrackers in his jeans pocket.

Out of habit, he did what he always did when he was about to be caught smoking.

He jammed the lit cigarette in his pocket and then he hit the pocket with the palm of his hand to put the cigarette out.

But of course it didn't go out.

It touched one of those little firecrackers.

I was off the hood of the car and running toward him before they even began exploding.

Those firecrackers went off, bang, bang, bang, one after another, louder and louder, or at least, it seemed louder to me.

Harry's face went dead white.

And then he was screaming and Mrs. Kline, the vice principal, was running, grabbing him, beating at his jeans, but of course by then all the crackers had gone off.

And Harry screamed real screams, nothing fake, real shrieks of pain.

Mrs. Kline shouted at a couple of large boys who were standing nearby, frozen in shock like everyone, and they picked up Harry and carried him past me as though I wasn't there. I'm sure no one saw me, they were all so frightened. They carried Harry to Mrs. Kline's car and put him in it and I could hear him crying and then the car door slammed and she drove off.

"Oh my God, what happened?" people were saying around me.

And, "Where is he going?"

And, "To the clinic, I guess."

Everything blurred. I wanted to vomit. Instead I started walking home, block after block, away from school, putting distance between me and what had happened.

The same thoughts kept screaming at me, as clearly as I'd heard Harry scream.

Why hadn't I argued with him about the firecrackers? Why hadn't I made him get rid of them?

I could have. I knew I could have. If I'd tried, if I'd stayed talking to him, he might have thrown them away or put them in his locker or anything at all except in his pocket. And more than that, if I'd been there, he wouldn't have lit the cigarette.

CHAPTER 13

The next day that's all anyone talked about at school, Hany Snider and how he set off firecrackers in his pocket.

I heard people whispering around me in class.

And when I hurried along the school corridor toward my last class, Carolyn fell into step beside me and said, "Now I guess you're glad you didn't have anything to do with that Harry Snider. His burns aren't half as bad as the trouble he's in."

"Oh! Have you heard how he is? Is he all right?"

She seemed surprised that I cared. "What I heard was that he got bad enough burns to keep him in the hospital for a few days."

"That's terrible," I said, thinking of the pain he must be suffering.

"No more than he deserves. He was probably planning to set those things off in front of somebody."

There wasn't anything I could say to defend Harry. She was right, he had planned to use them to play a trick on someone, though I didn't know who. But I felt guilty, anyway. I wanted to say something kind about him, do something for him. Maybe I could go to the hospital.

And would Harry want to see me? Only if I told him I was sorry we argued. Only if I let him think I was going to go on dating him.

As awful as it was, I knew I had to stay away from Harry. If I hadn't gone along with him on all those pranks, would he have continued? We were his audience, Tom and Lisa and mostly me. Tom and Lisa were tagalongs. I was the one who went with Harry by choice. And I helped him think up his last trick. Even though I hadn't meant to encourage him, I'd done just that.

After school when I headed for the bus, Paul came out of nowhere and caught my elbow and said, "Elvy. You want a ride home?"

Of course I did. Everyone on the bus would be talking about Harry, the same as they had been on the way to school in the morning, and I didn't want to hear any more.

Paul must have guessed that.

I couldn't look at him. His disapproval of me would show in his face, not for everyone to see, but I would see it. I stared straight ahead and let him guide me to his car. He had his hand around my arm. I wished he wasn't there, I was so unhappy.

At the same time, I didn't want him to let go of my arm. I had this feeling that he was the last person in the world who would ever touch me and if he let go, I would crumble to tiny pieces.

I felt like I hadn't slept in years. The previous night, all night long, as soon as I fell into an exhausted sleep, I dreamt of Harry, heard him scream, saw his face twist with pain. Each time I woke up shaking with fear.

The day had been a terrible blur. I hadn't heard a word in any of my classes. All I could see in my mind was Harry lighting that cigarette, his head bent over his cupped hands. And then he slowly raised his face. Slowly, slowly, through what seemed an eternity. He saw the vice principal. And even more slowly, while my voice froze in my throat, he did what he always did, he jammed the cigarette in his pocket.

"And I couldn't even shout," I said aloud.

"It happened in a second," Paul said, and I realized I must have been telling him the whole thing.

Tears poured down my face. "No, I knew! You see, I knew he had those firecrackers in his pocket!"

"Yes. But it's not your fault."

He pulled his car over to a curb on a street I didn't recognize, to give me time to cry it out.

"You don't understand!" I sobbed. "I knew he had the firecrackers. He showed them to me. I should have argued with him. I should have convinced him to get rid of them. Probably I could have done that! Instead I got mad and walked off!"

Paul pulled me into his arms, the way my father used to do when I was upset, and he murmured, "Shh, it's all right, Elvy, don't cry, please don't cry."

Which made me cry more. I felt so miserable, I couldn't think about where I was or who was holding me. For long minutes I sobbed, until finally my throat ached and my eyes burned and I didn't have any more tears.

Paul let go of me then. He pushed a handkerchief into my hand, a nice clean white cotton one that looked as though it had been ironed. I didn't know anyone used real cotton handkerchiefs. It was a lot better than tissues, though, for mopping up my wet face. I rubbed at my eyes.

Feeling a little better, I handed the handkerchief back to him. It was a messy wet wad.

"I'm sorry. I didn't mean to cry. Only I feel so guilty."

"Did you tell Harry to buy firecrackers?" Paul asked.

"No! Of course not!"

"Did you tell him to bring them to school?"

"No, but..."

"Did you tell him to light a cigarette?"

"No."

"So how do you figure you're to blame?"

Paul was being so nice, I started to cry again.

Very softly he said, "Is Harry that special to you?"

"I don't even like him," I said. As soon as I said it, I knew that was so. I didn't like Harry. He was not a nice person. He never took responsibility for what he did. Instead, he blamed everyone else and then retaliated by playing pranks.

"Then why are you so upset?" Paul asked.

"Because in a way, we were friends. I mean, I think he thought I was his friend. I think he wanted me to be his friend. And so I could have maybe done something to make him better. Maybe talked him out of stuff, like the firecrackers. And smoking behind the building. Stuff like that."

"Elvy, you can't blame yourself for the way Harry behaves. He's always behaved that way. What happened to him was his own fault."

"Are you saying he deserved to get burned?"

"No," Paul said. "No! That was an accident. Just a bad accident. He deserved detention or something like that, but nobody deserves to get hurt like that. I didn't mean that. I just mean, he did it himself. You didn't cause him to get hurt."

I rubbed at my tears with my palms.

Paul gave me back the wet wad of handkerchief.

"You'd better keep it," he said.

"Yeah, it's no good to you. I've worn it out," I said.

He laughed at that.

It seemed strange to hear him laugh. We hadn't done much laughing together, not since the day we baked cookies. I was right to want to keep that day forever.

And I was wrong to ever think I could. Nothing good lasted. Not for me.

I wanted to believe what Paul said about Harry, that it wasn't my fault he got hurt. But I didn't. Not really.

That would have been the easy way, to believe that Harry caused his own problems. I could forget about him.

Sure. I could desert him, right when he needed a friend. I could do that. Same as everyone did to me. When my parents walked out, did they look back and say, "Elvy needs us so we'll stick around, even if we have other things we want to do?"

No, they didn't.

I wasn't going to be like that.

To Paul I said, "I'm okay now. I better go home."

What had happened to Harry wasn't Paul's problem. It was my problem. And I had to solve it by myself.

Once Paul had said that I was taking out my anger toward my parents through the pranks with Harry. Maybe. If that was so, I wasn't the one who paid for my anger. Harry was.

I didn't want to have anything more to do with Harry, but I did want to do something for him. I wanted to give him a gift.

While I was sitting in Paul's car, drying my tears and agreeing with him, I decided what to do. I didn't tell Paul. Maybe I should have. It could have saved further grief. But listen, I'd made such a mixed-up mess of my life already, why would I suddenly make a sensible decision?

Right then, while I was assuring Paul that I was all right, I was planning the biggest mistake of my life, the one that made chopping off my hair seem like nothing. I mean, all that got hurt that time was a pile of hair, which had no feelings, and a lot of my pride.

This time I was going for the biggie.

I was risking my life.

And that wasn't the only life I risked.

CHAPTER 14

The water tower stood on four metal legs, with a rung ladder going up one side to the catwalk, one hundred feet above me. I stared up into darkness and saw the enormous black shape of the tower silhouetted against the star-filled sky. The tower looked a million miles away.

Not that I cared. Heights didn't worry me. And I knew I could climb the ladder. Anybody who can do three wheelies followed by a curb hop can climb a rung ladder. The big problem was reaching the ladder. When we were in the library building the book tree, Harry had talked about how to reach the ladder. He had figured it out with two of us helping each other.

Now I had to get there alone. I shouldered my backpack, which held a rope and a paint spray can. If I needed anything else, I didn't have it. I thought hard about what I was going to do and wished I could talk it over with someone.

Well, there wasn't anyone. I was on my own. Again.

The lowest rung of the ladder was ten feet above the ground to discourage climbers, and a chain link fence enclosed the four support legs.

There was a large, painted sign on the fence. Even in the dim light, I could read it. "State Property. Keep Off. Survivors Will Be Prosecuted."

Cute. I wondered what adult had thought up that one.

At least there wasn't barbed wire on top of the fence. When I first looked at it, I thought there was. But then, I hadn't looked at it closely, only from a distance. I hadn't wanted anyone to see me studying the water tower.

Now that I was standing right by it, I could see there wasn't any barbed wire. Just the metal points of the fencing.

I climbed the fence, clinging to its corner pole, wedging my toes into the chain links. When I reached the top, I tossed my backpack on the ridged edge and used it as a cushion while I worked my way over and inside. That was the easy part.

In the next step of this job, I was supposed to climb up on Harry's shoulders to reach the ladder. Once on the ladder, the plan was for me to drop him a rope which he could use to pull himself up.

"We could shinny up the leg," Harry had said, "but the reach over to the ladder looks too far. I don't think we could make it."

I could see now, standing below the tower and looking up at the ladder, that Harry was right, it couldn't be reached from the leg of the tower. But I would have to make it across that way now, wouldn't I? There was no other way to do it alone.

I took the rope out of my backpack, left the paint spray can in the pack, and shouldered the pack. Next I kicked off my sneakers and used the laces to tie them to the two ends of the rope. Then I looped the rope loosely over the outside of the pack, where I could reach it.

The metal pole was hard and cold beneath my sweating palms. I wiped off my hands on my shorts. I'd worn shorts instead of jeans so that I could grasp the pole with my knees.

"Here I go and I hope you appreciate this, Harry," I muttered into the darkness.

Getting a firm grip, I began to edge my way up. Pull with my hands, push with my bare knees and feet. Stretch up. Pull with my hands, push with my feet.

It wasn't easy, but the pole had a slight slant and that was some help. My arms ached. I didn't stop to rest. I knew that if I did, I'd start sliding back down.

I continued like an inchworm, up and up, until I was even with the lower edge of the ladder. It was off to my right. Stretching out one arm, I tried to touch it.

It was out of reach, as Harry said it would be, not far, maybe half another arm length. This was the point at which I would succeed or fail.

Pulling the rope free from my backpack, I swung it out, with a shoe as a weight, toward the ladder. It spun toward the ladder and the shoe hit a rung and bounced away, making a metallic echo.

I reeled in and tossed again. This time my other hand slipped on the pole and I slid down part way. Grabbing at the pole with both hands, I almost dropped the rope.

Starting over, I worked my way up, gripped tightly with my knees and one arm, and did another swinging toss at the ladder with the rope and shoe.

After several misses, I managed to loop the shoe over the lower rung. I let the rope slowly out until the shoe was five feet above the ground. Then I dropped the other end of the rope, also weighted with a shoe, to the ground.

I slid down the pole.

Shinnying up the rope wasn't as hard as going up the pole. I'd done rope climbing in gym class. The doubled-over rope was easier to hold onto. I left it looped over the ladder for my return.

The rung ladder was a cinch, except that it went on forever.

At first I counted the rungs. "Twenty-three, twenty-four, twenty-five ..." Between the thirties and fifties I repeated numbers or skipped numbers or maybe my mind was playing tricks. I kept thinking that I shouldn't be there at all. It's hard to count and argue with myself.

When I lost count, I stopped, hung on the ladder, and peered up into the star-filled sky at the water tower's black form. It rose above me like some evil castle in a fantasy film, larger and more terrifying with every step.

Did it matter how many rungs were on the ladder? I had planned to tell Harry sometime, just so he would know, but would I, even if I was able to keep count? Or was this it, one final gesture and then goodbye Harry?

He would still be sitting across the aisle from me in health class. I could still tell him the number of rungs.

And then I knew that I wouldn't. I would never mention the tower to him. He would know I had climbed it but he wouldn't ask me about it. Anymore than he asked about anything. That wouldn't be cool, not to Harry. He would wait, watching with those glittering eyes, for me to say something.

And I wouldn't. And then he would know for sure that we were through. And neither of us would want the other to explain why. To tell him in so many words that I didn't want to be his friend anymore was not possible. Not without saying things that sounded cruel.

Was that how it had been with my parents? When they parted, had they left all kinds of things unsaid? Was that why they couldn't really explain to me what happened? Didn't they know? Was it possible that a marriage could be like a friendship gone bad? It was simply over, with no one knowing exactly why?

By the time I reached the catwalk around the tower's base, I felt as though I had been climbing all night. I collapsed on the catwalk and looked out across the dark town. From that height I could see over the top of the school and the neighborhood houses. Only treetops were as high as I was.

Streetlights made crosshatch patterns in the silent world below me, casting their glowing circles against trees and streets and parked cars. Between their lights, the darkness was as deep as the silence.

I edged my way around the tower, entranced by the night. I liked the secretness of it, being up there unknown, unseen. I felt like a creature from outer space looking down on a new world. Would Harry have appreciated the view? Or if he'd been there, would he have been saying, "Come on, hurry up, let's get this done. Wow, they'll be surprised."

He had planned to paint our class year on the tower. That way, everyone could guess who did it but no one could blame him. I was going to do him one better.

I was going to paint Harry's initials on the tower.

He would love that.

There he was in the hospital with a burned leg. Stuck in bed. With nurses watching. So everyone would know he hadn't been near the tower.

And then magically his initials would appear on the tower. Everyone would know that HS stood for Harry Snyder.

Or maybe I'd paint, "Harry."

Yeah, that was better. I could paint his first name. So then everyone would know for sure.

After pulling the spray can out of my backpack, I twisted off the protective lid and found the spray button. I couldn't see the button in the dark, but I had studied the can and read the directions before I packed the can in the bag. I knew how the button should feel when the spray nozzle was turned away from me.

The paint was orange, of course. Harry had said something about using orange, that it would be more visible, so orange was what Harry was going to get.

And probably he would like his name facing the school, where everyone could see it from the school yard. Or would that be too obvious?

Harry loved secrets. He didn't really advertise what he did. It was the doing it and letting people guess that seemed to satisfy him. All right. This was Harry's choice.

Edging my way to the far side of the tower, where his name would not be seen immediately, maybe not for a day or two, I reached up and touched the metal side of the tower. I could paint Harry's name at the height of the railing around the catwalk. That way, from the ground a person would have to be standing at a distance and at exactly the right angle to see it between the railings.

And when someone did, they would tell someone else. And for several days the kids would walk out into the field behind the tower and stare up, moving around until they were in just the right spot to see.

Yes, I was sure that would please Harry.

Carefully I sprayed the "H."
And then I heard the sound of the rung ladder vibrating.
In the silent night, it sounded like thunder.
Someone was on the ladder.

CHAPTER 15

Setting down the paint can, I inched my way back around the catwalk. Below me the street looked deserted, but if it was the police, probably their car was parked out of sight.

Now what? There was nowhere to run. All I could do was stay on the far side of the tower and hope they wouldn't circle the catwalk. But if it was a policeman, of course he would. So maybe I would be better off to leave the spray can out of sight and wait for him at the top of the ladder. I'd be nice and polite and go back down.

And then they would take me to jail.

I could tell them I climbed the ladder for fun, just to see if I could do it. The way I skateboarded. Maybe they wouldn't be too mad. It wouldn't be like getting caught with the spray can. That was vandalism.

I held my breath to listen. The ladder was silent. Peering down, I couldn't see anyone in the darkness. Maybe I had imagined a sound.

Wouldn't a policeman call out and tell me to come down? That's what they did on TV.

I heard Gran's voice in my head saying, "Life is not a sitcom, Elvy."

Gran! What would she say when the police called her to tell her that her granddaughter was trespassing on state property in the middle of the night?

And as for finding the paint can, they didn't have to. Tomorrow they'd see the H painted on the tower. Vandalism. I'd be arrested for vandalism.

There it was again. The vibration on the ladder.

Then I heard a terrible clatter, like someone almost falling, a foot slipping on a rung, hands grabbing. My heart felt like it was sinking inside me, kind of pressing against my lungs and stopping my breath.

I whispered, "Who is it?" because I had this terrible feeling that I knew who it was.

"Elvy?" Paul whispered back.

I was both shocked and not at all surprised, and at the same time. Had it been lurking in the back of my mind, the thought that Paul might follow me? Not really, and yet, he did seem to turn up at all the wrong times.

"Paul! What are you doing?"

I heard that awful slipping noise again, a kind of metallic vibration followed by a thud. I half-expected the tower to begin to sway.

Moving around to the ladder, I leaned over and saw him, a long, dark form pressed tightly against the ladder, his arms wound around the rungs. He was almost at the top.

"Are you okay?" I asked.

"No."

"What's the matter?"

"I can't move."

What did he mean, he couldn't move?

"Are you stuck?" I whispered, thinking he might have wedged his foot between the rungs in some way.

"No."

"No? Then what's wrong?"

"I can't move," he repeated, in that odd flat tone that I never could figure out.

Kneeling, I reached down and grasped his arm near his shoulder. "Keep climbing," I said, and then I kept saying it, because I could feel him shaking.

His whole body shook. It was as though he was in an earthquake. And he was making the ladder vibrate.

"That's it, another step, put your hand there, yes, there, all right, one more step, you're here, hey, this is a flat ledge, it's got a railing, get up on the ledge, it's okay."

I didn't know half of what I was saying, I just knew I had to keep talking or Paul would quit moving and he would be stuck forever on the top rungs of the ladder.

Slowly, with me hanging onto him and pulling, he made it up onto the ledge.

"Sit down," I said.

He was on all fours.

I thought that if he sat next to me, his back to the tower, and looked out over the town, he could get a rest before we started back down.

He didn't do that at all. Instead he let himself down slowly, stretching out his arms and legs, until he lay perfectly flat on the catwalk, his fingers clenched around the metal rods of its floor.

"What's wrong?" I asked, kneeling near him.

At first he wouldn't answer. When I put my hand on his back, I could feel that he was still shaking. Sharp, fast little shakes, going through his whole body, like a person does who is terribly cold. But it wasn't cold out at all. Besides, I could feel the heat of his skin through his shirt.

"Paul! What's wrong with you? Are you hurt?"

"N-n-no," he stuttered.

"What is it then?"

"Height!" One word, loud and sharp, as though that's all he could say.

"Height?" What did that mean? I sat still, my hand on his back, waiting for him to explain.

When he didn't say anything more, I had to do my own thinking, and finally it came to me.

"You're afraid of heights? Oh! You're afraid of heights!" I exclaimed.

I'd seen a movie about a mountain climber who froze, spread-eagled on a cliffside, because of fear of heights. He was wearing some sort of special belt with a rope tied to it, and there were people above him hanging onto the rope so that he couldn't fall, and still he froze there on the side of a rock cliff, unable to move.

"If you're afraid of heights, what are you doing up here?" I demanded.

Paul didn't answer.

I couldn't remember what happened to the mountain climber. Somebody saved him somehow, but how? Had someone climbed down to help him? Or had they talked him into climbing up? Yes, I thought so.

Terrific. On a mountain a person could probably climb up a cliffside and then go down an easier slope on the other side. That wouldn't work here. The only way down was the same way as up.

I had to get Paul calm. There was no way anyone else could get him off that catwalk. Even a fire engine ladder wouldn't reach that high, would it? And how would I call a fire engine?

I imagined us staying there all night, finally being discovered in the morning. Everyone would show up for school and then run out to the school yard shouting, "Look at that," and point up at us.

"Great view up here," I said and tried to sound very casual, not the least worried about where we were. "Look, you can see clear over those houses."

Paul remained flat on the catwalk, face down.

"I never saw so many stars," I said. "Maybe it's because we're up above the streetlights. I think the streetlights block out the sky a lot, don't you?"

He mumbled. I couldn't understand what he said.

"Paul, I'm ready to go back down now."

In the movie, everyone around the mountain climber tried to remain calm except one friend who had hysterics. The others were furious with the hysterical friend. Watching the movie, I had been on the side of the calm friends. Now, I understood the hysterical friend. I wanted to shake Paul and shout at him.

Instead I tried to imitate the calm ones, making quiet small talk.

"One H is all Harry gets. I planned to paint his whole name, but I don't have to. We don't have to stay up here any longer. We can go down now. One H. It's done. Still, I think Harry will like that."

Okay, so Paul once asked me not to talk about Harry. The way I figured, right now, I'd be happy to upset Paul with thoughts of Harry. Then maybe he would forget to be upset about the height of the catwalk.

I rambled on, "I came up here to paint Harry's name, partly because I felt bad about him getting hurt. And also because I don't want anything more to do with him. It's sort of a farewell apology. Do you understand that?"

Paul actually mumbled, "Yes."

It was better than silence.

"See, I've been thinking," I went on, as nonchalantly as if we were sitting in his car chatting. "You're right, it's dumb to hang around with Harry. And I don't like him. I really don't. It's just, I didn't know anyone else. So now it's over and I'm calling it quits, but I kind of felt I owed him something."

Paul made a moaning sound.

"Yeah, well, maybe not, but I can't walk out on him. Not cold. I can't do that. Not with him in the hospital. And painting his name up here isn't such a big deal. Not for me. I mean, I'm not afraid of heights."

Paul made a weird, strangling sound. Maybe he was sobbing. I couldn't tell.

Still trying for a cheerful tone, I continued, "And I'm a good climber. Always have been. Very surefooted."

This time he said, "Stop talking. Just stop talking." Very clearly.

Figuring he must be feeling better, I asked, "What are you doing up here anyway? You're crazy, you know that?"

He said a clear, "Yes."

And then it hit me.

Why hadn't I realized before?

This absolutely crazy, insane, terrified, wonderful, sweet boy had climbed up that ladder because he had some idea that he had to save me. That meant he cared a lot about me.

Didn't it?

I could handle Harry and his crowd. I could even handle Paul when he acted like a bossy big brother.

But I couldn't handle anybody who cared about me. Every time somebody cared about me, I cared about them, and I was always the one who got hurt.

I shouted, "I don't want people sacrificing themselves for me! I don't want to be surrounded by martyrs! I have enough problems of my own!"

Paul didn't answer. He probably had no idea what I was shouting about. I wasn't too sure myself. The idea of Paul caring that much about me just about knocked me out. I didn't know what to think or how to handle my mixed-up thoughts.

What did I want? Maybe I did expect people to sacrifice themselves for me. Was that possible? Did I expect more than I gave? Hadn't I wanted my parents to stay together, even when they were miserable together, just to please me?

Hadn't I wanted Gran to be a TV sitcom cookie-baker?

Hadn't I wanted Harry to be a better person than he was?

Hadn't I wanted Paul to overlook all my faults and accept me as myself, even though I didn't do that for anyone else?

And why was I having all these brilliant revelations sitting on top of a water tower when what I really needed to do was figure out how to get Paul down in one piece?

"Hey, Paul," I said, calmer now, "you know what just hit me? My mom didn't want to leave me. Not really. She phones pretty regularly. Do you think she's as unhappy as I am? About having her gone, I mean?"

"I hope she's not climbing towers," he whispered.

Was he trying to make jokes? That was a good sign. Probably people who make jokes aren't quite as scared.

I said, "Considering how high the towers are in New York City, I hope not."

"Me, too," he said, which was another good sign. At this point I considered any coherent words from Paul as a good sign.

"I guess it will all work out. Maybe someday I'll even see Pop again. But I know they won't ever get together again. They have to live their own lives. But just the same, they're still both my parents. And I wish things didn't have to change. Listen, do you think we could start down now?"

In the movie, it was at this point that the climber got a grip on himself and began to slowly edge his own way to safety.

Unfortunately, Gran was right again. Life was not a sitcom. Or a movie.

And Paul was not a character in a script.

He didn't say what I wanted. He said what he felt.

He said, "No."

CHAPTER 16

So there I was, stranded between the stars and Eastside, perched high in the air on a balmy night with a light breeze blowing my bedspring curls around my head, and the nicest guy in town stretched out flat at my feet. And I didn't know what to do.

The only thing about which I was absolutely sure was that I had now done something dumber than chopping off my hair. And because I didn't know what to do, I told Paul about that.

"I was so mad at my mom, I cut my hair off with a manicure scissors. It was the dumbest thing I've ever done. And all Gran said was 'Sweep up the floor.' Still, what else could she say?"

Paul didn't answer.

"Okay, so it wasn't the dumbest thing I've ever done," I went on, carrying this intelligent discussion alone. "The dumbest was climbing this tower. I admit it. It was really stupid. There, I've said it. And I promise I'll never do anything like this again. Does that make you happier?"

He whispered, "No."

I was encouraged. At least he was answering. So he was still conscious. For an awful moment I was afraid he had passed out.

"Paul! You can't stay up here. Please. You have to climb down."

"I don't think so," he said. His voice wasn't shaking. It was dull, flat, kind of like a computer voice, like he was making final statements.

"Do you expect someone to get you off of here with a helicopter?" I asked. I meant it as a joke.

"Do you think they could?"

"Tell you what, I'll go down first and then you can follow after me. I'll be below you. I won't let you fall."

He actually laughed. Not loudly or happily, but a nervous laugh was better than nothing. "You're going to catch me?"

"No, I'm going to hang onto your ankles and get your feet set on the rungs so you won't slip. You'll see. It'll work."

As he was too frightened to move and I didn't think that standing up and switching places would make him feel any better, I got down on all fours and began to climb over his outstretched body.

"What are you doing?" he gasped.

"Going over you to the ladder." I really tried not to jab my knees into his ribs. I wasn't very successful.

"What for?"

"To climb down first."

He didn't answer.

"You are going to follow, aren't you?" I asked.

Still no answer.

I inched my way past his legs until I reached the ladder. When I was several rungs down it, I said, "Come on, edge backward, no, don't turn around and don't look."

When he didn't move, I said, "If you won't climb down, I won't either. I'll wait right here on the ladder. Until I can't hang on any longer. And then I'll fall. But don't worry about that. I don't mind. The important thing is that I will not leave you alone."

"Elvy, that's cheating," he whispered.

Maybe it was, but it got him moving. Flat on his stomach, he edged backwards toward the stairs, feet first.

I kept talking, chattering about anything at all, while he slid to the edge of the catwalk, until his legs stuck out in the air. I put my hand on his ankle and guided first one foot to a ladder rung above me, then the other.

"Keep looking up at the tower," I told him.

I didn't care where he looked as long as he didn't look down. If he did, and saw how far it was, he would probably go right back up to the catwalk. And never come down.

"That's it, okay, the next step, there it is," I said, guiding him, hand on ankle, step by backward step down the ladder. "I guess you were right," I said, to make noise and keep him thinking about anything except the height. "Yeah, you were right. I was doing all those dumb things because I was mad at my parents. I can see that now. The trouble is, if I care about people, then I get hurt. But if I don't care, then I have to be a hermit. Or spend my life with people like Harry. People I don't like."

Did he make some mumbled answers? Encouraged, I chattered away. "No more of this tricks stuff for me. I'm going to spend all my time studying. You'll see, I'll be a model student. Oh, and also, I want to learn more about cooking. You will still help me, won't you? Fine, I think I want to learn how to make spaghetti. You said you knew how to make spaghetti, didn't you? Or we could figure it out, couldn't we?"

Talk, talk, talk, Elvy-girl, I told myself, and if this boy never speaks to you again for the rest of your life, well, better that than leaving him up on the tower. So I kept it up, saying whatever came to mind whether it made sense or not, until I reached the last rung.

"Okay! We did it!" I shouted. "Now I have to go down the rope. Can you get down the last steps and to the rope by yourself?"

"I got up that rope," he said.

I could not imagine Paul climbing a rope. But he had, obviously he had.

We made it down the rope and out over the fence. Paul tore his shirtsleeve going over the fence. I heard a second rip but he didn't tell me what that was. All he mentioned was the shirtsleeve.

"I've wrecked this shirt," he said.

I threw my arms around him, I was so relieved that it was only a torn shirt, and not Paul in broken pieces.

When I realized what I was doing, standing in the dark yard behind the school hugging Paul Macintosh, with my heart pounding for no particular reason because climbing ladders and fences does not make my heart pound, I pushed him away.

I shouted at him. Now I wasn't saying whatever came to my head that I thought would keep him calm. Now that he had both his feet on the earth and the worst he could do was fall on his face from his own height, it was time to get truthful.

I shouted, "I don't like it when people desert me, but I don't expect them to break their necks for me, either! How could you have done anything that stupid! I can't believe you! You're always the smart one, the one who does things right! Don't you know that you could have been killed?"

Paul said, "Yes, but I wasn't, was I?"

"But you could have been!"

"Would that matter a lot to you?"

"Would that matter? Are you crazy? You're the best friend I've got in all the world!"

It was true, and I knew it. I hadn't meant to shout it, but I did.

"Then why do you want me to do wheelies?"

"What?"

"Wheelies," he said again. "I looked up wheelies in a book about skateboarding. It said a wheelie is when a rider balances on one end of the board to lift the other end off the ground. It leads into spins and a lot of other things that sound as dangerous as climbing a water tower."

"Paul, I don't want you to do wheelies! Or climb water towers! Or anything else dumb! I couldn't bear it if anything bad happened to you!"

"That's how I feel about you," he said.

And then he did something that scared me a lot more than climbing the ladder had scared him.

He put his arms around me.

I wanted to stay there forever. And if forever wasn't anything real, I'd take right now, I felt that happy.

I reached up and pulled his face down to mine and kissed him so hard I think I shocked us both.

So there I was, taking chances again.

END

Phoebe Matthews is currently writing three urban fantasy series. **Vampire Career** is the first book of the Turning Vampire series published by Darrk Quest Books. Here is the first chapter.

Vampire Career
Chapter 1

Vampire was never my career choice.

I was born with a severe heart defect and spent my childhood in hospital beds and waiting rooms, surrounded by dull green corridor walls and the smell of disinfectant. What the specialists told my parents is unknown to me. They tried to protect me from the truth, always saying that after the next treatment I would be a normal girl. When I reached my teens, my parents took me on tours of college campuses near our Seattle home and encouraged me to think about a career.

On my sixteenth birthday they gave me a snazzy little sport car. I had always been too frail to walk more than a block or two. The car allowed me to drive myself to school and around town. I think that was the year that I began to believe that I could be independent.

What is it about getting behind the wheel of a car and having all that control? Making quick decisions. Shall I go to the library or shall I stop at the beauty parlor and get my hair cut?

Maybe those decisions seem trivial to people who have made them all their lives. They weren't trivial to me. I had always been too frail to use public transportation, or to walk any distance by myself. Until the day I had my own car, my parents drove me everywhere.

With my own car I was free to change my destination without asking the driver if that would be convenient. Free to change my mind. Free to think I was a girl who had a future to plan. College.

Yes. All at once, I believed it was in my future. And, maybe a boyfriend?

The boyfriend wish was a secret I hardly dared admit to myself. The boys at school were polite to me. They held doors and sometimes asked me about assignments. I was an "A" student. I was also frail, so weak that after walking short distances, my posture sagged and I limped. My hair and complexion were as faded as I felt. Most of the time, the other students really didn't see me as they hurried by to join their friends.

I knew I was daydreaming when I thought about having a boyfriend. It wasn't going to happen. But I daydreamed, anyway. TV shows featuring teen romances were my favorites, watched whenever I had the TV to myself. As for novels, I loved them all, from Regency romances to the modern Young Adult collection at the library.

When I graduated from high school, I was still not well. But at eighteen I was an adult. That didn't mean much to me as I wasn't waiting for the day I could declare my independence. My family was functional, consisting of myself and my two parents who loved me.

Apparently, my age meant something to others.

A specialist made that clear when he looked me in the eyes and said, "Georgia, you might live for another year. Possibly two. I think you are old enough to make your own decision about what you want to do with that time. If your dream has always been to see Paris or to lie on a beach in Hawaii, you should do it now."

That was the day I grew up. I thanked him for his advice. Then I drove my little car out to a mall, found a space in a far corner and cried for an hour. I was so angry at my parents, I wept myself sick. Why had they lied? Why had they let me hope? Hadn't they known?

And then I realized that they had always put my happiness in front of their own. They had given up their own dreams for me, never taking the chance of leaving me in anyone else's care. And that's when I quit crying, grew up, and did exactly what the specialist suggested. I made my own decision.

Naturally, I had read the latest novels and seen movies about vampires and so when I made my choice, I knew where to look. Within a hundred miles of my home in Seattle was a place made famous by rumors of vampires. After thinking through all the future choices open to me, I picked the only one that might actually be possible.

At eighteen, I was off to college.

The college I chose was a small one on the Olympic Peninsula, closer to the ocean than to Seattle. It wasn't a college my parents had taken me to see, or even thought to suggest. What they had in mind, I realized, was something close to home so that they could reach me quickly.

Considering my choice, I needed to distance myself from them.

I did computer searches to locate a studio apartment for rent within easy driving distance of the campus. I made all the arrangements on-line.

And then I told my parents, "The sea air gives me energy. I always feel better when we visit the ocean beaches. I will miss you, but I need to try being on my own."

"I don't like you living so far away," my mother said.

"It's time for me to grow up, Mom."

"Yes, but is it time for us to grow up?" Dad teased. "How are we going to get along without you to tell us what to do?"

Neither of them had the heart to say, Georgia, you need to stay near us because you are dying. Perhaps they were still lying to themselves, believing that the doctors were wrong and I would make a miraculous recovery.

In the end, they agreed to my choice.

Their only request was that I wear one of those electronic locket gadgets that can summon a local emergency service with a touch. No doubt they expected a phone call any minute to inform them I was in a hospital ER or in a morgue. But like the doctor, they wanted me to have as much happiness as I could find. Unlike the doctor, they kept up the pretense to me and to themselves that I would have a long life.

"Georgie, darling, we'll go with you and help you settle in," my mother said.

With both cars packed, my mother drove me in my car, and Dad followed in his car. We drove from the city skyline of tall buildings to the country skyline of mountaintops and forests.

When we reached the Olympic Peninsula, we entered another world. At first, the road ran straight and inland, with glimpses of the water in the distance beyond communities of low houses. Then it curved toward the sea and cut so near it, we could smell the saltwater. On the other side of us, the Olympic Mountains rose sharply above their forested slopes to touch the sky with their snow-tipped peaks.

Dark firs towered above us, casting long shadows across the road. Fog drifted through the branches, pale, shimmering and carrying the clean scents of fir and sea.

If I hadn't been so afraid of what I had to do, I would have hugged myself for joy at the beauty of it.

We found the apartment building easily. My parents were relieved to see that it was on a pleasant street with neat front gardens and convenient parking. The apartment itself was small and clean. Of course my mother busied herself adding bright linens while my father checked the plumbing and appliances to be sure everything worked. Then they looked up phone numbers for a housecleaning service and a laundry that did pickup and pointed them out to me.

"I can keep one room clean," I protested.

"You'll have enough to do with college studies," Mom said. "Let someone else clean the kitchen and bath for you. And don't try to do any lifting by yourself. That's what laundries are for."

"If your money runs low, phone me," Dad said. "My bank can do an electronic transfer the same day."

After they hung up my clothes and shelved my books, they lingered, hugging me. I fought back tears. I would never see them again. I knew that. They suspected it, but for different reasons than mine.

"We can drive over any time you want company," my mother said.

"I know," I told her. "And I would like that. But, Mom, you've always been with me, doing everything for me. I have to learn to handle my own problems."

"We're so proud of you, Georgie," Dad said. "Promise us you won't overdo it. If you feel the least bit tired, you phone."

Every day of my life I'd felt tired. I said, "If I need you, I'll phone. I promise. And I'll email and tell you all about my classes."

It's not as though I had choices. Well, I did, of a sort. I could choose to die or I could choose to not die.

After they hugged me goodbye and reluctantly left me, I drove to the campus to meet with the counselor. I told her, "I have a heart condition that leaves me with very little energy."

She flipped through my folder and nodded. She had my medical records, dummied down to the level I had always been given. Inoperable condition kept under control with prescriptions and regular treatments. Nowhere on that record would anyone have written: Will probably drop dead within the year.

"I've picked a light schedule of classes four mornings a week. I hope that's all right. If that goes well, I can add more hours next semester."

"Very wise plan to pace yourself," she said. "By next semester you'll know how much you can handle."

"Yes, that's what I thought. And also, sometimes I need therapy for my back. This way, I can make medical appointments on Fridays and Saturdays."

"I can see you have thought this through carefully, Georgia. Let me know if there is anything I can do to help you."

She had already done everything I needed from her. She'd approved a schedule that set me free.

As I walked out of her office and into the long hallway toward the exit, I passed a young man. He wouldn't notice me. No one ever did. But I noticed him.

He was standing on a ladder reaching up to a ceiling light fixture with a screwdriver in his hand, his head tilted back so that all I could see of his face was the bottom of his chin. Hanging around his hips and dragging down his jeans was a belt heavy with an assortment of tools. His reach pulled his tee shirt up and left a wide stretch of tan skin bare, from his navel to his ribs.

Staring is rude, of course, and I wasn't thinking. I simply stopped and stared. That body could have been on the cover of one of my paperback romance books.

That's when I heard him laugh. He had a low, friendly laugh. I should have kept walking. Instead, I continued looking up as he bent his face down toward me and I saw that he was laughing at me.

"Hi. You okay?" he asked.

As usual, I felt weak. Or maybe I felt even weaker than usual. He had the loveliest brown eyes, that warm color of brown sugar. "Yes, of course."

"You almost bumped into my ladder."

"Did I? I'm sorry."

Again, he flashed that grin at me. "Not your fault. I'm the one with the ladder blocking traffic."

Embarrassed, I nodded and walked past the ladder and down the hall. He had laughed. He must have seen me staring at his body.

"Nice to meet you," he called after me.

Turning back, I watched him tilt his head upward again to look at the ceiling fixture he was repairing. His light brown hair matched his tan. Broad shoulders, muscular arms, narrow hips--he glowed with health. He was the sort of boyfriend I had dreamed about when I still believed I had a future.

Now I had no illusions. If I stayed and talked to him, he would be pleasant, and speak politely the way people speak to children and invalids. That's how men always treated me.

Not that it mattered any more. He was not at all what I needed to find.

That weekend I packed a small overnight bag, put it in the trunk of my car, and drove along the coast road.

Most of the Olympic Peninsula is filled by a National Park and National Forest. The Olympic Mountains rise above snow level. Between the mountain range and the ocean are rain forests and parks with hiking trails and campsites. At the western edge, the breakers of the Pacific Ocean crash onto long beaches.

Scattered between the forests and the beaches are small communities. Originally they housed the families of people working in the fishing or lumbering industries. Over the years the towns spread to accommodate summer tourists.

To all that natural beauty was added the usual tourist attractions: restaurants, gift shops, taverns, and hangouts catering to a variety of interests.

After checking into a tourist motel, I combed my dull, limp hair, put on a little lipstick, and dragged my weary body to a hangout that I'd heard was popular with college students. If the rumors were true, that made it the place to meet the type of person I needed to find. Time to hang out.

It was one of those places that couldn't decide what it wanted to be. At one side was a bar that offered snacks and drinks. Against another wall were pinball and shuffle board games. Mismatched tables and chairs circled an open bit of floor. At the far end on a small bandstand, five musicians shattered the sound barrier with their renditions of country western.

Possibly I could survive the music for an hour before collapsing beneath decibels. The food was beyond trying. So I ordered a coke and a bag of chips and settled into a corner to watch the crowd.

There were pretty women everywhere, healthy women with glowing skin and bright smiles, their eyes scanning the room. Like me, they were obviously hoping to meet men. Were they looking for the same sort of man that I was? I was small and thin and pasty white and my weak back gave me a twisted posture, nothing that had ever caught the attention of the boys at school at any time in my life.

I sat there, sipping coke, nibbling on the chips, and wondering if I had made the right decision. Perhaps I should have asked my parents to take me to Hawaii for the last months of my life, after all. Perhaps the rumors of vampires were a fantasy created to attract more tourists.

"May I sit here?" asked a deep voice.

I didn't quite catch his words over the noise of the band.

The man bent toward me, his hand on the back of the empty chair at my table, and repeated his question. Pale skin, dark hair, handsome face, and secretive smile. Dressed all in black, he looked my age except for the smile. There was something old and a bit too confident about his smile.

I nodded, unsure what to say.

"Or perhaps you would like to dance?" he asked.

I shook my head. "I never have."

"You've never danced? Then you must, of course you must." He reached out a long thin hand to me.

Eighteen years of hospitals had made me used to following strangers, within the confines of a populated building, to new and often unpleasant experiences. At least in this case I knew where he intended to take me.

Imitating the actresses on TV shows, I held out my hand. I was half afraid my back would give out and shoot pains through me before I could stand. It did that sometimes and then all I could do was sit down again.

Instead, he pulled me up so quickly and gently I didn't quite realize what was happening until there we were on the dance floor.

With his lean, hard body pressed against me and his arm around my waist, he actually held me up. I felt as though I was floating. For a moment he bent down to my level and brushed the side of his face against mine, and that was definitely a new experience. It made me a little nervous to feel his cool skin and smell the subtle scent of cologne.

He was incredibly strong. That was a good sign. Of course, I was such a weakling, most men seemed supernaturally strong to me.

We twirled and spun and slowed to drifting, surrounded by the steady rhythm of the music. For a few moments I felt like I was on a cloud.

When my feet touched the floor, I stepped back enough to look up at him. His eyes were as dark as his hair and as old as his smile. He kept his arm firmly around me.

"You're new here," he said.

I explained about attending college and then, because I really did not have months to waste on this project, I told him my name.

"I'm Dominic," he said. That seemed correct--slightly foreign, slightly old-fashioned.

When he talked, I stared at his teeth. They looked like normal teeth, what I could see of them in the moving shadows cast by the strobe lights. He surprised me by staying with me the whole evening, despite a parade of women who tried to cut in on us.

"My turn with Dominic," was the line.

Each time he'd say, "Sorry, love, not now," and whirl me away.

Those other women continued to flirt, even after they found other partners. They would dance past us and lean toward Dominic and make clever remarks and roll their eyes as well as their bodies.

"Save a dance for me," each would say.

He answered each request with a silent smile. And so I wasn't surprised when he led me back to the small table in the corner. What did surprise me was that he pulled out the other chair and sat down.

"Where are you staying tonight, Georgia? May I drive you home?" he asked.

If the circumstances had been different, I might have tried for a romance. I'd never experienced romance, not with my medical problems. True, I'd read every word I could find about Elizabeth Barrett Browning and had a secret dream or two in my heart, but I was smart enough to know that she had not been on her deathbed, plus, a Robert Browning is a rare occurence.

Might as well tell Dominic the truth. "Are you a vampire? Because I am looking for a vampire."

He grinned then and sorry to say, I didn't see any pointy teeth.

"A vampire? Why would you think that?"

"This area is famous for vampires," I said.

"Georgia, you've been reading romance novels."

I nodded. "But I've also done considerable research on the internet."

"And you found websites that promised you vampires in this neighborhood?"

"Something like that."

He pressed his cool fingers over mine. "And you've heard that a vampire can give you the most romantic experience of your life."

"I'm not looking for romance."

He sat back and stared at me, startled. "Then what is it you want?"

"I want to be turned."

He really did sound shocked. "Turned? Turned into a vampire? But, Georgia! You have to die for that to happen."

"I know."

"Well, and afterwards, when you're turned, you can never go out in the sun. You can't eat real food. You can't go home because if you do, no one will understand. Or if they do, they will no longer want you in the family. Believe me, there isn't a normal family around who wants a vampire sleeping in a box in the basement all day."

"I know all that."

"Vampires drink blood! Have you ever tried to drink blood?"

"No. But I will if I have to."

"Eeew." He looked away from me and I thought that he would

leave.

Had I misjudged? Except for the lack of fangs, he looked type-cast with the dark hair and white skin and cold hands and those very old eyes in his smooth young face. Plus, when we were dancing I had put my raised hand on the side of his neck. Years of experience as a patient had taught me the exact sites of pulses. He had no pulse.

There was no way to politely say that I thought he looked more like a vampire than anyone I had ever met.

"Do you know any vampires?" I asked quickly.

He drummed his fingertips on the table top. He tapped his shoes on the floor. He frowned and shook his head.

"Why, Georgia? Is there a reason?"

"Of course there's a reason. I am dying. And I am only eighteen. Somehow that seems premature to me."

That stopped him. He stared and stared and I thought he might sit there speechless until dawn, although if I was right and he was a vampire, he'd have to leave before dawn.

Finally he said, "Tell me your whole story."

And so I did. He watched, his face perfectly still, not giving away a thought. But he kept his dark eyes on me and I knew he was listening to every word and making a decision.

I'd been right all along. Dominic was a vampire.

"For more than a hundred years," he admitted. "In all that time, I've never turned anyone."

"You know how, don't you?"

"I never hurt anyone," he explained. "When I take blood I am very tender and romantic and gentle. Are you sure you wouldn't like romance? No? With a century of experience, I can kiss you to the edge of ecstasy so that when I draw blood, you won't feel it. And I am always careful to limit the amount. I would never leave you weak or faint."

"I'm weak and faint most the time, anyway," I said. "And as for drawing blood without pain, I've had blood drawn for hospital tests hundreds of times and it always hurts."

"Ah. I can insert a tooth more gently than a nurse can insert a needle. Isn't that odd?"

"Terrific if it's true," I said. "So how do you do the first part, the dying part? Do I have to wait until I die naturally? What if you aren't around?"

"That won't work at all," he said. "When the heart stops on its own, bringing back life is usually impossible. No, to be successful, I would have to drain you until you took that last breath, and then I would give you enough of my vampire blood to bring you back to life and turn you."

As that sounded like a solution to me, I asked him when he would like to do this.

"Georgia, do you think I take appointments? I am not a monster!"

Apparently vampires have rather tender feelings about some things. A century of experience hadn't hardened him the way I'd thought it would.

I explained my pain and my failing heart and my dreams and I kept on talking. In the end he said what all my doctors had been saying for years.

He said, "Very well. I can't make any promises about the results, but I will try."

He explained the procedure, which sounded like pre-op talk, and he set a time for the following night. As my life had been one long series of appointments, I knew I was lucky to find a specialist and get in for treatment so quickly.

The next day seemed endless. I drove to the nearby ocean beach to enjoy a last day in the pale sunlight slanting through the overcast. It sparkled on the crests of the long waves as they rolled toward the shore. In that final moment, each wave peaked and the light turned it to green glass before it curled in on itself and broke and shattered on the sand. The water drew back with a soft hiss to meet the next incoming wave.

I wanted to run along the beach and feel the ocean swirl around my ankles. I wanted the sun in my eyes. I wanted to soak in its brilliance and feel its heat because after today, I would never again see the sun. That seemed to me the greatest loss in becoming a vampire.

But when I opened the car door, the wind blew it shut. I fell back against the seat, gasping. For a long time I sat in my car in the parking lot, with the window down a few inches so that I could smell the freshness of the sea air and listen to the breakers.

A few tourists walked upon the sand, their coats billowing out around them, hair blowing across their faces. Occasionally a couple wandered by, stopping to embrace while the ocean spray flew around them.

If I did manage to get to the beach, I knew the wind would knock me over and someone would have to carry me back to my car. Instead, I rested against the seat back and sat facing the windshield and watched the sun weave its way through ribbons of clouds until it reached the horizon.

When the sun was gone and the sky faded to darkness, I turned the key and pressed the gas pedal and drove to a fast food take-out window to pick up a meal. After that there was nothing more to do than sit in the small motel room watching the TV, another long wait for an appointment, but at least I didn't have to spend it in a fake leather chair in a waiting room. Too tired to really enjoy my last meal, I picked at the hamburger and took a few sips of the milkshake.

Had he changed his mind? If he had, that was his choice.

Did I have the strength to go again and search again for someone else to help me? I was so tired I would have wept, if I'd had enough energy to do so.

***

Author's website is **http://phoebematthews.com**
 If you would like to be notified of new releases by this author, email mudflatbks at aol.com